EVELYN'S DAUGHTER

Talissa Tillman

In Loving Memory

Carrie, William, Larry, and John

ACKNOWLEDGMENTS

My sons Michael and Malcolm. I absolutely love and adore you. Everything I do is for you. Your love and encouragement meant the world to me. My beautiful daughter Latoya, you listened and never doubted. I love you. My sincere gratitude to my beta readers who inspired me to write the next chapter. And to you, the reader, thank you so much for bringing my story to life.

1
Mr. Hyde

"WHOSE IS IT?!" Mr. Hyde said from the other side of the door. They're getting on my last nerve. I covered my ears with my pillow. It didn't work. I still hear glass breaking and Mama screaming and cussing every time he hit her.

"Whose is it?!" he said.

"You son of a bitch, put your hands on me one more time, and you'll regret it for the rest of your natural life!" she said. They got quiet for a little while, but then he hit her real hard and tears stung my eyes. If Mama comes in here and catches me wide awake, I'll be in big trouble. She won't care that it's their fault. She'll say I'm trying to be in grown folk's business. I don't care about their business, I gotta pee that's all.

If I'm not careful, I'll look at those statues. They scare me because their eyes glow in the dark. So, I look over at my little sister Bunny and our baby brother Beau instead. We sleep together in the living room on the couch bed. They always sleep through the fights, but I never do. I can't help it if it only takes a whisper to wake me up.

Nana always said a bad thing can be a blessing in disguise. Like right now, if they didn't wake me up with their fight, I would've peed in our bed. I was having that dream again, the one where I'm already in the bathroom. I can feel the cold toilet seat under my behind and everything. The next morning, I'll be laying on top of a cold wet spot. I dream a lot, so Mama whoops my behind a lot. I always put my hands out and try to stop her. "Wait, mama, let me explain!" I cry, but she don't care.

1

"I put up with a lot of shit around here, but the one thing I can't stand is no pissy ass mattress. I'm gon' whoop your ass 'til it shake like jelly," she says. The first-time mama said that I laughed because I didn't believe she could really do it, but now I know she can.

Bunny and Beau are snoring. They're making a little sleeping song. I like them better when they're sleeping. If Nana was here she would say, "Lord, look at my little chocolate covered angels, them some good babies." Mm-hmm, she ain't never here when they be running all around the house, making all kinds of noise, and I'm the one who gets in trouble. "You supposed to stop 'em, you supposed to keep 'em quiet, you supposed to be the oldest," Mama always tell me. How should I know when Beau is going to the kitchen to pour a whole bag of flour on his head? Or when Bunny want to fill some balloons with water? She don't even know how to tie them up, but she'll keep trying until the bathroom floor is soaking wet.

"You can end all this shit right here right now!" Mr. Hyde yelled and made me forget what I was thinking about. Anyway, sometimes I can't tell if I'm still cute. Before Bunny got here, old ladies used to pinch my cheeks and say, "Oh my, how sweet." Now they're only pinching her. She hates it. Everybody calls me a big girl or they always telling me to be a big girl. If Uncle Ernest got one lollipop left in his old coffee can, it goes right past my face to Bunny's hand. "Uh-uh straighten up, big girls don't cry," he says when I start scrunching up my face. Make it so bad, she won't even give me one lick, no matter how much I beg. Bunny is still cute, but she better watch out. The last time our Aunts was over here, they didn't fuss over her that time. Instead, they pushed each other out of the way to pick Beau up. They put kisses on his cheeks and spun him around. And the last time we were at the big house, Beau got the last lollipop.

"Graham just lay down. Quit while you ahead." Mama said. Bunny's over there flip-flopping. She won't wake up, no matter how loud things get in there.

"That girl will sleep through a tornado," Mama said. It's true,

Bunny always sleeps in the shopping carts at the store or on the bus. She don't say nothing if Bunny falls asleep in church, but if she ain't woke by the time the preacher say we can go home, Mama will pinch her on her leg. I laugh every time Bunny give her the evil eye like she grown.

"Ouch, Mama don't do that," she says.

"Well wake your little ass up 'cause I ain't about to carry you," Mama tells her. When Mama cussed in church, I got away from her, so God could strike her down. I waited. Nothing happened. I forgot lightning can't come through the ceiling. When we got outside, Mama was chit chatting with the preacher's wife. I looked up at the sky. It was all clear. I only wanted Mama to get struck by lightning one time, so I could see it for myself. Some stuff people say just don't make sense. Like step on a crack break your mama's back. I step on every crack I see, then I'll run home with my fingers crossed. Mama be sitting straight up in the window and feeling just fine. What am I doing wrong?

Nana said God watches over us day and night, and he got the whole world in his hands. God gives me the creeps, I like Santa more. He only checks on you at Christmas time, and that's all right with me. I stole some candy cigarettes one time, and Santa still left presents under the tree with my name on them. But God's got a big book to write stuff in. I'm not worried, I'm not scared of God, or anybody, except Mama, she crazy.

"You can't fool me, woman!" Mr. Hyde said.

"Ain't nobody tryna fool you Graham you paranoid, just go to sleep," Mama said.

"Apparently, I been sleepin' for too long as it is!" he said. Mr. Hyde is Beau's daddy. We all got our own daddy, I'm glad he ain't mine. Beau ain't allowed to cry. If Mr. Hyde catch him crying he'll say, "Close your mouth boy, don't be cryin' in front of all these women. You king of the jungle!"

Mama ain't allowed to whoop Beau, but if he mistakes one of the statutes for a toy, she gets him good. Mr. Hyde always makes a big deal out of it.

"Woman I told you to put them damn things somewhere he can't reach 'em," he said.

"Negro please, if he touch my shit, I'm whoopin' his ass, period," she said.

"You keep hitting him all the time you'll make him soft, he'll be scared of women when he grow up. His ol' lady gon' be kickin' his ass too," Mr. Hyde said. Mama shook her head.

"You should hear how stupid you sound," she said.

"Call me what you want, but I can chastise my boy my own way. He do somethin' wrong, let me know, and I'll handle it," he said.

"Mm-hmm, *your* boy ain't payin' no bills around here, quiet as kept, you ain't payin' too many your damn self," she mumbled. I wish he would stop her from whooping me and Bunny's behinds all the time. He don't care if we be too soft and scared of women when we grow up.

I fell asleep for a second. Mr. Hyde yelled again and woke me up. I'm glad he did because if I pee in this bed, I'll get my behind whooped. And I'll have to scrub the mattress off with soap and Pine-Sol. Mama makes me wash the sheets out in the bathtub. Once they get wet, they'll be too heavy for me to wring out all by myself. Sometimes Bunny will come in to use the bathroom.

"Bunny come help me wring these sheets out," I whisper. I don't want Mama to hear me.

"Uh- uh, I ain't helping. I don't want no pee on me!" she says real loud. Now Mama knows I tried to be slick. Bunny gets on my nerves too, sometimes. All day she tries to get me in trouble. "Ooh, Goldie, um tellin' on you," are her favorite words. She always trying to get on Mama's good side. She stupid because Mama ain't got no good side, not that I know of.

"Woman, I said whose is it?!" Mr. Hyde yelled. Anyway, Mama smells like Juicy Fruit gum. That's how I know when she's close by. She chews it every day, she put in her dresser drawers, and way down in her purse. The smell makes me sick to my stomach, or maybe she does, I don't know. Her belly is sticking out like she got a watermelon in it, but it's just another baby. Mr. Hyde just want to know whose goddamn baby it is, that's all.

When she ain't got that big belly, and she put on a nice dress and high heel shoes, people will stop and stare at her. Sometimes a man will say, "Damn girl, you so fine I'll drink your bath water!" Sometimes they say, "Aw sooky- sooky now!" She really likes that one. She smiles real big, so they can see all her teeth. When she gets sad, I tell her she's pretty. It's like medicine, it makes her feel better. I keep trying to tell Nana that mama is crazy, but she don't believe me. She says she ain't crazy, she just ornery, like Poppa. "You just mad 'cause you ain't got no titties, all you got is raisins!" Aunt Sylvia said when they got into a fight. After that, I couldn't stop staring at her no matter how hard I tried.

"What you eyeballin' me for, girl?" she said. I wanted to ask her why she ain't got no titties.

"You're so pretty, Mama," I said instead. Anyway, Mama has fits. That's when she starts screaming at invisible people and throwing stuff around. When she's too tired to throw anything else, she'll sit on the window seat and light a Kool cigarette and stare outside. That's when she thinks of little ol' me.

"Goldie get in here and clean this shit up!" she says like I'm the one who did it. I bet I'll have to clean up the mess she's making in there right now. Maybe if she didn't have me to boss around, she wouldn't go crazy and break everything. People always want to know why she got so many statues in here.

"They bring me good luck," she says. She got Buddhas, snakes, elephants, some ugly dogs, and Africa ladies. I counted them, *forty-three.* She would never ever break a statue, she loves them too much. One-night Mr. Hyde came home from work while she was having a fit. He told her to calm her ass down, but she threw a lamp at him. After that, he grabbed the gold Buddha, her favorite one, then he held it over his head.

"Come on, break one more thing, and you can kiss his chunky

ass goodbye!" he said.

"You wouldn't dare," she told him. He turned the statue's booty toward her face.

"Try me," he said.

"All right, I'll stop, just put him down please," she said. So, she hurried up and sat on the couch. He put it back on the TV.

"He supposed to be watchin' the door dumb ass," she told him, and we laughed at her, and she had to laugh too. But she didn't forget to say Goldie go clean that shit up.

"I was born at night, but not last night!" Mr. Hyde said. So, when Mama has a fit, I know just what to do. I make Bunny take Beau to the kitchen and play. I stand behind the door with the broom and dustpan and I wait. Sometimes she will break down and cry. No matter how mean Mama is to me, I cry every time I see her cry. But I'm still sick and tired of cleaning up after her all the time. She even knocked over our fish tank, on purpose. I don't know why she did it because she was smiling at them, and tapping the glass to get them to move around. Anyway, I had the hardest time mopping up all that water and scraping up all those tiny pink, blue, and green rocks.

"I hate you, you make me sick!" Bunny said when she caught me in the bathroom dropping the goldfish into the toilet.

"But, I had to, they died." I flushed the toilet and watched them spin and disappear.

"And don't blame me, blame Mama," I told her.

Mama likes to fight. There's this lady named Miss Joanne who lives on the next street over. She always walks by our house switching her big ol' booty. And when she turns the corner, those nasty boys across the street say stuff like "Joanne got ass for days!" And even worse stuff I can't say. So, we was outside playing hopscotch when Miss Joanne stopped in front of our house. She put her hand on her hip and started hula-hooping her neck.

"Is y'all mammy home?" she said.

"Uh-huh, she home," we said.

"Go and tell her Miss Joanne want to have words with her."

"I'll go!" Bunny said. She rushed up the steps and skipped into the house. Bunny didn't know she came to beat Mamas behind. I knew because she said *mammy*. Bunny came back out and sat on the step close to me.

"My Mama said don't go nowhere, she'll be right wit'choo," she said. Miss Joanne threw her head way back and had a good ol' laugh. We looked at each other and shrugged our shoulders because we didn't see nothing funny. Mama came out wearing her best cooking apron, the one with frogs leaping over the flower pots. She took her sweet time drying her hands. When Miss Joanne fixed her mouth to say something, Mama slapped her, and they rolled out into the middle of the street. Mama was crawling all over her like a squirrel in a tree. Miss Joanne couldn't shake her off. I think she was screaming, "Help, get it off me!" but, I'm not sure. I put my elbows on my knees and rested my chin on my hands and watched the whole stupid fight. Mama's always embarrassing somebody. Other kids are always making fun of me. Poor Miss Joanne. She was running down the street like a puppy dog was trying to bite her booty. Her face was all scratched up, and she didn't even bother to pick her wig up off the ground.

"You fat bitch, don't get mad 'cause you got what you came for! I know my damn cornbread better not be burnt, or I'll whoop your ass again," Mama said to herself on her way back in the house. Oops, some giggles slipped out. I can't help it, I always giggle when I think about Miss Joanne's beautiful afro wig. It stayed outside for so long. We had a lot of fun with it. The little kids kicked it around. The big kids carried it on a stick and chased us with it. It got stuck in some bushes, and it scared people at night. Mr. Clarence, the wino, stopped to talk to it. "Who that lurkin' in the bush? Oh, it's you. You ain't thank I was ever gon' fine your ass, now did you? You got my money? Say what? You got mo' excuses than a Negro goin' to jail," he told the wig. When he tried to get down the street, he stumbled up three steps and wobbled back two. He kept doing that until he was finally out of our sight.

"No he ain't," Bunny said.

"Uh-huh, just wait a minute," I said. We watched the corner. Mr. Clarence wobbled back two steps, and we fell out laughing.

"See, told you," I said. I don't like to fight. One time I came home with mud in my hair and all over my clothes. I tried to sneak past Mama. She was hiding behind the "Good Housekeeping" magazine, so I started tiptoeing to the doorway. I was almost there before she asked me the same old dumb question.

"Did you win?"

"Nuh-uh."

"Why not?"

"Um, because she was way bigger than me." I stretched my arms out wide to show her how big Trudy was.

"Come over here," she said. I went, and she gave me a slap and hid her face again. I stared at the magazine, waiting for her to tell me why she had to hit me.

"The bigger they is, the harder they fall. Don't never let no heifer drag you through no damn mud. You got arms, legs, teeth, feet, and fingernails too. You better use 'em next time." Nowadays, if somebody want to fight, I just run. "You better run chicken!" they'll say. I don't care, I can't take any chances with Mama.

"FuckyouGrahamkissmyblackass!" Mama screamed. Uh-oh, she's running her words together now. Sometimes she gets so mad she forgets to breathe, and all her words run right into each other. It's kind of funny. Mr. Hyde don't know what she said. The first time he heard her running words he called me. I put my dolls on the floor and huffed when I got to the doorway.

"Yes sir, what is it?" I said.

"I need a translator."

"What's trains later?"

"No, *translator*," he said slowly.

"Yeah, I don't know what that means."

"You know what this woman said don't you?" Mama was up on her high bed folding clothes. I shook my head, yes.

"Now you tell me word for word, and I'll pay you two dollars."
He made the peace sign. I looked at her again. She smiled and
squinted her eyes, that's how I knew I could tell without getting in
trouble. So, I put my hand on my hip and rolled my eyes like fast girls
do.

"Um, she said she need a break, so take your *behind* to your
other woman's house before she *jack you* up." I knew not to say ass
or fuck. Mr. Hyde laughed.

"Is that all?" he said.

"Um, Uh-huh." I tried to grab the wrinkled-up dollars out of his
hand. He lifted me off the floor and swung me all around.

"You like roller coasters?" he said. "No, I hate roller coasters,
put me down!" I knew he couldn't just hand it over. He hates to let
go of his money. Sometimes he takes us to the store with him. Once
we get in the station wagon, he watch us like a hawk, just so he can
have a reason to change his mind. We never play with the knobs or
ashtrays, we don't roll the windows up and down, as bad as we want
to. We just sit tight with our fingers crossed. "Y'all get whatever y'all
want," he says when he turns into the parking lot at Kroger's. When
the check-out girl tells him how much he got to pay, he stands there
like a robot looking at the numbers on the cash register. Then he
squints his eyes at the checkout girl like she trying to cheat him or
something.

"For this little bit of grocery?" Mr. Hyde says. He don't care if
he got to pay five dollars, one dollar, or a teeny-weeny penny, he still
says "For this little bit of grocery?" The check-out girl knows all about
him. She sucks her teeth every time he gets in her line. "Aw, that's no
fair!" We cry after she tossed the cheese puffs, chocolate chip
cookies, and a big box of sweet cereal on the table behind her. He
only got a five-pound bag of potatoes, a piece of liver, some black-
eyed peas, a bag of white rice, and one big stinky onion. When he
opened his wallet to pay, it didn't close all the way because he put too
much money in it. "Cheap bastard," the checkout girl mumbled
behind his back. Anyway, he thought swinging me around would be

so much fun that I'd forget about the two dollars he owed me.

"Put me down, let go!" I told him.

"Just give it to her Graham," Mama said. Finally, he put me down and opened his hand. I got to be faster than him. If his hand balls back up before I get it, we got to start all over again.

"Thank you kindly," I said, when I got the money. I'm getting better at snatching. I went back to my dolls, but what did I forget? I asked myself. He'll take it back if he finds out I forgot any words. When I saw my Ken doll with no clothes on, I hit myself on the forehead and ran back to the doorway.

"And she said you got a...um...."

"Come on, spit it out girl," he said.

"She said you got a little, *you know*," I whispered. I knew not to say the real word that time too. After that, I went back to play in peace. I earned the money fair and square, so he couldn't take it back.

"So how the hell you explain all these damn scratches on my back huh?" he said. Mama screamed and laughed. Too bad, he don't ask me to trains late no more. I punched my pillow, I can't help it, I'm so mad now. I got to go through their room, down the hall through the kitchen to get to the bathroom. Holding it in is starting to hurt real bad.

"Go straight to hell Graham," Mama said.

"All right then, if that's how you want it," he said.

"No, let me go! Stop before you hurt my baby!" I heard the sound her body made when she hit the floor. I sat up straight. My heart is beating fast like I been running around the yard. Mama is still down there. I hear her voice from under the door. She ain't crying or screaming or cussing anymore, she's just praying for Mr. Hyde, asking God to have mercy on his soul.

The house is quiet now, except for the little sleeping song. I went to the doors and pushed them apart. All the lights are on. Mr. Hyde is already asleep. Mama's side of the bed is flat. I looked for a spot with no glass and jumped to it. I walked quietly to the kitchen. I stopped when I saw her standing at the stove stirring something in a big pot. She stared at the wall, talking to herself. Whatever she's cooking, I'm not going to eat none of it. Old people give her money to do their dirty laundry. The big silver pot is for boiling dingy white stuff. She won't touch them until she put on some big rubber gloves. "Nasty fuckers," she says if she sees or smell something bad on them. I saw a big bottle of bleach on the floor next to the stove. I didn't see any dirty clothes.

"Mama, I got to go to the bathroom." She didn't look at me. She kept stirring. I saw tears hanging from her chin, and then jumping into the pot. She stirred the tears in too. I started walking backward when I saw her black eye. Mama don't like nobody to see her when she don't look pretty. But, I stopped to tell her about the blood that was running down her legs.

"Mama, you're bleeding," I said.

"What you doin' out the bed girl?" she said. I pointed at the blood that covered her feet now.

"Um... I was... look Mama, you're bleeding," I said. She looked down and stared at the blood.

"Damn, damn," she whispered. She put the spoon down and came over to me. When she reached out to touch me, I moved away from her. I didn't mean to, I just get a little scared when she is too close to me. Mama don't ever touch me nice, she's always pushing, pulling, or yanking me around.

"I'm gon' be gone for a little while. Go on, get back in the bed and stay there."

"Where you going Mama?" I said.

"Me and Graham is on our way to the emergency room," she said. She went back to the stove and picked up the bottle of bleach and poured it all into the pot. She kept putting her eye over the hole to look inside, then she shook it over the pot. She did that over and over. I got scared.

"Ain't no more Mama, it's all gone," I said. When she started stirring again, I ran back down the hall, jumped over the glass, closed the doors, and felt my way over to the couch bed. Aw man, I forgot to tell her I had to pee. I know she'll be proud of me for getting back up. Mama put up with a lot of shit around here, but the one thing she can't stand is no pissy ass... I can't move. I heard a splash and Mr. Hyde screamed, "Evelyn!" The silver pot dropped on the floor and she ran down the hall. I'm just standing here with my eyes glued to the door in the dark. I don't know what to do. Mr. Hyde keeps making this awful sound, like a pig crying. After a while, I opened the sliding doors. Mr. Hyde sat on the edge of the bed in his underwear smoking a cigarette. He was as red as the devil and all bubbled up. The pot was rocking back and forth on the floor. Lots of times I heard people calling Mr. Hyde a pretty nigga. "You still with that pretty nigga?" men ask Mama. When her girlfriends come over to play bid whist they say, "Girl where you been hiding that pretty nigga at?" She always get mad and say, "That's for me to know and for you to find out." What are they gonna call him now? He looked at me and blew out some smoke. I jumped over the glass again and ran through the kitchen to the bathroom. I sat on the toilet, and I peed and cried. But when the pig cried, I flushed the toilet and dried my tears. I knew I had to be a big girl.

I followed the awful bloody footprints, they stopped at the back door. She forgot to close it. I looked out into the dark backyard and the cold air ran right through me.

"Mama, you out here?" I whispered. I heard some birds waking up.

"Mama?" I gave her one last chance before I closed the door. The pig cried again. Think Goldie, think... Oh, I know, I'll call Uncle Ernest, he always knows what to do. I went to the phone on the wall. I dialed two numbers until I remembered what Uncle Ernest told her before.

"I mean it, don't call me ever again," he said.

"So, you don't care if he be over here tryna kill me?" Mama said. He knocked on her forehead.

"Hello, is anybody home?" he said. She swatted his hand away.

"Stop it Ernest!" she said.

"I don't care if you get mad, I'm not runnin' over here every time y'all go at it. Especially when I know y'all will be all lovey-dovey before my knuckles cool off. I swear, you fools can't get along for five minutes, now you tryna have another baby. You should gather up them kids and come back home. Or stay your ass here until the shit hit the fan, but don't call me no more," he said. I put the phone back up on the wall.

I'm too scared to ask Mr. Hyde what I should do. I wish he could be quiet for a minute, so I can hear myself think. I know there's some number grown-ups call when bad things happen. What is it? I stood by the phone waiting for it to ring so I could tell them Mr. Hyde is red like the devil and crying like a pig. Night time turned into day time. I heard footsteps on the ceiling. Oh yeah, I forgot our landlord Mr. Pete lives upstairs. I kept knocking and kicking on his door until he opened it. He was fidgeting with his glasses and trying to tie the belt on his robe.

"For heaven sake gal, I ain't even had my morning coffee, what you need?" he said. I opened my mouth, but nothing came out, so I pointed toward our door. Mr. Pete looks scared now. He knows all about the fights. Sometimes he bangs on the ceiling, and one time he said he was gonna put their black behinds out on the street if they kept it up. He held onto the rail as he went down the steps, and knocked on our open door before going in. "Evelyn, honey, you all right in there?" Mr. Pete stopped and looked at Nana's chocolate covered angels sleeping on the couch bed. Mr. Pete jumped when the pig cried. He looked around to see where it came from. He walked toward the bed. Mr. Hyde was still sitting in the same spot.

"Robert?" Mr. Pete said. Then he went over there to see why Mr. Hyde was not answering when he called his name. Poor Mr. Pete, he probably never seen a real monster before. First, he took his glasses off and put them back on. Then he put his hands on his head and started going around in circles, and glass crunched under his hard-brown shoes.

"Oh no, you kids, what have you done? Lord have mercy Jesus!

How long he been like this? Where your mama at? Did she do this?" he said. Maybe that's why I can't talk, I'm not allowed to tell on my mama.

"Lil' gal, pick up the telephone and dial 911. Tell 'em a man here been burned horribly."

"911 what is your emergency? Hello, is anyone there?" a lady said.

"Um, Mr. Hyde," I whispered.

"Speak louder please."

"Mr. Hyde got burned... horribly. He need a doctor."

"Where has he been burned?" she said. I looked over at him.

"All over."

"How old are you?"

"Eight, almost."

"Where is your mommy?"

"Gone."

"Is the house still on fire?"

"No, it's Mr. Hyde, he on fire." The pig cried.

"What was that?"

"Mr. Hyde."

"Tell them to hurry, it's 459 Buena Vista Street!" Mr. Pete said.

"459 Buena Vista Street hurry up, please," I said. I hung up and ran back to the bed.

"Hold on son, the ambulance is on the way, they gon' fix you right up," Mr. Pete told him. Mr. Hyde's shaking hands reached for his cigarettes, but they fell on the floor. Mr. Pete picked them up and lit one for him. Mr. Hyde took a puff before he pointed to the chair in the corner.

"You want your trousers?" Mr. Pete said. He shook his head.

"I don't think we should," Mr. Pete told him. Mr. Hyde waved faster, he wouldn't take no for an answer. So, Mr. Pete is helping him get his legs in the pants.

"You got too much pride son," Mr. Pete said. The fire trucks made Bunny wake up. She sat up and looked around for Mama like she always do.

"Mama, I want Mama!" she said when she saw Mr. Hyde like that.

"Be quiet Bunny, stop screaming," I said. Beau woke up and I tried to cover his face. Mr. Hyde made that sound again, so Beau looked at him. I think he wanted to cry, but he's not allowed to.

"Did someone report a fire at this address?" the fireman said.

"In here," Mr. Pete said. He rushed into the other room.

"Oh shit. I'm sorry, I didn't expect... Hey guys bring a gurney, we got to get this man to the hospital, like yesterday!" he yelled over his shoulder. A man and a woman rushed in with a bed on wheels. They were sad to see Mr. Hyde like that.

"There's no way we can put him on a stretcher, his skin will stick to the sheet," he told the lady.

"You're right," she said. She was looking at all Mama's statues.

"Watch out Donald, there's broken glass everywhere," said the man standing next to Mr. Pete.

"Mr. Hyde, we need you to walk, can you stand on your own?" the lady said.

"Hyde? No, this young man is named Robert Graham," Mr. Pete said.

"I apologize sir, it says Hyde here on the chart," she said.

"Well I assure you that his name is Graham, not Hyde," Mr. Pete said. It's not their fault they got his name wrong. I'm the only one who calls him Mr. Hyde behind his back. One day he left me and Bunny in the station wagon on top of the hill. I climbed over the seat and pretended to be a race car driver. We were having fun, making race car sounds, but then I accidentally hit that stick thingy, and the wagon went rolling backward. We screamed all the way down until we crashed into a telephone pole. That's when I saw a strange man running toward us. He kept running and falling and getting back up and running until he got to the car. He was wearing Mr. Graham's clothes and swinging his arms over his head. The man grabbed me out of the car and shook me like a rag doll. "Look what you did to my fuckin' car!" he said. Then I knew it was him, but he looked like a monster, like Mr. Hyde. So, I been calling him that ever since. They made a circle around him and now they're moving like snails, still trying to get him to the front door. Bunny's still shouting I want mama at the top of her lungs. I'm getting sleepy, it's hard to keep my eyes open. I laid down and watched everything.

"That's it son, you gon' make it," Mr. Pete said. Mr. Hyde stopped moving and waved his hands at them.

"A few more steps sir," they said. He waved his hands until they got the message and let him out of the circle.

"Is there a problem?" the lady asked.

"I'm not sure," the man answered. Mr. Hyde forgot something. He made the pig sound all the way back.

They watched and waited. He went to the mantelpiece and felt around. I could see what he was looking for. He put it there every night after he counted it two or three times. Mr. Pete saw it too. He hurried over to help him get it all back in his wallet and into his pocket. Now he's ready to go.

"Well I'll be damned, if I ain't seen it all now," one fireman tried to whisper to the other. The lady turned her back and covered her face with her hands. Her shoulders were shaking. They all laughed, except Mr. Pete. I got mad at them. Don't they know he can't help it? Mr. Hyde, I mean Mr. Graham hates to let go of his money, that's all.

2

Home

WYLIE COYOTE WAS CHASING the Roadrunner with a knife and fork. Beau pointed at the TV and laughed so hard his whole body shook. I tried not to laugh because I saw this one before. I couldn't help it. Wylie Coyote is so funny, he's the one I like. He's just hungry that's all. I looked in the other room. Ain't no covers on the high bed. Ain't no broken glass or hot pots rolling on the floor. So, it was probably just a bad dream. Beau pretended to be the Roadrunner. "Meep meep," he said. I heard voices coming from the kitchen. If it wasn't a dream, there would be bloody footprints in the hallway. The hallway is clean too. I hurried toward the voices and the smell of oatmeal. Mr. Pete sat at the table with Nana, he tried to cool his coffee by blowing into the cup. I climbed on her lap and put my arms around her neck.

"Now don't you go blamin' yourself Pete," Nana said.

"Any other night I'd get to bangin' on the floor. Let's 'em know to knock it off. This time I said to hell with 'em."

"I done told them two a hundred times oil and water don't mix. I knew somethin' was bound to happen, but I never imagined nothin' like this. These young folks today, so full of rage," Nana said. I kept my head on her shoulder. She would make me go back to the living room if she knew I understood their every word. She told Mr. Pete that Mr. Graham was in critical condition, and it's a miracle he still alive. He scarred for life, and Mama will be all right over time.

"And the baby?" Mr. Pete said.

"Well Pete, I'm sorry to say the baby didn't make it." *I know what that means.* I felt too sick after Nana said that. I didn't touch the bowl of oatmeal she put in front of me. When I got back to the room, I heard "Captain Kangaroo" telling another story, but I didn't pay him any attention. Nothing could cheer me up now.

"Nana made oatmeal," I told them. They ran to the kitchen to get it.

"You babies come help me find your coats and things," Nana said after they got finished eating.

"Where are we going?" I asked.

"Home," she said.

"I can't go wit'choo Nana, I got to stay here and wait for Mama," Bunny said.

"Your mama will be there when she gets out of the hospital." Mr. Pete came down the hall and headed for the door.

"I'll be upstairs if you need anything Pearl," he said.

"Oh no, you done enough. I'm sorry about all this Pete, Lord knows," she said.

"How long that girl been cooped up in there like that?" Aunt Nadine said.

"Ever since she escaped from Western Psych two weeks ago," Aunt Sylvia said.

"She didn't escape, they let her go. It was self-defense," Aunt Tracie said.

"Self-defense my ass. It take a while to heat up a big ass pot of bleach water. Evelyn is pure evil," Aunt Sylvia said.

"She's your sister you should be on her side. Seriously, what kind of man beats on a woman? Especially one who's seven months pregnant. As far as I'm concerned, he asked for it," Aunt Tracie said.

"Be quiet Tracie," Aunt Sylvia said.

"What? I'm saying he knew her well enough to know better."

"Has anybody been to the hospital yet?" Aunt Nadine said.

"Me and Nolan went to see him this morning," Aunt Sylvia

said. They all stopped and looked at her.

"Child what he look like now?" Aunt Nadine said. She shook her head slowly.

"Only Evelyn would go and ruin a pretty nigga like that," she said.

"Is it that bad?" Aunt Nadine said.

"Is it that bad? Who cares? Ask her baby how bad it is," Aunt Tracie said.

"Well, I'm tired of talking about it. What's done is done. She need to come out of that room and see about the three who still living. They up here running around, getting into everything," Aunt Sylvia said.

"Y'all leave her be, she still in mournin'," Nana said from her bedroom.

Nana got more kids than old lady who lived in a shoe. That's ten. they're my Aunts and Uncles and they all live here in the big house. Auntie Althea is only two years older than me, and I got a Little Uncle, his name is Marcus. We was all in the backyard playing tag. Soon as I scraped my knee I went running through the big house to show Nana. She was sitting at the kitchen table mixing a bowl of cornbread. "Look what happened!" I say before I put my leg over her lap. If we get a boo-boo, she'll kiss it and make it all better. Even if it's a tiny scratch on my finger, she makes a big deal out of it. "My Lord, what done happened to my baby?!" she says. Sometimes she got to put her glasses on to see most of my scratches. I try to just watch her hands while she fixes me up, but I always end up staring at her cheek. Nana says dark skin can hide darn near anything. But if I stare long enough, I can see that long scar on her cheek. I look at my right hand. I can still see my scar from the time Mama whooped me and Bunny with her high heel shoe. My skin is too light to hide anything.

"What thoughts you hidin' behind them watchful eyes?" she said.

"Nana, how come I don't look like nobody?" I asked.

"Well, what about your Aunt Nadine? Y'all 'bout the same complexion."

"But Aunt Nadine got brown hair like everybody else. Why do I have yellow hair?" I watch her lips while she tells me some stuff about slave masters, and chickens, and roosters.

"But, I still don't see why I'm albino," I tell her.

"Who said you was albino?"

"Kids at school call me that sometimes."

"No honey, you stand out a little more, ain't nothin' wrong with that. No matter what they say, you be strong, keep your head up. You need a spoonful of sugar?" she said. We raced to her room and she reached into her special hiding place and gave me two chocolate squares.

It's three o'clock already. I looked out of the window and saw the top of my daddy's big afro. His car ain't got no top today. He was blowing the horn like crazy. I don't want to go with him, what for? He's just gonna leave me at my other Gramma's house. Soon as he sees me, he leans over and pushes the car door open. "Come on baby, I'm running late," he says. I get in and he speeds off. He stops in front of the candy store and carries me inside even though I'm too big for that. The man behind the counter puts whatever I want into a little paper bag. Now we're really on our way to Gramma Betty's. My daddy knows lots of people on Fifth Avenue. People always calling his name and blowing their horns at him. My daddy is handsome, he ain't pretty like Mr. Hyde was. His beard covers his face, so I can't tell if I look like him or not.

"Daddy, why I got yellow hair?" I asked. He twirled a toothpick between his teeth and stared straight.

"You take after my grandmother on my daddy's side. Her name was Clara Mae. That makes her your great-grandmother. She passed away back in '63. She was a beautiful woman."

"For real daddy?"

"I kid you not. She favored Angela Davis, 'cept she had

herself a natural blonde afro," he said. As soon as we get to Gramma Betty's, daddy reaches over me to push the door open. I get out fast, I don't want to hear him say he gon' be late for something. I didn't get a chance to ask him who is Angela Davis.

"Love you baby, be good," he said.

"I love you too daddy," I say quietly. I sat on the steps.

"Ain't you goin' in?" he said. I shook my head no. He laughed at me.

"Okay, go in when you ready. Don't eat all that candy at once," he said before he got behind another car. I watched the giant orange clock across the bridge. I wanted to catch the hands moving. I reached into my candy bag, all I felt was a bunch of empty wrappers.

"Girl get your behind on in here. How long you been on these steps?" My Aunt Loretta said from behind me. When I didn't move fast enough she yanked me by one arm. When we pass the living room, I see my rocking chair. My daddy gave it to me for my sixth birthday. I love that chair. They won't let me take it home. Savages don't know how to take care of nothing they say. Aunt Loretta pushes me up the steps and drags me to the bathroom. The tub is already filled with hot steamy water. She always pours too much Mr. Bubbles in the tub. It makes me all red and itchy, but she don't care. She still scrubs me like I'm a muddy kitchen floor. I start to cry.

"Stop crying, acting like you scared of water," she said.

"I'm not scared of water, I took a bath already Aunt Loretta."

"In water or dirt?" she said. After that, she holds the towel out in front of her.

"Stand up girl," she says. She lifts me in the air and puts me on top of the toilet to dry me off. I always read the poster on the wall behind her head. It says, "Children learn what they live". I learn a new line every time. Once I'm dry, she rubs pink baby lotion all over me. She squeezed a big glob of baby powder in my panties. "No, no!" I scream when she drags me to the kitchen to wash my hair in the sink. The hair washing is even worse than the bath. Gramma Betty came in from the deli she works at. She's all smiles. She stood in the doorway with one hand on her hip. Gramma Betty looks like the lady on the record with the big white flower in her hair. "Hi Gramma," I say while I try to worm my way out of Aunt Loretta's grip.

"What's all this fuss about?" she said.

"I'm sick of this Ma, they never wash or comb her hair. The last time they sent her it was all matted. I spent two hours trying to get all the knots out without cutting it. Be still! I swear if they send her here like this again, I'm sending her back the same way."

"Stop fidgeting and let Loretta fix your hair sweetheart," Gramma Betty said. When she's done, my head is aching because she parted it in a bunch of little boxes and put tight rubber bands in it. I go and stand in the mirror. I don't see my long yellow hair. I see red, purple, blue, orange, and green ribbons, and barrettes everywhere. I look like Bozo the Clown.

"You like it? It's pretty right?" she said.

"Uh-huh.

"Well, what do you say?"

"Thank you, Aunt Loretta." I walk down the stairs slow, so my heavy head don't snap my neck. On Sunday, all I got to do is go to church with Gramma Betty and eat Sunday dinner. After I help with the dishes, I rush to the third floor to get my bag. I packed it last night. I hug Gramma Betty and say I love her. I sit on the steps and watch the clock until my daddy drives up.

"Did you have a nice time?" he asks. I don't want to lie, so I smile instead.

"Your hair sure looks good baby, tell your mama I said to keep it up." When we pull up to the big house, my daddy keeps the motor running.

"All right baby, go on in. I sure don't want to deal with Evelyn's evil behind." I don't blame him for that. If she do catch him out here, she'll say "You ain't nothin' but a pimp and a drug addict, and I could use some damn child support." When he speeds away, she'll scream, "You better run, faggot!"

"What you bring me?" Bunny said. I want to say nothing,

except she knows my Gramma Betty always sends something for her and Beau. I gave her a bag from Kaufman's, she reached in and grabbed the fluffy pink sweater and a big rainbow swirled-lollipop. Shoot, I forgot to check inside the bag first. I could've kept the candy, and gave her a little piece of it.

"Gimme some," Little Uncle Marcus said.

"No, it's mine," Bunny said. He chased her inside the house. I took off behind them.

"Hey, leave her alone!" I said. Once inside I stopped in my tracks and sniffed. The big house smelled funny, like charcoal or something. When I got to the top of the stairs everybody was standing outside Mama's door.

"Evelyn, you come out of there right now!" Nana said. Gray smoke escaped from under the door. Uncle Ernest appeared at the top of the steps.

"I smell smoke, what's goin' on?" he said.

"Evelyn's room caught fire, and she won't come out!" Nana said.

"Everybody stand back!" he said. First, he banged on the door with his fist, then he dug in his pocket for his army knife. He tried to pry the lock open.

"Uh-uh, ain't no time for that, break it down!" Aunt Nadine said. Uncle Ernest pushed against the door with his shoulder until the door fell in and darker gray smoke rushed out in the hallway. We all coughed and covered our mouths. Through the smoke, we could see her laying in the middle of her burning bed with her arms by her sides.

"How can she even stand it?" Aunt Tracie said.

"Evelyn, you got to get up from there honey!" Nana said.

"Uh-oh she dead," Little Uncle Marcus said. That made Bunny cry.

"Don't say that," I told him. Uncle Ernest rushed in to get her. He waved the smoke with one arm and covered his mouth with the other.

"Girl get up!" he said. He grabbed her foot and she came to

life. She swung her arms and legs like a drowning person.

"Ma what's wrong with her?" Auntie Althea said.

"She coo-coo for cocoa puffs," Uncle Nolan said. Uncle Ernest took off his army jacket and beat the fire. The closer he got to Mama the more she clawed at him.

"Lord have mercy, bring her on out of there!" Nana said.

"No let me go, let me die!" she said. He dragged her through the doorway, and she started fighting him again. Uncle Ernest slapped her cheek.

"Cut this shit out, right now!" he told her. She was shaking like a leaf. Black smoke covered her face. When she saw us staring at her, she fell into Uncle Ernest's chest and cried like a sad puppy. Uncle Ernest put his arms around her. "Go ahead, let it all out," he said quietly while he moved her out of the way. We all ran to the kitchen and filled pots and buckets with water to throw on the burning bed. After we put the fire out, we all went about our business. The house was quiet again. I stood in Nana's doorway, my head was hurting so bad. She put a pillow across her lap and gave it a pat. I climbed on her bed and laid my head on the pillow, and she started taking all that stuff out of my hair.

"You make me sick!" I told Uncle Kevin because he reached over my shoulder, and grabbed the last pork chop. He knew I almost had my hand on it. "Snooze you lose," he said before he took a big bite out of it. Now I can forget about getting one, ain't nothing but crumbs left on the platter. This happens all the time because the big kids are so greedy. Sometimes Nana hides food from them or they'll eat it all in one day. But they always find it. Sometimes me, Auntie Althea, Beau, Bunny, and Little Uncle Marcus sit at the table with our bowl and spoon in front of us. She comes back empty-handed, and say she got to go to the store.

Me and Auntie Althea is helping Nana in the kitchen today. Her and Uncle Ernest came home from the Allegheny River with a gigantic Whiting fish. She put it in the downstairs kitchen in a big tin tub filled with water. I watched it trying to jump out of the tub. There's no way I could lose tonight because for once, there's enough everyone.

"Goldie, baby you done peeled too much meat off these potatoes, you got to be more careful. There's starving kids in Africa. Child, you think we poor? Lord know they would be happy to eat what we waste," Nana said.

"Oops, sorry," I said. I love her for caring about those hungry African kids.

"Ma, you put your foot in this fish tonight!" Uncle Paul said. Poppa followed his nose into the kitchen like Tuscan Sam. We all got quiet and watched him grab a plate and pile it with fried fish, potato salad, and turnip greens. He picked up a piece of cornbread, checked all the sides, and tossed it back in the pan. That's because Nana always burns it. We pretend to gobble it up. Uncle Nolan passes a bag under the table and we all drop ours in. Later, he'll take the bag outside, and she'll never know. We ain't rude like Poppa. Once the top of his head disappeared down the steps, we go back to eating. Nana was making fun of Uncle Ernest wrestling with the big fish, and we all laughed. I'm so glad we're back home at the big house, with Nana and all my Aunts and Uncles. After we ate our food, we lined up to get a sip of sweet coconut milk, but when my time came, the coconut was dry.

"See Nana, that's why they get on my nerves," I said. She laughed and messed up my hair some more.

"Next time you be first in line," she said like I ain't been trying.

3

Damn Savages

MAYBE I'LL GO TELL MAMA what Miss Juanita called me today. That will teach her. I don't even know why she called me a damn savage. Well, she didn't call me a damn savage exactly to my face. I knocked on the door and asked her if Tootie could come outside and play. She looked down at me, she didn't smile, and she didn't bother to call me any word grownups saved for other people's kids, like sweetie, baby, or dear. Even Mama calls other kids those nice names, *mean as she is.* "Tootie busy right now," Miss Juanita said before she shut the door in my face. When I was leaving their porch, I heard her say, "Tootie, didn't I tell you not to play with them damn savage's?"

On my way back to the big house, I tried to figure out why Miss Juanita would even say something like that. She ain't the only one who ever said it though. My name is Gwendolyn Renee Savage, not Gwendolyn Renee *damn* Savage. Why do they call us that sometimes? Well, I'm going to find out. I went straight to Nana's room and got the dictionary. She always say the most important books are the Bible and the dictionary. So, savage is a word and a last name, like brown, it should be in here. Okay, I found it. Savage, terrible, wild, one who is uncivilized. I look under the word uncivilized. Not polite or respectful.

I wrote everybody's name down. Nana was first on my list. I read the words again. Nana is perfect in every way, she never does anything wrong. I put a smiley face, and some kisses by her name. Next on the list is Mama. She don't know I'm out here watching her.

She's too busy staring out the window that's facing a brick wall. And she's smoking a cigarette and cussing out the invisibles. Make it so bad, it's past four o'clock, and she ain't even dressed yet. It's too late to start the day. Maybe Miss Juanita knows what she did to Mr. Hyde. I try to remember her before the baby died. She was always sad or mad, sometimes happy, but not that much. I want to stick my tongue out, but she always said she got eyes in the back of her head. Auntie Althea said she don't, but I don't want to find out the hard way, so I keep my tongue in my mouth. She turned her head around like a scary old owl and stared at me without blinking. I ran to the attic steps and sat. My heart is beating hard, and I try to catch my breath. I put a big fat damn savage check by Mama's name. Next, I tiptoed to the attic where Uncle Ernest sleeps. All he's doing is polishing his army boots. Sure, he looks innocent now, but he's not. It used to scare me when I went outside, and I saw him hiding and blending in with the trees. One time it was raining, and I saw his feet sticking out of the bushes on the side of the house. I called his name, and he whispered, "Be quiet soldier, dissimulate now." I got on the ground with him and crawled on my elbows. At least I got to take turns looking through the binoculars when we looked for the enemy. I had to wait until somebody come to snap him out of it.

"How come he do that?" I asked Nana when I stood by the warm fireplace and took off my soaking wet clothes.

"He been expose to that Agent Orange," she said. I don't ask her any more questions because it makes her sad. Kids won't come over to play with us no more. They're all scared they might end up like Miss Mary, Nana's old friend from church. One-time Uncle Ernest jumped out from behind the bushes and put her in a headlock.

"State your business!" he said.

"I stopped by to discuss the goodness of the Lord with Pearl," she said. Nana said she stopped going to church because people done got too uppity. Miss Mary didn't mind bringing church to the big house.

"That's not the enemy, that's Miss Mary!" we shouted. Nana must have heard all the commotion because she came running.

"Oh Lord, Ernest, honey, don't you recognize Miss Mary, my friend from church? You got to release her," she said. He looked up and watched some birds flying high. After a while, he realized he was safe at home, and not in the war. He let her go slowly, but he kept his eye on her in case she made any sudden moves. He always say that the enemy is tricky and full of disguises.

"Mary, I'm sorry, he ain't mean no harm. He been traumatized from Vietnam," Nana said. But she didn't care, and she kept looking back at him while she ran to her car. Nana said she was sorry over and over. But Miss Mary can't forgive.

"I ain't never been this humiliated in my life... I ought to call the police on y'all!" she said.

"*Oops there goes another rubber tree plant,*" Uncle Nolan sang, and his friends laughed.

"Hush your mouth. Now I done lost another good friend," Nana said on her way back in the house. Still, even after all that, I can't put a damn savage check by Uncle Ernest's name. It ain't his fault about the bad oranges.

Uncle Nolan is my favorite person in the whole world. The problem is that he carries a baseball bat everywhere he goes. He likes scaring people with it. I put a heart and a damn savage check by his name. Next is Uncle Paul, he might be home right now, or not. We call him a ghost. We don't see him for days, and then you look up, and he's coming out of the bathroom or sitting next to you at dinner time. But when Nana calls him to take out the garbage he's nowhere to be found. And people say that he's the one who's been robbing their houses in broad daylight while they are in their living rooms watching TV. He promised Nana they're all telling lies. I sneaked into his room to snoop around. I looked under his bed. I saw stuff...lots and lots of stuff. I put a damn savage check by his name.

Last on the list is Uncle Kevin. This is a hard one. Uncle Kevin is always very quiet, and he never bothers anybody. But, one time he went into this old abandoned house and drank some wine he found in the cellar. His seizures started right after that. We were playing in the yard when some kids ran back there. "Kevin fell in the street, he's dying!" they said. We hurried to the front of the house and there he was, on the ground with a crowd of people standing around him. He was shaking and only the white part of his eyes showed. We screamed and cried when the blood came out of his mouth. Uncle Nolan pushed through the crowd with that bat in his hand.

"Who did this to him!" he yelled.

"Nobody, we found him like this," they said. He tapped his cheek and tried to wake him up.

"Go get Ma!" he said. Nana held her heart when she saw him like that. Turns out he drank poison, not wine, and it messed up a part of his brain and caused the seizures. Try explaining that to these kids around here, they're still scared of him. They act like he's a monster. Well forget them, Uncle Kevin ain't no monster, or no damn savage, not to me.

So far, we only got three damn savages, and not as many as people make it seem. Oh, I almost forgot about Poppa. He lives in a room on the first floor, all by his self. He never says a word to anybody, not even Nana. Sometimes he comes in the kitchen to get some food, or to wash the tomatoes or green stuff from his little backyard garden. We always stare at him. We're just waiting for him to say something to somebody, but he never do.

Sometimes my Aunts and Uncles argue about Poppa. They try to figure out when he moved downstairs.

"No, it was when Paul hit him in the head with a skillet 'cause he hit you, right Ma?" Aunt Tracie said.

"Uh-uh, don't blame that on me," Uncle Paul said.

"It was when daddy gave you money for the light bill, but the lights still got cut off," Uncle Nolan said, and they laughed.

"It was when he lost his job at the Mill. And you went down to the welfare beggin' them white folk's after he told you not to,"

Uncle Ernest said from the doorway and scared everybody. I don't care why Poppa moved downstairs, I don't even like him that much. I just wonder why he took the TV with him. It's not fair. Nana keep saying she's saving up to buy another one, but that will take forever. Every Saturday morning, we race to his locked door. We scratch at it like little puppies do, and hope he have mercy. I can't go another week without seeing my favorite cartoons. Sometimes he makes us wait too long before he lets us in. He knows darn well that the *Looney Tunes* always come on early. Sometimes he don't open the door at all. Last time we sat there for a whole hour. Everybody gave up, except me. I stayed there for the longest time. Nana is always saying we got to have faith. But after a while, I realized that Poppa is worse than ornery, he's a mean old bastard. I stomped my feet all the way up the stairs. "Poppa you get on my nerves!" I yelled when I got to the top. I heard his door open. He probably stuck his head out to see who said that. I don't care, he don't know my voice anyway.

Most nights I sleep in Nana's bed. Sometimes Poppa stands still in her doorway, but when he sees me, he curses under his breath and goes back to his own room. Nana chuckles every time. Just to be sure, I look down and read some more words under savage. It said a savage shows no concern for the well-being of others and disregards the proper way to behave toward people. "Sorry Poppa," I said before I put a damn savage check next to his name, and then another one.

4
Nothin' for Christmas

AFTER HALLOWEEN, MAMA said she was sick and tired of living in the big house because she can't get no peace and quiet, or no damn privacy. So, she told us to pack our shit, and we moved to a little house in the alley, behind the big house. I felt sick to my stomach when she told us about it. I don't want to live by our self with her ever again. Bad things will happen. At least here in the big house, we have someone to protect us, and all these rooms to hide in.

Mama's been humming and smiling every minute of the day since we moved to this alley house. I was scared for nothing. She ain't whooped our behinds one time, and we ain't been all that good. Me and Bunny sat at the kitchen table drawing houses with happy stick families standing in front of them. Kids with happy mamas are the luckiest ones.

"Look at my picture I made Mama, you like it?" Bunny said.

"Uh-huh, it's real nice," she said.

"You like my picture Mama?" I said. She turned her back to me. When the phone rang, she jumped up to answer it. Mama laughs the most when she talks to other ladies on the phone. That's when I hang onto her every word.

"Child, after three damn years, my birthday finally fell on the weekend...I'm tellin' you there's gon' be plenty good lookin' men here tonight...please, that man keep me satisfied in and out the sheets...girl, you know me, I don't want too many heifers sittin'

31

around me and my man...uh- huh whatever, don't forget to bring the rum...the white kind. I'm gon' whip up some Pina` Coladas," she said, and hung up.

"Do you like my picture Mama?" I asked her again. She went back to the phone.

"Shit, I forgot to tell her to grab a can of Crisco for them chicken wings," she said. It's okay that she didn't say anything about my picture, she's busy getting ready for the party. I'll ask her later, or maybe tomorrow.

Mama's got another good man, his name is Mr. Charlie. He's the reason she's so happy now. I like him. He got us all this nice furniture and that floor model TV. He brings her flowers and stuff all the time. He ain't never hit her before, so she ain't got no reason to straighten him out. When Mr. Charlie is here, we know to be nice and quiet. Children are supposed to be seen and not heard. If he should ever talk to us, we know to pretend like we got good manners. We'll say yes sir, no sir, please, and thank you. That way, we won't chase Mama's good man away, like we always do.

Once the party started, I cracked the door open and peeked out. Mama's the prettiest lady in the room because she's the birthday girl. She's sitting on Mr. Charlie's lap, laughing, and popping her fingers, and swaying to the music. She got on a colorful party hat and some money is pinned on her tight blue dress. They're out there dancing, drinking, and stinking up our house with their cigarettes and reefers.

"Uh-oh," I say when Mama starts calling our names. She wants us to come out and sing that song for her friends. She make us do it every time she has a party.

"Aw man, I don't want to," Bunny said. Bunny never wants to. I want to because it's the only time our Mama ever smiles at me. Beau wants to, so he can run free. When we get out there, the microphone is already in the middle of the floor waiting for us.

"Evelyn know she got some good-lookin' kids," a lady wearing a short red wig said.

"Mm-hmm, two little Indians and a blonde," another lady said.

"For a small woman, she sure does get around," a man said.

"Please, I don't know what y'all heard, but all my kids got the same daddy," Mama said. They laughed until Mama started laughing for lying. When Beau turned five, she taught us how to be the Staple Singers. We know other songs, but when it's birthday party time, she wants us to sing "I'll take you there." Mama's friends love how I pretend to be Mavis, and the way Beau play the broom like it's a real guitar. Bunny just sings backup and dances. Once Beau steps out in front to do his part, the ladies clapped their hands and call him a handsome devil, and a little heartbreaker. When my part comes up, I put my mouth close to the microphone. Before the record got stopped, we fell on our knees to gather the loose change and dollar bills they threw at our feet. Mama said we could have some cake if we clean up afterward. On my way to the kitchen, I looked at Mr. Charlie. He smiled at us, sort of. Now he knows we got good manners, we're quiet as mice, and people give us money to sing and dance. He should be marrying our Mama any day now. Right after Thanksgiving, Mr. Charlie moved in with us. If we want to do any noisy stuff, we got to go to the big house. He still don't like us. If he comes into the living room and see us, he changes his mind and runs back to Mama's room. He's kind of like Poppa.

Every night Mama makes her good man a special dinner plate because he works late, and can't eat with us. She always covers it with aluminum foil and leaves it on top of the stove. One day we got up and Mr. Charlie's special plate was still up there waiting. Mama scraped the food into the garbage. She scraped it in the next day and the day after that. The next time she threw the whole plate in the garbage. She stayed in her bed drinking, smoking, and crying sometimes. Nana came over to see about her. "Lord child, you ought to know that man wasn't never gon' leave his wife and three kids for you and yours," she told Mama.

Mama tried to stay nice, but she couldn't help it, she ain't got no reason to be happy now. So, she's running around here whooping our behinds for every little thing.

"Who left this cereal box open? Go get the belt! Who left the TV on all night? Get the damn belt!"

"I know, go get the belt," Beau said when she hollered out his name from the bathroom. He left the toilet seat up again, and she fell in. When she kept whooping Bunny even though she was faking an asthma attack, we knew we was in trouble.

It's Christmas Eve, but we still don't have a tree, gingerbread cookies, or candy canes. Worst of all, no presents.

"Did Santa Claus die?" Bunny said.

"No, but maybe there was a bad snow storm, or maybe Rudolph broke his nose, or..."

"Or what?" she said.

"We been bad."

"I know I been good," she said. I looked at my brother sideways. "Beau?"

"Uh-uh, why you lookin' at me? I didn't do nothin'. You the one always be stealing candy," he said. He's right, Santa might be on to me. But why would he make them suffer? No, something ain't right. Santa wouldn't do that.

"Go ask Mama why Santa didn't come," I told Bunny.

"No, you do it," she said. If one of us got to wake Mama up, we'll never know why he didn't come. We were sad all day. She came out of her room to heat up some leftovers, but she looked so crazy we were too scared to say one word to her. We went to bed early because we had to be snoring when the sleigh landed on our roof.

In the morning, we came out with our fingers crossed. Santa still didn't come. Christmas morning looked like any other boring day.

"Okay, you can cry now," I told Bunny. Mama wasn't up yet, and she left a tall cardboard box in the middle of the floor. Beau looked wild-eyed, while me and Bunny started crying.

"Santa make me sick," I said.

"Me too, he so stupid," my sister said between sniffles. I was on my way to our room, so I could put some clothes on. I'm going to the big house to tell Nana we didn't get nothin' for Christmas. Beau was trying to get inside that big box.

"Hey look, here go some toys right here!" he said. We looked at him.

"This better not be no trick," Bunny said. We looked inside and then at each other taking back the mean stuff we said about Santa.

"Why did he leave all our presents in here like this?" Bunny said.

"Because of the snowstorm, he ain't have time to wrap 'em up," Beau said.

"Look, it's a Ms. Beasley doll!" I said.

"That's mine Goldie, give it here!" Bunny said. I hid the doll behind my back.

"Uh-uh, I asked Santa for one," I said.

"Gimme it!" she whined. She ran behind me and grabbed the doll by her big ol' feet. We were having a tug of war with it.

"Let go!" she said. I didn't ask Santa for no Ms. Beasley doll because she's funny looking, with her fat red cheeks and big glasses. I just wanted to see Bunny fall on her butt once I let it go. We fought over toys while Mama slept Christmas away. Bunny found a cowboy hat, plastic toy gun, and a sheriff's badge. She pointed the gun at us.

"Pow, pow!" she said.

"That's mine!" Beau whined.

"I don't see your name on it," she said.

"Okay, then I'm keepin' this stupid doll," he said. I didn't see the Malibu Barbie deep in the box. It was the only thing I asked Santa for this year. I knew how to get my doll. I tickled him until he let go. When our stomachs growled, we put on our coats and boots before we headed over to Nana's. Mama never opened her door. Once inside the big house, we yelled "Merry Christmas!" And ran towards the smell of turkey and sweet potato pie coming from the kitchen.

5
Spilled Milk

WHY DID I EVER TELL MAMA that my third-grade teacher spanked me with them ten taped up rulers? She keeps them on top of her desk, in plain sight so we know better than to misbehave. It was my turn to get some art supplies out of the cabinet, when Benjamin, the class troublemaker pushed me aside.

"Out of my way albino girl," he said.

"Don't call me that," I said.

"Okay, I won't ugly girl."

"Don't call me ugly either." He opened his mouth, and I punched him in his nose because I didn't want to hear it anymore. He sat in the chair next to her desk. He stuffed some tissues up his nose to stop the blood and snot from running out. That's what he gets for messing with me. He wasn't even bleeding all that bad. Anyway, Mrs. Nichols said she don't care what he called me.

"Who threw the first lick?" she said.

"I did because he keeps teasing me—" she stops me from talking by putting her long skeleton finger on my lips.

"What is our motto young lady?" she said. I'm not saying it because I don't want to lie. Mrs. Nichols says it for me.

"Sticks and stones may break my bones, but words can never hurt me." I'm trying to tell her she's wrong, words do hurt because they make me cry sometimes. Will she ever listen? No, she'll just play her song on the back of my thighs, and send me back to my seat. Mama look like her head is about to blow up like a balloon and pop.

"How many times she done put her cripple hands on you?!" she said.

"Seven times."

"She whooped you seven times since school started?"

"No, she only spanked me one time, but she tapped me seven times when she spanked me that one time," I said.

"Mm-hmm, how you know it was seven times?"

"Because she do it like a song."

"Show me," she said.

"Um, okay, it's like one two, one two, one two three," I said while I clapped out the rhythm the same way Mrs. Nichols does.

"Where she hit you at?" I turned around to show her. I touched the back of my thighs.

"Right here," I said. I turned back around, and she slapped me across my face.

"You should've told me the first day she did it," she said. I stood there holding my cheek. What is wrong with these people? First Mama tells me to fight or else she'll whoop me. Mrs. Nichols spanked me for fighting, and Mama slapped me because Mrs. Nichols spanked me, and I should've told her the first day.

When I'm sure Mama ain't paying me no attention, I run out and cross the alley to the big house. Nana takes one look at me and goes to her secret hiding place to get the huge chocolate bar. She gave me two squares, but I kept my hand out and shook my head slowly. It's gonna take three squares for me to get happy again.

The next day Mrs. Nichols wobbled around the classroom, with one hand on her hip. She's making sure we don't cheat on our tests. Wow, I never knew that one of her shoes is bigger than the other. "Your time has expired, pencils down, papers over," she told us. We waited for the little helper to pick up our papers. The classroom became quiet because it's jellybean time. Mrs. Nichols always handed out jelly beans after a test. Once the little helper put all the test papers on the teacher's desk, she rushed to her seat and folded her arms.

We were all ready and waiting for our jellybeans when the classroom door swung open and hit the wall. We jumped and turned our heads toward the door. My Mama stood in the doorway with her hand on her hip. Why, why, why? I ask while my heart beats out of control. Right away I pray, "Dear God, please make Mama disappear and I promise I'll never—"

"I want to talk to you, Lorraine!" Mama yelled. It's too late, nothing could stop her now, not even God. We watched Mama with our mouths open wide.

"I *said* I need to have words with you, Lorraine!" Mama yelled even louder. Mrs. Nichols calmly looked over her glasses at Mama.

"It's Mrs. Nichols, please address me properly. If you don't mind waiting in the hall, I'll get to you when this class has ended," she said. *Poor Mrs. Nichols.* She didn't know she said something wrong, but I knew. And she didn't know what's about to happen, but I sure did. Mama skated her way toward the desk. Mrs. Nichols looked like she just seen the boogie man. She tried to grab her cane, but Mama beat her to it. When she tried to stand up, Mama nudged her shoulder, and she fell back into her chair.

"What is the meaning of this?" my teacher said.

"Girl please, give me a damn break, we went to school together, and now you tryna act all high and mighty, talking like you better than some damn body. Mm-hmm, I know all about your ass, you sure ain't no angel." Mrs. Nichols look like she want to wring Mama's neck. If only she could get her cane and balance on it. But Mama won't even give her no breathing room.

"How can I help you Evelyn?" she said. Mama got all in Mrs. Nichols' face, but she didn't whisper.

"Look I'm only gon' tell you this one time. If you ever put your fuckin' hands on my kid again, I will drag you outside, and make you walk the plank bitch!" she said. Mama took the cane and laid it across Mrs. Nichols' lap real nice like.

"There you go *Mrs. Nichols*," she said. I slid as far into my seat as I could. Once again, Mama is acting crazy. Now she's up there straightening her clothes all slow, like she at home in the mirror by herself. She's checking for any broken nails. Now she's pulling and patting her hair in case it got messed up. She looked over at us like she didn't know this was a classroom with kids in it. She stared in my eyes for a second. "Please don't say my name, just get out Mama," I begged from inside my head. When she spotted them ten rulers I told her about, she snatched them off the desk.

"And give me these damn sticks!" she said. Darn it, she knocked the jar of jelly beans over. They made a lot of noise while they rolled all around the floor. Mama didn't even bother to look at them. She strutted her stuff out the door like a peacock with ten rulers in her hand.

The jellybeans were still rolling around everywhere. I watched the red ones. I happily traded any other color for a red. Mrs. Nichols finally got up and made her way to the intercom. She pressed the button and asked for Mr. Bill. We moved around in our chairs. I had to pretend like I didn't know my Mama either.

"Whose mother was that?" we whispered to each other. I turned in my seat and stared at Nay-Nay. She got cinnamon color skin and long brown hair just like that crazy lady. Now we're all staring at her.

"What y'all looking at me for? That ain't none of my mama. My mama ain't crazy," Nay-Nay said.

Ever since Mama came to my classroom, Mrs. Nichols been kind of mean to me. Whenever I raise my hand, she look right past me and calls on somebody else. I know she see me shaking my hand way over my head. Last time after a test, she only put six jellybeans on my desk, when everybody else got eight. Well, I got eight too, but two of them was black. They don't count, and she knows it.

So now, here she goes standing by my desk, and not saying nothing. I hope she ain't trying to get on my nerves today. I'll just write down the date that's on the chalkboard, *Monday, April 25th, 1977*, but I'm watching her from the corner of my eye. She got one hand on her hip, and one on the cane. I write my name next, *Gwendolyn R.*

Savage. Okay, now she's tapping her good foot on the floor. I'm just going to act like I don't see her. I got scared when she stopped tapping and started stomping.

"Dag, what I do Mrs. Nichols?" She stared over her glasses and raised her eyebrow.

"You know what," she said.

"No, I don't, I didn't do nothing," I said. She stood there waiting for me to answer a question she didn't even ask me. Like I can read her mind or something.

"What you want Mrs. Nichols?" I said while tears formed. I ain't in the mood today because of what Mama did to me last night. She looked under my desk and back at me a few more times. Shoot, did I steal something and forget to hide it? I leaned over to look under my desk. All I saw was a big puddle of water spread out under there.

"Well, what do you have to say for yourself?" she said.

"I don't know who spilled that water," I said. She looked up at the ceiling and shook her head.

"You've got to be kidding me," she said.

"But I didn't spill no water. I didn't...oh," I said once I felt a warm wetness in my underwear. But how did this happen to me? I'm not at home in bed dreaming, shoot, I'm not even sleeping. Anyway, I stopped peeing in the bed ever since we moved back home.

Maybe if I try hard enough I could make myself disappear. It didn't work, I'm still here, and I got to move. Mrs. Nichols is mad. She pointed at the door like I forgot where it was.

"Out, go to the nurse's office now!" she said. All the kids held their stupid noses. They moved to the far side of their desks, so I didn't get none on them. As soon as I got outside of the door by the yellow lockers, the floor rumbled like a train was passing through. They were stomping their feet and laughing at me. "All right settle down children, settle down!" Mrs. Nichols said. I walked into the nurse's office. Nurse Jane sat at her desk, doing nurse stuff, I guess.

"Hi Nurse Jane," I said quietly.

"Hello Gwendolyn, what's going on? You're not feeling well

today huh?"

"Mrs. Nichols made me come here."

"Why?"

"Because." She checked me out until she saw it.

"I see, did your mom send extra clothes for you?" she said. I shook my head no. The intercom buzzed.

"Wait here," she said. It's Mrs. Nichols. I can't understand what she's saying, but I know it's nothing nice.

"Very well, goodbye Lorraine," Nurse Jane said. She came over and put her arm around me.

"It's okay sweetheart, accidents happen, it's certainly not the end of the world. Here, put these on until your mom comes to get you," she said while handing me some dry clothes. I turned my back because I needed my privacy.

"Sweet Jesus," Nurse Jane said. She covered her open mouth with her hands.

"What's the matter Nurse Jane, don't you feel good?" I asked. She knelt in front of me and put her hands on my shoulders.

"Please, tell me, who did this to you, your mom?"

"Nobody did nothing to me Nurse Jane."

"What caused all those bruises on your back?"

"Bruises?" Oh, I didn't see my bruises, I only feel them. Last night Mama got mad and she beat me with the extension cord for no reason. It's the worst she ever done to me. She was going to kill me until Bunny started screaming, and Beau got a hold of the cord. He pulled it out of her hand and ran away with it. Then Mama came to her senses.

Nurse Jane takes me by the chin. I got nowhere to look except in her eyes. They're big and blue, like my Barbie dolls. She squeezed my shoulders softly.

"Gwendolyn, honey, look at me. Don't be afraid to tell me, I can help you," she said. I pulled away from her. Don't she know I'm not allowed to tell on my Mama?

"Very well Gwendolyn, if there's ever anything you want to

talk about, my door is always open. Okay love?" I shook my head. We heard Mama out in the hallway.

"Cripplebitchdon'ttellmeIain'tgotnocleanclothesformykid!" she said. When the door swung open, I pulled the shirt down and spun around fast. If she sees my back, she will think I showed it to Nurse Jane on purpose.

"What you doin' pissin' on yourself in broad daylight? Thought you outgrew all that," she said. Nurse Jane jumped to her feet and glared at Mama. Mama glared back until Nurse Jane sat down.

"Gwendolyn we'll see you tomorrow, and don't forget what I told you," she said.

"What that nosy white bitch call herself tellin' you?" Mama asked me when we walked up the alley.

"Um, she said next time to bring some clean clothes."

"Next time? Better not be no damn next time. I swear you ain't nothin' but trouble," she said.

Tuesday morning, I went into my classroom and sat down. After social studies, Mrs. Nichols limped over to my desk. I got scared of getting embarrassed again. I checked under my seat to make sure the floor was dry.

"Hello Gwendolyn, and how are you on this fine morning?"

"Very well, thank you," I said because she taught us to say that. Why is she being nice to me now? Nurse Jane probably told her about my back. Now she feels bad for whooping me because she knows Mama's taking care of it. Anyway, she's been treating me nicer ever since.

"Don't worry Gwendolyn, I have extra," she says whenever Mama forgets to pack my lunch. She even let me go to the Pittsburgh Zoo when Mama signed the permission slip, but she didn't send the five dollars. And she never gives me black jelly beans anymore. Now she calls my name as soon as I raise my hand, and she put smiley faces on my test paper. I have been picked to be her little helper some days. One time I opened the lunch she packed for me, and there was a pink comb and brush set inside.

"Don't tell the others," she said.

Today Benjamin and his stupid friend poured some water under my desk.

"Look, that albino girl peed again!" they said. I wanted to beat them up so bad. Mrs. Nichols been telling me I'm a smart girl who needs to exercise self-control.

"Hitting doesn't solve anything, you must find words to express yourself," she says. Hitting is all I know. I really want them to leave me alone. I think about what Mama would say to them and say that.

"Shut up, you stupid sons a bitches." They ran over to Mrs. Nichols right away. She bent down so they could whisper in her ear, while pointing at me. I thought she would be mad.

"Really?" she asked them. They shook their heads. She looked at me and smiled before she gave me a thumb up, and a wink.

It's getting hot outside. That's when they show movies in the park. Usually, it's a stupid Bruce Lee movie, but tonight it's Freaky Friday. Mama don't care where I go, or what I do all day, so I don't bother telling her that I'm going.

"Have your ass on them steps by the time the street lights come on," is all she would say anyway. If I don't, she won't let me in the house at all.

When I got to the park I saw Uncle Nolan with his girlfriend Rita. I sat on their blanket with them, and Rita gave me a whole box of Cracker Jack. I like her.

"Hush it, I can't hear," I told them because Rita kept slapping Uncle Nolan's hand and telling him to stop.

"I can't believe they switched Enter the dragon for that bull crap," Uncle Nolan said when we were walking home. But I loved it, and so did Rita. We were getting closer to my house.

"You aint comin' to the house?" Uncle Nolan said.

"Nope," I said. They kept going and said they would catch me later. I just had to tell Bunny and Beau what happened in the movie. Mama stuck her head out of the window, that's how she answers the door. She looked at me and then the street light and at me again.

"Sorry Mama, I was at the park. I saw Freaky Friday, it was *so* funny!" I said.

"Well good for you," she said before she shut the window. Deep down I knew she was gonna do that. She's trying to be funny. She just don't want to be bothered with me. Well, I don't want to be bothered with her either, she gets on my nerves. I crossed the alley and went in the big house. When I got upstairs, Nana was in her room reading her Bible by the lamplight. I went to her dresser and put on one of her cotton nightgowns. The gown swallowed me up. I crawled into her bed and fell asleep.

Little Uncle Marcus made a special signal for me, that way if anybody sees Mama coming from outside, they whistle and say, "The wicked witch is coming pass it on!" When the news gets to me, I'll run and hide. If she catches me having fun, she'll send me home for no reason. I slide under a bed or climb on the top shelf in a closet and stay there until somebody yells, "The wicked witch is gone!" One time they forgot to say it and I woke up behind the couch in the dark.

"Ooh, I'm a tell Mama you called her a wicked witch," Bunny said one time.

"But, I didn't say it, they did."

"So, I'm still telling." Bunny still always got to run and tell stuff. She loves Mama more than anything else in the world. So, Mama know she can count on Bunny to tell her everything. Bunny ain't got a whooping in a long time. The last time Mama took a belt to her behind, she had a real asthma attack. Now she's scared to whoop her, even when she knows she's faking. *Mama ain't slick.* She's giving me my own whooping's, and Bunny's too.

When I got to school this morning, I waited in line behind the others. I wanted to count all the red, gold, and green stars by my name. I had enough of them to know that I'm smart and special. Mrs. Nichols is proud of me for doing all my work. Most of all, she's proud of me for using words to express myself instead of my hands. I'm proud of myself too. I skipped to my seat and sat down. I saw the twins, Faith and Hope standing by Mrs. Nichols' desk. What in the world do they want with her? I made it my business to keep my eye on them. The twins dressed alike every day. Today they got on light blue dresses, laced white bobby socks, and super shiny black shoes. Mrs. Nichols stood in the hall waiting for the bell to ring. I still had time to check them out. Their hair was parted in the middle and held tight with some fluffy white ribbons. Our teacher came in and shut the door. She stretched her lips wide like Howdy Doody when she saw the twins. "My, my, don't you girls look especially pretty today?" she said. I felt scared. I put my hand on my fast beating heart. "Thank you, Mrs. Nichols," they said at the same time. I sneaked my other hand up to check my hair. It's all over my head like a lion, it had some knots in some places. Now I know why she gave me the comb and brush set. She wants my hair to be pretty like Faith and Hope's. I tried to use the comb, but some of the teeth broke. Mama always does Bunny's hair, but not mine. My Aunts said if they keep doing it, she never will. I look down at my clothes. I'm surprised to see the green pants under my old fashioned purple dress. I put my clothes on in the dark today. I don't remember leaving my seat or grabbing Faith and Hope by their ponytails, or bumping their heads together. But they are crying, and their ponytails are wrapped around my hands, so...

"Gwendolyn Savage! What on God's green earth has gotten into you?!" Mrs. Nichols yelled. I dropped the twins and turned toward my teacher. I kept my eyes on her secret mismatched shoes.

"Have you learned nothing?" she said. I wanted to say sorry, but a cat had my tongue. Mrs. Nichols don't look too proud of me right now. She pointed toward the door like she always do.

"You're suspended for the rest of the day," she said. I went to my desk to get my stuff. When I got to the door I turned around for a second. The twins were whining and holding onto each other. Mrs. Nichols fussed over them and tried to make them perfect again.

Mama did pack my lunch today. I told her Mrs. Nichols brings me lunch sometimes. So, she's showing off by making me a ham sandwich. It got lettuce and big red tomatoes falling out of it. I just needed to find the right place to enjoy it. I chose the steps leading to the school basement. After I ate my lunch, I fell asleep. In my dream, I'm a beautiful princess. I'm wearing a sparkling pink dress with white laced bobby socks. My yellow hair turned silky shiny black. It was parted in the middle with two fluffy white ribbons that helped it behave. Mrs. Nichols saw me, and she stopped dead in her tracks. "My, my, oh my, Gwendolyn Renee Savage, aren't you the prettiest little girl I ever done seen in this here school?!" she said. I looked down at her feet and they were perfectly fine. She started tap dancing. *Wow, she's really good at it.* She invited me to tap dance too, but somebody shook my shoulder before I could. I opened my eyes, it's Mr. Bill. He's the school janitor, and he's like two-hundred years old.

"Hey lil gal, what you doin' on these steps, shouldn't you be inside learnin'?"

"Huh, I mean, sir?"

"Why is you sleeping down there?"

"Because Mrs. Nichols suspended me."

"Well then, come up from there, and carry yourself on home," he said. I hoped Mama wasn't home. Then I could go tell Nana how Mrs. Nichols suspended me for no reason. She'll be on my side. She'll give me a spoonful of sugar. When I got to the alley I heard my favorite song, "*Bennie and the Jets.*" It sounds like mumbo-jumbo because it's playing different parts out of different windows. People are singing too loud or too squeaky. I spun around and around and sang along until I fell onto the steps. After the world stopped spinning I knocked on our door. Mama stuck her head out the window. She looked up and down the alley to see the other kids coming home from school too. But there ain't no other kids.

"What happened, the school burn down?"

"Nope." Mama always say she don't get no rest until our asses is in school. She jumped for joy when Beau started first grade. She's still in the window while the sun bakes my body up. I still hear the piano part of the song, so I move my head from side to side.

"Why the hell ain't you in school girl?!" she said.

"Oh, um, Mrs. Nichols suspended me, for no reason." She stared at me for a while.

"I knew it had to be that whore," she said. She slammed the window and showed up in the doorway.

"Girl, get on in here and have yourself a seat," she said. I did as I was told. I looked around the living room. The TV wasn't even on. It's always on when we're home. Mama still wasn't dressed yet. She's wearing her pink robe, not the one that looks like an old raggedy towel, but the satiny one. Her bedroom door was halfway open. I saw some big brown feet sticking out of her flowery bedspread. I looked at my own feet before she caught me being nosy.

She snatched the heavy black telephone off the table and it made that ding-ding sound. She put the phone on her lap. "Let me call this cripple bitch and see what the hell is going on. Hello, this is Evelyn Savage, I'm Gwendolyn Savage's mother—She in third grade, room one-oh-two. If you would let me finish, I'll tell you why I'm calling!" she said. That's probably Mrs. Lombardi on the phone, she works in the office.

"Her teacher sent her home—I don't know what for, especially since school just started thirty damn minutes ago. Her handicap teacher is just tryna fuck—hello?" she pressed the little button on the phone over and over. Mrs. Nichols gets on Mama's nerves, even if she ain't trying to. Mama said they went to Fifth Avenue High School together. But now Mrs. Nichols act like her shit don't stink because she went to college, and Mama didn't.

"Any jackass can go to college, big deal, if it wasn't for these damn kids, I could've went to some fancy college too. Let that heifer hop one mile in my shoes, see how good she do," she said before. She dialed the number to Larimer Elementary school again.

"For cryin' out loud, I just called a second ago—hello?" Mama look like the boogie man just jumped out the closet on her. She pushed the little white button over and over. Poor Mama. The teachers at my school don't like her, so they're hanging up on purpose. She took a deep breath and dialed the number again. "I'm callin' about my daughter and somebody keep hang—" She took the phone away from her ear. Now she's just staring at it.

"I hate you, you cripplema whore! I see why you got polio 'cause you a fuckin' bitch!" she said. She threw the telephone at the wall, and it broke in pieces. When she covered her face and started crying, I went over and tried to put my arms around her. She pushed me back into the chair.

"Get away from me, it's all your fault!" she said. She grabbed a statue off the side table and came toward me.

"No Mama, don't do that!" I said. It didn't matter how much I screamed and cried, she kept hitting me on top of my head over and over until I heard a man's voice.

"Evelyn, what the hell are you doing?!" he said. She stared at the statue for a little while, then she let it fall on the floor. She fell into his arms, and he held her tight and rubbed her hair.

"You don't understand...it's *her*, she makes me." Some red drops fell past my eye. I reached up and felt a big cut on my forehead. I held my hand there to stop it up, but when I let go, blood ran down my face like spilled milk.

They tucked my arms under the blanket, so I could hardly move. The hospital room was cold. I wanted to run when I smelled Mama's sweet gum. I wanted to run, I didn't know if she would hurt me again. I touched my head, this time it felt like spider legs on my forehead. A doctor put his face over mine. He held my eye open and shined a light in. Then he did the other one.

"Do I have a spider on my head?" I said.

"A spider? Oh, no, those are stitches, you got twelve on the top, and eight on the forehead," he said. He told Mama not to expect my hair to grow back where the stitches are. A nurse and a lady in a blue suit came in and stood at the foot of the bed with the doctor. All I got to do now is stick to the story I made up.

"I fell on a bunch of broken glass in the alley," I said. The doctor tried to trick me.

"So, how did you manage to avoid getting any cuts on your arms, hands, or knees if you fell on broken glass?" he said.

"Um... Because I was..." I looked at Mama for a second.

"Tell the truth Goldie," Mama said.

"I fell on some broken glass in the alley," I said.

"I don't know how it happened, she ran in the house all bloody before she passed out," Mama said.

"What a crock," the blue suit lady said.

"Excuse me, I beg your damn pardon," Mama said. I knew the lady in the blue suit would take me if I wasn't careful. She cut her eyes at Mama and rolled them hard.

"Is this what happened dear?" she asked me. I loved when grown-ups called me those nice names. I almost told.

"Uh-huh, yes ma'am, I fell." Mama didn't say sorry, but she must be because she took me to McDonald's, and the candy store. It's our own special day. But, when Nana found out what happened, she came over to see about me. She held my chin in her hand and checked all my sides.

"The doctor said we can't put no Band-Aid on it Nana, I got to let it breathe," I said.

"Baby, go on in the livin' area, I need to talk to your mama," she said. I went and sat right in front of the TV. The "Mickey Mouse Club" was on.

"You tryna kill that child?" Nana said.

"Is she dead?" Mama said.

"Evelyn, honey we need to get you some help."

"I ain't the one who need help!" Mama yelling at Nana made

me look in the kitchen. Her hands were on Mama's shoulders.

"Listen to me now, the lord works in mysterious ways. It don't matter how she got here, she here now so you got to love her. God gave you beauty for ashes," she said. Mama laughed like a wicked witch and shook herself loose.

"That would make it all better for you, wouldn't it Pearl?" Evelyn said. I never saw Nana mad before. I never even heard her say a cuss word. But when she left she slammed the door so hard that the statues started rocking. I'm trying to sing along with the "Mickey Mouse Club" kids, but it's kind of hard to concentrate. M-I-C... I just can't stop thinking. K-E-Y... How did I get here? M-O-U-S-E.

6

Good Moanin' Heartache

"CHILD, THE WOMAN IS PUSHING forty, if she ain't already crossed over. Walking around here half naked. Who she think she is?" That's what those other ladies want to know. They're talking about Mama's new friend, Miss Gazelle. She just moved across the street from the big house. If Mama catch anybody saying bad stuff about her friend, she will whoop their ass, she said so herself. Mama used to have house parties all the time, but now, she goes out to the bar with Miss Gazelle every Friday night. Sometimes she don't come back until early Sunday morning.

"Call me Evelyn from now on," Mama told us one day. She's just trying to be like Miss Gazelle because her kids call her by her name. I always sit on the bathroom floor to watch Miss Gazelle get brand new. She don't mind at all. She tilts her head and smiles at me after she puts on some fake eyelashes.

"How they look?" she said.

"They look like Miss Piggy.

"Good," she said. Then she covered her face with white powder. She pats the powder until the freckles and dark circles under her eyes disappear.

"Miss Gazelle ain't you done yet?" I ask.

"No, not yet," she says. After she put that black stuff all around her eyes, I jump up.

"Uh-uh, one more thing," she said. She smeared on lots of red lipstick before she put red kisses all over a tissue paper.

51

"Okay, go ahead and get it, girl," she said. I flew into the kitchen where she left the white wig. I come back and hand it to her carefully. After she puts it on, I stand back to get a better look. The wig is super curly, and it goes past her flat booty.

"Wow, Miss Gazelle, you look like a Barbie doll, almost."

"Almost?"

"Um, well." She laughed.

"Don't worry sugar pie, I admire your honesty," she said.

"Penny for your thoughts," Miss Gazelle said the next time I sat on the bathroom floor waiting for her to finish changing her face, and putting on a different white wig. It would be nice if she would wear a real dress this time, and not them same cut off shorts and swimming suit top. When it's snowing outside, she wears big fur coats, cowboy hats, and boots, but she's still kind of naked under all that.

"I wasn't thinking nothing," I said.

"But you look like you always got somethin' on your mind. I think you been here before girl. You got an old soul."

On Sunday morning, I stood in the kitchen by myself. I saw the lock turning. I waited. Evelyn fell through the door and crawled to the bathroom to let the party out. Her hair was still braided under the stocking cap. That long black wig she was wearing might be in her purse, or maybe it got snatched off in a fight. Now she's sitting on the floor next to the toilet saying, "Oh God, oh God, oh God." I pointed at her and giggled.

"What you laughin' at?" she said.

"I don't know what, stupid," I said. I ran back to our room and jumped in my bed. My heart raced because I got smart with Mama, I mean *Evelyn*. She won't even remember what I said today when she wakes up tomorrow.

"I said take y'all asses to sleep!" Evelyn said. We were jumping from one bed to the other and laughing and making all kinds of noise.

We knew she wouldn't whoop us, not while she got a man in there. *Boy, were we wrong.* When she busted through the door, we ran all over the room to avoid the leather strap, but it's no use. She's bigger and faster than us. Mama whooped us quick like we was the Three Stooges. I guess Beau didn't get enough. He keeps calling her.

"Hey, stop talking and go to sleep before she comes back," I said. But he wouldn't stop trying to find a name she would answer to.

"Mama... Lady... Evelyn get your booty back in here, I need you!" he said. We're really cracking up now.

"A'ight, laugh now cry later!" she yelled.

"Uh-oh, you better shut up boy," Bunny warned him.

"Hey Goldie, is you sleep?" Beau said.

"Yes, I'm sleep, what you want?"

"My arm broke," he said.

"Uh-uh you trying to get us in trouble again," Bunny said.

"No I ain't, Mama broke my arm for real." He found his way to the light and turned it on.

"Turn it off!" we said.

"Wait, look, don't y'all see it?"

"Uh-uh. I don't see nothing," I said. He pushed his arm until it swung back and forth fast. He couldn't stop laughing at it.

"Don't it hurt?" Bunny said.

"Man, it hurt bad," he said. But still, he liked to watch it swing.

"Beau, look out!" I shouted when Evelyn appeared behind him. The belt was wrapped around her hand one time.

"Y'all think I'm playin'?" she said. Beau turned around and gave his broken arm another push. He stuck out his bottom lip and put on his puppy face.

"Look what you did Mama, you broke my arm," he said.

"This ain't no good time for you to run off honey. I got my hands full with Kevin, Marcus, and Thea. Not to mention Ernest with all his troubles," Nana said. She was talking to the back of Evelyn's head. Ever since Miss Gazelle moved to Detroit Evelyn been staying in the bed all day holding the stack of pictures Miss Gazelle sent her. I sneaked into her room to look at the pictures. Miss Gazelle was singing on stage or sitting at a bar with lots of other happy people. On the backsides, she wrote stuff like, "Having the time of my life!" or "What's taking you so long?!" So, now she's leaving us to be with her friend. She ignored Nana and threw her suitcases in the trunk of the jitney car. I don't know why she can't take us, especially since Miss Gazelle took all her kids with her. Bunny ran and grabbed onto her legs like that would make her change her mind.

"No, get back, stay with Ma. I'll send for y'all once I'm on my feet!" she said before she slid into the front seat.

"Evelyn please honey, I ain't in no position to take care of three more kids." Evelyn stuck her head out of the car window.

"Nadine and Sylvia can help you. Or call their daddies. I got to get out of this God-forsaken city," she said.

When all the snow melted and dried up, Aunt Tracie took us to Detroit on the Greyhound bus. It was night time when we got there. She held Bunny and Beau by their wrist to keep them from wandering around. She opened the door of a waiting cab and pushed them in. We stopped at a house with soft yellow light coming from every window. When people opened the door, the loud music escaped. They were having a party. Miss Gazelle stood in front of a band belting out a song. She had on white shorts, a white swimming top and gold high heel shoes and a short white wig. They clapped and whistled while she sang her song.

We saw Evelyn standing next to a man, she nodded her head and smiled at him like she was some important lady, like Diana Ross. Aunt Tracie pushed them toward her and I followed. "Go on, say hi to your Mama," she said. Evelyn's teeth disappeared as soon as she saw us.

"Hi Mama," Bunny said. She threw her arms around Evelyn's waist. Evelyn squinted at Aunt Tracie and lifted Beau's arm.

"You still got this damn cast on?" she said. Most of the people watched Miss Gazelle, but some of them were staring at us. I wish we wasn't so dirty. The man raised his eyebrow.

"Are these *all* your kids?" he asked Evelyn.

"Yeah, they *all* mine, what about it?" she said.

"Well, enjoy the rest of your evening," he said before easing over to a lady wearing a tight red dress. Evelyn gave Aunt Tracie an evil look.

"What? Ma told me to bring 'em. She tired, so you got to take care of your own kids. Hey, don't look at me like that, I'm just the messenger, my job is done. You could at least say thank you," she said.

"Well thank you," Evelyn said. Aunt Tracie paid her no mind. She looked around the crowded room. A lot of folks was staring at her because she looks like Christie Love.

Every day, we play with Miss Gazelle's kids until we pass out. We have to stay out of sight when the parties are going on. Mr. Starks works in the kitchen all day because people want to buy beer or chicken with hot sauce on some Wonder bread.

Poor Mr. Starks, he got a hole in his neck. He got this little microphone that he puts up to the hole whenever he needs to say something. He sounds like a robot. Sometimes, we ask him silly questions just to hear him talk. "Ewe, that's nasty!" we say when he blows boogers out of it. Anyway, he takes care of us. He cooks for us and he washes our clothes. He says he don't mind, but sometimes he gets mad at Miss Gazelle and Evelyn. He'll grab his microphone and give them a piece of his mind through the hole.

"You hussies need to air y'all asses out. Shouldn't be running the streets all the time. Y'all need to see 'bout these here chillun. They should be in school," he said.

"Can you repeat that?" Miss Gazelle said. She's just making fun of him.

"Naw bitch, I can't repeat one damn word. How much breath you think I got? Anyway, you heard what the fuck I said the first time!"

We all laugh when we hear the robot cussing. I hope we stay here forever. But Mr. Starks is right, we should be in school.

Evelyn and Miss Gazelle got all dressed up last night. Evelyn had on a tight black dress and some pearls. Miss Gazelle had on some satiny black shorts and her itsy- bitsy matching swimming top. Oh well, at least the pretend diamonds on her neck and wrists looked pretty. She still let me bring her white wig after she put on the makeup. This wig is super short. I don't like it. I sat on the floor and watched while checked all her sides.

"Miss Gazelle, how come you don't dress like a lady?" I said.

"What you say sugar pie?"

"Um, I didn't say nothing Miss Gazelle." Then they went off to the Grande-Ballroom for a concert.

Later that night, Evelyn came home all by herself. She had her shoes in one hand, her wig in the other, and that wild look in her eyes. Then I started praying, please don't say it, please. "Y'all pack y'all shit!" she said. So, now here we are, in this homeless shelter, sitting on these bare mattresses. We're waiting for that lady with the bird face to finish talking mean to us.

"You will keep your children by your side at all times, if they're found roaming the halls unsupervised, your stay will be terminated immediately. This is the green room, there is a chart on the bathroom door. The green dots represent the times your family can shower and such, without any interruption. Breakfast is at eight am sharp, lunch is at noon, supper is at six," she said. She kept her eyes on us while she backed out and closed the green door. I hated the place already. It's so cold our teeth are chattering. It's warmer outside. The door opened, and the bird lady came back in. I don't know why she looks at us like that. She plopped some sheets and blankets on one of the beds before she backed out again.

"Stupid bitch," Evelyn mumbled. After we made the beds, we tiptoed to the bathroom. We came back quietly and slid under the thin blanket.

Aunt Tracie lifted her head and looked over at us to make sure we was asleep. Bunny and Beau was already making their sleeping song.

"Okay girl, spill the beans."

"It was just time to move on Tracie."

"Who moves on like this? Something happened, I know you." I stayed still and quiet as a mouse. I wanted to know why we left Mr. Starks' funhouse too.

"I didn't have to leave with you, but you're my sister, I'm on your side. I'm freezing, homeless, and cramped up on this cot, the least you could do is tell me why."

"Okay, I'll tell you, since you want to know so damn bad." We only went because she was obsessed with the lead singer. So, after the concert, she dragged me out to the back door. We stood out there for hours, like some desperate groupies. Once they realize they was horny the door swung open. I couldn't believe how easy it was to get close to a group as famous as they used to be. Anyway, the one she was after didn't seem too impressed with all her whoop-dee-doo 'cause he flirted with me all night."

"Child, what you do?"

"I ignored him. Then he swiveled his ass in her direction. She started flippin' her wig, she knew she had her hooks in him. He looked deep in her eyes and said, "Can I ask you one question baby?" She said, "Ask away sugar pie." Then he grabbed my hand and kissed it and said, "Who is this fine young woman here with you tonight?"

"Oh shit, what she do?"

"Girl, she turned beet red and said "Who her? She my maid, I brought her with me in case I spilled something on my shorts." Aunt Tracie sat up straight.

"What?" she said.

"Mm-hmm. They was all starin' at me like I was supposed to climb across the table and scratch her eyes out. But I couldn't move, I didn't say shit, I was in shock. After that, they hung all over her, takin' pictures with her. So, when they was halfway out the door, he asked her if she was going to make sure her maid got home safe. That old settler looked me dead in my eye and said, "She's a big girl, she should know the way by now."

"I can't believe you let all that slide, it ain't even like you," Aunt Tracie said.

"How could I beat the woman's ass while I'm stayin' up in her house with my three kids, and you?"

"I don't care, I would've snatched that cotton ball clean off her head, and let the chips fall. Then I would feel better about being here."

"Now I know she didn't give a damn about me," Evelyn said.

"I regret not tellin' her she sound like two cats stuck together when she sing," Aunt Tracie said.

"Yeah, that's it! *Good moanin' heartache*," Evelyn sang like a cat.

"*Good moanin' heartache*," Aunt Tracie sang in her own cat voice. They giggled at first, but now they're laughing too loud. They kept on trying to see who could sing it better until the door opened and light from the hall flooded the room. The tiny bird lady stood in the doorway like a sack of potatoes. When they stopped laughing, she backed out and closed the door. Now their beds are squeaking because they're trying to hold the laughter in. I know I better hold mine in.

"May I have your attention, please? If you arrived late last evening, you should know the building is closed from nine to noon," the bird lady announced.

"So, what we supposed to do for three damn hours?" Aunt Tracie said.

"You could use the time to find a job that leads to a paycheck, and perhaps a more permanent residence," she said. Aunt Tracie fixed her mouth to say something to the bird lady, but Evelyn elbowed her. After we ate we rushed to the green room to get dressed. "Shit, girl I ain't even got no clean drawers," Aunt Tracie said.

"Me either," Evelyn said. We cracked up when Aunt Tracie was trying to show Evelyn how to cut her pillowcase and make some undies out of it like she did.

"Oh, it's like a diaper," Evelyn said. The bird lady stuck her head in the room again.

"It is eight-forty-five, you must be prepared to vacate," she said. We stood on the sidewalk holding hands and waiting for the red light to turn green. Cars whizzed by and people walked or stood at bus stops. I wanted to ride the bus too.

"What now?" Aunt Tracie said.

"I don't know, let me figure it out."

"I can't believe they put kids out in the street like this," Aunt Tracie said.

"God bless the child that's got his own," Evelyn said.

"Look it's a park across the street," Bunny said. Beau couldn't wait to get to the park, so he ran into the traffic and fell. Cars rolled right over him. Evelyn and Aunt Tracie were too busy talking. I tugged on Aunt Tracie's skirt.

"Beau is in the street, under that car. Aunt Tracie—"

"Girl, stop pulling on my skirt. You gon' make my bloomers come loose," she said. When the light turned green, Evelyn realized her hand was empty.

"Where is Beau?" she said.

"Under there," I said pointing at a black car.

"What, why didn't you tell me?" Evelyn ran into the street waving her arms in the air.

"Please stop, I got to get my son!" she told the next man who rode over Beau. He ignored her and rolled over my brother. Then another car rode over him.

"Get out of the street lady! Are you out of your mind?!" one driver said.

"Are you trying to get yourself killed?" a lady yelled out of her car window. Evelyn jumped in front of the next car on top of him.

"Hey man, don't fuckin' move! I'm tryna tell you my son fell under your car." Beau was lying flat on his back as still as can be. The drivers looked surprised to a little boy crawling from under the car. They started honking their horns and screaming hallelujah! Evelyn scooped him up. "He's okay!" she shouted while carrying him the rest of the way. Once we got in the park, she pulled him behind the sliding board. We all knew what for.

"He's already scared enough, why can't you just talk to him?" Aunt Tracie said.

"No, he's too high strung, he could've got killed, he need to learn!" Some blackbirds flew out of the trees when her hand came down on his bare booty. She wanted him to cry, just to know he understands. But he ain't going to, not in front of all us women. He came out pulling his pants up while running toward the swings. We heard Evelyn crying behind the sliding board. Bunny started crying, so I joined in.

"Oh Lord. Y'all stop feelin' sorry for yourself. Go somewhere and play. I need to see about my crazy sister," Aunt Tracie said.

7
Graven Images

"I SAID GOOD DAY BITCH!" Evelyn yelled at the bird lady before we walked out of the doors for the last time.

"Leave that old woman alone. Besides, you might need to come back one day," Aunt Tracie told her.

"As Gawd is my witness, I shall never be homeless again," Evelyn said. Aunt Tracie laughed.

"Uh-uh, girl you are a mess," she said. The cab pulled up and we piled in and rode to our new apartment. I jumped for joy when Aunt Tracie said she was staying with us for a while.

Aunt Tracie is the only one who can calm Evelyn down. When she throws something against the wall, she says stuff like, "Damn, how much you pay for that? Or uh-uh, don't call that girl, you clean it up." When she sees Evelyn looking out of the window for too long she'll say, "Girl, why don't you go get yourself some beauty rest, I'll feed the munchkins tonight." For my tenth birthday, she baked me a cake with pink icing and gave me a present. I never seen a chocolate colored Barbie doll with a curly afro before. The box said her name was Christie, but I changed it to Tracie.

Evelyn's been going to that big tent revival on the corner. That's where she met a preacher she calls Prophet.

"Girl, he knew stuff about me, personal shit I never told a soul. So, I'm givin' God one last chance. Why don't you come to the tent with me tonight?" Evelyn asked Aunt Tracie.

"I'll pass," she said.

"Aw come on Tracie, you won't regret it. That tent is crawling with plenty of fine ass, sanctified men, all praying for a foxy brown girl like you."

"So, let me get this straight, you want me to come to church, pretend to catch the Holy Ghost, and speak in tongues, just to snag me a man?"

"What's wrong with that?"

"Girl, you need Jesus," she said.

"Well, that's why I'm going to the revival." Evelyn got saved and joined the church. These days she keeps her nose in the Bible. I like church lady Evelyn because she doesn't just whoop us. Instead she will up throw her hands up and plead the blood of Jesus. That gives us a chance to get our act together.

Me and Bunny stood outside our door listening to the strange voices coming from our apartment.

"What's that?" she said.

"I don't know." I opened the door and stuck my head in. Two strange ladies stood in the middle of the floor holding Evelyn's hands. They was praying and talking in them tongues. "Father God, we ask that you deliver your daughter," an old lady said. We went inside and watched them for a while. We made fun of them. "Praise Jesus bock, bock, bock! Help your daughter Lord cock a doodle doo!" Evelyn's right eye opened, and it told us to take our behinds to our room. We ran past them and shut our door.

"Who is those ladies?" Bunny said.

"Jehovah's Witnesses, I think."

"I don't like them."

"How come?"

"Because Mama said they just wanna come in our house to see what the hell we got." She peeked out into the living room.

"What they doing now?" I said.

"They sittin' on the couch, reading the Bible," she whispered.

"So, let's go dance for them," I said. Aunt Tracie always brings new records home. Bunny held up two good records. "Bustin' loose" and "Brick House" I chose "Bustin' loose". First, we did the robot, then the bump. Bunny started doing the spank. I tried to keep up with her. They're supposed to dig into their brassieres for a sweaty dollar, or at least feel around the bottom of their purses for some loose change to give us. Instead, they're just gawking at us like we're dancing butt naked. The song said to break it down, so we did. On our way up from the breakdown, the old lady surprised us with some whacks on our behinds with a rolled-up newspaper.

"You two cut this mess out right this instant!" she said. She didn't bother to say sorry for scratching our record when she lifted the needle. Our mouths flew open, I felt sorry for what was about to happen. Evelyn can whoop us until we're black and blue, but she go crazy if anybody else touch us. But she didn't do nothing. She's just standing there, looking kind of stupid, if you ask me. We can't believe she didn't straighten the old lady out.

"That worldly music ain't suitable for grown folk, let alone for these babies. Up here shaking their little tails all over the place. This is yet another way for Satan to steal their innocence," she said.

"Amen Mother Louise," the other one said. We watched the old woman walk around checking everything out.

"Let me just say, if Prophet come in here right now, he would hit the ceiling," she said.

"Why you say that? My place is clean," Evelyn said.

"It's the devil's den, with all these statues and whatnot you got on the surfaces. The bible tells us not to worship graven images. Sister, our God is a jealous God. That's why these babies ain't allowed to play with no dolls, it's idolatry plain and simple. From here on out, they can't dance or listen to them worldly records. Also, women ain't supposed to wear the garments of a man, so, get rid of them pants. The Bible tells us to turn away from the wicked ways of this world," she said.

"*Amen* Mother Louise," the other woman said. For heaven's sake. *Where is Aunt Tracie?*

"Notice anything different about me?" Evelyn asked Aunt Tracie when she came in from Wednesday night church.

"Nope, you still the ugly one," Aunt Tracie said.

"Girl stop playing and check me out," she said. She stuck her hand out and wiggled her fingers around.

"You been shopping at the five and dime again?" Evelyn started jumping up and down.

"I'm getting married! Ain't you gon' say something?"

"Uh-huh, do he know you got three kids, and you crazy as batshit?"

"I'm not crazy, I'm just disappointed about the way things turned out for me. If you had all these kids weighin' you down, you would understand. Anyway, he know all about them, and he still want to marry me. Girl, he worships the ground my ass walk on. He young." Aunt Tracie tilted her head.

"How young?" she said. Evelyn grabbed her arm and pulled her off the couch.

"Come to my room, I'll tell you all about him," she said.

Bunny was in the middle of the living room floor twirling all around in the blue satin dress. It's Evelyn's wedding day. I got on the same stupid dress, but I ain't happy. Now we got to move and change schools again. I'm tired of being the new girl, everybody picks on the new girl.

Evelyn stood in the front of the church with a regular brown-skinned man who was dressed like a penguin. A preacher asked them some questions and he said, "I do," and she said, "*I really do*," and they laughed. When they kissed everybody said aww and clapped their hands.

"Kids, come on over here. Come say hi to your new daddy," she said.

On moving day, New-Daddy came to help us. Every time they passed each other they kissed. *"Behave now,"* she said when he smacked her behind.

"Put it in the box with the rest of them," she told me. I held on tight to my Aunt Tracie Barbie doll. I love her most of all.

"No, I'm keeping this one!" I cried.

"What's the matter with her?" New-Daddy said.

"I told her she can't play with them dolls no more, but she won't listen. She give me the most trouble." I looked at Bunny. Why ain't she putting up a fight? Don't she know how serious this is? New-Daddy bent down and held my hand.

"Do you love the Lord?" he said.

"I guess so," I said.

"Well, he loves you for sure, and he don't want you to worship false idols. Inside the word idol is the word doll, you see?"

"No, I—"

"Josiah, it's getting dark outside, we ain't got time for all that. Girl leave the doll in the box with the rest of them," Evelyn said.

"That's a low down dirty shame," Aunt Tracie said. Me and Bunny was in the kitchen putting the last dishes in a box when Evelyn and Aunt Tracie came in.

"Come on Trace, come with us," Evelyn said.

"Uh-uh, that church crap ain't my cup of tea."

"Well, what you gon' do? You welcome to stay here, but the rent gon' be due come the first, and I can't help you with it."

"I know, anyway, Smitty say I can work at his bar some nights."

"Doing what?"

"Waitin' tables. What else would I be doing?" I knew Aunt Tracie couldn't stay with us forever, but I'm not ready to live without her. What am I gonna do now? Who's going to keep Evelyn from beating the living daylights out of me? *Maybe he will.* I looked over at them. New-Daddy was hanging all over her like a bee on a pretty flower. *Maybe not.* After we said goodbye to Aunt Tracie, I ran back inside and hugged her one more time.

"I love you Aunt Tracie," I told her.

New-Daddy stopped in front of another apartment building with red balconies all the way up. A man was in the hallway waiting for us.

"Ah, there she is, Sister Evelyn, welcome home," he said after he hugged her.

"Thank you, Deacon Williams," she said. He looked at me for a second. I remember him from the wedding. He kept bossing people around, telling them where to sit, when to stand up, and when to shut up. He had a wide flat nose, and no lips like a puppet on Sesame Street. I love puppets, but this one gives me the creeps. He grabbed New-Daddy's hand and shook it.

"Congratulations boy, you got yourself a real fine family," he said.

"Thank you, sir," our New-Daddy said. The man snapped his stubby fingers and dug in his shirt pocket for a white envelope.

"Hey, this is from Prophet," he said. New-Daddy looked inside and smiled. Now the creepy man is staring at me. He's scaring me.

"It's a little something to start you off with, Lord knows you got your hands full now," he said, before he walked away.

We were all so tired after we got everything out of the truck, but Evelyn still made us put the right boxes in the right rooms before we could go to sleep. New-Daddy showed us our room. Beau jumped on one of the twin beds.

"This is my bed!" he said.

"Let's go, son, boys don't sleep with girls. Your room is across the hall," New-Daddy told him.

"But Beau always sleeps with us," Bunny said.

"Well not anymore," he said. I didn't want him to go. Who's going to make us laugh when we should be sleep? Without him, the boogie man won't be too scared to come in here.

I miss Nana, we're not even allowed to call her on the phone. They said we got to forget our old family and our old life because they're all sinners who will only drag us to hell with them. We live in the world, but we are not of the world they say. The Saints in this building are our new family in Christ. We got to do whatever Prophet says and never talk back. And since we got baptized, we can burn in the lake of fire for all eternity if we sin.

"What's sin?" Bunny asked New-Daddy.

"Anything against the word of God."

"What's eternity?" I said.

"Forever and ever." I would tell him that my Nana said ain't no hell. She said if there is a hell, we already living in it. But I sure don't want to get in trouble.

8

She Need a Man

CHURCH LADIES DON'T EVEN try to look pretty. They don't wear makeup or nice long wigs. Their dresses are ugly and way too big. They walk too slow like they got all day or something. Except when they hear that Prophet is coming. That's when everybody comes to life, and the church ladies put on their best ugly dresses. Prophet is New-Daddy's daddy. Evelyn said she don't trust Prophet because he's one of them quadroons, whatever that is. To me, he looks like Jesus got old because his hair is long and wavy, and gray all over. But Evelyn says he looks like a pimp, whatever that is. On Sundays, we leave the building to go to the church. It has two signs outside. One says Promised Land Ministries, and the other one says corner store.

One Sunday two of the brothers came into the church pulling a big wood cross to the pulpit. It looked heavy. Once they got up there, Prophet showed us some weird looking hammer and nails.

"All right Saints, the time has come. I want to know who amongst you will stand and die to save the souls of humanity. Not one is willing to make the sacrifice? Jesus made it for you. Huh, Sister Claudette, what about you Brother Josiah, Minister Luke—anybody?" Nobody wanted to get nailed to the cross. Prophet said he would do it if God didn't ordain him to lead us to the Promised Land.

"Next week we gon' meet by the riverside and see who got faith enough to walk on water," he said, and the Saints laughed.

"Don't laugh, many of you are faking the faith. You'll step out on

68

the water with life preservers under your coats," he said, and the Saints said amen.

Evelyn and New-Daddy don't do that much smooching or behind slapping, like when we first got here. Most of the time they're arguing about Prophet.

"Seem like if I tell you I need a new pair of bloomers, you got to run and show your daddy my old bloomers, so he can decide if I really need 'em," Evelyn said. New-Daddy don't know what to say. He might be counting the scratches on the wood floor, that's what I do.

"Why Josiah? You work five sometimes six days a week, but you give him damn near every dime."

"I'm being obedient, and doing the Lords will by supporting Prophet," he said.

"Stop, you killin' me, you big dummy. He might be a prophet if you spell it P-R-O-F-I-T. Shit, if he a prophet, I'm the Queen of fuckin' Sheba. And why don't he live here with Mother Louise, huh? He out there somewhere eating steak and caviar, while the rest of us sit around waiting for some crumbs to fall off his table."

"What are you talking about? No one has missed a meal around here."

"I didn't say we did, I said he livin' like a king while we barely got two nickels to rub together. He might have all these other fools fooled around here, but not me." New-Daddy left a few minutes ago, but she was still talking. Shoot, she caught me staring at her. I couldn't help it.

"What I tell you about sneakin' around, listenin' to grown folks' conversations?"

"Um, you said don't do that," I said. I walked backward slowly until I was safe out of her sight.

Except for the arguments about Prophet, we're like a real family. We eat our dinner together each day. New-Daddy brings us a new toy from the five and dime store every Friday. This Saturday morning, after breakfast, Evelyn got us scrubbing the apartment from top to bottom. The sisters are coming here for tonight's prayer meeting. When they get here they just love everything.

"Sister Evelyn, you sure know how to pull a room together. I ain't never had fried chicken so light and crispy, you gon' have to give me the recipe. It sure smell like springtime in here, what is it?" they ask her.

"Potpourri, it's simmering on the stove," Evelyn says like she wish she was somewhere else. After there ain't nothing but bones and forks on their plates, I collect them and take them to the kitchen. When I get back they're flipping through their Bibles. They're pretending to read it, but they're just waiting for Sister Amina to hit the floor. She don't always do it, but she did do it tonight, right in our living room. So, they slammed their Bibles shut, and circle her. They join hands and try to boss the devil around.

"I command you in the name of Jesus to come out of our sister you ol' Devil. You ain't welcome here!" They say Sister Amina is possessed. With God's help, they're going to cast the devil out of her. They scream and pray at the top of their lungs when her eyes rolled back in her head, and blood ran out of her mouth.

"Come out Satan, stand down in the name of Jesus! Her soul belongs to the most-high!" they all screamed. Sister Amina is on the floor shaking like she got struck by lightning. They get on my nerves, so I went back to my room to draw pictures. I drew Uncle Kevin and Sister Amina. They were sitting in a tree, K-I-S-S-I-N-G. Maybe she ain't really possessed, she probably has seizures like my Uncle Kevin. Maybe she just need some of those little green pills. But, I'm just a kid. What do I know?

Sometimes I go around sticking my head into all the apartments. I start on the first floor and work my way up. I opened door one, and let my eyeballs roam. Sister Claudette is sitting at the sewing machine, making another ugly itchy dress that won't fit anybody. I wish I could make my own dresses. I'd make them pretty. One time a girl at school kicked me out of the blue. "What you kick me for?" I asked her. "Cause, I don't like your stupid dress," she said.

"You need something honey?" Sister Claudette said.

"No ma'am," I said and gently closed the door. We never lock our doors around here because they're all so goody-goody. Nobody here will burn in the lake of fire, except Evelyn, and me. I'm not going to heaven because of Brother Du Bois' candy store. He's at work, but anybody is allowed in here. All you got to do is pick what you want and leave the money. But I don't have any money. I just want to look at it and smell it. There must be more candy here than at Willie Wonka's. Why don't he just lock the door? *Why is Brother Du Bois leading me into temptation?*

I only helped myself to a box of Boston Baked Beans, one Chick-O-Stick, and hand full of butterscotch candies, at first. But then I couldn't get it out of my mind. "Come take me Goldie!" the candy told me over and over. And then I had the most awful dream. I stuck my head in Brother Du Bois' apartment and every piece of candy was gone! In the morning, I ran down there to check it out. It still here. But, what if Prophet say we can't have any more candy because God is so jealous? I hurried back to our apartment, and dumped all my books and papers out of my book bag. They say the truth shall set you free, so if I get caught, I'll just tell the truth. The devil made me do it. They'll pray for me, that's all. I grabbed boxes of candy and filled the book bag. It wouldn't zip all the way. I had to put some back. I peeked out to make sure the coast was clear.

The hardest part is hiding my riches from those two. I would tell Bunny about it, but I don't trust her. She'll help me eat every piece, but as soon as I make her mad, she'll run and tell Evelyn or New-Daddy all about it. So, at night, I sit on the floor munching away in the dark like a sneaky mouse. I think about the times my old daddy took me to the candy store. And Nana's chocolate squares, she called them a spoonful of sugar, she got that from "The Sound of Music." And when Evelyn rushed me to the doctor to get stitches. If I told the social worker that she didn't do it, she bought me ice cream and candy. She treated me nice until she stopped feeling guilty. I feel around to make sure I got all the wrappers. The bag is half empty already. I'll get some more on Monday when Brother Du Bois goes to work again. I ain't worried about getting caught anymore because he's kind of stupid, they all are.

We were in Sister Phoebe's apartment having another Bible study, when Brother Du Bois poked his head inside.

"Good evening, praise the Lord Sisters," he said.

"Praise the Lord, Brother Du Bois," they all said. Some of the Sisters smiled and looked at him funny. They probably want to marry him. I want to marry him too because of the candy.

"Is there somethin' wrong Brother?" Sister Phoebe said. He stepped inside and some of them started using the paper fans to cool themselves off, Evelyn too.

"Well Sister, I'm experiencing some problems." She raised her eyebrows.

"What kinds of problems?"

"Ah...Okay, I'm going to come right out and say it. Someone's been taking candy from my store." Sister Phoebe look like a train is coming right at her.

"There must be some mistake Brother Du Bois, are you sure?"

"I'm one hundred percent sure, I keep perfect records of my inventory, but things ain't been adding up," he said. All the prices are in plain sight, but whoever is taking the candy is not leaving any money, not even an IOU." She don't believe a word he's saying, nobody does. This is wonderful. If they don't believe his story, I will never get caught.

"Brother, we don't have that here. That's stealing," she half whispered.

"Exactly," he said. Sister Beulah Mae cleared her throat and raised her hand.

"What is it, Sister?" Sister Claudette asked.

"Well, I wasn't gon' mention it, but since we on the subject," she said.

"Sister would you mind finishing your thought, we're waiting?" Sister Claudette said.

"Lord, what we carryin' on for?" Sister Beulah Mae said.

"Something about some pastries went missing," Sister Phoebe said.

"Oh yeah, last week I made fifteen jelly rolls for the meetin'. After the prayer, I went in the kitchen to fetch 'em, but somebody beat me to it. I had 'round 'bout six left on the plate, and even some of 'em had bite marks in 'em. Now I know I forgets thangs from time to time, but, I thank I would recall gobblin' up all them jelly rolls by myself," she said. They laughed. I laughed the loudest, *Sister Beulah Mae is so funny.* I felt Evelyn burning a hole through me.

"Did you say some jelly rolls went missing?" she asked. I know, she's probably thinking about the time I kept her, and New-Daddy awake all night. "I don't know what's wrong with her Josiah, she just won't stop throwing up this purple goo," she said.

So, New-Daddy whooped me for the first time. He brought one of Evelyn's skinny dress belts down on my behind four times saying, "Thou, Shalt, Not, Steal.*" Thanks a lot, Evelyn, now everybody knows I'm a little candy thief.* New-Daddy took me to Brother Du Bois' door and made me ask for forgiveness. He said he forgave me, but these days he locks his door. I know because I checked, lots of times, just in case.

"Pretty soon y'all gon' get a new baby brother or sister," Evelyn said the other day. I pretended to be surprised. I saw her stomach getting plumper way before she told us. Besides, I figured it out, a baby in her belly makes her go crazy. That's why she's in the living room right now throwing stuff all around.

"I need a man!" she said over and over.

"You have to wait until she's done," I told New-Daddy when

he walked in. He's probably embarrassed because the whole building can hear her cussing. After she tired herself out she sat on the couch. I bet she wish she had a cigarette.

"Evelyn, why would you do something like this?" he said.

"You know damn well why, 'cause I'm mad as hell. How many times I got to remind you I need a man? A real man, a grown man, not some lil boy who too scared to stand up to his daddy!"

"You're right, I should have stood up to him, and now I wouldn't be married to some crazy woman! You think I wanted this?" he said while looking at all the things she destroyed. He slammed the door on his way out. Now she wants to know what the hell I'm looking at, *with my nosy ass.* I pointed toward the birdcage that she flung to the floor. The little blue parrot inside wasn't moving.

"Um, can I go see if Chips is okay?" I hoped he was playing possum, and waiting for her to stop. Nope, he ain't playing, he's gone on to birdy heaven. She always kills our pets. First the goldfish. One time the three of us were outside playing in front of our building.

"Y'all hear that?" Beau said.

"Hear what?" I said.

"It's a puppy, it's crying."

"It's probably a rat," Bunny said.

"Uh-uh, it ain't no rat, it's a puppy, rats can't cry." He listened for the sound again. He stuck his hand inside the couch and felt around. Then like magic, he pulled a puppy out. It was all black except for the white stripe down the front. It stopped shaking when Beau started to rub his fur.

"Please, can we keep it Mama, please?" we begged. She tilted her head. She probably thought about all the trouble the puppy could cause. "Hell no, go on, get it out. Don't bring no stray animals in my house, damn thing might have fleas!" she said. Beau could stretch his eyes out wide, so he looks like them sad kids on those old paintings. She couldn't resist that face. "All right, but y'all better clean up after it. The first time he piss or shit on my floor, his ass gon' be out of here like this," she said while she snapped her fingers. "Mama, she a girl," Beau said. "I don't care what it is, don't forget what I said." Beau always named his pets after food. He named the puppy Oreo. In no time, he taught her how to sit, and fetch. We would laugh at the many times he tried to get her to roll over, but she wouldn't.

"Bunny you ain't supposed to give my dog no potatoes!" Beau said.

"How come?" she said. Oreo answered her question by throwing up in the middle of the living room floor at the same time Evelyn turned the key. It all happened too fast, we didn't have time to clean it up. As soon as she came through the door, she saw it. She put her shaking hands over her mouth like a lady in a scary movie about to scream. But she didn't scream, she grabbed the puppy by her neck and raced into our room where she held her out of the window. We ran behind her.

"We sorry Mama, please Mama please don't drop her Mama, we'll get it up!" they cried.

"Aw, y'all sorry?" she said real nice like.

"She won't do it no more Mama," they begged. I didn't beg because I knew she wouldn't do it. Whoever heard of anybody tossing a puppy out of a window?

"I know it won't," she said before she opened her hand and let the puppy go.

"Now get in there and clean my damn floor!" she said. Me and Bunny held on to each other and slid down to the floor and sobbed. Beau watched her walk down the hall. He stood there staring at nothing for a minute. "I said get in here and clean this shit up off my floor!" she said. I remember thinking it was all my fault. I thought if only I had begged too, then maybe she wouldn't have dropped her. In the morning, we put on our shoes and tiptoed past her room.

"Don't worry about it, puppy dogs got nine lives, and they always land on their feet," Bunny said.

"That's cats, not dogs Bunny," he said. We hurried to the spot under our window. We expected to find Oreo's lifeless body, but we didn't.

"See, she must still be alive, anyway you can find another one, and Bunny don't feed it no potatoes," I said.

"But I love that one, I want her back," he said. Well, let her be the one to tell him what happened to Chips.

"What the hell is in South Carolina Josiah? We just got settled in here," she said. Evelyn went through the apartment checking the closets and cabinets. She's making sure we don't forget any important stuff. The last time we went to the church, Prophet said if we wanted to get closer to the Promised Land, we had to move to South Carolina. We stuffed everything into New-Daddy's new car. A raggedy old Pacer that was red, before it got painted green. We called it a space car. "Where in the junkyard did you find this monstrosity?" Evelyn said, the first time she saw it.

While we were on the road, the police made the cars stop on the highway. They checked the grown-folks' identification. Then they put Brother Du Bois into the back of their car and took him away. My heart started to race. But, what about the candy? Who will be in charge of it?

"What was all that about?" Evelyn asked New-Daddy when he got back in the Pacer.

"They're saying he has a warrant in Ohio."

"What for?" she said.

"I didn't get every detail, anyway, Prophet and Deacon Williams are going to stay back here with him, to see what's going on. They told us to go ahead."

"Sweet Brother Du Bois, who would've thought?" Evelyn said.

"What do you mean by that?" New-Daddy said.

"By what?"

"*Sweet brother Du Bois*," he said in a girly voice.

"I didn't mean anything by it Josiah, you're so jealous," Evelyn said. It was dark now. I watched the white lines on the road until I fell asleep. When I woke up, we were in the parking lot of this place with all these ugly brown doors.

9

Heartbreak Motel

"HOW MANY YOU GOT?" a thin, dark-skinned lady in a light pink worker dress asked New-Daddy.

"Well there's five of us and one on the way," he said with a wide smile.

"Single, double beds," she said. She handed him a key on a chain. She never smiled back. We bumped into other families trying to find the door that matched their key too. New-Daddy found our door and use the key.

"This is us," he said.

"Of all the damn rooms, *we* get thirteen," Evelyn said.

"That's just superstition, there's nothing wrong with this room."

"Yeah, we'll see. Couldn't we at least get one of them adjoining ones?" she said.

"They're for the bigger families."

"How long we supposed to stay here? I can't breathe in small spaces."

"Prophet said it shouldn't be more than a week or two."

"Mm-hm *Prophet said, Prophet said*," Evelyn said. New-Daddy hammered some nails into the walls and tied a rope to the nails. He tossed a wooly dark green blanket over the rope.

"Okay kids, this side is for me and your mama, and this here is your side."

"But, you said boys don't sleep with girls," Bunny said.

"I know, but this is temporary." I don't care if Beau sleeps with us, but I don't want to share a room with Evelyn and New-Daddy. Even with the blanket wall, it's creepy.

"Quit it! Move! I'm not touching you! Ouch, you stepped on my foot!" says everybody. After being cooped up in here for three weeks, all we do is fight.

"That's enough, cut it out. Instead of all this bickering, we should be thankful to have a roof over our heads, no matter how small. We got to have faith in Prophet," our New-Daddy reminded us. Evelyn whispered something.

"And what are you mumbling about?" he said.

"I said all you do is wait on your daddy to tell you when to jump and how high." She started to rub her swollen stomach.

"I done told you I don't need no little boy, I need—"

"Yeah, yeah, I know, you need a man. Well good luck finding one while looking like a beached whale," he said.

"A what? Boy, you got some nerve," she said. She looked around for something to throw at him. New-Daddy dashed through the door. We laughed because we knew they were only playing this time.

"Goldie get over here and fix y'all some eggs on this hot plate. Me and Sister Claudette got some business in town," Evelyn said.

"But I don't know how to make no eggs."

"Girl you done seen me make 'em enough times. Just do what I do, and you better not burn 'em." What is she talking about? I saw her cook the real kind, she cracks the shell, and they slide into the pan and turn into fluffy scrambled eggs. But, what am I supposed to do with this pack of yellow dust? I turned the package over and read the instructions. Step one, add four tsp of yellow mixture into a bowl. I almost forgot to plug in the hot plate. Okay, step two, Whisk together powdered eggs, water, and butter. Who they think got some butter? And what is a whisk? Step three, turn on heat to medium, stir until mixture is firm but still moist. "What does t-p-s mean? Shoot, damn it!" I screamed.

"Ooh I'm gon' tell Mama you cussed," Bunny said.

"Tell her Bunny, I don't give a goddamned fucking shit!" *Why not give Evelyn a real reason to whoop me?* I poured the whole pack of yellow powder into the bowl and put some water in it and stirred. I poured it in the pan and waited for it to dry up before I scraped most of the black, brown, but no yellow stuff onto a plate.

"Ain't you gon' eat it?" I asked Bunny. She looked at for a second and shook her head slow.

"*Uh-uh, I ain't gon' try it, you try it,*" she said. We started laughing. We pretended to be the boys on the Life cereal commercial.

"*Hey, let's get Beau, he'll eat it, he'll eat anything!*" We put the plate under his nose.

"Ewe that look like spit up," he said before he knocked the plate onto the floor.

"I know you did that on purpose," I said. These days, Evelyn makes me cook everything. Her stomach is too big now. "I don't feel like standing over no hot ass, hot plate," she said.

I snatched the note off the door and tried to give it to Evelyn. She wouldn't touch it.

"Read it to me," she said.

"It says a man-da-tory meeting will be held in Mother Louise's room at seven o'clock. Everyone must return all hot plates." Evelyn sucked her teeth.

"What is that four-eyed nigger up to now?" she said.

"Here, I'll carry it," New-Daddy said. Evelyn waddled down the corridor with our hot plate perched on the top of her stomach.

"No, I got it, I'm going to knock your daddy upside the head with it," she said. When we got there, Prophet was napping in a chair in the corner. Everyone in front of us went inside and gently put their hot plates in the big box that said hotplates. Evelyn tossed ours in from the doorway causing a loud noise. Prophet woke up and pulled his self together. He waited until the room was full. Some of them had to listen from outside.

"Anybody know why I asked you all to return your hot plates?" he said. They all agreed that they didn't know. Prophet sure is full of questions all of a sudden.

"Some of you think I done lost my mind, right Sister Evelyn?" he said. She shifted in the chair and twisted her face, so he knew she couldn't stand him.

"Can anybody tell me what this is?" he said. He held a piece of paper in front of him for all to see.

"This here is the reason you won't need your hot plates anymore."

"Well, what is it? I'm an ol' woman, ain't got no time for guessin' games Prophet. Wit' all due respect," Sister Beulah Mae said. They laughed at her like they always do.

"All right Sister Beulah Mae. This here is the deed to our own restaurant right here in Orangeburg County!" he said. They got excited while the paper got passed around. It made them do the holy dance, and Prophet sneaked out.

At least our room won't stink from whatever dumb food I used to make, like them nasty powdered eggs, or Scrapple. I hate Scrapple, I don't even know what it is, nobody knows. Way before the rooster crow, New-Daddy starts shaking our legs. We crawl into the Pacer, ride to the restaurant to eat delicious food. Prophet said the restaurant belongs to each of us, and this is only the beginning. Once inside the big restaurant, we sit at one of the round tables. Evelyn can't fit into a booth by the window.

"Can I take your order?" Sister Naomi said. I'm looking her up and down with a side eye. *I know who she is.* She's the little sneaky heifer who got a crush on New-Daddy. Sometimes I hear them arguing about her on their side of the blanket.

"I don't care about her, I love you baby," New-Daddy says, and then they make up like grown-ups do. We ordered pancakes, bacon, and fried potatoes with lots of ketchup.

"Wow, you guys got some big appetites," Sister Naomi said. After we eat we run around outside the restaurant while the grown-ups talk and drink coffee. When New-Daddy loaded us into the Pacer for the hundredth time, Evelyn is mad about it.

"No! Don't tell me to calm down. I can't sugar coat this shit, and personally, I ain't impressed. We ain't need to come all the way to Orangeburg South Carolina to eat what, when, and where he tells us to. And you see how they serve the same shit every day? Pancakes, bacon, meatloaf, mashed potatoes. You know what? I want some damn Chinese food, how about that? Some shrimp fried rice, or some pizza with extra cheese and pepperoni." She turned in her seat to look at us.

"Don't you kids want some pizza every now and then?"

"I want some pizza," Beau said.

"Me too," Bunny chimed in. I wanted some pizza too, but I didn't say so. Every time I say one-word Evelyn gives me a mean look. I freeze every time. I'm trying to build a big invisible wall around me, so she can't see me. New-Daddy's sister, Sister Sonya is the only one who can see my wall. She's trying to tear it down.

"You don't like to be touched, do you?" Sister Sonya said.

"Not that much," I said.

"And why is that?" she said.

"I don't know why."

"Well, stand still, I'm going to hug you. Are you ready?" she said. I shook my head no, but she put her arms around me anyway.

Sister Sonya is my favorite person. She's the only one who cares about me. Sometimes she'll stop whatever she's doing and give me a hug for no reason. She listens to me, like the things I say are important. And her face don't scrunch up when I come around. Every day I wake up she is on my mind. When I'm near her, I feel happy and safe.

"We ain't got no more bacon," Sister Naomi said after we came all this way to eat.

"No problem, we'll have the sausage links instead," New-Daddy said.

"Well Brother Josiah, we ain't got no more." We were all staring at her.

"What? It's not my fault. Our shipment didn't come in this month, it happens at all restaurants, it will be better next time," she promised. But the next time was worse than the last time, and each morning New-Daddy said we had to have faith. So, here we are in this almost empty restaurant, sitting at the round table, having faith. Sister Naomi rushed right over like she been waiting for us for a long time. She put one sweaty glass of ice water in front of each of us.

"Good morning Brother Josiah," she said.

"Is he all you see sittin' here?" Evelyn said.

"Good morning kids, *Sister Evelyn*, how are you?" Evelyn wasn't interested anymore, she hid her face behind the menu. The rest of started to order.

"Well, we ain't got—" Our eyes and mouths popped wide open when Evelyn slapped Sister Naomi across her cheek with a napkin.

"Stop tellin' us what y'all ain't got, and tell us what we can eat in this dump!" she said.

"All right, that's enough. Honey, control yourself," New-Daddy told her. He smiled at Sister Naomi.

"I'm sorry about that, you go right ahead and tell us what you got," he said. She looked at Evelyn and rolled her eyes good.

"Okay, we got eggs, the powdered kind. We got powdered milk and farina," she said. Everything was smooth sailing until Sister Naomi said they were out of sugar and butter. Evelyn picked up her glass of ice water and threw it at her. Now we're back in the Pacer, going back to the motel, hungrier than before.

"We could've used the money we spent on gas for food, you the only fool still driving your family out here. And how dare you correct me in front of that heifer, acting like you married to her instead of me!" New-Daddy kept his eyes on the road.

"You give him your paycheck, plus everything I get from welfare. He supposed to supply the food for the restaurant. Your daddy is full of shit. I hate that white nigger," she said quietly. I see her face in the window, she looks so sad. I'm on her side, I hate Prophet too. When we got back, New-daddy went inside Mother Louise's room and came out with our hot plate.

"What happened to that lady?" I asked Sister Sonya.

"What lady?"

"The one who gave us the keys when we first got here. She lived in the room with the big window, and she used to bring us clean sheets and towels, and those little soaps."

"Oh her, I don't know, I guess she's gone off somewhere."

"Did Prophet really pull snakes out of her belly?"

"That's what I heard, but I wasn't there," she said. Sister Sonya washed my hair because we're going to a funeral tomorrow.

"Why did Sister Amina have to die?" I asked.

"Deacon Williams said Satan attacked her in her sleep, and she choked on her own blood."

Sometimes a family will get in their beat-up cars, drive out onto the highway, and never come back. Prophet calls them jumpers. He always brings a new family to take their place. Prophet made the office into a jail. He calls it the isolation room. If the devil possesses you, they lock you in there and throw away the key. There's a lady in there now. I don't know her name or why she's in isolation. She looks like one of them giant dolls in the windows at Montgomery Ward. Her skin is black, not a different shade of brown like most people, but real black. Her hair is long and silky. I never seen a lady like her before. She's perfect. Some of the boys been throwing rocks at the window trying to get her to look outside. But every time she comes to the window, they run away.

"I'll tell you if you give me a kiss," Isaiah said. I put my cheek out.

"Okay, but just right here," I said. I punched him on the shoulder because he kissed me on my lips instead. I looked around to make sure nobody saw us. I wiped my lips off with the back of my hand.

"Hey, don't do that," I said.

"But, I sure do love you Goldie." Isaiah's twelve. He's always getting in trouble for touching girl's behinds, blowing kisses, and saying he sure do love us.

"Shut up, and just tell me," I said.

"Okay, she's a witch, she got black magic."

"What's that?"

"She put voodoo spells on the husbands, and make them do stuff they don't want to," he said.

"What kind of stuff?"

"I don't know," he said. I punched him harder.

"Hey, why you hit me again?" he said.

"Because you tricked me, you don't even know nothing."

"Uh- huh, that's what Sister Claudette told my Mommy, and Prophet said to stay away from her."

Sister Sonya asked me to be flower girl at her wedding. She said I get to wear a special dress all my own. I said yes. I hurried to room thirteen to tell Bunny. She was on the floor coloring. I stepped over her and sat on our bed. Evelyn is laying on the bed like a dying cow. She was due last week, but that baby don't want to come out. I think I know why.

"So what, I don't care," Bunny said when I told her about the flower girl stuff. I wanted her to be jealous because she's Evelyn's favorite. I wanted her to know somebody picked me over her.

"That's a shame, they gon' let that girl marry her own damn cousin. They gon' end up with a motel room full of two-headed babies," Evelyn said and roared with laughter. I don't care how many heads Sister Sonya's babies have, I still follow her everywhere she goes. Brother Hakeem, the cousin she's going to marry, always teases her about it. He calls me her little shadow.

It was getting dark out. Sister Sonya was busy getting ready for her wedding. She was moving too fast for me. I accidentally kicked her heels a few times. Deacon Creepy came up behind me and yanked me back by my shirt tail.

"Where do you think you're going?" he said.

"I'm going with Sister Sonya," I said while trying to wiggle myself free.

"No, come with me." He dragged me too fast, so I stumbled over my feet and fell. I stayed on the ground. He grabbed me and carried me under his arm like a football. I pretended to be an airplane. He opened our door and walked right in.

"Sister Evelyn, may I have a moment of your time?" She looked surprised to see him, but not surprised to see him yanking me around.

"What she done now?" Evelyn said.

"Is your husband around?"

"No, he's out making money to give to Prophet, but he should be back soon." He walked over to the bed.

"May I sit?"

"Whatever." He sat on the edge of their bed and cleared his throat.

"Sister, I don't have a heap of time, so I'm not gon' beat 'round the bush. Your daughter is possessed by a lesbian spirit." Evelyn looked at me and grinned.

"How you come to that conclusion, Williams?"

"Now I'm not saying for sure, but the way she runs behind Sister Sonya...well, it just ain't natural."

"Wouldn't surprise me none, I always had trouble out of her."

"Uh-uh, no you didn't!" I said.

"You see?" she said.

"As her mother, the responsibility rest on your shoulders. We got to do whatever it takes to rid this child of these demonic influences before it's too late."

"What you expect me to do about her? I'm a week overdue, I got other things to worry about." He put his stubby hand on her knee. She picked his hand up and dropped it to his side.

"Trust me, Sister, I'll handle it. Also, the good Lord gave me a message to give you."

"What the good Lord want me to know that he couldn't tell me his own damn self, Williams?" she said.

"He said whatever you done when you were out in the world, knee deep in sin, is all water under the bridge. Now let's bow our heads in prayer."

"Stop pushing me stupid!" I refused to move, so Deacon Creepy kept nudging my shoulder until we were standing in front of the jail.

"*She'll pollute the others, demonic spirits are contagious,*" he told Evelyn before he started dragging me down here.

"No, I don't want to go in there!" He grabbed one of my long braids with one hand and used the other one to unlock the door.

"Ouch, stop, let me go!" I screamed. Once the door opened, he pushed me inside and I fell on the floor. He slammed the door and locked it.

"Get up and quit all your wailing," the witch said. I was too mad to get up. I wanted to stay on the floor having a fit.

"I said stand up girl." I got up and let my eyes travel from the pink polished toes, past her silky hair to her beautiful black face.

"Now, dust yourself off. What is your name?" she said.

"Goldie."

"What they throw you in here for? You been out there raising hell, ain't you?"

"No, I ain't raised no hell, they said I'm a less bean." She stood there for a while and studied me.

"Girl how old is you?" she said.

"Ten."

"Ain't you got no mama?" I shook my head no.

"Well, go on, take the bed closer to the bathroom," she said. In the morning, Sister Ernestine opened the door and brought in two trays of food. She left the room without saying a word. We ain't had none for a while, but I could never forget the sickening smell of powdered eggs. Lately, we been eating mostly potted meat, or Spam or Scrapple. She stuffed a big forkful in her mouth. She looked like she just dug into a bucket of slimy snails.

"Oh my God, what is this?" she said.

"It's powdered eggs." She ran to the bathroom to spit the eggs out. I swallowed mine. She'll get used to it, we used to spit them out too.

"They're horrible, how can you stomach them?" she said.

"They're okay once you get used to them." For the rest of the day she ran to the window every time we heard a car outside.

"What you crying for girl?" the witch said. I reached up and felt the tears.

"I didn't know I was crying."

"How do you not know you crying?"

"Um, what is a less bean?" I said. She came over and wiped my tears away.

"You poor thing, you too young to understand it, let alone be it. It's too bad your mama is dead."

"She ain't dead."

"You said she was dead the night that baboon threw you in here."

"Uh-uh, you said did I have a mama, and I said no. I didn't say she was dead."

"Oh Lord, then where your mama at girl?"

"In room thirteen."

"Oh, I see, you been dealt a bad hand."

"What do you mean?"

"A mother who don't love you will make you wish you was never born, at times."

"Uh-huh she do love me, she's just ornery, she can't help it."

"Either way, you gon 'catch hell in this life."

"Do your mama love you?" I asked.

"I wasn't no older than you when my mama died, but she loved me. My aunt had to take me and my sisters in. She was bitter for it. She treated us so unkind. Girls like us got to have somebody to protect us Keep the vultures at bay. But don't you worry, someday your prince will come and rescue you," she said.

If anyone wants to know they can ask me, and I'll tell them her name is Valencia. She's twenty-eight, the same age as Evelyn, and she's going to marry her knight in shining armor. He's the one she's in the window waiting for. *And* if she's a witch, she's a good one.

"What you mean, y'all can't play with no dolls? They done went too far, I'm gon' have to talk to him," Valencia said.

"To who?"

"Never mind," she said.

Valencia likes to laugh. She sure got a kick out of the stories I told her about what goes on around here. I told her we weren't allowed to listen to worldly music or dance.

"When is the last time you heard some music?" she said.

"Ever since Mother Louise came to our house, I was nine. But, I still remember all the songs from the Staple Singers.

"You poor thing." She rummaged through her bag and pulled out a little radio. She found the closest outlet and plugged it in.

"You ready girl?" she said.

"Uh-huh, I think so," I said. She turned it on and adjusted the knob until we heard a squeaky lady voice singing.

"Yeah, this is my song!" she said. She started popping her fingers and singing along. I put my ear close to the radio and tried to understand the words, but I couldn't.

"What is she saying?"

"She said she love the nightlife." The sweet sound of the new music made me cry.

"Girl quit your blubbering, and come shake ya tailfeather!" she said. She did some dances I never saw before. I liked them, I tried to copy her.

"That's it, you got it!" she said.

"So, what they say about me?" Valencia said.

"Nothing."

"Aw, come on, pretty girl, tell me, I know you know."

"Nothing, for real."

"Okay, if you won't tell me, I'm gon' tickle it out of you!" She tickled me until I couldn't take it anymore.

"Okay, okay, they said you're a witch!"

"What else they say?"

"Um, you put spells on all the husbands, and you make them do stuff they don't want to do." I thought I hurt her feelings because she got quiet. But, then she burst out laughing like I tickled her this time. Later that night, the door opened, and somebody put some white bags by the door. Valencia snatched them up and rushed to the eating area. Just the smell of it makes it hard for me to move. I can't believe it. It's like manna fell from heaven.

"What's the matter girl, don't you like Kentucky Fried Chicken?" she said.

I hated being in isolation all by myself. Now I know how she felt. Last night I sat on my bed with the radio pressed against my ear. I saw some lights flickering on and off from behind the curtain. I watched the lock turn slowly from the outside. I looked toward the bathroom door. Valencia was in there brushing her teeth, I could hear her gargling. The lights flickered again. I went to the window. I saw a man on a fancy motorcycle that had red lights all around. He was putting on a show too, going around in circles, making all kinds of noise like vroom, vroom! She came and stood next to me, seeing the show for herself.

"My Knight is here!" she said before she started running around here throwing her stuff in her bag. The bike went vroom, vroom, vroom! She laughed and said, "Hold your horses." She put a light pink sweater over her white nightgown. She could hardly get her feet in the black boots she kept by the door. After she got them on, she hugged me, told me to take care of myself, and left me standing here. I looked out of the window in time to see her put big kisses all over the man's face. Uh-uh, it can't be, I argued with my own eyes. Uh-huh, it's him all right, my eyes assured me after I rubbed them, and looked again. Valencia hiked up her nightgown and threw her leg over the bike. She wrapped her legs around Prophet, the bike said vroom, vroom and they rode off into the night. I stood on my tippy toes and strained to see. The red lights got smaller and smaller, and then they disappeared.

Prophet forgot to lock the door last night, so in the morning, I freed myself. I made my way through the empty corridor. I heard loud voices coming through Mother Louise's door. I went inside.

"The woman is very high in the ranks of witchcraft. Jezebel reincarnated. She done got her hooks into Prophet. We need to fast longer, and pray harder," Deacon Creepy said.

"Well I can pray harder, but I'm already starving, I hope it count as fastin'," Sister Beulah Mae said, but nobody laughed that time. Deacon Creepy looked through me.

I opened the door to room thirteen. I smelled something new. It was wrapped up in a blue blanket. It's a boy! New-Daddy was holding him and making goo-goo sounds.

"Can I hold him?" I said.

"Hey girl, where you been?" he said. I glared at Evelyn.

"Nowhere. Aw, he's so cute, what's his name?" I said.

"His name is Joshua." He put the tiny bundle in my arms.

"Be careful, always hold his head up," he said. I never held a real baby before.

"Now you have two brothers," New-Daddy said. Beau put his finger in the baby's hand and he squeezed tight. We spent the next few days adoring baby Joshua. He was so sweet. He made us all feel happy and peaceful.

A few days later baby Joshua started screaming at the top of his lungs, he ain't stopped yet. They tried wrapping him up real tight to make him feel like he was back in Evelyn's belly. It didn't work. They tried massaging his tiny body. New-Daddy put him in the pacer and rode slowly around the parking lot before he brought the screaming baby back inside. Some of the sisters came to see about him.

"He got colic," they said.

"I don't know how he got it, none of my other kids ever had it," Evelyn said. They bought cans of baby formula because baby Joshua couldn't get no milk from Evelyn's raisins.

"How we supposed to sterilize his bottles on a hotplate? Somebody could've at least warned me before I married your sorry ass," Evelyn said. New-Daddy headed for the door like he always do when she starts up.

"Yeah go on, run to your little whore. Cry on her shoulder, faggot," Evelyn said.

They taped a new message to our doors today. Prophet wants the Saints to meet him at the restaurant at five o'clock. It also said there would be plenty of food to eat. Is this a joke? I wondered because the restaurant has been closed for a long time. We smelled the food from a mile away. When plates were placed in front of us, we hunched over them, and ate like wild animals. When Prophet walked into the restaurant, the Saints dropped their forks and stood up to praise him. Prophet nodded his head and smiled.

"Attention everyone. Quiet, please. Let's all gather around," Deacon Creepy said. They sat on the floor in a big circle, like we used to do in kindergarten.

Prophet stood in the middle of the circle and stared into the ceiling light for a long time. "I see Moses in this light," he said. We all looked at the light, we wanted to see Moses too, but only Prophet can see him. Moses must be saying something now because Prophet put his hands behind his back, and started walking inside the circle while nodding his head. "Lord I am but a humble servant," Prophet said. He turned and looked at all the faces in the circle.

"Brothers and Sisters, we are still in the wilderness, trying to get to the Promised Land, but we are not lost. Some of you don't even know where you are, or who you are. Each one of you have been hand-picked by God, but in these times of famine, all you do is complain. You're weak, always whining, crying the blues. You ain't no better than the Israelites. The word of God tells us to take no thought for our lives. Don't worry about what you will eat, or if you'll have a coat to keep you warm in the winter. The Bible says if he supplies the needs of the birds in the air, and every other living thing then surely...y'all don't hear me now."

"Preach Prophet!" they said. They clapped and waved their hands in the air while Prophet slowly wiped all that sweat off his face.

"I am simply trying to get you, Gods chosen people to paradise. There can be paradise here on earth, but you walk by sight, not by faith. And like the Israelites, you can't see the big picture. All you do is complain. Why we got to eat powdered eggs? What about when you ate like kings and queens here in this very room, huh? I didn't hear any complaints during them days. You only believe when your bellies are full. Many of you have jumped ship, but I say to you, rather you stay or go, I will obey my master!" After a while, Prophet got them running around and falling out. Prophet is standing in front of Evelyn and New-Daddy now.

"Hand me the baby Sister Evelyn," he said. Even with all the noise, for once, the baby is sound asleep. I hope Prophet don't mess it up.

"Saints as you all know, my daughter in- law is drowning the sea of demonic confusion. You must remember that the struggle of sin is within us. Which is why we Saints say we hate a thing, and yet we can't nip it in the bud, amen?"

"Amen," they shouted. Now, most of you have bared witness to what I'm talking about. We can't fault her, it's all beyond her control. For we wrestle not against flesh and blood—but spiritual wickedness in the highest places. If you know your Bible, you know Moses never made it to the Promised Land. Who led the Israelites after Moses died?"

"King Joshua!" they said. Prophet stepped back in the circle and held baby Joshua under the light. They got excited and started praising and doing the holy dance. Valencia came into the restaurant and kept her hand on the doorknob. She winked at me. She was wearing a black leather jacket, just like Prophets. He looked over at her, and she smiled. She tapped the watch on her wrist. Prophet walked over to Mother Louise, and put our baby in her arms.

"Mother dear, because you are a true woman of God, the Lord has instructed me to deliver this child unto you. He is malnourished. The enemy is relentless. We need you to be our rock and help us bring this prophecy to pass." I never seen Mother Louise smile before, but she's smiling down at her new baby. For some reason Brother Luke stood up and started singing "*Precious Lord,*" and the Saints lost their minds. New-Daddy held onto Evelyn while she cried her heart out. Prophet and Valencia gently closed the door behind them.

"I don't believe this shit, you just gon' sit up here and let them take our baby! Why he got to use my baby to pacify your old ass mother? It ain't my fault she too stupid to see he runnin' game on her ass," Evelyn said.

"Did you not hear a word Prophet said at the restaurant? Joshua is chosen," New-Daddy said.

"No, he'll say anything to keep layin' up in his mansion, with his whore, and we payin' for it. Did you see when she came in there today? She got some nerve to show her face. She probably put him up to this, *sneaky blue-black bitch*. Get out Josiah, I can't stand the sight of you!" she said. When he walked out, she closed the blanket wall. We heard her crying. Two days later she was still in bed. She crawled to the bathroom, and back a few times, but she won't eat any of the scrapple we made for her. New-Daddy didn't come back home this time. We saw him get out of the Pacer further down. We rushed toward him to tell him about Evelyn, but he disappeared behind door twenty-four. Sister Naomi lives there with her mother. Maybe he don't care about us no more since he ain't our real daddy, and baby Joshua is gone.

"You got to eat something Mama," Bunny said.

"Leave her alone, she don't want it," I said. I peeked through the blanket. I got a chance to get a good look at her. Her skirt is too snug around the middle. I just hope they ain't planning to take the one that's growing in her stomach right now.

10
Sands through the Hourglass

"SHE TOOK MY BABY!" a woman screamed into the quiet night. It didn't sound like Evelyn, but it must be. She's the only lady missing a baby around here. I was standing in Sister Ernestine's room, listening to all her chatter. I'm waiting for her to give us some scraps to eat. She has a toaster oven. I snatched the plate of biscuits from her and ran out. The Saints were gathered outside Mother Louise's door. "She took baby Joshua, he's gone!" Who could have taken our baby this time? Deacon Creepy ran past me like lightning, but I still got the creeps.

"Mother Louise, what's going on, are you hurt?" he said.

"No, my baby, he's gone, she stole him!"

"Mother Louise, please calm yourself and tell me who took the baby?"

"Sister Evelyn, she came to my door, she said she wanted to see him, I didn't see no harm in it, but soon as I turned my back she ran out with him!" I'm glad Evelyn came to her senses and took our baby back. I skipped toward room thirteen to see baby Joshua, I missed him, and I wanted to hold him again. Beau was laying on our bed squinting at the tiny black and white TV. I held the plate in front of him and he grabbed a biscuit. I put the plate on the small shelf.

"Where is Evelyn and the baby?" I said.

"I don't know."

"Well, where's Bunny?" He ignored me while concentrating on the fuzzy black and white picture on the screen.

"Beau did you see Bunny!"

"No, I ain't see nobody." I sat on Evelyn's bed and stared straight ahead at the tiny closet space. It looked different than before, bigger. I got closer to check it out. The old Samsonite suitcase is missing. Evelyn's tight colorful dresses she wasn't allowed to wear, all gone. Some of Bunny's stuff is missing too. Tears filled my eyes. I backed away from the closet until my legs hit the bed. I sat down and screamed at the top of my lungs. "Evelyn, you stupid cow, you left us!"

It didn't surprise me when she took Bunny with her instead of me. But why did she leave Beau? Ever since she ran off with baby King Joshua, the others ignore us, and nobody brought us anything to eat yet. They're out there saying Evelyn is possessed by the devil, and she's going to kill the baby. I know she's not gonna do that. *And where the hell is our New-Daddy?*

I hear my brother's stomach growling while he sleeps. I hate them all. My tears are all I've tasted for two days. I got up with the roosters, and put my clothes and shoes on. I sat on the bed until the sun came up all the way. I didn't want Beau to catch me, but when I turned around, his big eyes were watching my every move.

"Beau stay here, I'll be back," I said.

"You gon' leave me, you ain't never comin' back," he said.

"Uh-uh, I'm going to find us some food, that's all. I wouldn't leave you for all the tea in China," I said. He don't believe me.

"Okay, come with me if you want to." He sat on the floor and struggled to get his feet into his raggedy sneakers. I can't tell him I don't know where I'm leading him off to. Grown-ups get on my last nerve, I don't know too many good ones. Some of them pretend to be good at first, but they're all the same. We walked straight ahead and stopped at the motel sign on the highway. "Which way should we go?" Beau said. I looked at the sign, we never been this close to it since we got here. Somebody wrote heartbreak above the word motel with red paint. I decided to go the way I saw the jumpers go when they left this place.

We walked for hours. The sun stayed on our head and shoulders. Our throats were dry. I made sure we didn't take any turns or else we would be lost for sure.

"We should go back, ain't nothin' out here but grass. I should eat some," Beau said.

"If we keep going we're bound to find a store or something," I said.

"So, we ain't got no money." I wanted to cry, but I pictured Nana telling me to be strong and keep my head up. So that's what I'm gonna do.

"Let's go back I'm tired," he said.

"No, it's too late to go back now. Anyway, you remember what it says in the Bible?"

"Nope, what?"

"It says knock and doors will open. Prophet was right about God loving us more than the birds in the sky, and the fish in the sea.

"So."

"So, if he takes care of them, he'll take care of us because he loves us more than them."

"Then why we always hungry?"

"Because Moses wasn't in the light, Prophet lied, just so he could take our baby brother.

"Goldie, I can't read the Bible...I can't read."

"I know, I'll teach you." We walked a while longer before a house appeared like magic. I pointed toward the house.

"See I told you!" I said. I grabbed his arm and we ran through the tall grass. If it wasn't for the dresses, the stockings, and girdles on the line, we wouldn't believe anyone lived it the shabby shack. Two tired old dogs had spread out in the front yard. One of them raised his ear. Beau whistled.

"Come here boy," he said. It didn't budge. Beau kneeled in front of them.

"No, don't touch them, they probably got fleas or rabies."

"They ain't hardly got no teeth and this one is blind."

"Come on, stop messing with them." I pulled him away from the dogs and up three crooked steps. I knocked on the door softly. No one answered. Beau twisted the knob and he pushed past me. I followed behind him. "Hello, anybody in here?" he said. No answer. The shack was neat and clean inside. From where we stood we could see into the tiny kitchen. Something stunk so bad like somebody forgot to flush the toilet, a lot of times.

"Maybe we should wait until the people come back and we could ask them for some food," I said. He ran straight to the kitchen area. The smell got worse and worse. He opened the refrigerator.

"Just get the canned stuff," I said.

"Look, it's a whole cake in here!" I used the bottom of my shirt to cover my nose and mouth.

"Don't touch it. Beau, do you smell something?"

"Man, it stink in here, did you fart?" he said.

"Maybe, but it can't smell that bad." He wrapped some canned goods in the tablecloth.

"That's a good idea, okay let's go," I said. I stood by the door, I wanted to get out of there, so I could breathe, but he wasn't behind me.

"No, don't go snooping around."

"Hey, come look in here," he said from the doorway of a separate room. I pushed him out of the way.

"It's a lady, I think she dead," he said. The woman lay still, too still, her chest didn't go up and down.

"I think so too."

"What are you doing?" I asked him when we got outside, and he went back into the house. He came out with a bowl of water and a bag of dog food. He poured all the dog food out in front of the poor dogs. We got back on the road.

"Why she leave us?" Beau said.

"She had to save baby Joshua."

"What about us?"

"Yeah, what about us."

"Hurry up," Beau said.

"Okay, I'm going as fast as I can." I ripped the paper labels off and washed two soup cans with soap and water. I used a knife to cut them open. Three minutes later we were sitting on the floor making slurping sounds. This dead body soup is the best food we had in a long time.

"Shouldn't we tell somebody about that lady?" I said.

"Tell who?" Beau said.

"Yeah, you're right."

I opened the last can of food this morning, but Beau won't eat it.

"Ewe, I don't want it," he said.

"It's good, it's better than scrapple." He never liked tuna, but I thought it wouldn't matter since we're starving. After I ate the tuna, I went looking for something else for him. I saw Sister Sonya in the corridor. I called her name a bunch of times, but she looked the other way. She's not allowed to talk to me anymore. I squeezed my eyes together and told myself not to cry. I hate you now Sister Sonya.

"Hey lil' girl, what is your name?" said a man I didn't even know. He's new, but he'll be gone soon.

"Goldie," I said.

"Carry yourself to Sister Ernestine's room and get the cup of flour she promised my wife," he said. I didn't budge.

"Go on get the molasses out your behind."

"And *who* is you?" I said.

"Girl, I'm Brother Marion, now get on," he said. I don't know who he is to be bossing me around. That's why he got a girl's name. After I got the flour I stomped back to where Brother 'Maria' was waiting.

"Took you long enough," he said. I held the cup of flour out to him. When he reached for it I turned it over onto his feet. I thought it was funny, but he can't even take a silly joke. He just had to run and tell Deacon Creepy all about it. *Big crybaby.* Now they're trying to drag me out of room thirteen. I'm giving them hell. "No, leave us alone! Get your fucking hands off me! We're waiting here for our mother!" I said. But they still picked me up and carried me out. I got so scared when I saw tears running down Beau's face. This is bad, he never cries. "We got to stay together!" I said. I kicked and screamed while they carried me down the corridor. I heard my brother screaming my name "Goldieeee! Goldieeee!"

My tears made it hard for me to see. I'm trying to count the numbers on the doors as they carry me past them. *Twenty-two, twenty-six, twenty-nine.* No, that's thirty, that's his room! They took me inside and dropped me like a hot potato. It smelled like a whole bottle of Pine-Sol got spilled on the floor.

"Sister Lucinda, I'll have you mind this child. Keep her inside, she is not to see the light of day," he told his wife. She sat on one of the beds and stared at her husband. His hand was already twisting the doorknob.

"For how long Deacon, a day, a week?" she said. He stared at me. I stared back. "Creep, creep, creep!" I screamed from my eyes.

"Indefinitely," he said.

Sister Lucinda takes a hundred showers a day, her legs and hands are cracked and ashy like elephant's skin. She supposed to use lotion, but she don't. Sometimes she gets close and sniffs me. "Wash," she says if she don't like how I smell. She don't talk to me unless she's making me do something. When I ask her a question, she won't answer unless the answer is one word like yes or no. I want to run away but I don't know where to go and I can't leave without Beau. Every time Sister Lucinda closes the bathroom door, I sneak to the window to see if anybody's out there. The sun always stings my eyes. One time I saw Beau out there running around with the other starving kids. I tapped on the window to get his attention, he looked at me for a second before he looked away. Maybe he's scared to look at me, he might get in trouble if he waves, or maybe he don't even know me anymore.

She is not to see the light of day. Those words been floating around in my head for a long time. I'm trying to find a way to ask Sister Lucinda how long indefinitely is. In case it came and went without her realizing it. But indefinitely got to be shorter than eternity. New-Daddy said eternity means forever and ever. Sister Lucinda kept a flowered blanket to separate the beds. It's always open because Deacon Creepy don't sleep here.

"Sister Lucinda, how come Deacon Cree...I mean Deacon Williams don't sleep here, with you?" No answer.

"Sister Lucinda, how much is two plus two?"

"Four."

"Sister Lucinda, can puppy dogs fly?"

"No."

"How long is indefinitely?" I asked quickly trying to trick her. It didn't work.

Sister Lucinda goes around cleaning the clean room all day. When she's done, she sits on the edge of the bed and waits for a dust to fall, then she runs after it like a kitten chasing a big ol' ball of yarn. I want to get out of here. When Deacon Creepy first brought me here, it was March, I think. It's August now.

Every day at the same time I go and sit in front of the blank TV screen. I'll fold my legs and watch the clock. When it strikes one, she reaches over my shoulder and turns it on. "*Like sands through the hourglass, so are the days of our lives,*" the announcer says. I sit as still as an oak tree. I don't understand what they're saying, but they're the only voices I'll hear for the rest of the day. At night, I rock myself to sleep while saying like sands through the hourglass over and over. Now it's October.

"Me and Deacon Williams got some business to take care of in Charleston. You'll stay next door 'til we get back," Sister Lucinda said. Those are the most words she ever said to me. I can't believe it! I'm gonna get out of this room. I don't care that I'm only going to room, twenty-nine. *I'm going somewhere.* I stepped outside and sucked in the pine sol free air. My eyes didn't hurt at night. A lady I didn't know opened the door and smiled at me. Once I got inside she put her hand on my shoulder.

"You must be Goldie. Well look at you, you're a ray of sunshine. Just call me Sister Katherine," she said. Her cheerful voice made my ears ring. All this time Sister Lucinda wouldn't talk to me, so I read the Bible every day. I had to wait for "Days of our lives" to hear any other voices. Sister Katherine got three little girls. They ran around in circles, screaming with laughter.

"How long y'all been here?" I said.

"I believe it's been a month, give or take a few days," she said. I asked her a hundred questions, so I could hear her answers. Seeing those little girls made me realize how big I am. Sister Lucinda didn't have any mirrors in our room. Mirrors are vain. "Women of God should not give into vanity," Prophet said. I went into the bathroom. Good, the mirror is still attached to the medicine cabinet. I stared at myself for the longest time. I pinched my arm to make sure it was really me. The black around my eyes made me think of raccoons. My hair was in four fat braids off my shoulders and away from my face. I forgot the color of my own hair. I shut my eyes tight to keep the tears from stinging them.

I was afraid for the little girl. That's why I snatched the baby doll from her. She fell on the floor in a fit. Her mother picked her up and held her and rocked her.

"What did you do that for honey?" she asked me.

"She ain't allowed to play with dolls." She took the doll from behind my back nicely and gave it back to her screaming daughter and she closed her mouth.

"It's okay, I made these myself. See? The face is flat, no graven image."

"Oh, sorry. How do you make them?" I said.

"I used a pair of socks for the body, and the hair is made of yarn," she said while she caressed the pink yarn hair. I had to have one. I yanked my good brown socks off my feet.

"Can you make me a doll out of these?"

"Sure, if it's okay with your mother."

"She ain't my mother," I said.

Early in the morning, the little girls were giggling and running around the room. Seeing them so happy and free, and not afraid made me want to cry. I wanted to hurt them, but I wouldn't. I know it's wrong to feel that way, they didn't do anything to me. I picked up my unfinished doll and tried to concentrate. I got to hurry up because I'm eleven, and as far as I know, twelve is the cut off age for playing with dolls. I worked fast. I dug through the basket of yarn to pick a color for the hair.

"Mommy, somebody's knockin' on our door!" the girls said. Damn, they're back already, they will never let me keep my doll, even with its flat pancake face.

"Please answer that Goldie," she said from the bathroom.

"I can't, I'm not allowed to."

"What? Be still girl," she told the one who was in the bathroom with her. Now they're banging on the door.

"Goldie, please tell whoever that is to come back later!" I opened the door, and the light of day blinded me.

"Sister Katherine is busy, come back later," I said.

"Oh shit, Goldie it's me," said this strange lady. She smelled like something sweet that turned my stomach.

"Girl, come on here. I came all this way to get y'all!" she said. I moved backward.

"No, why you tryna run away from me?" she said.

"I can't see, I don't know you!" I said. She pulled me outside and forced me into the back seat of a car. I would have fought her, but I was blind.

"Watch her, she confused, she might try to run away," she told a person in the backseat who reached over me and locked the door.

"Beau, where are you!" It's Mama! Come out if you can hear me! Don't be scared baby!" she said. I could see shadows now. She's right, she's our Mama, Evelyn.

"Somebody please tell me where my son is?!" she said. When my eyes got used to the sun, I saw my brother standing behind her. He tugged her furry coat sleeve and she spun around and saw him too.

"Beau?" He stood there staring at her with sad eyes.

"Do you remember me?"

"You Sister Evelyn, ain't you?" he said. She almost cried before she pushed him into the backseat. He climbed over me because I didn't move. I needed lots of air. Two police cars and a shiny black car surrounded us as we eased toward the heartbreak motel sign. The Saints stood outside their doors and watched us escape. We rode for a while before the cars pulled onto the side of the road. A man in a dark blue suit, and a tan cowboy hat got out of the black car. He walked up to Evelyn's window. She smiled up at him.

"You should be fine from here," he said.

"I can't thank you enough Mayor," she said. He smiled at her.

"Glad to be of service," he said, before he tipped his hat and walked back to the black car. They turned around and went back the other way. We kept going straight. We passed a sign that said, "Thank you for visiting South Carolina!"

11
Yellow Bitch

"DID YOU SEE THEM DUMB looks on their faces," she asked the man who was in the back seat with us. I was watching her like a hawk. I glared at the stupid fur coat she had on. Look at her, sitting up there just chit chatting away like she only left us here a few days ago. It was eight months!

"Yes, I saw them," he said.

"Mm-hmm, they didn't know who they was messin' with. I got the mayor of South Carolina on my side!" She told him how she walked right into the mayor's office, and showed him a little leg, and told him a sad story about her kids being held hostage in some motel out on the highway. She tossed two sticks of Juicy Fruit gum into the back seat. What's wrong with her? I picked them up and threw them back in the front seat.

"Y'all don't want 'em?" she said. No, we don't want no funky gum. I wished I could put my hands around her neck and squeeze.

"*Like sands through the hourglass. Like sands through the hourglass,*" I said.

"What did she say?" she asked the man.

"Something about some sand or something," he said. I loosened my braids and shook my hair out. The wind grabbed it through the window. I loved how the sun felt on my scalp. Beau laughed at my flying hair. I could see her staring at me through the mirror outside the car. Then I remembered, she hate me.

"Hey Evelyn, we should stop and get these kids something to eat," the man said. After we ate, we dozed off. I opened my eyes in time to read the sign before we passed it. It says, "Welcome to Florida, the sunshine state."

"Look Beau, a peach tree," I said when we stopped in front of the wide country house. I knew we wouldn't go hungry with a tree in the yard. The house stood all alone with nothing but space and grass. This is good, no more living inside a tiny box. But why did we come here instead of going home to Nana?

Bunny came out of the house. She ran toward us with her arms stretched wide. I braced myself for a great big hug. I tilted my head when she threw her arms around Evelyn instead of us.

"Mama you're back, I missed you!" she said.

"Girl, I only been gone three days." *Are we invisible to her?* I cleared my throat.

"Oh, hi Goldie, hi Beau," she said. The car we came in eased off, and we followed them up the walk to the beige house. An old woman watched us from the doorway. The cane she held kept her from tipping over.

"Kids, come meet Miss Hattie," Evelyn said. She told the old woman our names. She nodded her head toward me.

"Well who this here one belongs to?" she said.

"She my daughter, I already told you about her Miss Hattie."

"My Lord, how many mo' you got?"

"That's all of 'em."

"Well, them is enough. They ought to tie up your tubes," she said. We waited for Miss Hattie to back out of the doorway, and boy did it take a while. Once inside we saw a big girl sitting in a chair holding a baby. Her face lit up when she saw us. She jumped up with the baby and pushed him into Evelyn's arms.

"Here go your baby, the other one upstairs sleep," she said, and ran out the front door.

"Well thanks a lot, *lard ass*," Evelyn mumbled.

"What's his name?" I said.

"His name's Joseph, here hold him," she said handing him over.

"Hi Joseph," I said before I kissed the sleeping baby.

"Bunny, where is Joshua?"

"He upstairs, you want to go see him?" I held back my tears when I saw baby Joshua laying there. He was sickly, and too little to be a one-year-old.

"What's wrong with him?" I asked Bunny.

"He got pneumonia."

"What's that?"

"I don't know, but he can't eat no food, he just gon' throw it all back up.

"Goldie come get this baby!" Evelyn yelled while I was in the bathroom brushing my teeth.

"Which one?" I said.

"Don't get smart with me, whichever one is crying." It's baby Joshua, he was in such misery. I held him close and rocked him. I hummed, *"Hush little baby"* softly in his ear, but I knew it wouldn't do any good. This baby don't need no song, he need a miracle, so that night when I prayed I asked God to fix Joshua.

Why did she come back for me if she hates me? It don't make sense. She can't stand the sight of me. All she do is give me evil looks. She scares me. I need a spoonful of sugar. I need Nana.

"Goldie come change these babies! Come fix 'em somethin' to eat! Get em, get 'em!" she says like I'm their mama. She won't feed them, and she never changes a diaper. If she get one whiff of baby poop, she almost throws up. Sleep is the only free time I get, but she don't mind waking me up. What did she do before I got here? I look over at Bunny. She's small for nine. I'm only a year and a half older than she is. I want to share my secrets with my only sister. I want to tell her that I hate Evelyn's guts, but I know better.

After a while, baby Joshua swallowed some of the watery grits that I been making for him every day. I'd pretend the spoon was an airplane. Every time he swallowed a drop, I did a silly dance, or I'd clap my hands and cheer. "Go Joshua!" He would laugh, swallow, and clap too. In no time, he wanted to eat rather I danced or not, and that's how he got so chubby.

Every day after I put the babies down for a nap, I rush into the part of the house where Miss Hattie sits all day. I plop in front of the TV. Miss Hattie makes fun of me every time, but I don't care. I can't miss "Days of our lives," I'm starting to understand it. "Child what you know 'bout them soap operas?" she says.

We were all in the upstairs bedroom. The sun shined bright and the breeze made it a perfect day. I gathered things for the picnic we were going to have under the peach tree. I found a great book that Uncle Nolan used to read to us when we were little. It's called "Green Eggs and Ham". They're going to love it just like we used to. Bunny was sitting on the floor between Evelyn's thighs getting her hair done, so we're waiting on her.
"Where did you sleep when I left y'all?" Evelyn said.
"Huh?"
"You heard me, where the hell did you sleep?"
"Um, in Sister Lucinda's room."
"Before that when I first left." I tried to remember before that.
"In our room with Beau, until Deacon Williams made us leave."
"Did Josiah ever touch you?"
"What you mean?"
"Don't play dumb you yellow bitch, you know what the hell I'm talkin' about." She's right, I do know what she means. I think my oatmeal is going to come back up, and not just because Evelyn is nasty to think something like that, but mostly because she called me a yellow bitch. And Bunny sitting there like she don't care.

"Answer me!" she said.

"No Evelyn, daddy never touched me like that," I said.

"Mm-hmm." She parted another section of Bunny's long thick hair.

"What about Williams?" she said.

"No, but he treated me mean all the time."

"Mm-hmm, that nigger was waitin' to see if I was coming back for you, fuckin' pedophile. Ain't no tellin' what plans he had. She shook her head and laughed. Girl, you better be glad I came back when I did. I could've left your ass there. I should take you back, you mess with me, I will," she said.

"Goldie go to the basement and get those clothes I left in the dryer and the ones on top, and hurry up, don't have me waitin' all day!" Evelyn said. I did all that while she stood up there and watched me struggle up the steps with the heavy bag.

"Where you want them?"

"Put 'em right here." I felt afraid even before she pushed me by my forehead, and I went tumbling down.

"What's all the commotion?" Miss Hattie said from the back.

"It ain't nothin' Miss Hattie, that clumsy girl done tripped on the stairs," she said.

"You need to keep them lil' monkey's quiet, I'm trying to hear Bob Barker." I looked at Evelyn with questioning eyes. She had a smirk on her face. She moved her lips without sound. But still, I know what she called me.

Evelyn and Bunny are stuck like glue, so Bunny think she's grown. Beau can't stand to be more than a few feet away from his mama. He's scared she'll disappear if he turns his back on her too long. She pushes him away like some annoying mosquito. "Go on, get from under me, go outside and play," she tells him.

I stood at the sink washing the dishes. Evelyn came into the kitchen and stood too close to me. I tried to ignore her. My heart started beating faster, and sweat covered my forehead and started to drop. I kept washing the dishes. She reached into the dishwater and pulled out a knife. She stood there just holding it. My body trembled, and I fell to the floor screaming and crying. I heard her giggle. The old woman made her way to the doorway.

"What in the world wrong wit' her?" she said. Evelyn twirled her finger around her ear.

"She touched," she half whispered.

"My Lord, is she?"

"Please pray for me Miss Hattie, I always had trouble out of this one."

"Mm-hmm, I see. Well carry her on to the doctor, so they can 'scribe somethin' for her. Lord know I don't need this foolishness 'round my house," she said before she waddled out of our sight.

"You gon' get us put out... you yellow bitch," she mumbled.

12
Ain't God Good?

SUICIDE: INTENTIONALLY ENDING one's own life. I heard Nana say it's the only sin God won't forgive, but I would rather die now and deal with God later. I can't live with this evil woman for another day. I'm really going to do it. *That will teach her.* I threw the dictionary back in the kitchen drawer because it just says what it is, not how to do it. When I turned around, I was surprised to see Joshua walking to me, all by his self. He should've taken his first steps already, but because of the sickness, he was barely crawling. I picked him up. He put his arms around my neck and laid his head on my shoulder. We needed each other to survive.

"Okay, I'll stay," I promised him. Evelyn appeared in the doorway.

"Y'all pack y'all shit, we movin' to St. Petersburg. I ain't puttin' up with that old biddy for one more day," she said.

The house we moved into belonged to some other church folks. We can only live in the back of the house. The front has everything a real church has. Evelyn is supposed to be a preacher now. She held services four days a week, and twice on Sunday. She turned over the offerings she got from the church ladies instead of paying actual rent. She wears a green and white robe with a big gold cross in the back. They believe whatever she says when she's wearing it. She's up there singing God's praises now, but she says God ain't nothin' but a big ol' faggot in heaven who just love to watch women suffer.

"Ladies, ladies, ain't God good? I said God is good, ain't he?" Evelyn said.

"Amen! Hallelujah! God is good!" the church ladies agree. Once they start falling out, I got a hand full of sheet squares that are just big enough to cover their fat, slain in the spirit behinds with. Soon as Evelyn get to singing and crying some onion inspired tears, I know I got to get the money. She may be pretending to be in deep prayer. But when the plate is passed I see the slit in her eye. She's counting it up from way over there. Later tonight she'll say, "I saw two tens, three fives, a twenty, twelve ones and some change, how much is that?" She can't count too good, but she sure can remember money she saw from a distance.

I want to go to school but she need me here. I hope the people find out and make her send us. Beau's almost eight years old and he still can't read. I got some paper and crayons and tried to figure out the secret to reading, so I could teach him.

"See every letter is like a piece of a puzzle, and each letter got its own sounds. They have to fit together to make a word," I told him. Beau was sounding out the first letter of the alphabet when Evelyn slapped me good. Why don't she want him to read? When she left the house, I got our papers and crayons out, but he said he don't want to learn anymore. I don't believe him.

This morning while I stood at the kitchen sink, Evelyn caught me off guard by beating me with the broom handle. I waited until she caught her breath. I wondered what her excuse was this time.

"You know you ain't supposed to be wearin' no damn pants," she said. I almost laughed in her face. I knew it wasn't because I'm wearing pants because she bought them. Oh no, she beat me because New-Daddy showed up here last night. He played with the babies, ate dinner with us, and told us some scary stories. Later, they disappeared behind her bedroom door. When she woke up this morning, she went stir crazy. She started running around checking every room, the closets, the backyard, the front porch, behind the pulpit, and inside the clothes hamper, but he was long gone. And that's when she thought of little ol' me.

I heard a strange voice outside, so I went into the church-room and peeked through the curtains. Evelyn was on the porch talking to a man standing in the grass. He had on a hot black suit and a dusty old hat.

"You mean to tell me you ain't held no meetings all month?" he asked Evelyn.

"You callin' me a lie? I done told you they ain't been putting shit in the plate," she said. His eyes lit up and he shook a finger at her.

"No, *you said* you ain't held no meetings at all."

"I did not say that."

"I came to collect, not to hear any excuses. I'll be back in a couple of days. Give you time to get your house in order," he said.

"All right, you come on back in a few days. I'll be here with bells on." As soon as that man drove away, I got my behind out of the window. I pretended to be straightening the tambourines.

"Get me that cheddar cheese color envelope in my closet," she said. It was full of money. She poured it on the bed. I gave her a funny look.

"Girl shut up and help me count it," she said. I put all the same money together to make it easier to add up.

"How much is it?"

"Six hundred and eighty-one dollars," I said.

"Damn, we need more than that. Y'all better be on your P's and Q's tonight," she said.

I passed the collection plate. When they put money in, I smiled and said "God, sure is good, or "Praise the Lord my sister." But, if they didn't put anything in, I tilted my head and gave them a look like shame on you, trying to cheat God, *after all he done did for you.* Evelyn showed me exactly how to do it. They usually dug deeper after that. I try not to look at Bunny while she's doing the holy dance because I know she's trying to make me laugh. So, those are our jobs, I collect, she dances, and Evelyn plays with God. I put the overflowing collection plate behind the pulpit. And then a black cat flew over our heads like a bird, making the church ladies shriek. I was alarmed. Was the cat a part of the act? The service ended instantly.

"Minister Wallace, I ain't even know you had no cat," one lady said.

"I don't," Evelyn said slyly. All the windows and doors were shut because the sunshine state is chilly in February.

"See now, that there is a bad sign," said a hefty woman who was stuffed into a beige dress. She stood up and gathered her hat, and Bible. The others did the same. Any other night the church ladies hung around after the service. They would eat up the desert we made, and chat about the goodness of the Lord, or the slyness of the devil. But now they were stepping over each other to get out and a few of them got stuck in the doorway for a moment.

"What, y'all leaving so soon?" Evelyn said following behind them. "But, I baked a cake, it's German chocolate," she said sweetly. After they were gone, I went in search of it. I looked under the beds first. "Here kitty." I quickly opened the closet to catch it off guard. "Here kitty." Either a black cat flew over our heads or Evelyn is a real witch. I sat on the floor with my back against the bed. "Here kitty-kitty-kitty."

"Hurry up," Evelyn whispered while she stood in the church, peeking through the curtains. After we dressed the sleeping babies, she made us turn off every light in the house.

"Mama somebody in the backyard," Bunny whispered.

"It's the cab, I called it earlier. Y'all go get in, and keep them kids quiet," she said. We piled into the backseat of the cab and waited for Evelyn to come out.

"Where to?" the cab driver said when she slid into the front seat.

"Damned if I know. Anywhere but here," she said. The top of

the driver's head was polished, but he had some hair on the sides. He adjusted his rear-view mirror and stared through it. It seemed like he was counting us.

"You got enough dough for a motel or somethin'?" he said.

"I ain't got a dime to my name," she said in a sugary sweet voice. The cab driver rushed to the curb and slammed on the brakes.

"I got enough to pay you!" she said, and he eased back onto the road.

"Uh, there's a woman's shelter over on Corey Avenue. It's called Haven House I believe. Y'all might be able to stay there tonight. They'll take anybody, long as they got the beds."

"Okay take us on over there," Evelyn said. A woman opened the door.

"I'm sorry, we ain't got no beds free right now," a lady said as soon as she opened the door and saw us standing there. We heard the cab sneak away from the curb.

"What am I supposed to do with five kids and not a dime to my name?" Me and Bunny held a baby in our arms. Joshua squirmed and whined. She looked at all our sad faces. I get off in a half hour, you can stay with me, but only until some beds are free here." Evelyn threw her baby free arms around the woman.

"I prayed for a miracle, and God sent us one of his angels in the flesh," she said. I held in my laughter. The woman smiled and pointed at a brown car parked on the curb.

"Y'all wait inside there until I finish in here," she said.

"Bless you, ma'am," Evelyn said.

"Please, just call me Marta," she said. The lady was very round, and she jiggled like Jell-O as she walked toward her car. Marta told Evelyn she lived with her husband. They been married for twenty-five years, and they got nine kids, but most them is grown now. Once inside the house, we followed close behind her. She tip-toed through the almost dark living room and stopped in front of a man snoring in a reclining chair. She shook his knee, and then his shoulder.

"Ralph honey, wake up, I got some people I want you to meet," she said. He opened his eyes and tried to focus. All six of us stared down at him. He looked up at us like we were a bunch of big headed aliens. He ran his hands over his face.

"Aw Marta, how many times we done talked about this? You can't keep bringing your work home honey," he said.

Marta is a Jehovah's Witness, so Evelyn has been pretending to be one too. On Saturday, they go out knocking on doors while we run around in the yard all day, enjoying the warm sun. They have a real tree house and a few tire swings. At Marta's I'm not a little mama, here I get to be a kid. Marta's daughters got babies of their own. They don't know I can take care of babies just as good as they can. But I know lots of stuff, like no matter how good things are here, we'll have to leave soon. Oh, and Evelyn keeps pulling her shirt down because she can't zip her pants up all the way. So, that one-time New-Daddy showed up, was when they made baby number three, all for me.

I stood there with my arms folded across my chest. I refuse to pack anything like she told me to.

"Girl did you hear what I said?" Evelyn said.

"I'm not going anywhere with you!" I ran to the backyard and climbed the ladder to the tree house. I pulled the ladder up with me. They called me from the ground, but I ignored them.

"You can always come back to see us baby," Marta said. I heard one of Marta's daughters laugh, and say "She's so cute." *Cute my eye, I ain't playing, this is serious.*

"She still in that darn tree?" Evelyn said.

"She say she ain't never coming down," Marta said playfully.

"If it was up to me you could stay you're behind right here, but what am I supposed to tell Ma?" Evelyn said. Wait, what's Nana got to do with this? I stuck my head out of the curtain. She glared at me with her hand on her hip. She probably wanted to call me every name in the book for causing her so much trouble. But, she got to keep up the angel act in front of Marta.

"Ma's here in Florida, she got a nice house and everything," she said. Why didn't she say that in the first place? I love Marta and her kids, and even her grumpy ol' husband Mr. Ralph. But Nana is here. I dropped the ladder and got my behind out of that tree. Miss Marta chuckled while I ran past them waving and blowing quick goodbye kisses.

13
Reunited

I HATE HER, SHE TRICKED ME. I mean, why would Nana move here? She lives in a big house in Pittsburgh, where we belong. The cab stopped in front of a house with lots of tall windows. Who really lives here? What terrible things are gonna happen to me behind those walls? Suddenly I feel nervous like I want to run for my life. I can't live alone with Evelyn. I bet she can't wait to start acting crazy again.

"Look, there go Nana!" Bunny said. We all jumped out of the car and ran toward her. She stretched her arms out wide like she wanted to scoop us all up at once.

"Oh Lord, how long it's been since I seen my babies?"

"Three years," I said.

"Goldie, honey look at you, all grown up. And who we got here?" She meant the chubby two-year-old on my hip.

"This is Joshua." Joshua put his head on my shoulder. He didn't like to meet new people. But when Evelyn carried little Joseph over, he leaped right into Nana's arms like he knew her all his life.

"This is Joseph," I said. She kissed the baby's cheek.

"Come on, let's all go 'round back, everybody waitin' to see y'all," she said. I smelled smoky barbeque that made my mouth water. It wouldn't be a Savage cookout without Al Green telling us we *ought to stay ta-getha.* Uncle Ernest was handling the meat on the grill.

"Uncle Ernest!" I said. He didn't answer, but I know he see me standing here.

"Uncle Ernest?"

"I'm sorry ma'am, but do I know you?" he said.

"It's me, Goldie." He looked me from head to toe and shook his head.

"Let's see, I got a niece by that name, but she's 'bout yea high," he said while pushing his hand close to the ground.

"I don't recognize you. You a grown woman."

"Stop playing Uncle Ernest, you know it's me." He placed the big pitchfork on the grill and gave me a tight squeeze. I love being reunited with my family. I'm going to pretend that it was all a dream, no not a dream, more like a long, scary ass nightmare. We're back with Nana, so everything will be smooth sailing from now on.

There's something wrong with Nana. She was drinking so much when we got here. But, we were celebrating, all the grown folk was carrying on that night. But she's been carrying on, all by herself, for five days and counting. I've never seen her like this, I think she's broken.

After a few months of carefree living, Mr. Barnett, the truancy officer came to round us all up. He had papers on every school-aged Savage in the house. The weird thing about Mr. Barnett is his missing arms. We don't take him seriously. He likes Nana.

"Pearl, my dear, I certainly understand what you're up against. Teens can be very taxing," he told her. We watched in amazement when he took off his shoe and used his foot to lift the cup and sip the black coffee without spilling one drop. Another time, he dug his wallet out of his front shirt pocket. He laid it on the floor, opened it and took out a dollar. He held the dollar between his toes and pointed it at us.

"One of you kids be a dear, and go to the store and purchase a cold bottle of Pepsi for me, please," he said.

"No, you go get it, I'm not touching it," we whispered. We

pushed each other toward the foot. Nana kindly took the dollar from his toes.

"Stop misbehavin', and run get Mr. Barnett a cold pop," she told Uncle Marcus.

Since Evelyn couldn't produce any of our school records for the last three years, we had to be tested. I passed the tests and went straight to the fifth grade, but Bunny wasn't reading at the right level and Beau couldn't read at all.

When I got home from school today, Evelyn was stretched out on the couch, the baby is due any day now, and Joseph is laying across her thighs. "Here get him, he been gettin' on my nerves all day," she said like she's been babysitting for me. She hardly gave me a chance to put my books on the table. It's getting harder to keep up with Joshua and Joseph. They're both walking and exploring things.

Damn it, I told her not to leave the same diapers on them all day. Now I'll have to work extra hard to keep them from getting rashes. Every day I fall asleep at school, when I get my graded papers back, they're all bleeding because of red marks. One teacher wrote lacks initiative on a test I failed. My science teacher wrote "See me after class," but I walked on by his desk when the bell rang. And my social studies teacher wrote you've got to be kidding me, and a big fat red F on my paper, just because I filled in a-b-c-d all the way down the multiple-choice test.

Everybody's too busy living their own lives to help me out. Aunt Sylvia and Aunt Nadine would help, but they went back to Pittsburgh. Nana's got her hands full now with Aunt Tracie. And Uncle Kevin's seizures have gotten worse. He's also losing his common sense. Somebody chases him home every day. That's because he always says whatever comes to mind. If he spots a man talking to a woman, he thinks it's his duty to warn her.

"Don't listen to him, he just want to stick it in you," he'll say.

Once he said that to a young-looking woman who stood at the bus stop with her son. The son chased Uncle Kevin all the way into our living room. We explained Uncle Kevin's situation to the angry man. Occasionally he'll go into a bar and wait for the bartender to put a drink in front of somebody and he'll snatch it, guzzle it, and run. Once he tried to get in on a crap game in the alley by throwing food stamps on the pile of money and... *Well, he got his ass beat that time.*

"You should keep him in the house, he gon' get hurt out here," a chaser will tell Nana after she apologizes for Kevin. Sometimes they find Uncle Nolan in the window. They stop dead in their tracks. They all know about Uncle Nolan, but not everybody knows Uncle Kevin is his little brother. "I didn't know he was your brother Savage, my mistake," they say. Uncle Nolan has a wooden bat for occasions like these, he wrote savage beast on it with some red nail polish. It looks like dripping blood. He'll stand on the island in the middle of the street, swinging the bat like a black, five-foot-three superhero. "And the name is Savage!" he says proudly.

Uncle Nolan was always the best storyteller. But none are as funny as his real-life adventures. One-night he ran into the house with blood on his hands and shirt.

"What happened?!" we asked.

"Y'all be quiet before Ma come in here," he whispered.

"So, what happened?" we asked again. He peeked out of the curtains while holding his side.

"A'ight, meet me upstairs and I'll tell y'all." Once we got upstairs, we waited impatiently.

"Okay, first me and Johnny got a pistol. We devised a foolproof plan to rob Wells Fargo on 125th street."

"Man, you ain't rob no Wells Fargo bank, not even in your wildest dreams," Uncle Ernest said.

"Then how you explain this big brother?" he said before throwing a small bundle of blood-stained money into the air. We ran over to see if it was real. It was.

"Man get to the part where you got shot," Uncle Ernest said.

"Okay, I'm gettin' to it. Anyway, the tellers acted all scared, but they tripped a silent alarm without us knowing. When we got outside, five-o was on our asses. Then everything went in slow motion. I was like "Shiiit!" and Johnny was like "Fuuuck!" Then we hopped in the car and took off. I should've been the one driving the getaway car, but you know Johnny never let nobody drive his buggy."

"Then those cops shot you in the back, right?" Little Uncle Marcus said.

"No, then Johnny took out his gun and started firing off at the pigs. So, I said "Nigga is you crazy? Stop shootin' at them damn pigs, watch the goddamn road man!"

"And the cops shot you?" Little Uncle Marcus said.

"Nah man, why you keep sayin' that?"

"For the last time, who shot you?!" Uncle Ernest said.

"Johnny shot me when I jumped in the back seat at the same time he was firing off at the fuzz. This ain't nothin' but a flesh wound." We were silent for a few seconds after that. We didn't want to laugh with him standing there bleeding and all. But we couldn't hold it, and we fell on the floor laughing like a bunch of Cheshire cats.

"Boy, you never cease to amaze me," Uncle Ernest said before he left the doorway.

"Aunt Tracie, do you remember the time Beau fell in the street, and all those cars rode over him? No answer. What about the time you gave me my first black Barbie doll? It was the last doll I ever had..." She don't say a word. She is not the same person we left alone in that apartment and she never will be. Her mind is gone. Every day she sits in front of the TV, talking to herself. Laughing at only God knows what.

"What happened to her?" I asked Auntie Althea.

"Ma said somebody put something in her drink when she worked in some bar in Detroit."

"Put what in her drink?"

"I don't know, drugs or something."

"Why would somebody do that?"

"Because, there's evil people in the world, ain't no other way to explain it.

Aunt Tracie has been going outside asking people if they got a cigarette. Everybody bums cigarettes around here, that ain't no crime. It's just that she don't bother to put on a stitch of clothing when she does it.

"Nolan, Thea, Goldie, Lord have mercy. Somebody, please go get Tracie, she done got away from me again!" Nana yells. We'll grab a raincoat or a bathrobe and run after her. Uncle Nolan is the only one who can talk her into coming back in, she gives the rest of us pure hell. The neighbors freeze when they see her easing on down the road, butt naked, without a care in the world.

Evelyn's wish was finally granted. After her water broke, she was hauled off to the hospital in a noisy ambulance. A week later she came home with another baby boy. Jeremiah, another J from the Bible. He's so adorable, it's just that I really wanted a girl this time.

14
Sweet Tooth

"TELL HER I SAID TO KISS my black ass," I told Little Uncle Marcus. He just stuck his head in my doorway and said Evelyn said Jeremiah's diaper needed to be changed.

"Okay," he said. I heard him running down the stairs. I jumped off the bed and ran after him.

"No, wait. Don't tell her," I said, once I realized he absolutely would tell her that. I came back to my room and collapsed on my bed. I don't care if the babies are crying, or wet or hungry, not now. There's no way I can deal with them right now. Some of my back teeth are rotten and the throbbing pain is too much to stand. I can't stop crying for myself let alone soothe baby Joseph while he's teething. It's not like I didn't know about the cavities before now. I just never thought they would ever hurt like this.

"Love and happiness" played from a speaker in the downstairs window, so it could be heard in the backyard. I went to the window and peered outside. Another cookout, I should have known because Al was crooning away. I never thought I'd say this, but I don't want to smell or eat another piece of grilled meat for a long time. These cookouts are an excuse for people to get drunk. I spotted Evelyn sitting on some guy's lap. He whispered in her ear and she swallowed every syllable. I hope she's not trying to make another one. I can't afford it. I went out to the backyard and headed in her highness's direction.

"Evelyn, can you please take me to the doctor? My teeth hurt."

I stood there, holding both sides of my face until she realized I wasn't going away.

"Where the hell am I supposed to get money to pay a damn dentist? That's what you get, goin' around here eating candy like it's going out of style." She's right, I been eating too much candy since forever. I'd rather eat candy in place of real food. I don't always brush my teeth at night, and now look where it's gotten me.

"Okay I'm sorry, but can't you take me anyway?" She grinned while the man-chair whispered more stupid stuff in her stupid ear. I stomped my foot.

"Evelyn!"

"Didn't you hear me say I ain't got no way to pay some damn dentist, go on somewhere!" she snapped. I turned around and ran back into the house. Lying cow, she could take me if she cared to. She didn't have any money when Bunny had a real asthma attack, but she practically carried her to the hospital on her back.

Without thinking it through, I rushed straight to Nana's room and snatched Uncle Kevin's seizure pills from her dresser. The bottle was half full. I went to the dining room and got into the closet. It will all work out because everybody comes in here for one thing or the other. I won't die, I'll just get sick. I slid to the floor and swallowed two at a time until they were gone. I tossed the empty bottle outside of the closet door. After a while, I felt nauseous and I had trouble breathing. All I see is a thin slice of light coming from under the door. A dark shadow crossed the light.

"Kevin, what is your pills doing out here on the floor? Oh, Lord, it's empty, Kevin!" Nana said.

"Ma did you call me?" he said.

"Honey, where your pills? You know these got to last you."

"I don't know Ma, I took one this morning and I still had plenty left," he said.

"We got to find 'em," she said before she opened the closet door. Well, it's about time. If I die I will haunt her for taking so long to find me.

I opened my eyes and checked out my surroundings. I was in a cold hospital room. Miss Juicy Fruit is in here too. I felt like somebody pulled my guts inside out.

"They had to pump your stomach. I can't believe you got me down here with this bullshit. On second thought, I do believe it, you ain't been nothing but trouble since the day your ass was born," Evelyn said.

"I'm sorry."

"You should be sorry bitch."

"You forgot the adjective. You're supposed to say you should be sorry, you *yellow* bitch." She opened her mouth wide enough for me to see down her throat. She was about to let me have it, but somebody knocked on the door. It was a doctor, he eased into the room.

"Okay Mrs. Wallace, here are the forms I mentioned earlier. I need your signature. She signed the papers without reading them.

"That should take care of everything, in a few minutes she'll be transported to the facility."

"What is he talking about?" I said. I ignored the pain and sat up straight anyway. The doctor acted as if I wasn't there.

"Good luck to you ma'am," he said before closing the door behind him.

"Evelyn where are they talking about taking me?"

"They gon' lock your ass up for tryna kill yourself." I wanted to jump out of the bed and run for my life, but I had to roll off instead. It took me five minutes to stand straight.

"Uh-uh I'm going home, I wasn't trying to kill myself, and you know it." Like a turtle, I made my way to the door. Two giant men dressed in milky white uniforms blocked the doorway.

"Going somewhere young lady?" one of them said. I didn't have the strength to fight. Who am I kidding? Even with strength, I could never push past these Incredible Hulks.

This is weird, I can't believe my luck. A few hours ago, I was at home in pain. Now I'm riding in the back of a gray van in even more pain. Was it necessary to put me in this jacket that makes me hug myself? Some of the other kids had my same taste in outerwear. The van made some stops along the way and another bewildered looking kid climbed aboard. Why does she always do these things to me? The van stopped again, and the doors flung open. "Okay, end of the line, everybody step down," said one of the gigantic men. The sign on the building says Children and Family Crisis Center.

"What city is this?" I asked one of the Hulks.

"We're in Sarasota my dear," he said. I felt another knot forming in my stomach. How am I supposed to run away from here? Once inside they unbuckled the weird jackets. A chubby dark-skinned nurse handed each of us a tiny pill with a small plastic cup of water. But I didn't want to see another pill.

"What's it for?" I asked.

"It will keep you calm, it won't hurt you," she said.

"I'm calm already, I don't need it."

"You have to take it. Don't give me a hard time, come on open up." She looked like somebody's mama, but not mine so I got nothing to worry about. I swallowed the pill, and gulped the water down.

"Good girl, who's next?" she said. The guard led us through a maze-like hallway. He unlocked the door to a huge room, with a high ceiling. There were kids everywhere. The guard passed us off to a man wearing green hospital clothes. He read our names off a chart.

"I'm right here," I said when he called my name.

"You're in room Seven, right behind the ping pong table. Okay, you're all free to go get settled in. Join the rest of us when you're ready," he said. I wanted to be alone. The room had a twin metal bed with a thin uncomfortable looking mattress, a desk, and chair. They covered the windows with wire making it impossible for me to jump out of it. I sat on the bed and tried to make sense of all this. Okay, this is where they put you if you try to kill yourself on purpose or not. Something stinks in here. I lifted my arms and sniffed. Oh, it's me. I could hear the others playing ping pong and yelling. While I pictured Evelyn getting run over by a bus, my neck tensed up. It felt like I put my own self in a headlock. I stared at the blinding white light in the ceiling because I didn't have a choice. What is happening to me? I tried to straighten it, but it wouldn't budge. I can't even swallow my spit, so it ran down my chin and neck. I tried to call for help, but my tongue wouldn't cooperate. I walked around the room touching everything until I got lucky and found the doorknob. I opened the door and heard loud laughter.

"Been there," said one of the kids.

"Oh dear," the resident said. He took my elbow and led me back to my room.

"Here, sit back on the bed. What color was the pill they gave you during intake?"

"Wa wink won."

"What? Oh, the *pink* one. You're having an allergic reaction, it happens all the time. Don't move, I'll be right back." He didn't take long, but it felt like forever with my neck like this, and the drooling. It's about time, I thought when he re-entered the room.

"I'm going to give you a little shot." I stuck my arm out urging him to hurry up.

"No sweetie, this goes in your rear, it may sting a little but don't be alarmed." After the shot, my neck straightened, and my frozen tongue thawed out instantly.

"All better now?" he asked.

"Uh-huh, I'm all better now," I assured him. But, five seconds later I was crying my heart out. I got scared. I had every reason to be sad, but this was a weird cry, like a cartoon baby cry.

"Gwendolyn you're off your rocker because of the medicine. That also happens often, you'll be fine."

"Can you make it stop?" I said when I started laughing like a hyena.

"No honey, you're gonna have to ride it out," he said. I laughed and sobbed my way through a long, and much-needed shower. The resident came in and put a boring gray sweat suit on the bed. All the kids were wearing them.

"How long do I have to stay here?" I asked him.

"That will be determined by your assigned counselor on Monday," he said before he closed the door. He blew his whistle.

"Rusty, that's enough, get down from there, and go to your room!" Thank goodness, the laughing and crying stopped. I crawled under the blanket and pulled it up under my chin.

The next morning, I panicked as soon as I saw the wired window. *Where am I?* A few seconds later, yesterday came back to me. The pain, the pills, the pump, I'm safe in the nuthouse. The morning light was blinding, so I closed the curtains. After a slight knock, a heavy-set woman with a short, no-fuss haircut came in. She was all smiles.

"Hello there, you must be Gwendolyn, I'm Stacy. I'm one of the weekend residents.

"Hi," I said.

"We're headed for the cafeteria in ten minutes." The others were already in line and ready to go. They were moving like zombies. They must be all drugged up.

"What is your name dear?" a lady asked.

"Gwendolyn Savage." She handed me a covered tray with my name on it. I scanned the area for a non-crazy table to sit at. I know all about crazy people and the sudden moves they make. I sat next to a girl who I recognized from the van. I took the top off the tray. What kind of zoo are they running here? Eggs, toast, no jelly, and white milk, this must be a mistake. I looked around the room like Columbo. Okay, it's just as I suspected, the other trays are covered with blueberry muffins, orange juice, pancakes, and chocolate milk. My mouth hurts like somebody's been drilling inside it, but chocolate milk is still all I need right now. I covered my tray and carried it back to where the nice lady sat.

"Excuse me, ma'am."

"Yes, what is it dear?" *She ain't slick, she knows exactly why I'm here.* I took a deep breath.

"Um, I didn't get any chocolate milk or muffins, only eggs and toast."

"Let me see, you are Gwendolyn Savage, you arrived yesterday, right?"

"Uh-huh."

"See it says right here, you're not permitted to have any sweets."

"Why not? I just need one chocolate milk."

"Well my dear, sugar is a stimulant. I must follow the chart. I saw some covered trays stacked on a shelf behind her head. I knew some of them were fully stocked. I don't care about no chart, I know she has the power to give it to me.

"That's all dear," she said. I tried to scare the old lady into giving me the goodies.

"Just give me the damn milk! *Okay, lady?*" I said. She blew her whistle, and the guard floated in our direction. I suddenly saw things her way. I sat with my arms folded refusing to eat anything on my tray, but nobody cared.

At lunch, a mousy brown-haired girl slipped me a chocolate milk under the table. I snatched it and gulped it down like I been in the desert for days.

"So, what are we in for?" she said. Her eyes darted all around the room, never settling on one thing. I turned my back to her. She tapped my shoulder. I shouldn't have taken the milk if I didn't want to talk to her. Nothing in life is free.

"Let me guess, you offed your mom and dad, and then you tried to off yourself?"

"What?"

"Okay, okay, I got it this time. You stabbed your teacher in the neck with a number two pencil, and then you tried to off yourself by jumping off the roof, right?"

"Why does everything end with me trying to off myself?"

"Duh, this is the suicide ward remember?"

"Oh, I forgot, but that's not what happened. Please leave me alone."

"Jeez, lighten up lady. Anyway, my name's Paula Sansone, slit wrist and waited to die in a tub of water," she said, holding her hand out to me. I hesitated until I saw the thick healed slashes on her wrist. I put my hand in hers.

"Gwendolyn Savage, overdosed and hid in a closet," I said.

Paula was unshakeable, she spent the rest of the day giving me the inside scoop, as she called it.

"Yeah, so, like I said I know what's going with everybody in here," Paula said. A boy named Rusty walked past us again. Whenever he's in this room he walks in circles, nonstop.

"Except him, I don't know what the fuck is wrong with him," she said. I laughed with her. When the pool table was free, we jumped at the chance to play.

"So, how do you like it so far?" she asked.

"What's to like? It's a jail. Anyway, I'm going home Monday, after I talk to the counselor."

"Uh-oh, you're in denial, it happens to the best of us."

"What do you mean?"

"I'm not saying you're not getting out, you probably will, but it won't be on Monday."

"How do you know?"

"Because anybody who comes through those metal doors, has to stay for two weeks. By then, they'll pump you up with a bunch of pills and potions. Your head will get all screwed up. They'll increase your dosage, add more time, and before you know it, you'll be celebrating your sixteenth birthday in this place." I threw the paddle against the wall and headed for my room. A resident blew the whistle on me.

"Gwendolyn, calm down now!" he said.

"Have a seat, Miss Savage," the counselor told me without looking up from her desk. There were pictures of happy white people all over her office. Some half dead plants sat on top of the file cabinet. A collage of serious looking papers was tacked on the wall behind her head.

"Would you like to discuss what happened last Friday afternoon?" she said.

"Yes, I do. See it was all an accident. I didn't, I mean I don't want to ever die."

"You swallowed a lethal dose of seizure pills. What did you expect to happen, exactly?" I thought about what Paula said. This lady is the key to my freedom. I got to play my cards right.

"Okay, first I asked my mother to take me to the doctor because my teeth were rotten, and it hurt bad, but she said she needed money. I only took the pills because I needed to get to the hospital. I meant to ask them to help me. But I passed out...had to have my stomach pumped." She sat quietly, twirling a green and gold pen. I wondered if she even heard a word I said.

"Okay Gwendolyn, I'll see you at the same time this Wednesday. By then you may be prepared to be honest and talk things through." *No, I can't stay here another day.* I rushed toward her, she reached for her whistle. I held my mouth wide open.

"Look...you see?" I said. She started looking all around in there.

"Oh my, you poor girl, how long have you been like this?"

"Um, for like, eternity," I said. It wasn't easy, but my plan worked. The pain is gone, but so are some of my back teeth. The dentist gave me a mirror.

"They couldn't be saved, no more candy young lady," he said.

"No sir, I will never eat candy again." Paula was right, I did have to stay for two whole weeks. Not one Savage arranged to pick me up. The last time I called, the phone was temporarily disconnected. I called my friend Danny and asked him to pick me up. He promised me he would find a way to get to Sarasota. My new looney bin friends formed a goodbye line. Paula stood in front of me with her arms stretched out and we hugged quickly.

"Sorry I was so mean to you at first," I said.

"Hey, no sweat," she said.

"Maybe you should stop swallowing the pills," I whispered to make sure the residents couldn't hear me. She put her thumb up and winked as if we shared a top secret.

"Gotcha," she said.

I owe Danny my life for rescuing me. When one of the Hulks walked me through the doors, he was standing next to his father's shiny black mustang. He opened the door for me and I felt like a princess in a fairytale. But most of all, I felt like I mattered to somebody. His father looked back at us and smiled.

"Well, now I see what all the fuss was about son, she's a beauty," he said.

"I told you," Danny said. As soon as they dropped me off I went through the house looking for Uncle Kevin. I found him in his room putting another cardboard airplane together. I sat next to him.

"Hand me that glue right there," he said. I handed it to him and watched as he carefully lined a wing and stuck it to the body.

"Did you have any seizures while I was gone?"

"Yeah, I did. Ma had to get me some more pills." I put my arms around him.

"I'm sorry Uncle Kevin, I'll make it up to you, I promise."

"That's okay," he said. I went into the kitchen and bumped into Evelyn. She gasped like she saw a ghost.

"How you get out of that place? I ain't signed no papers," she said. I ignored her. Did she think she could lock me up and throw away the key? Do I look like Rapunzel or some damn body?

15
Ain't Misbehavin'

"FIVE DOLLARS! THE HELL I'm gon' do with five dollars?" Uncle Paul said, when I asked him to babysit.

"You could buy a pint of Thunderbird or some Wild Irish Rose," I said.

"Girl, I ain't on the sauce," he said. He's trying to see if he could squeeze more out of me. I stomped my foot on the kitchen floor.

"Come on Uncle Paul, I ain't got no more money," I said. He snatched the five.

"Go 'head on girl," he said.

"Thank you kindly," I said as I headed for the door.

"You better have your behind back by eight o'clock," he said.

"Why?"

"Girl, you know the liquor store close at nine."

"Where you headed off to?" Uncle Ernest asked when he caught me trying to sneak past him.

"I'm going over to Danny's house to watch a movie," I said.

"A movie huh? What time you plan to be back on base?"

"What time is it now?" He checked his special wristwatch.

"It's eighteen forty-five."

"I'll be back by oh twenty-two hundred hours."

"Be back here by oh twenty-one hundred hours, and not one second past."

"I'll try Uncle Ernest."

"Or else I'll come looking." I knew he meant every word. Ever since they found that girl's body in Maximo Park, he has been watching us night and day.

"We don't live nowhere near Maximo Park, and ain't nobody killing no black kids anyway," we told him.

"Just because they found her body in the park, don't mean a damn thing. Could've been grabbed right off the street for all anybody know. How soon y'all forget about them kids in Atlanta, every one of them was black." He peered at the other houses. They didn't know it, but Private First-class, Ernest Savage is on the case.

When Mr. Freeman said he would pay one of us twenty dollars to clean his camper, I quickly volunteered. I already got a list of the stuff I'm going to buy. I've never had that much money in my life, except for the time I stole a twenty-dollar bill from DeeDee and nems coffee table. They had the funhouse on our street. DeeDee and nem got double the people and triple the problems in their family. If anybody go missing, they're just hiding out over there. Miss Mabel, can't tell one kid from the other. DeeDee and nem are my friends, I didn't want to do it. But it was the first thing I saw when I walked through the door. It begged me to set it free. DeeDee used her body to barricade the front door.

"Uh-uh, can't nobody leave 'til we search all y'all!" she said. I wasn't worried because I already stuffed the twenty into my panties. They wouldn't dare look there, would they? After patting us down and still coming up empty, Miss Mabel called the police to report the theft.

"Hey, how about it? Whoever took the money come clean, have a heart huh, you won't hold it against him or her, would you ma'am?" he asked Miss Mabel.

"Sure, I'll forgive you, whoever you are," she said looking from face to face.

"But I didn't take it," the other kids said.

"Me either," I said. Who did Miss Mabel think she was fooling? If I confess, she would whoop my ass good for stealing from her house. No thanks. To make matters worse, DeeDee's sister Lucrecia, came into the room pointing a black water gun at the policeman. He drew his real gun and pointed it at her stupid head.

"Drop it!" he said.

"No, don't shoot, it ain't real, it's a water gun!" we shouted.

"Get on the floor!" he said. She stood there, still pointing the water gun with a silly grin on her face. Every family had a crazy. We got Aunt Tracie, and DeeDee and nem got Lucrecia.

"Get on the fucking ground now, final warning!" he said.

"Lucrecia get your *ass* on the floor," Miss Mabel said calmly, and she did.

"Now slide it over," the policeman said. He snatched the toy gun off the floor and examined it.

"It's a fucking water gun," he said.

"Told you," Lucrecia said from the floor.

"All right, get up," he said. He took loud and deep breaths. He grabbed her by the chin to keep her from looking off into space.

"You came this close to getting your little head blown off, never, ever point a gun at an officer, real or otherwise," he said. After that he didn't care who took the money, he just wanted to get the hell away from DeeDee and nems.

Mr. Freeman picked me up and dropped me off in some empty field where the camper was. There was filth on top of the dirt, but like Mary Poppins, I whistled while I worked. About an hour later the small door opened.

"Hi Mr. Freeman, I'll be finished in a minute." He scanned the camper.

"You've done enough, come here have a seat at the table," he said. Mr. Freeman took out his wallet and gave me two ten-dollar bills. I was disappointed because I wanted twenty ones, so I would look richer. I snatched the money and tucked it into my sock.

"Thank you, Mr. Freeman," I said. The aroma coming from the bag he brought in with him put me in a trance. He pushed the bag toward me.

"Go ahead, it's for you," he said. I grabbed the bag and tore it open. He sat quietly while I chowed down on the cheeseburger and French fries. Mr. Freeman is so nice they way a grandfather should be. He asked me the same dumb questions grown-ups always ask.

"So, do you like school, what grade are you in, do you play any sports, do you know what a blowjob is?" I put my finger in the air to say I had to swallow the delicious food before I could answer.

"Uh-huh I like school, I'm in the sixth grade, I play baseball sometimes, but I don't want to blow dry my hair." He chuckled and kindly explained what a blowjob was. My heart start beating with fear and anger. I threw the rest of my burger at him. I wasn't satisfied so I threw the fries one by one until there were none left. I got the hell out of there.

"That bastard bet' not bring his ass back here again!" Auntie Althea said after she found me crying about it. But Mr. Freeman did bring his ass back the same day. I watched from the upstairs window as he pulled into the backyard and stepped out of his truck. He held a bottle of whiskey like a sweet-smelling bouquet.

"Hey Pearl, you in there?" he said. Auntie Althea is our queen bee. Whenever she told us to do something, we did it like little worker bees.

"Get the trash can and dump it all over the bastard's truck!" she said.

"Why?" Uncle Marcus said.

"Just do it!" she yelled. Once the truck was covered with garbage and plenty of dirty diapers, she reached inside and pressed on the horn violently.

"Pearl, your kids done put trash all over my truck!" he said from the doorway. Nana came and stood in the doorway beside him.

"Thea, why y'all kids misbehavin' so?" she said.

"We ain't misbehavin', old Mr. Freeman been misbehavin'. Go ahead nigga, tell her what you said to Goldie!" We followed him and Nana into the kitchen.

"Pearl, I don't know what these kids is talkin' about, he said.

"Oh really, *would a blowjob hep you ramemba?*" she said. The cat had his tongue. That gave her time to go to the closet and return with the savage beast. She swung the bat wildly. We all said, "Whoa" and got out of her way. Even Nana took a sobering step back.

"Uh-oh, you better haul ass mister!" Little Uncle Marcus said. Old Mr. Freeman ran out and jumped into his garbage-filled truck and he left a dust storm in the yard. When the dust settled, Auntie Althea stood with the bat over her head. "And don't bring your ass around here no more!" she said. We thought we were in big trouble with Nana since he took the whiskey with him. But instead, she slapped her knee and hooted until tears streaked her cheeks.

"Y'all come on in here, leave that ol' man be," she said. When it got dark, I met Auntie Althea in the bathroom like she told me to.

"You ready?" she asked.

"Uh-huh, I'm ready," I lied. Inside I screamed, "Are you crazy or something?! As poor as we are!" I took a deep breath and placed the two ten-dollar bills in the sink, and she set them on fire.

16
Another Think Comin'!

"LORD KNOWS I'M HELPING in every way I can," Nana said. She was sitting in the backseat of an unfamiliar brown car. She had on that very familiar short, and nappy gray wig. I hate it because it makes her look like old Kizzy from Roots. Last week, I took it upon myself to hide it. I was trying to save the Savages from more embarrassment. But, when I found her ransacking the house looking for her "good wig," I pretended to find it in the back of her closet. But next time, I won't fall for it, she ain't getting it back. Nana's always pleading with somebody. I don't know why she even bothers. Who is it this time?

"Well thank you Pearl, you helped a whole lot," Evelyn said in her usual nasty tone. *I should have known.* Because if it ain't one thing it's my mother. I sat on the curb behind the car.

"Honey you scorned right now, come in the house 'til things calm down some."

"She a grown ass woman, let her go ma," Uncle Nolan said.

"Evelyn please leave that boy be," Nana said.

"Ifhethinkhegon'leavemewit'threekidsandlayupwiththatwhorehe gotanotherthinkcomin'!" Hmm, that was the longest running word I ever heard, I didn't catch it all.

"Ma'am I don't mean to interrupt, but I got other places to be," the driver said.

"Hey, don't disrespect my mother, mother-fucker," Uncle Nolan said.

"Whoa young blood, listen up, I know she's your sister, but she called me. She said she needed a ride. That's what I do, I pick peoples up, and carry 'em where they want to go for a price. The rest ain't none of my business."

"Man, forget this shit, excuse my language Ma," Uncle Nolan said before he got out and slammed the car door.

"Hey man, careful with my door, it ain't new, but it's new to me," the driver said. He saw me sitting here. The look on his face said I tried and I'm done.

"Evelyn come with me, let's talk it out," Nana said.

"Reggie, can you kindly ask my mother to get out of your car."

"Ma'am, please." Nana finally stepped outside the car. She didn't see me. I watched her walk into the house. She looks like the weight of the world is on her shoulders. She's going straight for the bottle. The smoke from the tailpipe made me cough as the car sped off. From what I gathered, she's running out on us because Josiah left her with three babies.

"Hey, why are you sitting on the ground, and what are you so happy about?" Danny said. I used my hands as a shield and looked at him.

"How long you been standing there?" I said.

"Not long."

"Well, you shouldn't sneak up on somebody like that." If I want to stay friends with Danny, I'll have to keep him away from the Savages. His family is so different from mine, his parents are still together, and they both got good jobs. One time a book of food stamps fell out of my pocket, he picked them up and asked me what they were. I told him it was like monopoly game money and he believed me. He has an older brother, and those are all the people who live in his house. He gets to do fun stuff, like taking karate lessons and going to Disney World more than once a year. All the furniture in his house matched and was placed in the right rooms. Not like at our house. We have a couch in our dining room, a deep freezer in the hallway, and the bed on the porch where Uncle Norman sleeps, in case of an ambush. One day, he'll insist on coming in the house.

Sure, he'll try to overlook the crazy stuff at first, but eventually, it will all be too much. His friends will start teasing him, and he'll be forced to find a nice normal girl. So, I'm going to quit him before he quits me.

Five days have passed and still no sign of Evelyn. Is it me, or is the sun shining brighter than usual? Bunny is starting to go crazy, and it won't be long before Beau realizes she's been gone longer than what he's used to. Normally, after being gone for days she'll come home to sleep off a hangover. The next day she would wake up, wash up, get dressed and go again without mumbling one word to any of us.

Evelyn didn't leave us like I hoped, she's in jail, that's all. She had to settle the score with Josiah. She went over to the trailer park he lived in and put three bullets in his behind. One for each baby he left her with, or something like that. Anyway, he ain't dead. He couldn't walk for a while because he was paralyzed. It was printed in the St. Petersburg Times and on Channel 10 news. A bunch of women got together and tried to get her out of jail. They're calling Josiah a deadbeat dad. They say he deserves exactly what he got. She's been in jail for seven months. She calls collect every day. I avoid talking to her. But she told Bunny it's nothing like you see on TV. She's having the time of her life, making lots of friends, and getting lots of beauty sleep.

"You can't go to school today honey," Nana said.

"How come?" I said.

"I need you to dress the kid's real nice and clean for me." She's more herself this morning, she wasn't drunk or hung over.

"What they got to get dressed for?"

"Your mama's trial start today," she said.

"What they need to go for? They didn't shoot nobody."

"Stop being ornery, before I take a switch to you." I shake my head. Nana has never taken a switch to anybody.

"The lawyer wants that judge to see she got six kids to care for," she said.

"You mean they might let her go because of us? So, it's okay to kill somebody as long as you got kids?" Nana wasn't listening to a word I said.

"I wrote a letter to the court telling them she didn't mean no harm, she just wasn't in her right mind," she said.

"Dang Nana, why did you do that?"

"Well don't you want your mama to come home?"

"No, I don't, I hope she gets the electric chair. I hope we never see her ever again, we better off without her."

"Hush now, don't ever say nothin' like that, she still your mama no matter what. Besides you too young to understand matters of the heart."

"But—" She put her hand up to shut me up.

"Go on now, help me get them kids ready," she said sternly. I stomped up the steps. Nana got some nerve to say I don't understand matters of the heart, I understand plenty.

A bunch of sweaty women crowded into the courtroom.

"Who are they?" I asked Nana.

"They're spectators honey," she said. A door opened, and a bunch of people came out and sat together on one side of the room. I knew they were ladies and gentlemen of the jury. The door opened again, and they brought Evelyn in. The awful orange jumpsuit or the handcuffs didn't stop her from grinning or waving back at all the excited women. The guard removed the handcuffs and she sat next to her lawyer. She swung around in her chair.

"Hi ma, how y'all doin'?" she said. She playfully stuck her tongue out at Uncle Nolan. The lawyer cleared his throat and nodded toward the jury box.

"Oh, right I forgot," she said. She turned around and tried to look sorry.

"Oh my, she's adorable, so petite, she couldn't upset a fly. It must have been self-defense," the spectators said. Evelyn's lawyer had pale hair and a peach face, and he wore glasses. He came over and arranged us like we were going to take a family picture.

"Okay Pearl, just make sure these older ones are holding a babe in arms when the judge comes out. Now if you guys want your mommy to come home, just look super sad, no playing around," he said. Nana gave me a stern look when she saw the corners of my mouth curling in the wrong direction.

"You're a big girl, can you manage to squeeze out a tear or two for your dear mommy?" he asked me. I shook my head no.

"She will," I said pointing at Bunny.

I used to watch Perry Mason late at night. When the judge banged his wooden hammer, and said, "Case dismissed!" I wanted to stand on the table and scream "Your honor, I object!" like they do on Perry Mason. It's all Josiah's fault, all he had to do was come and tell the jury what happened, and show the ladies and gentlemen of the jury, the three holes she put in him. Josiah's lawyer hesitated to tell the jury that his client was in the jail next to the woman's jail where Evelyn was in. He said Josiah and his father, Vernon Wallace was apprehended while attempting to rob a bank. And Josiah Wallace was shot, for the fourth time, by a St. Petersburg police officer. The judge flung his hammer down, folded his arms, and waited for the women to stop laughing.

"Mrs. Evelyn Wallace, due to the lack of evidence, you're free to go," the judge said.

"Hallelujah!" Evelyn said.

"And try not to shoot anybody else," he said.

"I won't your honor, I promise."

"Because next time, I will throw your ass under the jail. Do you understand?"

"Yes your honor, I understand, I'm free!" she said. She spun around and waved at the ladies. They stood, they cheered, they even whistled. That's when I managed to squeeze out more than a few tears.

17
Dirt

"DAMN EVELYN, AIN'T THESE the slave's quarters?" Uncle Nolan said. He dropped our old dusty rug on the living room floor and took a ten-second tour around the house.

"Well this is all I can afford right now," she said.

"I don't like it here, why can't we stay at Nana's?" Bunny whined.

"My probation officer will send me back to jail if I didn't find a house and a job".

"They can do that?" Bunny asked with a worried look on her face. I tilted my head and smiled. The thought of her going back to the slammer excited me, those were some of the best days of my life.

"Hey, get the molasses out ya' asses and bring the rest of that stuff up here," Uncle Nolan Joked.

"Please, I ain't never goin' back to jail. I'm gon' make damn sure I don't get caught next time."

"Wow, Annie Oakley ain't got shit on you," Uncle Nolan said.

A week later, Evelyn got a job working in the kitchen on a cruise ship. Every day she falls through the door smelling like fish. After she lands on the couch she starts barking orders. "Somebody bring me a glass of water! Somebody come change this channel! Somebody close this window! Somebody open this window, its hot as hell in here!" She got some damn nerve, *changing my name to somebody.*

Christmas is here and we ain't got nothing to show for it. Ever since we left the heartbreak motel, Evelyn went back to doing all the things she used to do. I can't believe she's having a party here tonight, but by eight o'clock people were crammed into our tiny kitchen. It's a good thing people still bring food to parties. Aunt Tracie is sitting at the table having a deep conversation with somebody nobody else could see. Uncle Nolan keeps glancing over at her, he wants her to get up. He's itching to get a card game going. Bunny's friend Lisa is spending the night, she even brought some Christmas candy. The boys never had a Christmas before, so they don't know what they're missing. I managed to beg up a few dollars. The toys I got for them will crumble by morning. By ten o'clock the party people are having a good time. I saw Aunt Tracie trying to squeeze through the crowd. I moved down on the couch to make room for her, and her "special friend".

"Aunt Tracie, why are you laughing?" I said. She's staring at the barest part of the wall.

"No reason," she said. Ever since Nana got the doctor to switch her medicine, she'll answer if she wants to. Uncle Nolan got his card game going now. They're in there slamming cards, and cussing up a storm. "*Master Blaster*" by Stevie Wonder's is exploding from the speakers. Everything that wasn't nailed down was jumping to the beat. I rubbed my temples and focused on the stupid Christmas tree on top of the TV. "It's twelve inches tall!" the box bragged. I want to rip it to shreds. It would be better not to have one at all.

"Y'all come on sing for my friends!" Evelyn said in her tipsy voice. I can't believe she's making us do this now, especially since we're not as little or as cute as we used to be. I'll be twelve in two weeks. Once we got their attention, Lisa placed the needle on the record. I stepped out front to sing over Mavis, but I swear this is the last time.

After midnight, the tiny house started to air out. "All right girlie, let's do it again," they sang happily as they staggered down the steps. Evelyn said she was going to a bar with Uncle Nolan and his friend, but first, they had to take Aunt Tracie home. After they were gone we played games and ate the rest of the cold fried chicken, potato salad, and Christmas candy.

"Hey, why you do that!" Beau said when I dropped the little raggedy Christmas tree deep into the garbage can.

"Because it's stupid, and it ain't even real," I said. I snatched a drinking glass off the counter and dropped it in there too.

"Mama gon' git you," he said.

"No, say Mama gon' get you, *get* you," I said. Beau was having trouble talking right. He said pit for put, and wit for what and stuff like that. I always correct him if Evelyn ain't around.

After midnight, I noticed that not a creature was stirring, except me. A bright light was coming from our room. I went to turn it off. They were all sound asleep. Aw, they look so cute with their arms and legs all tangled up. I couldn't tell what belonged to who. It would have made a perfect picture.

Lisa was in my spot, so I went to the kitchen to clean up a little. Somebody left a pack of Benson and Hedges on the table. I laughed at the long name. Oh, what the heck. I took one out. I had been curious about cigarettes for a while. I lit it and inhaled some smoke. I choked and felt a little light-headed. I picked up a half-full bottle of beer and swallowed some. Yuk! How can they stand it? Smoke is disgusting, and beer isn't even sweet. I ran over to the sink to spit it out. I rinsed my mouth out and turned off the kitchen light. I checked the door, it's locked. I put the chain on and pulled out the couch-bed. Evelyn sleeps out here because her room ain't no bigger than a jail cell. I climbed under the blanket. The Midnight special was on. The band playing was called Kiss. I wish they were the Bee Gee's. These guys are so weird because of all that white clown make-up, and that one is always sticking out his...

Somebody's here, standing over me, I just know it. Maybe it's Evelyn, she probably wants me to get out of her bed. I tried to get up, but somebody held me down. Now I know it's not her, she ain't this big and she smells like *Cashmere Bouquet* soap, and sweet gum, not musty stale sweat. It's a strange man. He put his hand over my mouth and I tasted the dirt.

If you scream or try to fight me, I'll kill all them kids back there," he whispered in my ear in a raspy voice. His hot, and stinky breath was stuck in my ear.

"But I'm a kid! I'm a kid too!" I screamed from inside my head. He climbed on top of me while one dirty hand pushed my panties down and the other still pressed hard against my mouth. I couldn't breathe. I dug my nails into his filthy fingers. "Okay, but you better not make one sound. Is a lil' pussy worth your life?" he whispered. When he moved his hand, I tilted my head to let the spit run out of my mouth. I refuse to swallow the dirt.

I'm paralyzed. Dirt didn't bother to close the door. I just been laying here watching the porch light swing. Every time the wind blows, I hear the life in the trees, and death in my bones.

The freezing cold air forced me to get up and close the door. I'm standing in the middle of the tiny floor wishing I could go back in time. But where would I go? I never felt safe anywhere anyway. Except when we lived in the big house. I went in back to our room and turned on the light. Unlike me, they were unchanged, still innocent, and still alive. I feel good about that.

"Lisa, wake up, please," I said while shaking her gently. Lisa looked younger than me, but she just turned thirteen. She probably wasn't used to being woke up in the middle of the night.

"What's the matter, why are you crying?" she said. I put my finger to my lips and motioned for her to follow me. We sat on the floor in the small space between our room and the bathroom. After I told her about Dirt, she put her arms around me and we started crying.

"Did you lock the door?" she said.

"I thought I did, but I guess I forgot to."

"Why didn't you wake us up?"

"I couldn't."

"Why is all my damn lights on?!" Evelyn said as she stepped over us and went into the bathroom. We could hear her peeing. She made sounds that said she had been holding it for a long time.

"What y'all sittin' there crying for?" she said on her way out.

"Miss Evelyn, somebody came in here," Lisa said.

"What, who the hell you let in my house?!"

"Hey Evelyn, I'm headin' out, you cool?" Uncle Nolan said.

"I'm always cool," she responded. He peered over her shoulder and saw us. The look in his eyes changed.

"Move out my way," he said pushing her back toward the living room.

"What's going on here?" he said.

"Somebody came in here and did something to Goldie," Lisa said. Our eyes locked and a sorrowful look filled his.

"Y'all get up from there," he said. He tried to wake Evelyn, but she was already sleeping in the very spot I died in. I couldn't sleep, I sat at the kitchen table next to Uncle Nolan, and he dozed off. I watched the house get brighter by the second.

"Bye Goldie," Lisa said as she headed for the door.

"By Lisa, thanks for the candy," I said.

"Was he young or old?" Uncle Nolan said.

"Old."

"How old?"

"I don't know, like, fifty." Evelyn let out a quick laugh. Uncle Nolan ignored her.

"Was he fat or thin? You remember what he was wearing?"

"A leather coat, I think."

"Can't you see the girl is lying? She let some little nappy head ass boy in here and now she tryna cover it up, she sneaky like that."

"Evelyn, shut up. It had to be somebody who saw us leave last night. Ain't nobody gon' just come back here. I called Ma, she said to call the police. But first I got to see what's up with that cat who lives up front. Put a jacket on Goldie," he said.

"No, I don't want to."

"I need to know if it's him, I ain't gon' do nothin' in broad daylight." I refused to move. He disturbed the salt and pepper shakers when he slammed his fist down on the table.

"Put a damn Jacket on! I'm sorry I didn't mean to yell, just do what I say," he said. The man up front stuck his head through the light green curtains. He opened the door when he recognized me.

"Hey man, what's happenin'?" Uncle Nolan said.

"Can I help you brother?" he said.

"Sorry to bother you, but can you tell me how to get to the Coliseum from here?" I watched the man as he gave us directions. I knew it wasn't him, he's normal sized and his hands are too clean.

"How you know for sure?" Uncle Nolan asked me on the way back. I couldn't tell him about the dirt. I didn't swallow it, but I tasted it.

"I just know," I said. The police came and wrote down everything I told them. They said I had to go to the hospital to get checked out. That nurse wanted me to spread my legs apart, so she could look inside me.

"No, no, don't touch me!" I swung my arms and screamed until she let me go.

"Go away!" I yelled from inside the bathroom. Bunny is twisting the doorknob like a maniac.

"Mama, Goldie won't let me use the bathroom!" she said.

"Girl hurry up, it's more people in here besides you," Evelyn yelled. I ignored them. Anyway, I can't move now if I wanted to, I'm staring into the toilet trying to figure out what those bugs are. Ever since that night I been itching in my private area. We don't have a bathtub, but I took lots of showers. It didn't help, I couldn't sit or stand without the urge to scratch. All I could do was cry. So, I came in here and sat on the toilet and scratched, picked, and pulled. Bunny's still trying to break the door down. She'll just have to wait. After I thought I got all of them, I flushed and watched them spin around and disappear. I'll never tell anybody about the bugs, not Auntie Althea, not even Nana. Evelyn banged on the door this time.

"Bring your ass out of there right now!" she yelled. I washed my hands and flushed the toilet again, just in case.

"It's about time," Bunny said while pushing me out of her way. I sat on the floor against the wall to avoid that disgusting couch. I saw Evelyn moving around in the kitchen. "Let's do it again" *was* playing on the stereo, *again.* I closed my eyes and thought about the last time I heard this song. I see the three of us jamming. A couple was sitting on Evelyn's bed looking out at us. Aunt Tracie on the couch laughing at the wall. Lisa fluttered in and out like a busy bee collecting money in a hat. The boys were in the back having fun. The others are watching the show from the kitchen, and the other two doorways, *except him.* He's standing close enough to reach out and touch us. He wore a long black leather coat. Something about him gave me the creeps. I kept singing, but I was thinking, as soon as he's gone, I'm gon' throw that glass he's using in the garbage. Who would want to drink after somebody with hands so... dirty?

"Did you hear what I said, girl?!" Evelyn said.

"Huh, what you say?"

"I said get over here, and wash the dishes over, you left spots all over these plates." I went to the doorway of the kitchen.

"Fuck you, wash them yourself," I said.

"Ohhellnoyoulittltebitchwhothefuckyouthinkyoutalkin'to?!" she said. Her head darted around the kitchen for something to draw my blood with. I didn't hang around to see what she found. I ran all the way to Nana's house. I ran straight into her arms and sobbed into her bosom. I breathed in deeply, searching for the chocolaty scent I used to love. I found it hiding under the heavy odor of whiskey.

"It's gon' be all right after while baby." She didn't mean to lie to me, but she just did.

Me and Auntie Althea stood in the middle of Uncle Nolan's studio apartment. I told her who I believed Dirt was, and she dragged me here to tell him.

"I'm saying, you might be confused, I been known' him for years, from back home, since I was a kid, he been like a second father to me, taught me everything I know about mechanics. He wouldn't ever do no shit like that, not to me," Uncle Nolan said.

"Mm-hmm, well the world is full of perverts Nolan. Look at how pretty she is," Auntie Althea said. Uncle Nolan looked at me like her never really did before.

"You know what, now that I think about it, I got things mixed up. Come on Auntie Althea, let's go home," I said. I didn't want them to argue.

"No wait," he said. He rubbed his temples, and picked up the phone and dialed a number. "He stay across the hall. We gon' nip this in the bud right now. I'm tryna find the mother-fucker who—hey man, it's Nolan, I need to holla at you real quick... Nah, I can't tell you over the phone... It can't wait until later... Damn Earl, it ain't like you to be asking me no twenty questions, just come over here for a minute man." A few seconds later he twisted the doorknob. Uncle Nolan locked it on purpose. He knocked.

"Answer it," he said.

"I don't want to," I whispered.

"Hurry up," he said.

"I can't."

"I'll do it," Althea said.

"No, not you Thea," he said. I opened the door with my eyes cast to the floor. My body trembled as my eyes traveled upward. They stopped at the black dirt caked on his hands and embedded into his nails. I slammed the door in his face. I didn't need to see anymore.

"Wait, be still," he said. We stood like mannequins, listening, waiting, and watching the door until the shadow of his feet backed away and the door across the hall closed. From behind me, I heard Uncle Nolan crying.

"That fucking bastard!" Auntie Althea said.

"Be quiet Thea," he said. I watched him light his cigarette and inhale deeply. He let the smoke out in smooth circles. The tears were gone.

"Y'all go home," he said. We gathered our stuff and headed toward the door.

"Goldie, wait. The cops said they was gon' come back and ask you some more questions, didn't they?"

"Uh huh."

"Tell 'em you don't know nothin' else. And don't say nothin' to nobody, ever, not even Ma, you too Thea." We shook our heads and left the building.

"I ain't nothing but trouble, right Auntie?" I said as we walked. She shook her head no.

"But Evelyn always says I am."

"Don't believe anything she say about you."

"How come she hate me?"

"I think she's jealous of you."

"But why? She made me."

"I don't know everything Goldie. I'm just trying to keep going crazy my own self. Why don't you just stay away from her?"

"I want to, but I can't leave them. I promised."

Auntie Althea said not to worry about Uncle Nolan because he can take care of his self. But I can't help but worry, it's been two days since we left his apartment and we haven't seen or heard from him. I'm staring out of the living room window just hoping to see him coming up the walkway. I felt a tap on my shoulder, so I turned around.

"You lookin' for somebody?" Uncle Nolan said.

"Uncle Nolan!" I said excitedly while giving him a bear hug.

"Whoa, be careful. My hand, it's busted," he said. Bandages covered his right hand. Some blood seeped through.

"You got to go to the doctor with me. They gon' show you how to clean this out, and pack the gauze so it don't get infected."

When we got to the doctor's office, I gasped when I saw Uncle Nolan's hand. The skin that should have covered his knuckles was gone, his bones were exposed. The next day he left a note on Nana's bed. It said not to worry about him and he loves her. Who's gonna take care of his hand now? I went through the house looking for Nana, she was in the kitchen cooking. A half empty bottle of gin sat close by on the table. I sat next to her and grabbed a large potato to peel.

"Baby don't peel too much meat off that potato. Child, they got—"

"Plenty of starving kids in Africa, I know," I said.

"Mm-hmm, Lord know they would appreciate what we waste," she said.

That night I tossed and turned on the couch in the dining room. A few minutes after I fell asleep. The loud banging on the front door woke me up. There were red and blue lights flashing outside. Nana came running out of her room. She was wrestling with the zipper on her housecoat. She stood in front of the door and put one eye over the peephole. I pulled the curtain back to see what I could.

"It's a police car," I said.

"Oh Lord, Marcus, Kevin, Thea! Tracie ain't done run out of here, did she?"

"No, she's here." I laughed because she always does that when the law darkens our doorstep. Whoever ain't in the house is the one who's in trouble she always says. Nana opened the door. Two police officers were standing on the enclosed porch. It's a good thing Uncle Ernest went back to Pittsburgh to get help from the VA hospital. Otherwise, he would already have one in a headlock and the other one would have to shoot him.

"Evening ma'am, are you Mrs. Pearl Savage?" a lady officer said.

"Yes, I'm Pearl, can I help you?"

"I'm Officer Cooke and this is Officer Burrell," the man said.

He reached out to shake Nana's hand, but she only stared at it. He put his hand away.

"We came across the report concerning your grand-daughter Gwendolyn. Is she here with you?" he said.

"What you after her for?"

"Ma'am, please don't be alarmed, she's not in any trouble, we're here to take her into protective custody, at least until we get more information on the perpetrator."

"He could be watching, you never know," she said. Nana thought for a second before she stepped to the side to let them in. I want to tell them not to worry because Dirt will never come near me again. But, what if they ask me how I know? Finally, the lady notices me standing there.

"You must be Gwendolyn. Can you tell us anything more about what happened the other night?" I shook my head no.

"We want to take you to a safe place, okay?" the man said.

"Okay."

"You should ask her mama first," Nana said.

"Ma'am, we've already spoken with her mother, she sent us here," he said.

"I got to go home to get some clothes and stuff," I said.

"Everything you need is in the backseat of the squad car, your mom packed enough for a couple days," he said. I hugged Nana and told her not to worry about me.

"Watch your head hun," she said before I slid in the back of the police car. I saw a brown paper bag on the seat.

"It's only for two days, right?" The lady turned and smiled.

"Two days tops," she said.

18

Trans Am

"WHAT IS THIS PLACE?" I asked.

"This is a temporary group home," Officer Burrell said. A stout brown skinned girl stood in the doorway.

"Hello Maxine, how are you?" Officer Cooke said.

"I'm fine, thank you, come in please." The enclosed porch was made out like an office with a big brown desk and chairs.

"How are Mr. and Mrs. Hobbs?" he said.

"They're doing okay, they were asleep when you called."

"Will it be a problem?" officer Burrell said.

"We have two empty beds, so it should be all right," Maxine said.

"This is Gwendolyn Savage," he said. Maxine smile and nodded.

"Please to make your acquaintance," she said.

"We're gonna go now, we'll see you real soon Gwendolyn," Officer Burrell said.

"But, I don't want to stay here, I changed my mind," I half whispered. She put her hands on my shoulders.

"I've known the Hobbs for years, trust me, you'll be fine here," she assured me.

"Two days, right?"

"Sure kiddo, I'll swing by and take you back home myself."

"Okay, goodbye," I said reluctantly.

"Not goodbye, see you later," she said.

"I'll show you your room, and we'll go over the house rules in the morning," the girl said. I followed close behind her. Soft golden lights lit the hallway. There were many closed white doors with gold knobs. She opened the last door on the left and flicked the light switch.

"Hey, turn the damn light off!" a girl said instantly. There were two sets of bunk beds in the room. Two girls slept soundly while the one on the top left bunk covered her eyes and cursed Maxine.

"I'm getting a new girl settled in Priyanka, I need the light for a minute thank you," Maxine said.

"Get the fuck out of here," she mumbled. She flung herself around until she faced the wall. Her long light brown hair fell and reached the bottom bunk. She reminded me of Cousin It from the Adams Family. I'm glad I don't have to sleep under her. Maxine opened and closed the drawers until she found an empty one.

"You can keep your belongings in here." I opened the paper bag to see what Evelyn put in there. Great, one pair of shorts, and two t-shirts, all dirty. Maxine read my mind.

"If your things need to be washed, I'll do it in the morning," she said. Cousin It huffed and puffed and kicked the ceiling. I stretched my eyes in question.

"Don't worry about her. Here is a gown for you to sleep in. And here are your toiletries," Maxine said. I took the gown and the clear baggie that contained toothpaste, soap, deodorant, and other important stuff.

"Thank you," I said.

"No problem. I'll see you in the morning," she said before gently closing the door.

"Hey, can you turn off the fucking light?" Cousin It said. I quickly turned it off and slid into the bottom bunk and silently cried myself to sleep.

I opened my eyes to the sounds of yelling, laughter, doors opening and slamming, and other signs of wildlife. I sat up, all three girls were gone. I put my shorts and t-shirt back on. I bumped heads with a girl coming into the room when I was leaving.

"Sorry," I said.

"No sweat, it happens all the time around here, you'll get used to it."

"Hey, Good morning Goldie. I was just about to wake you up. Come with me, I'll show you around. If there's time we'll go over the house rules before brunch," Maxine said. Why she wasted her time telling me when I could to take a shower, how to use the sign in and out sheet and what chores I got to do all month is beyond me. Come Monday, I'll be long gone. She dropped me off back at the room.

"Could I have something to eat?"

"Of course, brunch will be ready at eleven-thirty." Waiting for the clock to strike eleven-twenty-nine was torture. I followed my nose toward the most delightful smells. From the doorway, I counted ten heads sitting at the big round table. They stopped whatever they were doing to check me out. I stood still, so they could get a good look at me. This way they could decide if they like the new girl who came in the middle of the night, or not. I don't give a damn what they think, I'm just getting this part over with. After them wenches sized me up, they went back to their conversations. I sat in an empty chair across from Cousin It. From the front, she was a pretty Indian girl.

"She's in our room," she said dryly.

The kitchen is not hidden behind walls, so I could see the old black couple standing at the island. They must be the Hobbs. They were busy, chopping, mixing, and tasting. Be patient, I told my stomach when it started doing cartwheels. "All right girls, come and get it!" the old man said. They stampeded toward the island, snatching up bowls and platters of food to place in the middle of the table. I went over to help, and Maxine grabbed my arm.

"Mommy, daddy, this is Goldie, she got here last night."

"Hello sweetheart, were so happy to meet you," Mrs. Hobbs said.

"Another pretty one," Mr. Hobbs said.

"Come a little closer honey, give us a hug," Mrs. Hobbs said. She smelled like the stuff old folks always rubbed on their bodies. Mr.

Hobbs could barely raise his shaky arms to hug me, but he managed.

"Now go on and get you some brunch," he said. More food than I ever seen at one time sat on the table top. Stacks of pancakes with real maple syrup, mounds of scrambled eggs, bacon, fried potatoes, all kinds of fruit. The main attraction was a big platter of pink chopped meat. The girls practically stabbed each other's fingers with their forks trying to get some of it.

"What is that?" I asked the little white girl sitting next to me.

"It's deer meat," she said before stuffing a forkful of it in her mouth.

"You're kidding, right?"

"Nope, it's good, you should try it."

"No thanks, I'll pass."

"Have you ever tasted rabbit before?"

"No." She picked some up with her fingers and pushed it in my face.

"It tastes like chicken." I slapped her hand away and, the rabbit landed on the table.

"I said I don't want none, and if I did, I wouldn't eat it out of your hand, I don't know where your hands have been." I peeked over at Maxine and the Hobbs. Good, they didn't see that. I stuffed myself with everything except the Bugs Bunny, and Bambi meat. After the brunch, we spent our time playing games and watching TV in the until the Hobbs came out and fired up the grill. They served hot dogs, hamburgers, potato salad, and the best baked beans I ever had.

"How do you know?!" Cousin It said.

"Because I heard Mrs. Hobbs tell Maxine to get a bed ready for her," Donna said. She only takes her thumb out of her mouth to talk, then she pops it back in.

"Thank God they put the new girl in her bed. Now they can't stick her retarded ass back in my room," Cousin It said.

"But, now she in our room," another girl chimed in.

"Who y'all talking about?" I said.

"Some girl who was supposed to be gone for good," Donna said.

"Yeah, and she's ugly as shit, and she smells like dried up period blood," another girl said. I cringed.

"Why is she coming back?" I said.

"Because her no good, trifling ass mother didn't show up for court again," Cousin It said.

"If she was my daughter, I wouldn't claim her ass either," another girl chimed in. They slapped high fives. Donna shivered like she was suddenly freezing.

"That bitch gives me the heebie-jeebies," she said.

Maxine bossed us around in the nicest way. "Do it now, please, thank you," she says before anybody gets a chance to protest.

"She ain't much older than us, how come she gets to tell us what to do?" I asked Donna.

"She's the Hobbs' daughter. She came here like the rest of us, but they adopted her and her sister Darlene. She's away at college," she said.

"So, how old is she?"

"Fourteen."

"Fourteen going on forty," another girl added. Sunday was another delicious food eating, lazy fun-filled day. Some old crusty preacher came and preached a boring sermon. Afterward he tried to get us to accept Christ as our personal Lord and savior. We all refused. Reverend what's his name, must get paid in leftovers because he didn't leave until every bit of them were gone.

On Monday morning, I went into the dining area. Six boxes of cereal and two gallons of milk sat in the middle of the table. I felt relieved because the other food constipated me. A girl sat alone at the table eating a bowl of frosted flakes. She must be the girl everybody hates. Nana always said don't judge a book by the cover. *Okay, I'll try not to.* She saw me and waved excitedly as if I were a mile away instead of two feet.

"Hi," I said and took a seat not too far but not too close either.

"What your name is?" she said.

"Goldie, what's yours?"

"Erma." Some of the girls came out and were hesitant to sit at the table, or they sat as far away from her as they could. Others huffed and turned around. These stupid cows are getting on my nerves. She can't help the way she looks, and she don't stink like they said.

After breakfast, I put my clean shorts and tee-shirts back in the paper bag. Maxine said the toiletries were mine to keep. I went out to the office porch to wait for Officer Burrell. Some of the girls' school buses screeched as they came and went.

"Why ain't you coming to school with us?" one of the girls said.

"Miss hot stuff is going home," Donna said without even taking her thumb out of her mouth.

"Oh," she said. I didn't blame her for being jealous, they all are. But I don't want to stay out in the middle of nowhere, with a bunch of mean cows. Not to mention the old people frying skunks and whatnot. They caused a wind storm when they ran out the door to catch the school buses. Some of them got on a short bus. I watched the cars cruise by. Not one happened to be a police car. What's taking them so long? Minutes later, a shiny new Trans AM pulled into the driveway. It's the same color as a Hot Wheels car I got for Joshua one time. The package said the color was electric blue. A rich looking woman got out of the hot car. She wore a nice beige skirt suit. Before coming to the door, she straightened her clothes and ran her hand over her already perfect short hair. I didn't care who she was. I looked past her prissy behind. I continued to watch the road. It's already eight o'clock. Where is that damn police woman? She rang the doorbell although we were staring right at each other.

"Maxine somebody's at the door! Maxine!" Oh, I forgot she went to school too.

"Who is it?" I asked.

"I'm Luanne Michaels," she said as if I should've heard about her.

"Well, what do you want?"

"I'm here to see Mrs. Hobbs," she said.

"Okay, I'll tell her."

"You can let me in," she said. I ignored her. She could be an ax murderer for all I know. Mrs. Hobbs sat comfortably in the plush reclining chair. Mr. Hobbs was propped against the headboard of the bed, watching TV. The ceiling fan whirled around making a little noise. I knocked lightly.

"Mrs. Hobbs, it's a lady named Luanne Michaels at the door."

"We'll let her on in, she's the social worker, she came here to see about you," she said. What does she want to see me for? I went back and opened the door.

"Come in, you want me to go get Mrs. Hobbs?"

"No, let her rest, please. You're Gwendolyn Savage, right?"

"Uh-huh, how you know my name?"

"I know all the girls here. She sat at the desk like she owned the place. She cracked opened her leather briefcase.

"I work for child welfare. I'll be handling your case. I'd like to have a few words with you."

"Okay, but I really don't have time."

"Why don't you have time?"

"Because I'm going home. Officer Burrell is on her way to get me right now." She seemed unaware.

"A decision has been made by the family court judge. You will remain here until I can find a home for you," she said. My head throbbed, and my mouth got watery. What is this lady talking about? Again, I stood in the window with my back turned to her.

"Gwendolyn, come away from the window." Tears escaped my eyes. Something told me officer Burrell is not coming.

"Gwendolyn come sit down," she said sternly. I threw myself into a chair.

"I understand how you feel, and none of this is your fault," she said.

"Then why are you trying to keep me here?"

"Your eleven years old, and you were assaulted in your home. That is the one place where you should be safe and protected. Instead, you were left alone with much younger children. This should never have happened."

"But, they're safe with me. Anyway, I protected them. I wanted to fight, but I didn't make a sound." She only stared at me for a while.

"Um, the judge declared you a ward of the state."

"So, what does it mean?"

"Well, until your mother answers to the court and proves she can be a fit mother, you will remain under the protection of child welfare. Listen, you're just too young to understand how lucky you are. You kids could have been killed." She took a sheet of paper from her briefcase.

"These are your school transcripts. Your grades are well below average and your attendance is poor. Why have you been truant?" I folded my arms across my chest defiantly.

"Don't you like school, is the work too hard for you?" she asked nicely.

"No, I like school, but sometimes I'm too tired."

"Why are you tired?"

"Because if one of the kids get sick, or when Evelyn was in jail that time." *Oops, I said too much.*

"Here's my card, call me if you have a problem here, although I doubt you will. I looked but didn't touch the card.

"The Hobbs are good people."

"My Nana is good people, I'll stay with her from now on." She gathered her papers and briefcase.

"You're better off here with the Hobbs, until I find you a more suitable home, somewhere where you can be a child, not a mama," she said like she knew me. Please as soon as Miss high and mighty drives away, I'm out of here, they can't keep me.

"And don't even entertain the thought of running away. You will be placed in juvenile hall. There are no comfortable beds or weekend brunches in that place. I don't want to appear harsh, but, it's my job to protect you, even against your will. She got some nerve, pressing her stupid business card in my hand. Don't lose it, call me anytime, for any reason." I don't like this Luanne Michaels, or her stupid, shiny ass electric blue car.

All weekend I bragged about going home. I told everybody my people was waiting for me and whatnot. After three o'clock they start falling through the front door. If I'm extra quiet maybe they won't see me. "You still here? What happened, thought you went home?" they said with smirks on their faces. *Damn, they saw me.* I tried to act casual about it.

"The judge forgot to sign the papers," I said.

"You're gon' have to make up a better story than that," Cousin It said. The other girls laughed. They were just glad that I wasn't special, and nobody wanted me either. That night Maxine officially added my name to the chore board.

"The other girls will show you the ropes when you get to school," she said.

"But I don't have anything to wear," I said. She unlocked a closet that had lots of neatly folded clothes and shoes.

"Problem solved," she said. Tuesday morning, I was ready to go. I sat at the table trying to decide which cereal I wanted. That girl, who nobody likes, beat me here again. The other girls came to the table all at once. They were anxious about something. When Erma went to the bathroom, Cousin It rushed over and spit into her bowl, and ran to the doorway to watch for her.

"Hurry up," she said. They took turns spitting in the bowl and rushed back to their seats and tried to look normal.

"Did everybody do it?" Cousin It said.

"No, not *everybody*?" somebody said.

"Who's left?" she said.

"That new girl," they said. Now they're all staring at me.

"Hurry up before she comes out," the ringleader said. I felt helpless. I didn't have anywhere else to put my pain. Ain't nobody coming to get me. I'm a prisoner here. And I have thirty days' worth of chores to do. When I got up and spit into the bowl, they all laughed. *I think they like me.* They straightened up when Erma came back out and sat.

"Did you wash your filthy monkey hands?" Donna asked her.

"Yeah," she said. They all waited on the edge of their seats. Poor thing. She lifted her spoon and scooped the cereal. We all saw the spit stretching from the spoon to the bowl. She had to see it too. She stared at all our faces, her eyes pleaded for mercy before she opened wide.

"No don't eat it, we spit in it!" I blurted out. They all sucked their teeth and slammed their fists on the table.

"Aw man, you're such a stupid butt hole!" Donna said.

"Oh, suck it Donna! You're all weirdos. Come on Erma, forget them, I'll be your friend," I told her. I wasn't sure if I made the right decision. Erma was strange. But I remembered Uncle Nolan always said if you don't stand for something, you'll fall for anything. Erma is still sitting at the table looking like a lost puppy. She's scared to move.

"Oh my God, Erma, will you please get your ass up?" I said.

19
You'll Be Sorry

"HEY THERE LITTLE LADY, you need a ride?" A strange man in a rusty white truck asked after he eased up beside me. When I got off the school bus this morning, I didn't go into the building. I thought wishing I was home was enough to get me there, but now I'm lost. A voice in my head told me that I knew better than to get into a car with a stranger. I told the voice to shut up and mind its own business because I'm going home one way or the other. It's been two weeks. I didn't do anything wrong. Besides, I can't spend my birthday at the Hobbs'.

"Where you headed?" he said.

"Ninth Street, is it far from here?" I said.

"It is, but I'm headed that way, hop on in." We rode without saying anything. He stared ahead but I knew he watched me in his own way. *Shifty-eyed bastard.*

"So, you like school?" I knew that was coming.

"Mm-hmm, I like school just fine mother-fucker," I said under my breath.

"Excuse me," he said.

"Oh, I said yes sir, I like school, thank you for caring."

"Well didn't you have school today?" I knew where the questions were leading because the man licked his lips after each sentence. When I saw the big flea market Nana always goes to, I jumped out of the truck. I knew my way home from there anyway.

"Hey girl, get back here, you little hussy!" I spun around and showed him two middle fingers.

"Go to hell, you fucking pervert!" I said before I disappeared into the woods. I feel safer with lions, tigers, and bears. I ran fast and free through the trees until I came out on the main street. When I got to the garage house, the entire place had been cleared out. I sat on the empty floor. When I find Evelyn, I'm going to tell her I'm sorry. You shouldn't cuss at your mama no matter what. Besides, the Bible says to honor your mother and father, no exceptions. I should love her more, the way the others do, they never complain. I know, I'll start calling her mama again.

"Goldie that you baby?" Nana said while fiddling with her glasses.

"Nana, since when do you need your glasses to see people?" She laughed.

"Your Nana done got old," she said.

"Not to me," I said. I gave her a big squeeze.

"Them people know you here?" she said.

"Who cares what they know? I'm never going back there." Even through the bifocals I could see her sad eyes. She hated to see any of us suffer.

"Don't worry, things are going to be different this time Nana."

"You know I ain't forget your birthday baby, wait till I get some money, I'm gon' get you somethin' real nice hear?"

"I know you didn't forget, it used to be your birthday too," I said, and we laughed. When Nana had to send for a copy of her birth certificate, she found out I wasn't born on her birthday, but seven days later.

"I don't even know how I could've made a mistake like that," she said.

"It could happen to anybody," I said. After Nana wrote Evelyn's new address down, I snatched the paper and headed out the door. I didn't mean to be so rude. Maybe she didn't notice.

I opened the gate to the house and flew up the steps. My heart raced. I missed them like crazy. I can see them through the sheer white curtains on the door. Evelyn's back is turned. She's standing at the kitchen sink or something. I turned the doorknob and I stepped inside.

"It's Goldie!" Joshua said. They came over and covered me with hugs and kisses. Evelyn appeared in the doorway.

"Hi... Mama," I said.

"What you doin' here?"

"I... I just—"

"You get on out of here!" she said. I was crushed. I started crying. I wanted to kill her.

"No, I don't want to go back there! Why?" I said.

"I don't want no trouble, so get!"

"No, I didn't do nothing wrong!"

"You done got me in trouble with them peoples with all them lies and shit you told the social worker!"

"What lies, what shit?!"

"Now I ain't got to put up with your ass no more. Get the hell out before I call the police on you!" I folded my arms across my chest.

"No, I'm not going."

"You want to try me?" she said, before she left and came back with a stupid stick.

"All you know is violence, I hate you!" I ran outside and crossed the street.

"I hate you more, you yellow bitch!" she screamed from the porch. Now she's slamming the door over and over. It would close easily if she would just stop slamming it. My brothers were crying.

"Shut up, she ain't nothin' to be cryin' over!" she said. I've been standing here staring at the house for a while. Every few minutes she will peek through the curtains to see if I'm still standing out here. I am.

The electric blue car caught my eye. Luanne Michaels parked and got out. I just been wandering around until I landed on the beach. I sat on a picnic table. If I wasn't heartbroken, seeing Luanne trying to walk and keep her heels from sinking into the sand would have made me laugh. Earlier I dialed the number on the card she gave me. But when she answered, I couldn't get any words out. I managed to squeeze out some sobbing sounds. "Gwendolyn, tell me where you are," she said. *How did she know it was me?* "I'm at the beach." Luanne made it to the table. She brought lunch and we ate without any words. She let me sob in peace.

On my twelfth birthday, I watched the girls excitedly decorate the game room for the party I didn't want. They're in it for the ice cream, and birthday cake. Luanne stopped by and gave me a pink boombox with a cassette player.

"Thank you, Luanne, I've always wanted one of these." This is the first birthday party I've had since Evelyn married Josiah.

"Go on and enjoy the party, you deserve to have fun," Luanne said. Luanne's right. Last night, I prayed that God would show me what I'm doing wrong, so I can stop doing it. If I don't figure this out, I will be ripped away from Bunny and my brothers forever. They need me to protect them from her. That's why I'm running away from the Hobbs again.

I laughed to keep from crying. Anyway, I'm all cried out. Just two weeks ago, I stood on this same corner staring at Evelyn's house like I am now. She kept slamming the front door, saying she hate me and calling me names. At least I don't have to worry about that today because ain't nobody home. Ain't no curtains on the windows. All that's left is a sign in the grass that says for rent. No, I'm not gonna cry, or go running to Nana. I know she loves me, but she can't do anything but pity me. I ain't calling Ms. Trans AM either. I'll get back to the Hobbs on my own. As I walk I write a letter in my mind. "Dear Evelyn, someday you'll be sorry."

20
Burning Bridges

"ERMA, LET GO," MAXINE SAID. The two days tops turned out to be three months. After that, Luanne got me an extension for another month while she tried to find me a foster family. Then one day she shows up all excited. "Gwendolyn, I have found the absolute perfect home for you!" she said. I kept my word with Erma about being her friend, her only friend. I understand why she's holding on to me this way, but now it's getting kind of creepy. "I'll call you, so we can hang out sometime," I said. She still won't let me go.

"If you're my friend, you should be happy for me." That worked.

"Now don't forget what I told you," I said. I got tired of taking up for her all the time. One night I locked the door to the game room. I told her I wouldn't unlock it until she kicked Cousin It's behind good. Turns out that girl was all talk. Erma turned her every which way but loose. After that, the others weren't so quick to mess with her anymore. "See, you got arms, legs, teeth, feet, and fingernails just like they do, so use them," I told her. I hugged the Hobbs and a few girls who didn't think I got the cooties from Erma.

"You are going to love it here, you'll see," Luanne said as she excitedly pushed the doorbell. I looked at the sky and faked a big ol' yawn. Luanne ignored me, she wasn't about to let me ruin her moment. She loved her job. "Helping less fortunate girls is what I live for," she said once. I guess Luanne comes from a rich family. How else could she have this good job, and this great car? She probably

170

never had a hot dog that didn't have that fancy mustard on it.

We never passed through the gates of the estate homes. We rode for two minutes before she pulled into a long driveway. The house was perfect, except for the three scary beanstalks towering over it from the backyard. A robust light brown skinned woman opened the door. She wasn't bad looking she just had huge bags under her eyes, like Mr. Magoo. Her smile said she was happy to see us.

"Well, hello there!" she said cheerfully. I was startled by her Darth Vader voice. I should ask her to say Luke, I'm your daddy.

"Hello Margaret, I'd like you to meet Gwendolyn," Luanne said like she created a match made in heaven.

"Y'all come on in here 'fore you catch cold," she said although we were sweating from the heat as it was. We followed her inside. A little six-year-old boy jumped out and started making silly faces at me.

"Go sit your bad self on down," the woman said in a playful tone, but still that voice is frightening. They moved on, but I lagged. I needed to check things out. There were three small steps that led to the sunken living room. I skipped them and let my body roll down onto the soft gray leather couch. I took my shoes and socks off and dug my toes deep into the plush gray carpet. A thick layer of dust covered the expensive glass coffee table. I leaned over and scribbled wash me and quickly erased it. I laughed at my silliness. I heard Luanne call my name. I went up the three steps and followed their voices into another nicely furnished room. They were each sitting at opposite ends of a red and white flowered couch.

"Where are your shoes?" Luanne said.

"Who needs shoes in here? My feet ain't dirty." Luanne patted the empty space on the couch. I plopped down between them, and let out an exaggerated breath before folding my arms across my chest. Luanne stretched her eyes wide and tilted her head to the side. That meant straighten up and fly right, or else. I forced myself to smile, and she relaxed.

"You's a pretty lil' light-skinded blonde hair girl. What you mixed with?" the woman said. Lately, anybody a shade darker than me wanted to know what I'm mixed with. I gave Luanne a taste of her own medicine by twisting my face into a question mark.

"Uh, Gwendolyn isn't bi-racial. Both of your parents are black, right Gwendolyn?" Luanne said.

"Mm-hmm, child day sho' is," I said. Luanne looked at me and smiled sweetly. Translation, *when we get outside your ass is mine.*

"Oh yeah? See, I done told them gals down at the shop there's black girls with real blonde hair in the world. They swear on they life it ain't no such thing. Wait 'til I carry you over there, Miss Charlene gon' have to eat her words." Me and Luanne locked our eyes that time. I pointed at the little boy.

"Who is he?" I said.

"This is Anthony, my great-nephew. Come say hi." He shook his head no and stared at me.

"We calls him Tony, what they calls you," she said.

"They *calls* me Goldie ma'am." I felt Luanne burning a hole through me. I crossed my eyes and stuck my tongue out at her super-fast before that woman could catch me. Nephew Tony caught me. He looked like he wanted to tell, but I stopped him with a cool stare. While we were getting acquainted she called me Goalie. I wanted to correct her, but I didn't want to get on her bad side. Besides, she probably couldn't do any better, she's country as hell.

"Uh-oh, you got split ends. Lucky for you I do hair. I owns a beauty shop," she said while inspecting the terrible condition my hair was in.

"Oh, gee golly wow," I said. I knew Luanne wanted to shake me.

"Mm-hmm, it's called Why Be Nappy?" she said. After that, I let my guard down. This lady looks scary, but she's sweet and funny. I can't help but like her.

"All right, I must go. I'll check on you guys in a week or two," Luanne said. Like always she stood up and carefully made sure she was a ten before making her next move.

"I'll walk you out," I said.

172

"No, you, stay *here*," she said as if I were an untrained puppy. After Luanne left, there was an awkward silence between me, Nephew Tony, and the nice big boned woman.

"Come on Goalie, I'll show you your room," she said. That boy has not let go of her leg since Luanne left. She's dragging him around like the extra weight ain't nothing.

"Here it is!" she said but it sounded more like ta-dah! I pinched myself. I loved the expensive glossy white furniture and a canopy bed. She carefully matched the bedspreads to the pink and white wallpaper. The room was fit for a princess, or a big ass baby. Her eyes danced all around. She seemed proud of it.

"You like it?"

"I love it ma'am," I said honestly.

"Aw Goalie, you ain't got to call me no ma'am, I ain't that old," she said.

"Then what you want me to call you?"

"You can call me Margo, or mama if you want to."

"*No, I don't want to, I just met you, lady,*" I said to myself. There was a mystery door, it was shut, and she forgot to show me what was behind it.

"What's in there?" I said.

"That's just my room, I keep it locked up, so this ol' knucklehead can't get in there," she said while tickling the boy.

"Ain't that right bad butt?" she said.

"Yup!" he said excitedly. I'm saving all my love for my own little brothers, but this kid is kind of cute. The three of us were having dinner at a humongous table with twelve chairs. There was an oil painting of her over the fireplace. She was younger, her under-eye baggage hadn't arrived yet. She had on a navy green uniform like Uncle Ernest had when he was in the army.

"I didn't know women could be in the army," I said.

"Oh yeah, I served for twenty years. I retired Sergeant Major."

"Is that good?"

"That's very good, especially for a black woman, hell any color woman."

"Where is his mother?"

"She up there in New York, just tryna get herself together."

After a few days, I realized this charming house was crawling with lizards, the way a house in the ghetto had water bugs and roaches. They were cute at first, but now they're driving me crazy. The carpet is thick and I'm constantly stepping on them. I heard if you chop off a lizard's tail, it would hop around until the sun goes down. I wanted to see for myself. Wow, it's true.

I'm the only one who walks to school around here. Every morning I feel the breeze as kids cruise by on their cool shiny ten speeds. Most of the seniors drive themselves to school. I don't even know that many grown folks who can afford a car. They all have rich parents. They look at me like I'm the Loch Ness Monster when they pass by. No one ever asks if I need a ride. I know they know exactly where I'm going. *Assholes.*

The Sergeant never leaves the house without Nephew Tony. It's like he's her responsibility alone. So, I always have time to study and no excuse for a bad grade. I don't like going to that uppity school. But I really like my English teacher, Mrs. Arndt. She shows us how to pronounce words the right way and how to construct a sentence by using punctuation. She doesn't want us to say stuff like me and you, I'ma be, or y'all, but it's hard not to. I raise my hand whenever I know the answers. Two gum popping, hair twirling heifers approached me after class one day.

"What y'all want?" I said.

"We want to know why you be kissing Mrs. Arndt's ass all the time?" they said. I pushed past them.

"I'm not kissing her ass. I refuse to be as witless as the two of you," I said, over my shoulder.

"What am I supposed to buy with this?" The Sergeant said after she opened the envelope with a one-hundred-dollar clothing allowance check, sent from the state. She dug deep down into her own pockets when it came to me and Nephew Tony. She never tells people I'm her foster child. She couldn't fool the women at the hair salon, they know she never had any kids.

"Far as I'm concerned, you is my daughter. I'm gon' be adoptin' you," she said.

"You can try, but you'll be wasting your time," I said under my breath. Anyway, no matter how much money she spends on my clothes, it don't work. Them uppity ass kids ain't fooled for a second. They know I'm not one of them. They can tell I never had any silver spoons in my mouth. That's why they don't make room for me at their lunch tables or invite me to their parties. The boys only associate with two kinds of girls, the rich and the easy, not that I care.

It's Saturday so The Sergeant will be at "Why Be Nappy?" for the rest of the day. Five months have passed, and she still hasn't left Nephew Tony alone with me. I have never stepped foot inside her room. I know I'm the reason it stays locked. Miss *call me mommy* 'cause I's gon' be adoptin' you, don't trust me as far as she could throw me. I'm the stranger in the house. I used a small kitchen knife to pick the lock. I walked into what looked like a fancy hotel room. Oh my God, there's a bathroom in here! The bathtub was on one side, and the shower was on the other. The walls were made of mirrors. Everywhere I looked, there I was, looking all sneaky. I thought I walked into another bedroom. Soon I realized it was just a closet big enough for someone to sleep in. Lots of new dresses with price tags were hanging up. I picked one up off the floor, it was shiny, and emerald-green, size fourteen. The red tag screamed, "On sale!" One hundred and thirty dollars. I realize how poor I am. I opened another mystery door and found myself back in the bedroom. The fancy round bed was unmade. The dressers were crowded with expensive perfume, jewelry, and makeup. Of course, dust bunnies covered everything on it. I lifted a bottle of unopened *Chanel no. 5.*

I blew the dust off. It's Nana's favorite. When I was little, she would take me in Gimbles Department store for a sample of it. They always gave us a quick spray and locked it behind the glass. They never once asked her if she wanted to buy it. Even though I was little, I knew them ladies looked down on Nana and me. I placed the perfume back on the dresser and locked the door behind me.

"Go on now, while the sun is still high," The Sergeant said. I was in the sitting room, lying on the couch, and reading a "*Jet*" magazine. Apparently, the mini skirt is making a comeback. I stared at the beauty of the week and wondered if Uncle Nolan has her on his wall with the rest of them.

"You hear me girl?" She said.

"No, you do it, I ain't going back out in that forest ever again." Did she forget what happened last week? I was out there hanging clothes when I got the feeling that I wasn't alone. I stood as still as a block of cement while my eyeballs scanned the yard. I didn't see anybody, so I reached for another damp towel. Whoever said to be still while you're standing toe to fangs with a snake is a damn fool. I high tailed it toward the house. I didn't bother to look back. I fell through the back door and landed at The Sergeant's feet.

"Goalie what you doin' now?" she said.

"Snake!" I said out of breath.

"Where 'bout?"

"Between the clothesline and the shed!"

"I know you ain't scared of no little garden snake."

"Uh-uh, it's this big black anaconda, and it was chasing me!" Okay, it wasn't an anaconda, just the biggest snake I ever seen in my life. The Sergeant wasn't fazed when I told her about it, and now she's forcing me back out there.

"Goalie, go on now, 'fore the sun go down," she said.

"No, put them in the dryer."

"Girl you know I can't stand no clothes from the dryer, all that static." I grabbed the basket and headed for the back door. I don't appreciate her bossing me around like this, treating me like some damn foster child.

I know he's out here watching me. When I got by the shed, something as light as a feather brush up against my ankle. I dropped the basket and ran back toward the house, and smack dab into her pillow like chest.

"Move Margo!" I said. She chuckled.

"Once you hang them clothes, I'll move." There's no way I'm getting past her. I walked back toward the line, keeping my eyes on the ground.

"He out there?" she said.

"Probably."

"Look in the pail over yonder."

"What for?"

"It's a surprise."

"What kind of surprise?"

"See for yourself." I hung Nephew Tony's pajamas on the line while I ignored The Sergeant, I needed to keep an eye out for the python. I glance over my shoulder, she was guarding the door, looking like a lumberjack.

"Man, you get on my nerves!" I moved toward the pail with caution. I gasped and looked back at The Sergeant. I felt sorry for the anaconda-python. I mean, did she have to chop it up like that?

"See, you ain't got nothin' to worry 'bout, I ain't gon' let no ol' snake harm my baby," she said.

"I'm bored, there's nothing to do around here," I told The Sergeant.

"There is plenty to do, why ain't you made no friends in these estates?"

"Because I don't like these kids around here Margo, they treat me like shit." She shot me a disapproving look.

"Oh, I meant crap, I didn't mean to say shit."

"Well, if you let 'em get to know you, I'm sure they'll like you just fine."

"Who cares? I ain't about to beg them to like me. Why can't I go to my old neighborhood, where my friends live?"

"Because I don't want no daughter of mine 'round all them heathens."

"Heathens? You mean as in black people?"

"No, I mean as in black people who don't know how to act, as in niggers." I don't know why The Sergeant thinks just because she got a little money, she's better than regular folks like my family. Sometimes she'll hold a paper bag next to me and Nephew Tony's arms and faces. It's her way to tell if we been out in the sun too long. If we ain't brighter than the bag, she won't let us go to the beach or pool for the next few days. One time I went to the pool and purposely laid out in the sun until I got a shade darker than her bag. When she saw me, she faked a heart attack, like Fred Sanford.

"Thank God you got good hair. Y'all gon' have to stay in 'til this heat wave is over," she said.

"What heat wave Margo?" She gets on my nerves. She expects me to sit in this pink ass room, brushing my yellow ass hair, staring in the mirror, and having private ass talks in my head, like Marcia Brady, or anybody who's light, bright, or damn near white.

Luanne checks on me once a month. She told me Evelyn didn't show up for court today because she moved out of the state.

"Where did she go?" I asked.

"I don't know. So, we're going to start adoption proceedings with Margaret."

"Uh-uh, no way."

"Why would you say that? I thought you liked Margaret. Gwendolyn, you've got a good thing going here."

"I don't want a good thing going Luanne, I want my family."

"Margaret loves you."

"She don't love *me*, she loves her nephew Tony, who is her blood. But when it comes to me, she loves when I'm lighter than a paper bag. She loves my "good hair," and she'll *love* anybody who has it." Luanne raised her brow and looked at me like she's seeing me for the first time.

"Go on little girl," she said.

"Okay, I like Margo as a person, but nothing more. She never talks to me about my life before I came to live with her. It's like she unwrapped me from a box like I'm something she ordered from a Sears catalog. If she really loved me, she would want to know what I been through or care what hurts me. That ain't real love, at least not in my book." Luanne seemed exhausted. She took a deep breath and exhaled.

"Listen, Gwendolyn, I understand what you're saying, but I'm your social worker, not a miracle worker. I'm doing the best I can for you. So, you dream about being reunited with your family, that's fine, but what will you do in the meantime? How will you live? Well here is where I come in. Your well-being is what concerns me, not your feelings. I'm sorry, but unless your mother comes riding in on a white horse, or any of your relative's step up to the plate, *this* is your home. And that ain't bad my dear. Plenty of girls would kill to be in your shoes." She opened her car door and slid in. "If you need me, call me," she said because she means it.

On my thirteenth birthday, The Sergeant threw me a party. She let me have half a glass of pink champagne, and I wanted more. Some of the snobby kids from the estate showed up. I wasn't impressed with their Prada this or Gucci that. The Sergeant must have begged their parents to make them come. Anyway, they kept their noses up like one- thousand-dollar bills were taped to the ceiling. Thankfully, my gay friend Thomas came with some of his friends. They really knew how to party, they were loud and wild, and they danced like nobody's business. After they sang happy birthday, we devoured the cake and punch. Later, The Sergeant said she had a surprise for me in the garage.

"It's not a snake in a bucket, is it?"

"Girl, go on out there and see what it is." Thomas covered my eyes and gently led me toward the garage.

"No peeking. Okay, open them."

"Man, that's bad," one of his friends said.

"It's fierce!" another one said while doing that finger snap thing they always do. I'm at a loss for words when I see the expensive white ten-speed bike with gold trim wrapped with a big pink bow. Now I know how Miss America feels. My hands shook uncontrollably when I tried to cover my wide-open mouth. I ran back inside and put my arms around her without words. "You're welcome," she said.

Man, I wish I never got this damn beautiful bike because riding over to see my real family, is all think about. It's Saturday, so those two will be at the shop all day. I'm all alone, and I'm bored. That's it, I'm going to "Negro-land" today. The Sergeant will never know if I get back on time. Shit, I almost forgot. I rushed to the kitchen and got the small knife to open the door to The Sergeant's hotel suite and snatched the unopened bottle of *Chanel no. 5.*

When I got to Nana's, there was loud music and laughter coming from the backyard. I looked out of the window and saw her sitting at a table with a built-in umbrella over her head. She had a drink in her hand, the half empty bottle of gin sat close by. They're all having a good ol' time, dancing, singing, laughing, and eating barbeque, while I suffer over there with that rich lady. I waited for her to come to her room.

"Close your eyes and hold your hands out Nana." I placed the perfume in her hand and she opened her eyes. So far she's just staring at it.

"Look Nana, it's your favorite, remember? It's the real thing too." She shook her head sadly.

"Uh-uh, you ain't got to do that for me, you hear?" My feelings are hurt. Why does she care how I got it? How else are we ever going to have anything if we don't take it? I put the bottle on her dresser anyway, I bet she'll be excited about it when she sobers up. I spotted a stack of pictures of my brothers on her dresser. They were all dressed in red and white jerseys. I put one in my pocket.

"What if I pull down my britches, and invite her to kiss my booty?" I asked Thomas.

"Not even then," he said.

"But what if I—?"

"Goldie, your foster mother is not allowed to hit you for any reason, it's against the law, they'll throw her ass in jail."

"Hmm, very interesting," I said.

"But, she might get you in a headlock before you get a chance to dial 911, so be careful," he said.

I just had to see what The Sergeant would do when I got out of line. When she told me to come in the house, I told her I'd come in when I got good and goddamn ready, and to my surprise, she did not whoop my ass. I started skipping school because a good talking to didn't faze me. I pretended to be like Robin Hood by stealing her stuff and giving it to the less fortunate. She never says anything about it, like she don't care. One night The Sergeant comes in my room to remind me that I'm a sweet girl, but I ain't been acting like one lately.

"Is you smokin' marijuana plants with that boy across the street?" she said.

"Get out of my room!" I said. She came toward me and I accidentally scratched her arm. I didn't mean to do that. She might have wanted to choke me, but she headed toward the door.

"Why you do me like this Goalie, when all I try to do is love you?" she said. Honestly, I didn't know why I did these things to her. I threw my big biology book at her. Thank God, I missed.

"Get out of here Margo!" I screamed.

Now I hop on my bike and cruise over to Nana's every chance

I get. Living behind these gates is as boring as living in a graveyard. When I got there, I called out, but no one answered. It's only four o'clock, but the house is dark and lifeless. I clicked the knob on the TV, but nothing happened. I checked behind the TV, it's plugged in. The light in the hall didn't come on. I opened the refrigerator, there is never a light in here, but it stinks inside. So, Nana couldn't pay the light bill this month, and Florida Power did what they always do. Lord knows I didn't miss days like this.

I might as well ride down the street and see who's at Leslie's house. We used to call Leslie frog- dog behind her back because it's hard to decide which one she looked like the most. Anyway, I wanted to show off my Rolls Royce, that's what Thomas calls my bike.

"Hell no, ain't nobody allowed to ride it. And you better not touch it either," I told Frog-dog's little sister Anna before letting myself in their house. She kicked my heels as she followed close behind me.

"Please can I ride it one time, please?" she asked again.

"Are you deaf or retarded?" I said. She punched me on my arm. I slapped her harder than I meant to. She put her hand over the handprint I left on her cheek.

"Ooh I'm gon' tell Leslie," she said. When I saw Frog-dog galloping from the side of the house, I remembered that I'm not one of her favorite people. She used to always charge up the hill to the bus stop to slap me for messing with her "Sustah's". They were such good liars. I bolted through the door and tried to jump on my bike before she could get to me. *Damn, she's on all fours.* I couldn't get my leg over my bike. I had to keep both feet on the ground.

"Hey Goldie, you hit my sustah?" she said. I walked backward away from her and my bike.

"What? No, Leslie, I didn't hit your sus-sister. I'd be crazy to touch *your...*" Without thinking it through, I dug into my new leather Rainbow Bright purse and produced a small pair of scissors. I held them out in front of me.

"Back off, leave me alone or..."

"Or what, you gon' stab me?" she said. *She's right, bad idea.* I eased my hand back in my purse and tried to shake the scissors off, but somehow, they ended up in her top lip. Oops, I didn't mean to do that, it was a reflex from when she went upside my head. Blood ran out of her lip and down her chin and stained her dark gray t-shirt. The scissors were stuck on my fingers and still in her lip. I didn't want to make matters worse. That's why I tugged and yanked until I was free to run for my life. I didn't mean to split her lip.

I'm a good runner, I'm only thirteen, all muscle The Sergeant says. But running uphill wasn't as easy. I looked over my shoulder and saw a mob of kids running behind me. Damn, they're all muscle too. I almost made it to the top, but Levi caught me. He's Frog-dogs brother. He had a crush on me before, but it must have worn off. We were both out of breath.

"Goldie...Why you...Stab...Leslie?" he said.

"It was...By accident...The scissors got...Stuck." The mob was a few feet away from us when Levi tripped me and laid me in the grass. I know, blood is thicker than water. I looked at him like a sad puppy and hoped he didn't black both my eyes.

"You better haul ass," he whispered. I crawled away at first and he pretended to try to catch me. I tackled the rest of the hill, but when I reached the mini-mart my legs gave out and I fell and put myself in a ball. They kicked and punched me. Some of them spit on me.

"All right, get off her, back up!" a man said before he picked me up and placed my feet on the ground. I was wobbling and whatnot.

"You all right?" he said.

"Uh-huh," I said after I realized all that blood on me wasn't mine. The man tried to tear me from the crowd and a girl slapped him on his back. The man drew back his fist.

"Do it again, I'm gon' knock your little ass out," he told her.

"But she stabbed my cuzin," the girl said.

"Yeah, in the mouf!" another kid yelled. The man peered at me and shook his head. His eyes landed on Frog-dog. She looked like she dipped her face into a pot of spaghetti sauce.

"I'm sorry about that, but regardless, I won't stand here while fifteen kids beat up one girl, now back off!" he said. He stood in front of me like a human shield. None of them wanted to go through the big man to get to me.

"Get in the burgundy car over there," he said. He didn't have to tell me twice. Once inside the car, I hurried and locked both doors. I looked around for the big man. Another man came over and tapped on the window. I rolled it down halfway.

"These yours?" he said. He opened his palm and showed me a pair of twenty-four karat gold earrings. They were stunning perfect little roses with a diamond stud in the center. I caressed my naked ears. I couldn't think straight because they knocked a few screws loose in my head.

"No, I don't think so," I said. But how did you know so much about them? I asked myself. Oh shit, I borrowed them from The Sergeant's jewelry box this morning.

"Yes, they're mine, thank you," I said. I grabbed them and tucked them safely under my bra. Ain't no way she wouldn't have missed these babies. I looked toward the mini mart a saw the big man flirting with a pretty woman behind the counter.

Uh-oh, Frog-dog is on her way over now. I rolled the window up super-fast. She put her snout right on the glass, so I knew she wasn't playing.

"You best watch yo' back, cuz when I ketch you, I'm gon' kill yo' ass!" she said.

"Shut up, with your stupid Frog-dog face, I ain't scared of you!" I lied. I was so scared that I started laughing like a mad scientist. Oh well, I may as well go all the way. I put two firm middle fingers against the window. The big man walked toward his car, whistling like he didn't have a care in the world.

"Go on, go home, so your mama can carry you to the hospital. You're bleeding all over my car," he said. He unlocked his door and slid into the front seat. When he rode past the mob I made sure to give them two extra firm middle fingers. The big man adjusted his mirror and caught me.

"Hey, cut that out," he said.

"Oops sorry," I said. He laughed slightly and shook his head.

"You one tough cookie, that's for damn sure," he said.

"Goalie where you been? I was worried sick about you," The Sergeant said from the kitchen. I tried to sneak into my room, but she stepped out and saw me.

"My God, girl what happened to you?" she said.

"Nothing."

"What's that in your hair and all over your clothes?"

"It's blood Margo. You know it's blood, but it ain't mine."

"What you mean? Oh my God. What did you do Goalie?"

"I got in a fight, it ain't no big deal." She sat on the flowered couch and stared at me for a few seconds.

"Bring your bike inside and go wash up. Try not to get any on the furniture. I couldn't move, instead I stood there glaring at her sad saggy face.

"Did you hear me Goalie?"

"My fucking name is Goldie not Goalie!"

"All right, Goldie, bring your bike in please."

"I can't."

"Why not?"

"They got it."

I saw Luanne's Trans AM parked in the driveway. It's too soon for a home visit. I went inside and saw her in the hallway talking with The Sergeant. Their mouths slammed shut like they been caught gossiping.

"Hi Luanne, what are you doing here?" She looked at me with some dumb expression. The Sergeant looked at everything but me. There was a mound sitting in the corner by the door. It was all my shit.

"Whatever," I said. I grabbed my bags and dragged them out to Luanne's car. I tried to pretend like I didn't care. Luanne kept silent until she backed out of the driveway and got on the road, and then she let loose.

"I can't believe you, do you realize how hard I worked to get you this placement?!" she said.

"So what, I don't care," I lied.

"Oh, so you a bad girl now, huh? You don't need anybody, right? You plan on going through life burning bridges?"

"That's right, I am a bad girl, but I ain't burnt no bridges, I don't even know what you're talking about." She waved her finger in the air.

"Oh yes, you have certainly burned a bridge here today, make no mistake about it. One day in your life you will realize, but then it will be too late!" At the red light, she looked at me and shook her head. "And now, some other little girl is gonna come and snatch up all your blessings."

"Why are you talking like that?"

"Like what?"

"Like sleeping in a forest under a canopy bed is a kiss that makes it all better. Did you forget what happened to me, and why I'm here?"

"No, I didn't forget, but this is serious Gwendolyn, life is serious, and the path you're choosing is—"

"Save the bullshit Luanne."

"What did you say?"

"You heard me."

"How is it bullshit?"

"Because, I get in a little bit of trouble, and here you come in your Trans AM, transporting me from one bad place to another. Y'all didn't even give me a chance to say goodbye to Nephew Tony."

"I'm sorry I didn't have time to... No, you wait a damn minute. Is this what you consider a little trouble? She laughed. Do you think this is the first time she's called me? Huh? I have been begging that dear woman to give you another chance for months! But this last thing, with the blood, well, that was the final straw baby." I folded my arms across my chest because I was too old to cover my ears and scream la-la-la I'm not listening!

"She put up with all your mess. The back talk, the staying out late, and the stealing! How could you steal from her, when she freely gave you whatever you wanted?" I angrily turned toward the window and stared out of it.

"I guess no one ever taught you not to bite the hand that feeds you," she said.

"Whatever, I'm glad I'm leaving, that lady got on my damn nerves. I hate her, and I hate you too Luanne!"

21
Damaged Goods

"A FOSTER HOME IN THE GHETTO? This ain't what I'm used to," I told Luanne when she pulled into the driveway. The house was painted pale pink with white trim. The front door and all the windows were covered with black iron bars. It was an old house, but still, the best looking one the street. Cars rode by with loud rap music blasting from those gigantic speakers they put in their trunks. Small kids were running around playing tag. People are sitting on their open porches sipping beer, talking loud, and blasting music of their own

"Seriously, I'll pass on this one," I said.

"Please get your behind out of this car," Luanne said.

"No, I'm not ready yet."

"Look, this may be your last chance. I haven't told Kelley your exact age.

"Why not?"

"Because Kelley's girls are from ages sixteen to eighteen. Let's hope she likes you when she sees you."

"Like me? You mean like a doggy in the window?"

"Stop being dramatic," she said. She's pissed at me for messing up my perfect life and saying I hate her. She should know I didn't mean it. I love her. I crawled out of the car.

"Luanne, before we go any further, there's something I need to know."

"What is it?"

"Okay so, when we get in there, do I wag my tail to accentuate my cuteness? Or should I go for the dignified puppy, and tuck it in?"

"Girl if you don't grab those bags and come on. And you had better wag the hell out of your tail. I'm running out of ideas here," she said.

A caramel-skinned girl with chestnut colored hair answered the door. Her face was covered with hundreds of freckles.

"Hey Luanne," she said.

"Good afternoon Crystal," Luanne said. The ironclad door had a sign on it that said Armor Guard with a picture of a knight on a horse. We waited while the girl tried to find the right key. We followed her through the foyer and into the living room. We sat on the expensive plastic-covered sofa, while the freckled girl stood in the doorway with her arms folded.

"Is Kelley here? I don't see her Cadillac out front," Luanne said.

"No, but she called ten minutes ago, she said she on her way." Luanne placed her briefcase on her lap and opened it.

"She must be at church, huh?" Luanne said.

"Yeah, that's all she ever do," freckles said. Luanne chuckled.

"Some things never change. I'm sorry, where are my manners? Crystal this is Gwendolyn," Luanne said.

"Hi," we said at the same time. I felt something lurking over my head. I looked up at the ceiling and saw this humongous chandelier. It was like a bunch of diamonds.

"Y'all want something to drink?" freckles said.

"No thank you, we're fine," Luanne spoke for the both of us. Man, I wanted some red *Kool-Aid*, I know they got some. Ten minutes later, the back of my thighs started to sweat and stick to the plastic. Finally, we heard heels click-clacking through the foyer. A fiftyish brown-skinned woman appeared in the doorway. She wore a nice off-white skirt suit, with a big matching hat with feathers and bows and shit.

She smiled at Luanne. I knew right away she had false teeth. Luanne put the briefcase on the floor and went over to hug the lady, but the over-decorated hat got in their way. They had to settle for holding hands.

"It's good to see you again Michaels, it's been quite a long time," she said.

"Kelley, this is Gwendolyn Savage," she said while sweeping her hand in front of me like I'm something to win or lose on "The Price is right". The woman was checking me out, way out. She scrunched her nose. She sure don't seem too impressed with my light skin or my good hair. I don't think I'm a puppy she wants to keep.

"I know, she's a little young, but she's mature for her age," Luanne said.

"Well you know I'd do anything for one of my girl's. Welcome, ah... what you say her name was?"

"It's Gwendolyn Savage."

"All right Savage, welcome to Kelley's. So long as you follow the rules around here, we should get along fine," she said.

"Why did she call you one of her girls?" I asked, Luanne when we walked outside.

"Because I came to Kelley's at sixteen. Before that, I moved from one foster home to another. At eighteen I found a job and a roommate. Eventually, I was accepted at Saint Petersburg College."

"What, you didn't have rich parents and that fancy mustard?"

"Nope, no rich parents, and no Grey Puopon on my hotdogs.

"Wow, who would have thought?"

"No one because I've never allowed my circumstances to define me. Gwendolyn, you are intelligent, you can be anything you want to be. There's no excuse for why you can't make something of yourself as well." She glanced at her watch, I knew that meant she had to go.

"Okay, if I need you I'll call, I said. A sad expression came over her face.

"What is it?"

"Gwendolyn this is the last time we'll see each other."

"Why?"

"I don't work with kids in group homes, I specialize in finding permanent foster homes, and facilitating adoptions."

"When were you going to tell me?"

"All the girls have one counselor; his name is Scott." She came in for a hug.

"Don't touch me please," I said. She waited a few seconds and hugged me anyway.

"It's not because of anything you've done. It's my job. I'd stay with you if I could." When Luanne's hot wheels disappear around the corner for the last time, I thought I smelled smoke.

"I prefer to be addressed simply as Kelley. Once we had three girls named Theresa. That frustrated me, so I started calling the girls by their last names," she said. The kitchen had a long yellow counter and twelve red stools. Restaurant style, nothing about it said home.

"We attend church every Sunday, through rain, sleet, and if it should so happen to snow. Also, you must join the youth choir or the usher board. If you miss curfew you lose your privileges and allowance for a week. You must complete your assigned chores every day." My mind went somewhere else while Kelley went down the list of do's, but mostly don'ts.

"Violence won't be tolerated, are we clear Savage?" *Whatever, you don't scare me, Mr. Ed.*

"If not, your next stop will be juvenile hall. I've read your file." She cleared her throat.

"Do you need birth control, young lady?"

"What's that?" She raised her brow and looked down at my hips, up at my new titties, and dead in my eyes.

"Mm-hmm, well, if you get caught, you on your own," she said.

Me and Kelley are like oil and water, we just don't mix. We argue every day of the week. The other girls are so grateful that they hardly look her in the eye when she speaks to them. They only say stuff behind her back. *Cowards.*

"Why not?" I said.

"You must be sixteen to have men company. Those are the rules, no exceptions," Kelley said.

"But my friend Thomas don't count, he likes boys not girls."

"Sweet Jesus, he funny? In that case, he ain't never to step foot in my house. I don't go for that kind of foolishness," she said before turning her attention back toward the TV. I folded my arms across my chest and glared at her.

"Ooh, I can't stand you!" I said. She looked alarmed and snatched up that black book she used to keep track of our doings. She sounded out the words as she wrote them down. "No allowance for Savage."

"What's that for?" I asked one of the girls when I saw a huge white banner that said, "Congratulations Perkins!"

"It's for our last Theresa, she turned eighteen yesterday, she's leaving tomorrow," freckles said.

"The damn thing should say good riddance and don't let the doorknob hit you where the good Lord split ya!" Jacqueline said. They laughed and slapped fives.

"Shit, you might have dimples deeper than Shirley Temple's. You could know all the words to "The Good Ship Lollipop," but you ain't getting adopted!" one of them declared.

"Uh-uh, Kelley ain't fallin' for it!" another girl said.

"I know, you might follow every rule, go to church every Sunday morning and Wednesday night, join the choir and the usher board, but the second you turn eighteen, and them checks stop, Kelley want your ass out!" freckles said.

"How old are you?" Jacqueline asked me.

"Almost fourteen," I said.

"Oh well, you can relax, but don't get too comfortable," she said. They cracked up all over again.

This new girl named Vanessa is in Theresa's room now. She's

nice and all, but there's just something about her. Sometimes when I'm bored, I'll write all twelve of the girls' names on a piece of paper to see who's the prettiest. Rose is always number one. Anyway, no matter how many times I do it, the new girl lands at the bottom of my beauty tree. She's after Jacqueline, who I hate, but I must be fair, Vanessa is last. I checked the visitor's board to make sure what's his face was penciled in for tonight.

"What you reading the board for? Ain't nobody coming to see your little ass," Jacqueline said.

"Man, stop breathing down my neck!" I told her. She's right, thanks to Kelley's age, and no funny boys rule, ain't nobody coming to see me. I'm checking to see if Vanessa's boyfriend is coming to see her tonight. Normally I wouldn't give him a second thought, but lately, he's all I think about. He's short and chunky and even though he tries to hide them, he got titties too. The problem is he acts like he don't like me either. The other A lot of the boyfriend's will sneak a peek at me when they come to visit. But he acts like I don't exist. I don't understand. *She's last on the list.* Unless he's trying to say I'm at the bottom. I'm not on the list because I'm only fourteen. I'm not allowed to have a boyfriend and I don't want one. But they all know I could get one if I was allowed to. Anyway, like I said, I don't want one. I stood in the full mirror that's nailed to my door. Now let's see, my good pink bathing suit and cut off shorts? Check. Blue and pink striped leg warmers? So cute. Hair running wild like Miss sexy Diana Ross? Check.

At seven-fifteen, I sashayed out to the foyer. This is as far as any boys are allowed to go. I saw them kissing one time, even though it's against Kelley's rules, they took a chance and did it anyway. Vanessa and her stupid boyfriend are already on the love seat, hugging. I'm sure they won't mind if I practice my made up modern dances out here. I put my pink cassette player on the floor and pushed play. First I did some stretching, and then slow movements. It's called a warm up. They gazed into each other's beady eyes, acting like nothing existed around them. Okay fine. I removed the slow music from the cassette player and put in my other tape. It's called "Super Freak" Once the song starts I let myself go. I'm twisting and turning and shaking it like I'm all grown up and sexy like Miss Tina Turner.

"Why don't you go to your room and dance?" Vanessa said.

"I'm practicing."

"Practicing for what?"

"None of your business." I shook my shoulders just enough to make my titties wiggle. It hurts a lot because I just got them, but I can't stop now. I started spinning around and around like I didn't have a bit of home training.

"Don't look at her, she's trying to get attention," Vanessa said. I got dizzy from all that spinning. I stopped and waited for the room to be still. When it did, his eyes were all over me, hers too. *Mm-hmm,* I knew it! My work here is done. I was getting my cassette player when my cheek crashed into Vanessa's open palm.

"Girl, I know you didn't!" I said. I did windmills and karate kicks, but she still managed to get me in a headlock.

"Let me go lard ass!" The boyfriend is sitting on the loveseat laughing.

"Wiggins, please release that Savage this instant!" Kelley said. She dropped me like a hot potato. Rick James was getting super freaky now.

"Savage turn that recorder off!" Ladies, you know fighting is strictly prohibited," Kelley said.

"She hit me first Kelley. I was out here minding my own business, doing my dances," I said innocently.

"Is this true Wiggins, did you attack her?"

"Yes ma'am, but ask her what she did."

"No, I want you to tell me." She looked at her boyfriend for help. He stared at the shiny black and white floor tiles. Vanessa ran out of the foyer. Damn, I didn't mean to make her cry.

"Young man, it's time to go. Savage lock the gate behind him." Once he got on the porch he stopped and gave me the googly eyes he only gave her before.

"Ewe, what you eyeballing me like that for stupid?" I said.

"I hate you, you're such a bitch," he said. I stuck out my tongue and slammed the Armor Guard. After Kelley got Vanessa's side of the story, she called me into her bedroom. She gave me some speech about my body language, the green-eyed monsters, how looks ain't everything, and a man of my own someday.

"So, you're not going to send her to JV after she tried to cut off my air supply?" I said. She peered over her glasses and raised one eyebrow a little higher than usual.

"Girl, if you don't carry your little fast tail out of here," she said. I huffed and charged off to Rose and Mya's room like I always do when I want to be babied. They are the only sisters here, and they adore me. Wait until I tell them how that stupid new girl tried to choke me for no reason. They'll be on my side. Once outside their door, I heard my name. I stopped to listen.

"I like the little girl, I'm just saying she don't look no fourteen to me. She must be sneaking around with somebody. I mean how big is them titties planning to get?" Mya said.

"She's just a kid, she didn't know what she was doing," Rose said.

"Please, she knew. I don't care how young she is, I wouldn't want that high yellow heifer shaking her behind or swinging her hair in my man's face either. Hmm, I wouldn't leave Silas alone with her if he was on life support. I don't blame Vanessa, I would have gone upside her head too."

"You're crazy," Rose said.

"Would you leave her alone with Calvin?"

"Mya, get a grip, I'm not worried about him or that little girl. Unlike you, I trust my man, anyway, she's just acting out. There's no telling what she's been through." It hurt to hear how Mya really felt about me. I tiptoed across the hall to Jacqueline's room. Where is it? I know she didn't wear it today. I looked in all the drawers first. I had to be as quiet and careful as possible. Things have been coming up missing lately. I don't want anybody to find out I took them. I got on my knees and felt around under her bed until my fingers hit a shoebox. I found the watch hiding under a stack of old letters. I always knew I'd take it since the day she rolled her eyes at me. It's the prettiest watch I ever seen. It's gold with a little heart. Taking it tastes like a spoonful of sugar to me.

"I know you stole it!" Jacqueline said.
"No I didn't!" I said.
"Yes you did, give it back or else, I swear I'm gonna hurt you!"
"I didn't take your ol' ugly watch!"
"Everybody know you steal Goldie!"
"And everybody know you pee in the bed at sixteen, Jack-ass!"
"So what, at least I ain't let some nasty man climb on top of me!" she said. They stopped whatever they were doing, and stared at me. Now it's my turn to run out of the room. I fell on my bed and sniveled. How did she know about that? I never told a soul here. Kelley, who else? Luanne had to tell her about me, but it ain't nobody else's business. And now my secret is out. When people find out what happened to me, I feel so ashamed. Sometimes I have nightmares, and those bugs are crawling all over me. I hate Kelley. To make things even worse, I heard two boys at school talking about me.

"Man did you see them titties though?" said boy number one. He was spinning a basketball on one finger like a Harlem Globetrotter.

"Nah man, I don't care how fine she is, she's going home in a white van regardless," said boy number two. He had on a stupid red Hawaiian shirt.

"The last time I got some good head was from inside that white van. It's too bad I can't recall her name though. Anyway, I don't discriminate," said number one. He kept twirling the ball.

"My daddy told me not to ever mess with no damaged goods. He would hit the roof if I came home with her. I'll bet she got all kinds of diseases and shit," Hawaiian shirt said. They walked by me with smirks on their faces while I stood paralyzed.

I went to Nana's house a while back, but they fucking moved somewhere. I'm still waiting for them to find me, and rescue me. Me and Kelley bump heads all the time. Every week she threatens to put me in JV. Lots of girls come, and go before you get used to them. Vanessa got our counselor to move her to another home. Some Puerto Rican girl is in her room already. I like the way her name rolls off my tongue. Chiquita Marita Rodriguez. From day one she said if anybody comes up to her singing that banana song, she'll knock their teeth out. But she can't stop it from playing inside my head.

So, Chiquita's from the boogie down Bronx. *That's what she said.* Anyway, she's going to be a rapper like Sweet Tee. She begged Kelley to let her group practice in the backyard, but she says no every time.

"This is a Christian home, and the Lord ain't too fond of music that don't glorify his holy name. Pastor Holcomb preached on the subject last Sunday.

"But I'm no Christian, I'm Protestant," Chiquita tried to explain.

"Either way you ain't got no business loafing around no gang of boys. Soon as your belly start sticking out, them heathens will be impossible to find. Kelley is a dream crusher.

"Maldito Caballo Dientes La Perra!" she yelled when she came into the TV room. I didn't understand a word she just said but I knew exactly how she feels. I smiled at her. Finally, somebody hates Kelley as much as I do.

Me, Chiquita, and the gang was hanging out in the laundromat when two of the boys got to wrestling. The grown folks were agitated but too afraid to confront them.

"Hey, y'all kids go outside with that shit!" a man said. He was stretched out in a chair with a hat covering his face. My heart skipped a beat. I'd know that voice anywhere.

"Oh my God! Uncle Nolan?" I said. He lifted his hat. He got a full beard now, but I know my favorite Uncle.

"It's me, Goldie," I said.

"I know, I'm just surprised to see you," he said.

"I can't believe it, when did you get back?"

"A few months ago."

"Why are you on this side of town? There's a laundromat on Ninth Street."

"Ma just moved into a house around the corner."

"Seriously? I live around here too!" I said excitedly.

"Oh wow, is that right?" he said. He seemed different, I'll have to figure out why later. I'm just so happy to see him. Chiquita and her boys headed for the door. She eyed Uncle Nolan distrustfully.

"Hey Chica, you are coming or no?" she asked.

"Nah, I'm staying here for a while."

"Cool, but you better not miss the curfew," she said. I helped him take the clothes out of the dryer. We folded them without saying too much. I know he checked me out when I wasn't looking. I sneaked glances at him too. He looked much older, although he couldn't be more than twenty- four. He's probably thinking how much I've grown in three years. Normally he would have me rolling on the floor with a funny story, but he didn't offer to tell me any. We carried the clean clothes to Nana's new house in silence.

"Hey ma, I got a surprise for you," Uncle Nolan said when we entered the house. My heart sank to my feet when I saw my precious grandmother collapsed on the bed like that. She seems even worse than before. I looked at Uncle Nolan with questioning eyes. He went over and shook her. It may have been easier to wake the dead.

"Ma, wake up," he said shaking her harder. She struggled to sit up. She stared at me and blinked a bunch of times, but before she could finish saying "Oh my God, where you find my baby?" My arms were already wrapped around her.

"You see how the Lord work? He done brought the mountain to Mohammed," she said when I told her how close the group home was. Auntie Althea screeched when she came in and saw me sitting next to Nana. We hugged and jumped around together.

"Don't I get no hug?" a man with a deep voice asked. I turned around and saw my Little Uncle Marcus. He had grown taller, and now he had huge muscles, and a mustache to go with them.

"Goldie, I could bench press you," he said.

"But don't forget, I'm still the oldest. Where is everybody else?" I asked.

"Tracie's in the back and Kevin should be getting chased home any minute now," Little Uncle Marcus said. We laughed because the truth is funny sometimes. All I wanted to know was where Evelyn took my family, but I didn't want to ruin our reunion. I went through the house looking for a space to call my own.

"I'm so glad I don't have to go back. That lady don't care nothing about us," I told Nana. She didn't respond, instead, she picked at the lint on her brown polyester pants. Don't she care that "them people" ain't treating me right?

"Didn't your friend say something about a curfew?" Uncle Nolan said.

"I don't care, I'm staying here from now on."

"That's all right with me. I ain't seen my baby in all this time. You stay here with your Nana," she said.

"Ma she can't stay here, remember what the judge said?" Uncle Nolan said. She looked at me sadly, like her hands were tied.

"What time is your curfew?" Uncle Nolan said.

"Eight o'clock." Uncle Nolan is getting on my nerves. Why is he acting like he can't wait to get rid of me?

"Okay, I'll walk you," he said. I shot him a mean glare.

"I don't need nobody to walk me, the house is across the bottom of this damn street!" I said.

"Detroit," Auntie Althea said.

"Why did you wait so long to tell me?" I said.

"You know why."

"But I love them, plus they need me, and you know it." How am I going to get to Detroit? I'll have to save every allowance if Kelley ever stops finding reasons to take it. Every day after school I go straight to Nana's. Each night at seven-forty-five, my chariot turns back into a pumpkin, and I become damaged goods again.

After all these years, Nana has found herself a man. His name is Butch, he's got a wrinkled puppy face. He works at a glass factory. He helps her keep the lights on, and put more food on the table. They remind me of Romeo and Juliet if they were drunk every minute of every damn day. So many times, we had to drag them out of the corner bar. At any given moment, you could find them both passed out on the front steps, just like Jacqueline said.

"She think she so special 'cause her people stay across the street now," Jacqueline claimed every time we got into it. She's jealous, they all are. Sometimes the other girls talk behind my back. Jacqueline is the only one who got the nerve to say hurtful things to my face.

"Hey hot stuff, wasn't that *your* Aunt walking around half naked with her hair all over her head? You should use your allowance to buy *your* Aunt some cigarettes." Or "I just saw *your* grandma and her man, and boy oh boy, they couldn't even make it up the five steps to the door." When they dragged me off her, I had a nice sized clump of *her* nappy hair in *my* fist. I threw it at her. "I ain't ashamed of my family bitch, at least I got one!" I said.

"You are a little troublemaker Savage," Kelley said after three or four of the girls got together and claimed I stole their crap.

"If you take anything without asking or get into one more fight, your tail will be out of here! You were supposed to be mature, that's what Michaels told me, but you are skating on thin ice sister." I want to tell Kelley to kiss my black ass, but I can't risk getting sent to some baby jail. I got to get myself to Detroit.

I tried to be good, but Kelley started it that day I walked by the chandelier room. That nosy old biddy from Prayer Towers Church was sitting on the plastic covered couch sipping tea.

"That one's grandmother lives right across the street, but she drink," Kelley tried to whisper. I stopped dead in my tracks, my blood was boiling. We weren't even allowed in the chandelier room, except on Christmas, or when the social worker came, but I went right in there. I got close enough to smell that Poligrip on her gums.

"I heard you, Kelley, don't say that shit about my Nana, take it back!"

"Fine, I apologize."

"Oh no don't apologize, say you sorry bitch!"

"Don't you dare raise your voice and curse me in my house lil gal!"

"So what, you wouldn't have this house if it wasn't for us...Plus I heard you used to be a prostitute! Is it true Kelly? Did you used to sell tail? Is that how you paid for that chandelier?" I said while laughing and pointing at the ceiling.

"You see, that's exactly why I don't want you going around there. You always come back with your chest all poked out, and thinking you can sass me!" she said.

"I don't care, I hate your horse teeth butt!"

"But here you are, in my house, with my horse teeth, and not with your precious grandmother!"

"I'm here because they put me here!"

"Mm-hmm, they put you here because your mama ran out on you, and the judge won't let you go over there and live with her. She's a drunk, and the rest of them ain't right in the head. I ain't got to be sorry for telling the truth!" The raggedy old church lady sat there getting an earful, and loving every minute of it.

"What you looking at? You old shriveled up raisin," I said. I headed to my room.

"From now on you come straight home from school. If you want to visit your grandmother, she's got to go and petition the court because if anything happens to you, it will be my fault."

"Whatever," I said. Once inside my room, I slammed the door as hard as I could.

"If I hear you been over there, I'm going to call the agency and tell them to come get your fast tail. Lord knows I'm too old for this foolishness," she said.

I didn't go back to Nana's for a while. Not because Kelley told me not to. I'm just tired of them. When I heard that Butch passed away on the third step leading to the house, I was humiliated for real. I avoided making eye contact with Jacqueline, but I could feel her looking at me with that stupid smirk on her face.

I can always find Uncle Nolan standing on the corner, in front of the pool hall, going in or coming out of the bar.

"I need Nana to go to court and petition for me to visit. I want to have weekend visitation," I told him.

"So now she got to go beg some fuckin' judge to let her see her own granddaughter?" he said. We walked through an empty lot. Some men whistled while others ogled me from inside their cars. It didn't bother me, I liked it when they looked but couldn't touch. No man will ever touch me again. Uncle Nolan grew more agitated with each passing second.

"What the hell you got on?" he said. I looked down at my clothes I was wearing what I always wore, short shorts and a cut off t-shirt.

"Didn't anybody teach you to wear a bra?" he said.

"Like who, your sister?" I said jokingly.

"Seriously, how many men gon' end up in jail or worse behind your fast ass?" he said. I stopped dead in my tracks.

"Fuck you, Uncle Nolan," I whispered.

"What?"

"I said fuck you!" I turned around and ran. I could barely see through my tears.

"Goldie, wait, I'm sorry!" he said. But, it's too late to turn back now. For the first time in my life, Uncle Nolan cut me down. Ever since I was little he was my guardian angel. One time when I was eight years old in the third grade. He was the same age I am now. I was skipping down the alley when he saw me.

"Come here Goldie, what happened to your face?" he said.

"I don't know," I said. He picked me up and carried me straight to the big house and upstairs to Nana's room.

"Ma, look at her face."

"Oh Lord, let me see," she said. She inspected the red and purple bruises on my left cheek.

"Somebody ought to beat Evelyn's ass black and blue," he said.

"She didn't do it," I said.

"Don't lie for her, I know she did it!" he said.

"Uh-uh, she didn't do it, Nana."

"Well, who hit you, baby?"

"I don't know."

"How do you not know who put them marks on you?" he said.

"I'ma tell you okay?"

"Go ahead, tell us," he said.

"Okay, so, like every day at recess, somebody keep punching me in the face. I don't never see who it is."

"Every day?" he said.

"Uh-huh, at recess," I said. The next day in Mrs. Nichols' class, we did math problems, we finished our art projects, went to lunch, and at recess, I got my punch. Afterward I saw Uncle Nolan coming across the yard, dragging a little boy by the collar.

"You know this fool?" he said.

"Uh-uh."

"Let me go before I kick your butt!" the boy said while punching the air like a tiny boxer. Uncle Nolan tried to keep from laughing at the boy.

"Why you keep hitting my niece?" he said. The boy folded his arms across his chest and pursed his lips. We waited for his mother to come out of the principal's office.

"He got a little crush on her, you didn't have to put your hands on him," she said.

"Whatever you say lady, look at the marks he left on her. You better make sure it don't happen again or else," he told her. He gave me a piggyback ride to Rimini's bakery and bought me a giant cream puff. If only I could turn back time, I would have kept my big mouth shut. I wouldn't be here, away from Bunny and my brothers, and my uncle wouldn't be tormented.

"Savage, you are a menace, a delinquent, and a nuisance," Kelley said.

"Oh Kelley, stop exaggerating, I can't be all that shit!" I said. So, it's official, she's taking me to court, the date is set. I couldn't help it, all those times I called her Mr. Ed and I might have called her an old ho' once or twice. Yeah, I know, I'm messing up, again. So, until they cart me off to baby jail, I'm going to say what I want, do what I want, and take *whatever* I want. I ain't even going to school today. Our teachers know who the "damaged goods" girls are. If we're late for homeroom, they'll sound the alarm, and send their bloodhounds after us. I have no reason to care anymore. So, when Kelley's van driver, handyman and secret lover, Mr. Sherman dropped us off in front of the school, I thought why pretend? I went in the opposite direction of the school. He rolled alongside me.

"Schools in the other direction young lady," he said.

"Oh Sherman, just mind your business and drive your van man." Two hours later I sat on an empty beach twiddling my thumbs. Who knew skipping school alone could be this boring? After treating myself to lunch at McDonald's, I took my lovely gold watch out of my pocket. I still had three hours to kill. I should have asked Chiquita and the gang to skip with me. I love hearing them practice. Maybe I can help them write rhymes, because I can't rap for shit. I sat on a park bench trying to recite the words to "Rapper's Delight". The macaroni so soggy, the peas are mushed, and chicken's hard as wood. *Wait, that's not right, is it?*

With two hours to go before I could get back into Kelley's, I strolled by Nana's street, it had been a month since I saw any of them. I spotted a small Jar Tran moving truck in front of the house. I picked up the pace until I reached the truck. Nana and Uncle Nolan were inside. I caught him putting the key in the ignition.

"Nana, you were moving without telling me?!" I said. She was startled, and she looked guilty as hell.

"No baby, we was comin' around there to get you."

"I'm supposed to be at school. Was you coming to my school? Do you even know what school I go to? Just give me the address, I'll find it later."

"We goin' on home this time baby," she said.

"Home? Oh my God, Nana, you were gonna leave me in Florida, by myself!"

"Hush now, you know I wasn't hardly gon' leave my baby," she said. I folded my arms across my chest.

"Mm-hmm."

"Run on back and get your stuff, we gon' be right here waitin' for you," she said.

"Ma you know you can't take her out of this state, they'll charge you with kidnapping," Uncle Nolan said.

"How in the world can I be kidnappin' my own flesh and blood? Run along and hurry back sweetheart," she said. I eyeballed her distrustfully.

"All right, but when I get back, you better be here."

I don't believe this. I've been at Kelley's for over two years, and in all that time, the Armor Guard was always locked. No one got in or out without the gatekeeper's key. The backyard had a high fence with no way out. Kelley kept a girl on door duty twenty-four hours a day. But today, somebody is sleeping on the job. The gate is unlocked, and no one is hanging around. I could have taken anything I wanted. I wanted to break into Kelley's boudoir and stomp on all her church hats, but I didn't have time for all that. I always knew that when Kelley called my name, she was calling me a savage on the sly. If I take everybody's stuff she would have a field day.

I darted around the house putting everything I borrowed or stole on each girls' bed. I reached in my pocket for Jacqueline's watch. I admired it for a second. I hated to part with it. Supposedly, her mother gave it to her before she went to jail. I kindly placed it under her pillow. *Oh, fuck her, she should've been nicer to me.* I put the watch back on my wrist. I dragged my bags over the pavement as fast as I could. Good, the truck is still there.

"Okay I'm back, I'm ready to go, scoot over Nana," I said half out of breath. She didn't budge.

"Nana, move before I climb over you," I said. Uncle Nolan jumped out of the truck.

"Girl, if you don't bring your ass back here," he said.

"Right, I got to put my stuff in the back first, I'll be back," I told Nana. I was surprised to see that the truck was empty, except for some mattresses.

"Thea, Marcus, Kevin, Tracie, y'all come on! We got to hit the road, we already behind by thirty-five minutes. If we don't get this truck back we gon' lose the damn deposit," Uncle Nolan said. They came out the house and rushed past me and climbed into the back of the truck.

"What the heck y'all doing in there?" As soon as it became clear I gasped.

"I know we ain't riding in the back of no stupid Jar Tran truck like some damn savages!"

"So what, we was in here burning up the first time you came," Uncle Kevin said.

"Uh-huh, and you was like, Nana don't leave me, you better be here when I get back Nana," Little Uncle Marcus mocked me, and they cracked up.

"Well, how we supposed to breathe?"

"Girl get your ass on up there, you been livin' with rich folks too long," Uncle Nolan said. Our eyes locked, and his said he was sorry.

I threw my arms around him.

"Me too Uncle Nolan," I said. I climbed into the truck. I stood there facing him.

"But you know this is some bullshit," I said. He pulled the metal door down and everything went pitch black. They burst out laughing again. When the truck took off I fell.

"Get your ass off my foot, Goldie!" Uncle Kevin said, and they laughed again.

"Man, this is some hillbilly, underground railroad, Mexican's running for the border bullshit!" I said.

22

The Ninth Hour

"HELLO, WHO DIS?" a girl said from the other end.

"Bunny?" I said.

"Yeah, who dis?" she said.

"It's your only sister," I said. Getting Evelyn's phone number seemed harder than finding my way out of a maze with a blindfold on. Mainly because Nana didn't want me to go back with her. But what else could I do? I missed my sister and brothers more than anything in the world. Once I got the number, I dialed it right away.

"Oh man, what up doe Goldie, how you been doin'?" Bunny said.

"I've been all right I guess. So, how have you guys been?"

"We been chillin' out."

"So, is Evelyn there?"

"Oh, um, she ain't really home." She lied for Evelyn, but I didn't know why.

"Well when she really gets home, tell her I really need money for a bus ticket." She didn't respond.

"Bunny!" I yelled.

"Oh, okay, I'ma tell her," she said. Anyway, two weeks have passed since then. The next time I called, Evelyn answered the phone.

"Hello, who is this?" she said. I couldn't speak.

"Hello?" she said again. My heart pounded wildly, I could hardly catch my breath. Talking was out of the question. What if she tells me I can't come period? What if— "Goldie, I know it's you, come on down here if you want to," she said casually and hung up.

When the bus driver announced our arrival in Detroit, I damn near stepped on the backs of the other passengers to get my ass off the bus before them. I dragged my bags over to the first pay phone in sight.

"Hello, who is this" Evelyn said?"

"It's me, I'm here at the Greyhound station."

"Oh damn, I didn't even know you was comin' today."

"I see how you could forget after three years."

"All right, I'm on my way," she said. Three hours later and here I sit, looking kind of homeless.

"Excuse me, Miss, would you mind taking a picture with us?" a young man asked. The terminal was crawling with men. Most of them were wearing crisp military uniforms, just like these two.

"Sure," I said before I stood between them. I tilted my head and smiled brightly. Each time I sat down another uniform approached me. "Hey pretty lady, would you please?"

"You know, it's okay to decline," said an older woman, who was sitting next to me.

"What do you mean?"

"Just smile politely and say no thank you," she said. Another soldier boy came toward me with a camera. I smiled and said "No, thank you," before he could even ask.

"You're a fast learner," the woman said, and we chatted for a short while. A handsome young man came toward us. I was about to smile and decline, but she jumped up and threw her arms around him. She laughed and rocked him during their embrace.

"Oh, baby let me carry something," she said when he picked up all her luggage.

"I got it Ma-dear, relax," he said.

"Your people on the way?" she asked me.

"Yes ma'am, they'll be here any minute."

"You take care of yourself, you're such a lovely girl," she said.

Another hour went by. I looked left and right, everyone I stepped over was long gone. I watched people get off buses, stretch their arms wide, and simply go on their merry way. Others stood in lines and boarded buses. The only thing out of the ordinary was me since I had been sitting here for six hours. I only have fifty cents to my name. After spending my last seven dollars on a corned beef sandwich, a bag of potato chips, and one ice cold Vernors pop, I dragged my stuff to the pay phone. I'm beside myself when Evelyn answers the phone again.

"Hello, who is this?" she said.

"Evelyn, you *know* who it is, I been waiting for you for over six hours now!" *Okay calm down, I'm sure she has a good reason for not being here yet.*

"Girl, when you called this morning I fell back to sleep, I was tired as hell," she said.

"You're still a fucking bitch," I mumbled.

"Hey, you still there?" she said.

"Evelyn, will you please wake up and come get me, please?" She sucked her teeth.

"Okay let me try to find a ride." I sat down and tried to entertain myself with the conversations around me while I waited.

"So, how's the family?" "They doin' fine." "Aunt Mamie got the sugar, they tryna save her leg." "Oh lord, not little June bug! How much time they give him?"

By the ninth hour, the workers were looking at me sideways. I wanted to scream. How could she leave me here for all this time? Instead of dragging my bags back to the pay phone, I went outside and jumped into one of the waiting cabs.

"Where you headed to?" the driver said. I peeked at the paper and told him the address.

"That's off Jefferson Avenue, right?"

"Sure is," I said trying to sound confident, otherwise he might take the scenic route, and I wouldn't know the damn difference.

"Right over there we have the Renaissance Center," he said.

"Why are you telling me?"

"Well, I figured since you're new in town."

"Who said I was new?" The meter was already at seven dollars.

"*Okay,* you don't need a tour then," he laughed. He stopped in front of a shabby gray house.

"End of the line, eighteen-fifty," he said.

"I have to go in and get it."

"No problem, leave your bags here please." The house wasn't bad. All it needs is a fresh coat of paint. I went up the unstable steps and knocked on the door. When Bunny appeared, we screamed like we saw the same ghost. We hugged. She's small for her age, not even five feet tall.

"Dang Goldie, how you get so big?" she said.

"I'm not so big, you're just small."

"Well Mama went to get you, why you ain't wait for her?"

"I waited for nine hours, I ended up catching a cab here."

"Oh, for real? She probably couldn't get no ride, where your stuff," she said looking around.

"My bags are in the cab, I need eighteen dollars to pay it."

"Damn, I ain't got no money on me. Anyway, it ain't no eighteen dollars from no Greyhound, this mo'fo tryna get over on you." She shuffled down the steps like a boy.

"Hey man, what you tryna pull? You know it ain't it no eighteen dollars from downtown," she said.

"That ain't what the meter says," the driver said. He seemed amused by Bunny. Who wouldn't be? Especially since her big personality did not match her tiny frame. I didn't recall her being this pretty, her skin was brown with a red tone. Her hair didn't curl tight like mine. Hers was naturally wavy, and her features worked together to make her fine.

"Ah come on man, this my sister, cut her some slack, plus my mama can pay you on the fiteenth, come back on the fiteenth," she said. *I know she can talk better than that.*

"Nah, I need my money right now baby. So how 'bout I just keep her bags until the *"fiteenth,"* unless you got it?" he asked little Miss Bunny.

"Who me? Let me check," she said patting herself down and reaching into her top pocket and pulling out a cigarette.

"Aye you got a light?" she asked him.

"Girl you something else," he said while giving her a light. She looked across the street.

"What up doe, you got me?" she said to a man sitting on his steps waving money in the air.

"Do you know him?" I asked.

"Nope, I ain't never seen the nigga before. This how we do it in the three-one-three baby!" she said, while shuffling across the street.

"A'ight man, good looking out!" she called over her shoulder with the cigarette dangling from her lips. I'm in shock, *the driver is in love.*

"Here, I got yo' money man, she said handing him a crisp twenty-dollar bill. Keep the change, you ol' gold digger." He laughed.

"What did you call me?" he said.

"You heard me, nigga. Did I stu, stu, stutter? You got some nerve. Go 'head on somewhere, mister eighteen dollars from the Greyhound."

"Boy, if you wasn't so damn cute," he said before driving away.

"Bunny you shouldn't smoke, you're only thirteen," I said.

"I'm fourteen, anyway Mama know I smoke, she be borrowing squares from me." She showed off by blowing perfect rings into the air.

"Well, you're too pretty to smoke."

"Dang Goldie, you just got here, chill out, here take a hit," she said while pushing the cigarette toward me. I slapped her hand away and it fell to the ground where it belonged. She picked it up and brought it back to life.

"Damn, squares don't grow on trees Goldie," she said. A car

pulled up next to us and Evelyn bounced out showing the world her thighs and teeth.

"Girl, there you go. We was downtown lookin' all over for you. Some people said they seen you, but they ain't know where you went," she said. She had on a black and white mini skirt set, clearly made for girls me and Bunny's age. Embracing her firstborn child, who she ain't seen in three years, obviously wasn't on her to do list.

"Girl look at you, you a brick house for sure. Turn around, let me get a good look at you," she said. I was turning when I saw my three baby brothers on the porch. I stopped spinning and ran toward them. They stood close together like triplets joined at the hip. They had sad faces like wise old men. I reached out to hug them, but they moved away from me.

"Hey Joshua, don't you remember me?" I said.

"Uh-uh," he said while shaking his head slowly.

"Boy this our big sister Goldie, y'all know who she is," Bunny said. Evelyn happily sashayed into the house and we followed behind.

"Hello there, may we take your coat? Or perhaps you'd like something cool to drink?" the roaches asked me politely.

"No, thank you, I'm fine, but I suggest y'all pack your shit and go because there's a new sheriff in town," I warned them.

"You can have any one of these empty rooms," Evelyn said. I found myself standing in the kids' room. Their beds were broken and scattered everywhere, and the mattresses were bare. Evelyn's room was fit for a queen. I went to the kitchen and lifted the top of a pot that sat on the stove. Some chicken and rice had been thrown in. I could smell that the chicken hadn't been cleaned well before it made it into the pot. It's okay, I'm here now.

"Aye what up Miss Lady," Beau said from the kitchen doorway. I dropped the lid back on the pot and turned around. We hugged each other tight. I stood back to get a better look at him. He had the same mischievous grin all boys have once they realize they're fine. His hair had grown out, now he's sporting neat cornrows. At eleven he's as handsome as he can be.

I spent the entire night staring at them and hanging onto their every word. All this time they had each other, while I had no one. Bunny and Beau told some crazy stories and I told them a few. We reminisced until it got dark and the little ones passed out. I held Joshua so tight while I carried him upstairs. It hurt my heart to lay them on the broken beds.

The next morning, I tied a scarf around my head and stood on the steps. Didn't I tell you creepy fuckers to get the hell out of town? I used the broom to sweep and crush roaches. They were lined up along the ceiling. But why? Maybe they heard about me, and now they're migrating to a part of the house I didn't about. I laughed and got back to the business of sweeping and crushing. Ugh, they got my skin crawling. This would take all month, perhaps longer. It don't matter, I'm going to win this war.

"Evelyn, can you give me some money for some roach spray and some boric acid?"

"Girl, what you know about boric acid?"

"I know all I need to." She went somewhere in her head. I stomped my foot. "Evelyn give me some money, please!"

"Bunny I need you to help me get this house together, you know this ain't right, we never lived like this before." Bunny is lazy, but she hates to feel guilty.

"A'ight, what you want me to do?"

"Let's start by trying to put these beds back together."

"Okay, but, the kid's gon' keep jumping on 'em."

"They can be taught not to jump on them."

It only took a week to get the house in order. I chose the room on the first floor next to the kitchen. It's really a dining room, but a room is a room. I wish it wasn't painted in this God- awful shade of blue. Well, it beats the alternative of sleeping upstairs, next door to

Evelyn. Last night, I stretched out on the couch to sleep. She came in and watched me for a while. The only light was courtesy of the moon. I pretended like I didn't know she was there. She used to watch me through cracked doors when I was little. It used to scare me. Anyway, I ain't scared of *Mommie Dearest* anymore, but it don't mean she can't hurt me.

I planned to spend this Friday night on the couch watching a good old Elvis Presley movie when Beau came running in the house to hand me a note.

"What is this?"

"I don't know, Mama said to give it to you," he said. I read it twice to make sure I read it right the first time. "GOLDIE, TAKE YOUR ASS UPSTAIRS RIGHT NOW! AND DON'T COME DOWN UNLESS I TELL YOU TO!" Is she serious? Who am I kidding? The crazier things seem, the more serious she is. I suppose she don't this man to know she got a daughter as old as me. How come Bunny never gets a sour note? She's almost as old as I am, except she still looks eleven or twelve. Until she opens her mouth and starts cussing like a forty-year-old sailor. On my way upstairs, in my mind, I can hear Aretha Franklin singing "Rock Steady". I hum along because I intend to do just that. Besides, still waters run deep. One wrong move and I could be separated from my sister and brothers forever this time.

Sometimes Bunny will come in and hand me a note, but they're from boys around the neighborhood. They say they seen me going to or coming from the store, and they really want to get to know me better. I'm not used to getting this much attention from boys my age. I ball up the corny notes and laugh. I already got to cook and clean and watch three kids. I don't have time to let anybody know me better.

After the boys had their baths and said their little prayers, I tucked them in for the night. There was a knock on the door. I'm always tired, but not too tired to spend time with Matthew. He's Bunny's boyfriend's older brother. I don't recall when it started, but every night he comes around and we sit and talk. We have kissed, but only a few times, and he's okay with it. I hurried to the door to let him in.

"Oh, it's you," I said when I saw Fredrick.

"Bunny here?" he said.

"Nope, not at all," I snapped. I think Bunny's too young to have a boyfriend. I'm afraid this little Casanova will get her in some trouble she couldn't easily get out of.

"You know where she at?"

"Nope, can't say I do," I said dryly.

"Can I come in and wait for her?" I looked over his shoulder hoping to see Matthew coming down the street.

"Maybe she's at the arcade playing Pac man," I said.

"I already checked, she ain't there." He shifted from one leg to the other a few times.

"Man, I got to use the bathroom, Miss Evelyn always let me in when Bunny ain't here." I stepped aside. As soon as I closed the door, Fredrick pushed me onto the couch, and laid on top of me and tried to stick his tongue down my throat all in one swoop.

"Fredrick, what are you doing?!" We're about the same age, except he's shorter and thinner than me. How can he be so much stronger than I am? I tried getting from under him. He squeezed my titties like a maniac.

"Girl you fine as hell, finer than any of these girls around here," he said. Like it justified what he's trying to do to me.

"Come on baby, kiss me back," he said pressing his lips on mine.

"Little boy, get off me!" I said while he held my arms at my sides. I squirmed beneath him trying to break free.

"So, you really like that punk huh?"

"Matthew is your brother Fredrick."

"I don't care, any man who be with you all night and don't try to get none is a damn fool."

"He never told you?" I said.

"Told me what?"

"Whenever he comes here, we spend the night doing it, and doing it." He slowly opened his palms and my titties went their separate ways.

"For real?" he said.

"Mm-hmm, so if you want me to keep this a secret, I suggest you get your little ass off me now." It worked. Once I heard Uncle Nolan say no man wants to go anywhere his brother has already been. Once again, he was right. Fredrick had a leg on the floor when the front door opened. My stomach turned when I smelled the Juicy Fruit gum.

"What the hell is going on in here?!" Evelyn said. This is all I need, now that me and Bunny are getting closer. Evelyn is always trying to divide us by our skin tones.

"Sorry Miss Wallace," Fredrick said before stumbling out the door with his tail tucked between his legs. She slammed the door behind him.

"I knew you was a sneaky ass snake!" she said sounding like a snake herself.

"What? No, I'm not, I didn't do anything." Her expression said bullshit.

"Evelyn, he came in here and jumped on me."

"I know what I saw whore," she said. She strutted into the living room to wait for Bunny to come home.

"What up Gee?" Bunny said in her usual cheerful way. She headed straight to the living room.

"What up Mama, you got a cigarette?" she said.

"Here, you gon' need it after you hear this," she said. What kind of a mother would tell her daughter something like that? Oh yeah, the mother from the Black Lagoon would.

The next morning, I stood in the kitchen getting breakfast ready for the boys when Bunny came in. She didn't speak to me. I know what it's like to be betrayed by somebody who's supposed to love you.

She don't know me well enough to know I'd never do that to her. She's my baby sister. I love her so much. I had better say something before she walks out.

"Bunny, I let him in to wait for you, and he jumped on me. I was fighting him off when Evelyn came in."

"I believe you, I know how Fredrick is, he always be trying to get with somebody, he a dog."

"Yes, he is," I said. Evelyn let out a wicked witch laugh.

"All right Bunny, you can fall for her shit if you want to, I done told you, you can't trust no yellow whore, sister or not!" she said.

23

Decent Shoes

"HEY, WAKE YOUR LAZY BUTT UP!" Evelyn yelled from my doorway. Lazy? I don't know what she did all night, but I was up until one in the morning, washing the kid's clothes, and hanging them in the basement. That old rusty dryer waited until I got here to stop working. I used my pillow to cover my head.

"Please, I'm tired, leave me alone," I mumbled.

"Don't get smart with me, you supposed to take these papers to the high school, and get them filled out. Them people downtown won't keep you on my case if you ain't in school. Hell, you ain't bringing a dime in here, and you eating me out of house and home." Please, she exaggerates. How much government cheese, white rice, and free grapefruit juice can I stand? Every month, she auctions off most of her food stamps, so she can buy the finer things in life.

It's the beginning of November, school started back in August. I'm not going this year. For one thing, what would I wear? All my clothes screamed Florida, in the summertime at that. I only have one pair of green flip flops, and some sharp white pumps that Nana got me last Easter. She refused to get them at first. She said three-inch heels was for grown women. I sat in that shoe store pouting until she finally gave in. But now, I can't stand the sight of them.

I stopped by Evelyn's room and tried to stuff my size eight and a half foot into her size seven shoe. The prince would never choose me, not with these feet. I got two pairs of nice jeans, but when I tried them on, they barely went past my ever-spreading hips. Every time I settle on a bra size, I grow out of it. This month I'm a 34DD. Please don't get any bigger, I pray. Why some girls wish for these things is beyond me. They're heavy as hell, and the top button on my shirt never closes.

I walked to the school wearing a thin pink jacket. I'm freezing. Southeastern High School. I've heard people call it the jungle. I can only imagine why. When I stepped through the doors, I barely noticed the place. After I registered, they gave me a class schedule. I'll give it to Evelyn, so she can show the people downtown. I made a beeline for the door. I won't be setting foot back in this place again, not this year anyway.

"Stop it Evelyn!" I said when she woke me up the next morning by banging on a pot with a big metal spoon.

"Uh-uh, take your ass to school!" she said.

"Since when do you care if I go to school or not?"

"I don't care, I just don't want no truancy officer comin' around here, gettin' all up in my business."

"Well I don't have nothing to wear, not even a good coat, can you give me some money?"

"Child please, you better get out there and use what you got to get what you need."

"Ugh, that's disgusting, I'll pass."

"What, you think you better than somebody?" I fought the urge to jump out of bed and choke her. I sat on the edge of my bed. Finally, I got up and walked to my closet like the bride of Frankenstein. After I grabbed the coffee can I hid up there, I poured its contents onto my bed. I've been keeping the change from the cigarettes and whatnot. She's the last one to depend on for my personal hygiene stuff. But what kind of clothes can I buy with twelve dollars?

After only ten minutes in the thrift store on Jefferson Avenue, I'm screaming inside. Everything looked like something Thelma or

Willona from Good Times would wear well. But this is Detroit, 1983. I can't go to school in no purple bell bottoms, or this plaid dress with a white doily for a collar, or heaven forbid anything polyester. It's too bad I didn't pay attention when The Sergeant tried to teach me how to use the sewing machine. But I was hard headed back then. I left the thrift store with a few interesting garments. Some of the pieces were as low as thirty-five cents. Nothing costs more than a dollar. Transforming them into something presentable would be easy enough. If this don't work, I may have to start stealing.

I stepped through the doors of Southeastern High School for the second time. A woman sat at table with a lost and found sign behind her head. I rushed toward the table.

"That's it right there, the red one," I told her. She smiled warmly. "I'll bet your mother paid a pretty penny for this, its real leather," she said. I looked over my shoulder nervously. I yanked the coat from her hands.

"Yeah, she did." Hopefully, the real owner won't recognize it. I'm sure they sold more than one. If anybody dares to approach me about it, I'll go damn savage on their ass.

Some girls at school said they liked my skirt and asked me where I got it. This one is two-toned, pink in the front and red in the back. I saw it in "Teen Vogue" magazine and copied it.

"I got it in New York," I told them. I lied confidently because I knew all about shopping in New York. The Sergeant took me there when she went to visit her sister. We spent a whole Saturday afternoon bartering on the sidewalks.

"They must not sell shoes in New York," one girl told the other. The first week nobody mentioned them. I guess I'm trying their patience. They reminded me that Labor Day had come and gone.

"Why she keep on wearing them white shoes?" one girl asked her friend as they walked by.

"I don't know, maybe they her favorite, or she might be color blind."

"You tell her."

"No, you should tell her."

"Her mama should have told her." They laughed. Stupid cows. Why do they care what I wear anyway? Does my steady diet of government cheese leave them constipated? I think not.

Damn, this is my third slip and fall of the day. I should just stay down here and take a nap. I'd been deceived by ice covered with fresh snow. I got up and dusted myself off.

"Hey lil girl, go home and put on some decent shoes!" somebody yelled. I looked around to see who said it. A heavy-set dark-skinned woman struggled out of her car and stared at me. But she can't be talking to me, I don't even know that lady.

"Yes, I'm talking to you, please go put on some decent shoes, and stop trying to look cute," she said.

"These are all I got ma'am."

"Stop lying," she said.

"Okay, whatever," I said. I turned around and kept trying to walk without taking another dive.

"Wait, you Evelyn's daughter, right?" I stopped, but I didn't say anything.

"Well that explains it, what's your name?"

"Goldie."

"I heard she had another daughter who came to town, but you don't look nothing like her," she said. I watched her struggle to get herself back under the steering wheel. She reached over to unlock the passenger side door. "Come on, get in," she said. I stood there staring at her. I don't know. Is she even allowed to drive legally? I mean, isn't there a weight limit like in an elevator?

"Look, lil girl, I just got off work, I'm tired, and I'm hungry. Let's go," she said. I opened the car door and slid in. The nerve of some people. Once inside the car, I tried not to stare. It's just that I'd never seen such an unfortunate looking woman.

"What's your name?" I asked, after a few minutes.

"Millie," she said while keeping her eyes on the road. Finally, she turned into the Northland mall parking lot.

"You ever been here before?" she said.

"No, I've only been at home, school and back home. Except for that one time a guy took me to Skate Land." When we entered the mall, I headed straight to the Picway shoe store. She turned her nose to the ceiling and strutted past the cheap store and stopped in front of Thom McAns instead. She placed a pair of black ankle boots and a pair of pink and white sneakers on the counter and handed the salesman her credit card.

"Ah, Adidas, great choice, all the kids are wearing these," the salesman assured us.

"You hungry?" she said.

"No, you've done enough for me already."

"I didn't ask you all that, I asked you if you were hungry."

"I'm always hungry, I'm a growing girl."

"Okay, so where do you want to go?"

"McDonald's please."

"All these different restaurants around here, and you want to eat there?"

"You asked."

"Your mama need her ass beat," she said pointing a French fry in my direction. I didn't know what to say, I didn't appreciate her talking about Evelyn like that, true or not.

"*And* she be running around with all them different men." I tried to keep quiet, even though my temperature was rising. She bit into her second big mac making half of it disappear.

"She don't even take care of her own kids. Seriously, she ain't nothing but a—"

"Whoa wait a minute," I said. I pushed the Thom McAn bag and the tray of food toward her and stood up.

"What's wrong with you?" she said.

"Millie, I appreciate the food and the decent shoes, I mean I needed...need them, but I won't sit here and listen to you talk about Evelyn like that."

"All right, all right, calm down, I'm sorry. I got a little carried away, besides, you probably got that Patty Hearst syndrome."

"What?"

"Nothing, never mind. Eat the rest of your food before it gets cold. You need some meat on your bones," she said.

"Can you lend me some?"

"Oh, okay you win this round," she said. When she reached over to grab one of my fries, I slapped her hand away playfully. By the time she dropped me off in front of my house, I felt like we had known each other forever.

"Thank you, Millie," I said.

"You don't have to thank me."

"Well my Nana taught me better than that, so thank you ma'am."

"Okay, you're welcome. Lord you already starting to be a pain in the butt," she laughed. Millie has a job at the cable company, her own apartment in the building her parents manage, and her own car. I want to be just like her.

Millie's mom said she would pay me to clean some of the empty apartments. Now I can buy a few things for school. None of the apartments ever needed to be cleaned. I guess they understand, I have my pride, and I don't want to be treated like a charity case. Although the apartments are clean, I spic and span or mop and glow them anyway.

Millie is still having a hard time keeping quiet where Evelyn is concerned.

"Did you see the mess she had the nerve to have on today? Running around here like some ol' teenybopper."

"Of course, I saw it, we live in the same house," I reminded her.

"Oh, that's right, sometimes I forget y'all is even related," she said. We were in her parent's room stretched out on their big comfortable bed. Millie is only twenty-six, but her parents are old as Methuselah.

"They were close to fifty when they had me," she told me.

"That's nasty," I said. Millie's' mother calls her the miracle baby she waited all her life to have. But still, old people doing it, and having babies is just gross.

As soon as I opened the door to Millie's parent's apartment, I wanted to turn right back around. Millie was having another pity party. She was perched in front of the mirror, scrutinizing the reflection like she had never seen herself before. This meant she ain't taking me and my brothers to Belle Isle like she promised. Slowly she turns toward me and once again it looks like she's about to sneeze, but I know she's not going to.

"Uh-uh don't ask me, I don't want to hear it," I say and cover my ears.

"Why couldn't I look like my mother instead of my father?" she said.

"Damn it, Millie!" I said. Who cares if she's about three hundred pounds, six feet tall with a face that couldn't be camouflaged? We've tried everything, but no amount of make-up helps. We've even tried pulling her awful mushroom wig down until it brushes the top of her stubby eyelashes.

"Stop it, how are you supposed to see, or breathe?" I said after she yanked the wig over her nose. Other times out of nowhere she'll blurt out.

"I'm ugly, ain't I?" I used to say, "No you ain't ugly." Lately, my response has been "Aw, you ain't that ugly." But honestly, I do think she's ugly, I mean I know she is. She looks like a burnt Mrs. Potato head and a baby hippo from behind, but so what. Her parents love her, I love her. And she's got a fine Spanish boyfriend who must love her because he's fine and can have whoever he wants, and he wants her. She should just shut her mouth and count her blessings. I'm getting tired of all the whining.

A week later I walked into Millie's parent's apartment and there she is, adding salt to her mother's homemade meatball soup, by crying into it. I walked right past her to the cabinet. I grabbed a bowl and put two scoops in. It's the best I ever tasted. After I crumble a few crackers into my bowl. I looked at her and analyzed her face. She looked at me like I held a gun on her and might shoot her down.

"*But, you're so damned...uugggly,*" I said mimicking a line from the Planet of the Apes. We just watched it two nights ago, so that line is still fresh. She surprised me by laughing. Her shoulders shook like some old washing machine on the spin cycle. She rolled onto the floor. I called her mother from the living room. I pointed to the large vibrating heap.

"Something's wrong with her!" I said.

"Ain't nothin' wrong with her, she simple is all," her mother said. Millie picked herself up off the floor and regained her composure.

"I'm going to get you for that when you least expect it," she said.

"Woo, I'm shaking in my boots," I teased."

24
Purpose

"NEGRO PLEASE, YOU GOT some damn nerve," I said when a fine Egyptian eyed boy tugged on my skirt, and accuse me of making it myself.

"You shouldn't be ashamed of it. I like it, it's dope," he said.

"If it's so dope, why did you ask me if I made it?"

"The stitching is a dead giveaway, but you have good vision.

"Hey Adrian," a girl said when she walked by.

"What's up Brenda? Looking good girl," he said. *She looked okay.* She had on a pair of jeans with cool graffiti designs, a lot of kids were wearing them.

"Guess who made those?" he said.

"No way, you're kidding, right?"

"I'm Adrian Moss. I'm a fashion designer, all these fools know me around here," he said.

"I'm Goldie, pleased to meet you." We ended up skipping two classes just to talk. Designing clothes is his passion and purpose for living, he said. I was forced to make my own clothes, I wouldn't call it a passion. I didn't know about rushing, or how to trim a garment or the proper way to stitch this skirt.

"It's okay if people know you made something, as long as they can't *tell* you made it. You got to learn how to hustle if you want to get anywhere in this world. You understand?" If you got talent you need to work that shit. Let all these players know what time it is," Adrian said.

227

"But I don't have a sewing machine, I can't do all that by hand."

"I got this old singer I could sell you. You do know how to use one don't you?" I shook my head no. He snapped his fingers in the air.

"Girl you better work it," he said. *Damn, he's gay.*

Ever since we met, I've been going to Adrian's house twice a week. He's teaching me the tricks of the trade.

"Never do anything for free, not even fixing a zipper or replacing a button. Even the nicest people you know will try to get over on you, it's human nature. You got to be tough, don't let anybody take advantage of you. You understand?" he said. I nodded my head, but I wasn't really listening, I got lost in his eyes. I took a roll of cash from my bra and peeled off three fives. It's a partial payment for the lessons, the singer, and an old dressmaker's dummy. I am aware that it's all worth so much more than he's charging me.

"Thank you, Adrian."

"You're welcome honey," he said, while tucking the cash into his imaginary bra. *I hated when he did shit like that.*

I don't like calling attention to myself. So, Adrian took care of the advertising for me. Apparently, his sculpted body didn't come with any shy bones. Suddenly girls who didn't know me from a can of paint gave me their money. They wanted me to make outfits they saw in magazines, but couldn't afford. None of it seemed that hard to do. Most of the time, all they wanted was a blue jean skirt with a matching vest. I can do that in my sleep. But soon they hunted me down and begged me to make the same outfit Janet Jackson wore to the BET Awards. "Sure, no problem," I said after I snatched the tens and twenties out of their hands. Honestly, it was all about the money.

"Can you make my prom dress?" A senior asked me a few weeks later. I looked at her like she punched me dead in my stomach. The thought terrified me.

"Girl please, she'll have you looking like Cinder-fucking-rella.

You understand?" Adrian said while doing the finger snapping thing that reminded me we will never be more than sister girls, his words, not mine.

"If the price is right," he added. His word was good as gold, but he should slow down when it comes to offering my services. He's the smartest boy I've ever known. He's a hard worker, and he hates laziness.

"Get your work done, you can sleep in your grave," he says. So, yes has become my middle name.

"But, why did you say I could make a prom dress when I never have before?" I asked Adrian.

"Don't worry, you got time, prom is months away. I believe in you, but you got to start believing in yourself. Self-doubt is like mud in your wings. Get rid of that shit, and you'll be flying high. The sky is the limit, always remember that," he said.

"Damn it, Adrian, can you stop being so goddamn wonderful, and fabulous, and sweet and whatnot? Please just be a jerk," I joked, and he gets it. I'm not the first girl to ever fall in love with his dimples that are so deep, you can stick your finger in them. His almond toned skin was too smooth. His hair and clothes were always flawless, and I imagined his body was perfectly sculpted underneath. He clapped his hands in front of my face like a school teacher.

"Goldie, pay attention sweetie, we don't have all night," he said.

"I know, we never will," I mumbled.

She don't have to say a word, I smell her standing in the doorway watching me while I work on a second lacey ass prom dress. I got half in advance, so it's top priority. I hate being broke, so I'm trying to save more money than I spend. But, it's not easy when Evelyn wants every dime I make, she's such a greedy goat.

"How much you gon' get for that one?" she said.

"I don't know yet, it depends on how it turns out," I told her. I never tell her how much I make. Wasn't she the one who always said not to let your left hand know what your right hand is doing? Well, as far as I'm concerned, my left hand is standing in the doorway.

"See how long it last your ungrateful ass. You can't lend me a few stinkin' dollars, after all I done for you?" she said the last time I refused to give her any more money. Forget her, I'm doing this for me and my brothers. This is my way of using what I got to get what we need. Most of the time I don't get to sleep, until one in the morning. I'll work until my fingertips are numb. Day in, and day out, I still have to remind myself not to fantasize about Adrian. It's clear that he's not going to switch sides any time soon. Hell, his boyfriend is just as pretty as I am, from a distance, *meow.*

"Hey Goldie, you wear a size seven, right?" Adrian said when he bumped into me in the hallway. I gasped before putting my hand on my hip and rolling my neck around dramatically.

"Negro please, you got some damn nerve. I wear a size five."

"My sincere apologies ma'am, I should get my pupils dilated," he said.

"That's exactly what you need to do, check 'em."

"Too bad because I made these for you," he said. He held up a pair of cool white jeans with a sexy cartoon version of me with colorful angel's wings. I couldn't contain my excitement as I reached for them. He took a giant step back.

"Too bad I got the size wrong," he said. I tapped myself on the forehead with an open palm.

"You know what? I just remembered I do wear a size seven. But, in Paris, I wear a six. Detroit adds ten pounds, because of all the fried chicken and mashed potaters. *You understand?*" I joked.

"Mm-hmm, that's what I thought," he said. I snatched the jeans and thanked him with a big hug, and a kiss on his cheek.

The boys said they wanted a hamster. I went to the pet store and picked out the best one. Lucky for him, Evelyn hasn't had a fit since she got her tubes tied. So, this furry critter should die of natural causes. Anyway, Mr. Hamster lives a colorless life. Every day, he eats, sleeps, and poops in his tiny cage. He climbs on the wheel and goes nowhere fast. "Believe me, I know how you feel," I told the rat. I go to school, come home, and take care of my brothers, mindlessly sew, go to bed, and wake up to do it all over again. I try to ignore the voice telling me that I'm lonely, bored, and boring. Matthew doesn't come around anymore. He said our relationship wasn't really going anywhere. "Baby, I can't be around you anymore without wanting you," he said. Bunny has Fredrick and a herd of girlfriends, and she lives at the arcade. If she ever invited me into her world, I wouldn't fit in any way. I often wonder where Beau goes all day. For all I know, he could have another family somewhere. Joshua, Joseph, and Jeremiah don't need me as much as I wished they did. They're happy running around the house or playing in the backyard rain or shine. When they're hungry, or they need someone to put a Band-Aid on their scrapes, I'm always right here waiting. Even Evelyn has a better social life than I do. These take your ass upstairs notes are really adding up.

I smelled smoke the moment I stepped through the door. My nose led me upstairs to the kids' room. It was coming from the closet. Some clothes were on the floor burning and spreading fast. After putting the fire out, my mission was to find out who the hell has been playing with matches. A tiny cough stopped me in my tracks. I turned around, but no one else was in the room. I waited to hear another cough. I followed the sound to the top shelf of the closet and found Joseph in a ball.

"Joseph, how did you get up there?" I stretched my arms out to him. He hesitated.

"I'm not mad at you Joseph." He let himself fall into my arms.

"Did you start this fire?" He shook his head.

"Why Joseph?" He pursed his lips. I grabbed his shoulders and forced him to look at me.

"Why did you do it?"

"Because Mama whooped me for no reason," he said. We sat

on the floor while I held him on my lap.

"Promise me you will never do that again, no matter what."

"Okay," he said. Oh God, what if I had gone to the fabric store instead of coming straight home? Now I know for sure that they are my true purpose in life. I have to protect them from her. It's hard to believe that some animals eat their young, but they do.

25

Who You Callin' a Sidekick?

THANK GOD, IT'S FRIDAY. I'm eager to join the herd stampeding through the front doors. I was standing at my locker when I saw Layla Washington gliding in my direction. She's the most popular girl here because she looks exactly like Vanity from that sexy singing group. All the men and boys go crazy for that type. Who cares? Looks ain't everything. I always thought she was a real trip, walking through around in slow motion like she owns the place. They're all too scared to touch her highness, so they part the Red Sea when they see her gliding through the halls. I wonder what would happen if someone did touch her? She would probably disintegrate, or maybe the fool who touched her would turn into a toad. Hmm, I don't know, but I'll be damned if I ever bow down to that stuck-up heifer. *Am I in her way?* I don't think so. Anyway, this is my locker, so she can go around me. She snapped her fingers close to my face.

"What's the matter, you deaf?" she said. She knows I'm not deaf. But, I am at a loss for words. I mean, she was appealing in passing, and despite all the stuff I just said up close she was fucking unbelievable. She didn't even have pores. I managed to squeeze out one word like what, or maybe it was ma'am.

"I said I like your coat," she said. We were wearing the same coat in different colors. Hers is black patent leather and mine is red leather. Thank God for things lost, and found. Otherwise, she didn't have any reason to talk to me.

"Thank you, I like yours better," I said awkwardly. The satisfied look on her face told me that I was safe, I said the right thing.

"Is that your real hair?" she said.

"What, you think I'm wearing a wig, or weave or something?" She grabbed a chunk of my hair, and studied it like she's trying to decide if something is worth buying or not.

"No, the color, is it natural?" she said.

"Uh-huh. Your hair looks like mink on a fur coat," I said then I mentally kicked myself. *Be cool, stop kissing her ass.* She's just a girl. She puts on one sock at a time. Her doo-doo probably stinks like the rest of ours, although I doubt it. She must have felt the small group of girls, standing behind her burning a hole through her back. Slowly she looked over her shoulder and rolled her ridiculously long eyelashes at them. They scattered like a bunch of Quasimodo's.

"So, who you hang with?" she said.

"Nobody really, except Adrian sometimes."

"Who, the sissy?"

"Uh-huh, I guess," I said.

"What's your name?" she said. *Shit, what is my name?* I know it starts with a C, no a G.

"Uh, Goldie?" I said. One bead of sweat crawled down the side of my face. I hoped she didn't see it. After she walked away, I stood there frozen, breathless. My palms were sweating too. I opened my hand, and gazed at the piece of paper she scribbled her phone number on.

I stood in the bathroom far back from the mirror, checking myself out from all angles. Layla always wears black so I'm wearing this tight black mini dress. Would she look down on me if she knew it was just a Goldie original? I was headed to the mall, but ended up in the fabric store instead. Wearing the jeans Adrian made for me is not an option, apparently I wear a size eight now. That's it, I'm going on Dexatrim. My eyes are perfectly lined. I look like a naughty feline. After making sure not one strand of hair was running wild, I put on my gold necklace. Someday I'll have a real one with a diamond heart, but tonight, this will have to do. Shit, it's tarnished in some spots. After tonight I'm tossing it before my neck turns green.

"Where you think you goin'?" Evelyn said from the doorway. I ignored her. After taking one last look at myself, I quietly walked past her, I'd fight her if I had to.

"Uh-uh, I got a date tonight, you better have your ass blah blah blah—." I couldn't hear clearly from the other side of the door.

"It's Like That " by Run-D.M.C. blasted from the kicker in the corner. These party people were far from high school age. They were on fire though, stomping out the beat instead of dancing to it. Layla ain't even here yet. She had the nerve to call me earlier to tell me not to be late. Several men huddled in a corner. They were fired up about something. It's probably a dice game. How can they see? The house was lit with dim red- light bulbs. The DJ changed the song, so now they're trying to match Prince's dove cry, but they sound awful.

"No thank you, I don't drink," I said after a man offered me one.

"Then what you up in here for girl?" he said. I checked out the decorative Stacey Adams shoes that most of the men were wearing so proudly. Girls like Layla probably had to make a grand entrance. Every time the door opened my neck swung in its direction. A man in his late twenties, who was a dead ringer for Morris Day, moseyed over to me confidently. I stopped him dead in his tracks with my evil glare. "Damn baby, you cold as ice," he said before moseying over to the next one. Twenty minutes later I realize I'm a damn fool. Well forget her, stuck up heifer, I should have known she was gonna blow me off. I headed for the door. I saw something swinging around in the middle of the man circle. *Hair*. There's only one person I know who's blessed with hair like that. I squeezed through the men. Layla smiled wide when she saw me. "Hey girl, you came. What took you so long?" she said. I ended up having enough fun to make up for all my hamster nights. I had my first taste of alcohol, which made me loosen up. When men asked Layla to dance, she took me with her. She's used to being watched, she worked the room like Carmen Jones worked that cafeteria. Men pressed money into her palms, and they got a kiss on the cheek. All the Cindy Lou's in the room were green with envy. Some of them threw their hands in the air when she walked by. She didn't steal the spotlight, she brought it. And somehow a little of her light spilled onto me. I was important for being with her. Hours later, I asked Layla why the room wouldn't stop spinning. "Okay, the party's over!" she said. Her gigantic friend Tank threw me over his shoulder and carried me outside. He put me in the backseat of his car. Even though I'm high as a kite, or drunk as a skunk, or whatever they say, I knew without a doubt, that I had hit the friend jackpot.

"I don't get it, I'm doing everything right," Millie said. Me and Layla were hanging out in the basement with Millie. She's disappointed because nobody wants to buy her fancy beauty products.

"Well, what's the problem?" I asked.

"Okay, I spent sixty dollars to sponsor a party for the ladies to come and see all these wonderful products. Anyway, they came, ate all the food, and left without buying one darn thing," she said. When Layla looked up from the magazine. I gave her a serious if you can't say anything nice, don't say anything at all stare. Why waste my time? If she doesn't say whatever comes to her mind, her head will explode.

"Millie please, get real, who's gon' buy beauty creams and potions from a damn boogabear?" she said. I threw my hands in the air and shook my head.

"What do you suggest I do, Miss Thing?" Millie asked her.

"Yeah, *Miss Thing*, what she supposed to do?" I said. Layla's frustrated with having to school us all the time. She rolled her eyes.

"Y'all ain't never gon' get nowhere in life. It's simple, we'll come to your stupid party and tell them bitches we're twenty-five, and we use this shit. What is it, Avon or Mary Kay?"

"No, it's called Jafra cosmetics," Millie said while handing her a jar.

"See ain't nobody even heard of this shit before. And whatever you do, don't put your mug on the package," she said. No matter what

Layla says, she says it sweetly. Nobody realizes she's cutting them to a stump. Layla is a wolf in sheep's clothing. I wish I could be more like her.

Millie was skeptical about lying at first, but she couldn't afford to lose the three hundred dollars she already spent on the starter kit. On Friday, the whole place was overflowing with women from her mother's church.

"I'll take one," a woman said. Layla grabbed her hand and pressed it against her own twenty-five but still looks, and feels sixteen-year-old flawless skin."

"Make it two," she said. Man, or woman, it hardly matters, they all fall under her spell.

"Ma'am, you should try this special firming cream kit. It's only eighty dollars," Layla said.

"Eighty dollars?" the woman said. Layla put her face close to the older woman's face and shook her head in pity.

"Ma'am, if you want women like me, and Goldilocks over there to come and run off with your husband, keep on walking around looking all dry. I tried to help you," she said. I shot her a disapproving look.

"What? I'm just tellin' it like it is," she said.

"Okay I'll take it," the woman said. *I can't' believe she fell for that.* Before the ink dried on the receipt Layla was on to her next victim.

"Do you put those perms in your hair?" another desperate woman asked her. Layla wasn't prepared for any hair questions.

"Bitch, my hair was as nappy as Roberta Flack's before I started using this...scalp massage oil," she said. Oh, no, she called the Pastors wife a bitch. I got to get out of here before the gates of hell opened and swallow us whole. After all the satisfied customers were gone, we sat on the floor and counted the money.

"Wow, we made the three hundred back, plus tips," Millie said.

"Told you, you got to run a game on them ho's," Layla said. I shook my head in disappointment.

"What?" she said.

"Only you would sit here and call them nice church ladies ho's," I said.

"Please, when them bitches get down on bended knee, they're just practicing," she said. As hard as we tried not to, we fell out laughing.

Layla modeled her new clothes, paid for by numerous suckers around town. I laid across her bed, flipping through the latest issue of "Ebony" magazine. I barely looked up. I didn't need to. It didn't matter what she wore, whatever it was, she wore the hell out of it. How anybody could be a size two and still shapely at the same is beyond me. Anyway, that's dope, or fly, or bad is all she needs to hear.

"Where, I mean *who* did you get that from?" I asked when a certain outfit caught my eye. She can never remember their actual names. She snaps her fingers and says, "You know, the red Camaro?" I shake my head no. "Cheesy teeth?" I cringe and shake my head harder. "Goldie think, he's the one with the bitch butt." I don't want to laugh, but I can't help it because the image of that man's ample ass comes into my mind.

"We should be the ones in them magazines," she said.

"I guess we could be." I lied to keep the peace. In the modeling world, with these titties, I'd be too womanly, and she would be too much to deal with.

"I heard being pretty ain't enough, you have to be the right height and weight. Oh, and you have to be, what's the word, it's on the tip of my tongue?"

"You have to be photographable," she said.

Once Layla decides she wants something, she goes for it. So here I am running behind her to what she claims is a respectable modeling studio.

"Are you sure this is the place?" I said. It was a house, not a real studio. And it's in bad shape, like one step above an abandoned one.

"I don't trust this," I whispered, as we followed behind the bulky, and disheveled man who let us in.

"Right this way," he said.

"Did you tell anybody we were coming here? Why are we going to the basement? This don't seem right, it's creepy," I said.

"Would you stop complaining? All of them high-class models started out in places like this."

"Which ones?"

"Which ones what?"

"Which ones started out in the basement of some abandoned house?"

"Um, Beverly Johnson, Karen Alexander, and that white girl who did that movie where she was naked on some island, and she got fucked. What's her name?"

"How should I know? I ain't never seen any movies like that." The basement was damp, and dim like a cave. The man didn't bother to introduce himself. He grabbed the camera and pointed it at us.

"All right look happy, look sad, look sexy," he said in between the ten clicks.

"That's it?" Layla said.

"Y'all some bad mother fuckers, y'all don't need no extra shit," he said. Layla took twenty-five dollars from her purse and handed it to him.

"Pleasure doin' bit-niz with you," he said.

"When can we get the pictures?" Layla said.

"If they turn out right, I'll let you know."

Ever since I got to school this morning kids have been staring at me. Once I got in the cafeteria it got worse. Staring became whispers and then pointing and laughing. They can't touch my reputation because it's in the sky. I'm an angel, nobody has any dirt on me yet. I hurried to the bathroom to check myself out, even though it wasn't my time. Two boys were huddled together snickering about something when I came out.

"What y'all laughing for?" I said.

"We saw what you did," they said. Layla stepped into my path.

"God, what is going on today?" I said. She batted her baby doll eyes at me.

"I got something to show you, but you got to promise you won't get mad," she said.

"What is it?"

"You gon' get mad?"

"How do I know? You got to show me first." She handed me a stack of pictures. Why did she think I would get mad? Maybe because she's the "photographable" one. We took these in a dank dungeon last week. Here's one where we look happy, the next one is sad, this is supposed to be sexy. We looked stupid. By the fifth picture, my chest tightened. By the eighth, I couldn't breathe. By the tenth, I fell back onto my locker. Okay, pictures of Layla and me, spread eagle on a bed with red satin sheets are floating all around the school. Mr. ten- clicks pasted our faces to the bodies of women, who didn't mind doing some of the nastiest stuff I ever saw. My reputation is six feet under now.

"Can't people see those ain't our real bodies?" I said.

"They know," she said.

"I mean those bodies are much browner than ours. Plus, they're years older than us. I mean, it would take forever for our titties to flatten out like that. And we need to have some babies for our stomachs to get all loose and poochy and whatnot. And those stretch marks—"

"Okay Goldie, if you really think it's not us, then I believe you," she said while laughing at me.

Me and Adrian were hanging out in the school library trying to find fashion books. The selection was minimal. We found an empty table in a corner. After graduation he's running off to some fashion college in San Francisco, California. I don't know what I'm going to do without him.

"You know what they say," he said.

"No, what?"

"Birds of a feather flock together."

"That's true."

"Then why do you flock with the likes of her?"

"Here you go again."

"That's right because I love you, you're my sister girl. I'm going to look out for you, always. You understand? Layla is love with her own reflection. She will never have your back.

"Aww, I love you too Adrian, but I think you're just a tad jealous of Layla. Or maybe you're afraid she could turn you. I waited for him to stop laughing.

"I'm serious, be careful," he said.

"Of what?"

"She's using you as a sidekick."

"What's a sidekick Adrian?"

"It's like, she's Lucy, who *everybody loves*, and you're Ethel Mertz. You understand? She's the Lone Ranger, and you're Tonto. She's Batman, you're—"

"Okay, shut up boy. At least I know what *you* think of me, Adrian."

"It's not what I think, it's the role you choose to play. That girl will get you into a world of trouble if you're not careful. And besides, you're just as sexy as she is." I tilted my head and looked him dead in the eye to call his bluff.

"Your right, but you are pretty as hell, and you have a good heart," he said. He's never steered me wrong before, but he's wrong about Layla. She could be friends with anybody, and she chose me. Layla is the cure for my loneliness. Because of her, I'm somebody.

"Come to my house first thing in the morning," Layla said. She's excited because tomorrow is my birthday, but to me, it's just another day.

"You only turn sixteen once," she said.

"You turn every age once," I said.

"Dang, what a sourpuss. You better be the life of your party tomorrow night," she said and hung up. When I got to her house, Layla was bright eyed and ready for whatever the day would bring. She went over to the couch where her mother slept and shook her roughly. Evelyn would kill me if I did that.

"Girl go on and leave me alone," Miss Ann said groggily. Layla shook her again.

"What girl?!"

"It's Goldie's birthday today, say happy birthday," she said.

"Oh, happy birthday lil girl."

"Thank you, Miss Ann." Layla took some money from Miss Ann's purse and we headed for the door.

"Where y'all harlots off to so early?"

"We fixin' to go to school," Layla said.

"Mm-hmm, if y'all going to school on somebody's birthday, my name is boo-boo the fool."

"Bye-bye, boo-boo," Layla said right before she closed the door carefully. Once outside we went in opposite directions.

"Goldie, where is your ass going?" she said.

"I'm going to school, ain't you?" I said. She twisted her face like she accidentally drank some spoiled milk.

"Oh my God. Nobody ever goes to school on their birthday. Seriously, Goldie, you want to have that memory for the rest of your life?" She stopped in front of the house with the red door.

"Uh-uh, I ain't going in there," I said.

"Why not? This is my friend's house," she said.

"Layla, this is the weed house, and I'm not going in there."

"Girl, weed man is a friend of mine. Anyway, you promised to smoke some with me, last time you chickened out."

"I just don't like it, that's all."

"Goldie, it's your birthday, you're supposed to party like its nineteen-ninety-nine."

"Why, what happens in nineteen ninety-nine?"

"Girl, come on," she said pulling me closer to the house. A cock-eyed man opened the door.

"What up Lucky?" she said. He smiled wide and stepped aside dramatically.

"Get on in here girl," he said.

"Did I wake you up?"

"I don't give a damn, you look better than any dream I'm ever gon' have. What can I do for you?"

"This is Goldie, my home- girl, it's her birthday, hook us up."

"A'ight, happy birthday, how old is you baby?"

"She sweet," Layla said.

"Oh, this is a big one. Sixteen, twenty-one, and thirty, those the best birthday's you'll ever have, it's all downhill from there," he said.

"We ain't got all day Lucky," Layla said.

"Oh yeah, right. I bet y'all gon' get buck wild tonight huh?"

"Mm-hmm, something like that," she said.

"Well damn, can I come?" he said.

"Please, nigga, your ass is done seen all your best birthdays. Man, just go get the shit." He laughed like she fed him a spoon of honey instead of vinegar.

"A'ight, y'all go on in the living room, I need to run upstairs for a second," he said. We had only been sitting for a minute before I heard the familiar sound of plastic unraveling. I shot her a mean look.

"What?" she said.

"It's only eight o'clock in the morning, don't play dumb." She knows exactly what I'm talking about. Those damn hot Cheetos. I can't stand them things, but lately, she's been eating them night and day. Of all the bullshit I let her get away with, this one thing vexes me.

"Shut the fuck up Goldie, and don't worry about what I be eating," she said while tearing the bag apart at the top.

"What I eat don't make you shit okay?" she added before she

poured a bunch of them into her mouth.

"Ewe," I said but she could care less. She's just chomping and chewing.

"Oh, and soon as I get this weed, you better smoke it with me. Shit, you know how much weed cost these days?"

"I thought you said it was free."

"It is free, *chomp chew, chomp chew, swallow...*but I might still have to tongue kiss that mother-fucker," she said. She made sure she got every single crumb before folding the bag and putting it back in her purse.

"Are you serious?" I said.

"Bitch, where you been? Niggas love it when a ho ain't got their money. I hated her vernacular. I hated for anybody to call me a bitch. Layla talks like she stepped out of some Iceberg Slim book. In her world, you only fit into three categories, bitch, nigga, or ho.

"Last time I had to let that nigga suck on one of my titties," she said.

"Who sucks just one titty?"

"Lucky ain't got no two-titty weed, you got to go up on Mack Avenue to get the two-titty weed," she said in a dead serious tone.

"Is that why he's cockeyed?" I said. She tilted her head to think about it. We laughed so hard we couldn't put the brakes on. Layla started waving her hands wildly. I held my breath. *Either my mind is playing tricks on me, or Layla just threw up an entire bag of hot Cheetos all over the weed man's coffee table.*

"Oh shit, give me some tissue," she whispered. I patted myself like Bunny does when she ain't got your money. I shook my head from side to side in slow motion.

"I ain't got none," I whispered back. We heard footsteps coming down the stairs. Her eyes changed from human to wild animal. I'd never seen her like this, *she's becoming unglued.* We stared into each other's eyes like they do in those western movies. I stretched my hand out to her and whispered, "No Layla, please don't." But she was a quicker draw than I was. *Bang-Bang, she shot me down.* Her lips were already pressed against the table. *Damn.* She quickly used her coat sleeve to rid the table of any trace of the orange-red goo. Weed man was clueless as he came in the room whistling and carrying a small yellow envelope. She snatched it and pulled me out the front door.

"Thanks Lucky, we gotta go," she said.

"Why y'all leaving so soon?" he said.

"I forgot to do something for my mother!" she said. Once we got outside I couldn't stop laughing.

"I can't believe you did that, you're so nasty!"

"Whatever," she said.

"But, why did you do it? All you had to do was—"

"Look, I'm okay from here," she said.

"What do you mean? We're supposed to hang out all day until the party.

"Did you not hear me say I got something else to do?" she said as she walked away.

"You didn't mention it before. You'll be at Millie's tonight, right?" *She'll be there, she's my best friend.*

"Goldie come on, this is the second time I lit these candles!" Millie said.

"Wait a few more minutes, please," I begged.

"If we wait any longer your birthday will be over," she said. By ten o'clock I knew she wasn't coming. People eased out the door since we were out of beer and food. Most of them are only here to see her up close anyway. Millie wrapped the rest of my cake for my brothers.

A few days later, Layla had the nerve to knock on my door. I'm still mad at her. She's standing in the grass now. I never told her she couldn't come in my house, she knows from never being invited. She probably thinks our house is dirty or something, but I just don't want her to ever meet Evelyn. Especially since her mother worships the ground she walks on. One time I saw Miss Ann staring at Layla. It was obvious how much she adored her. I went into their bathroom where I flushed the toilet and ran the water, so I could cry my heart out without anyone knowing.

"What you want Layla?"

"I need my pink fingernail polish," she said. I tilted my head as if to say, *aren't you forgetting something*? She must have amnesia.

"Wait here." I knew she wanted me to admit that it was my fault that she didn't come to my party. I shouldn't have laughed at her. I handed her the nearly empty, flaky bottle.

"Next time you better close my door, lettin' out all my damn heat, stupid yellow bitch, you don't pay no bills around here!" Evelyn said before she slammed the door. Layla looked at me like we were playing one on one, and she just dunked on me.

"Damn, was that your mother?" she said.

"Who else could it be?" I said.

"So, there's a party tonight, be ready by nine o'clock. Tank is gonna take us over there," she said.

These days Layla's reputation is at less than zero. People are saying she'll do anything for a few pieces of silver. I know she loves money, but who doesn't? I don't judge her. Silk blouses, leather skirts, and gold chains cost money. Besides she's found a new hobby, riding in nice expensive sports cars "I can't be seen on foot," she says. She don't care if they come with a wife, or worse, a drug dealer. On the rare occasion that we don't have a ride, she constantly looks over her shoulder.

"Are you dodging the grim reaper?" I asked her.

"You never know," she said.

To keep from being lonely, Millie will let anybody crash at her apartment. She acts like she don't know what goes on out here when she goes to sleep.

"Don't do anything I wouldn't do," she says.

"Like she could ever do shit, fucking grizzly Adams looking bitch. She ain't never seen no part of a ding dong," Layla said. Layla had a foul mouth, why she uses a safe word for dick is beyond me.

"Unless she walked in on her daddy takin' a piss," some boy she brought with her added.

"She does have a boyfriend," I said.

"Where he been all this time?" she said.

"He lives in another town."

"Have you ever seen the nigga, in the flesh?"

"No, but I have heard them talking on the phone sometimes, I think."

"Mm-hmm, you *think*, but you ain't never seen the nigga 'cause the nigga don't exist.

"Please stop saying nigga all the time Layla. I'm not trying to be square, but it ain't ladylike to cuss all the time."

"Okay, wait a sec, I'll be right back," Layla said. She came back with the framed picture of Millie's boyfriend. She always kept it on the nightstand.

"Here, check this shit out," she said.

"Don't need to, I have seen it plenty of times already."

"Girl, you believe everything somebody tells you." She started taking the frame apart.

"Don't do that," I said. She held the picture and waved it in front of me. I couldn't ignore the finely printed words on the back of it.

"Bitch, this is Chico, from Chico and the fucking man," she said like a ghetto, Nancy Drew.

"Give it to me before you tear it," I said. I put the paper back into the frame and tiptoed into Millie's room. She was snoring like a hibernating bear. I carefully placed her dream lover back on the nightstand. I'll never tell her I know about Chico. I went back into the living room. Layla was smoking a joint with the rest of the freeloaders. So, how does one break up with a best friend?

"Come with me this last time," Layla said.

"But you said the last time would be the last time. No way, I'm not doing it again." Early this summer she begged me to go to some motel with her.

"All you got to do is sit in the corner and look delicious," she said. When we got there, a white man in his fifties opened the door. He looked like he had been boiled and needed a few minutes to cool down. He spoke like he had a mouth full of cotton. "Are you Cherry?" he said. "Mm-hmm, and this is Peaches," she said. I glued my ass to the chair in the corner. I didn't know exactly why we were here, it's clear what this man had on his mind. But would she really do it? Well, that's on her. All I got to do is look delicious, like plastic fruit. They were sitting on the bed. He poured liquor into three paper cups. A minute later "Cherry" undid some of the buttons of her hot pink silk blouse.

"Hey, why is she staring like that? She looks nervous," he said.

"Who Peaches? That's how she look every time she get close to a fine man like you," she said.

"Ah you have to wait your turn honey," he said. I felt nauseous, but I tried to keep it together. She took her panties off from under her skirt and threw them in the man's face. He sat there sniffing like a bloodhound. "You ready daddy?" 'Cherry' said. *Please don't be ready.* She got closer to him and did some sniffing of her own. She jerked her body back and covered her nose in disgust.

"What's wrong sweet cheeks?" he said.

"You smell like a fucking skunk! Come on Peaches, let's get the fuck outta here." He tried to pull her back. Uh-uh, mama can't get down like that," she snapped. He lifted his arms and sniffed each pit. He realized all the forbidden fruit was about to walk out of the room.

"It ain't that bad, but I can wash, I'll take a shower, you wait here, enjoy the gin," he said. He disappeared behind the bathroom door. Seconds later the shower turned on.

"What now Cherry?" I said. She put herself back together

minus the panties, she didn't want them anymore. She opened the bathroom door and dragged the man's plain brown pants out with her foot. She took out his wallet and peeked inside. Her face lit up.

"Bingo," she whispered.

"Did you say something sweet cheeks?" he said from behind the steamy shower curtain.

"I said if you want to taste my cherry, you better scrub your ass good!" she said.

"All right sweet cheeks, I will," the old horny man said. She grabbed me by the arm and we headed out the door. She tossed his pants, and empty wallet into the first dumpster we passed.

"No Layla, count me out this time," I said.

"Fuck it, I'll just get somebody better to do it," she said.

26
Rock Steady

"WELL, IF IT AIN'T THE ONE and only Miss Gracelyn Marie Savage," I said while walking up to Bunny. I decided to come to the arcade and see what all this "Pac man" fuss is about. The place was overrun with kids from the neighborhood. I knew I'd find her ass in here, our house is her second home. "Candy Girl" exploded out of a big speaker in the corner. She didn't answer me right away. She was in a trance, I could see the colorful ghosts running around in her eyeballs. She used every muscle in her tiny body to play the game.

"Girl, don't be saying my gov'ment name in front of my peeps." Five minutes later she said, "Anyway, you hangin' out in the cut now?"

"Something like that," I said. She kept her eyes on the prize, but when the ghost backed the "Pac man" into a corner and gobbled him up, she banged on the side of the machine.

"Oh, hell no, okay y'all asses is mine!" she said. Once the quarter went into the slot she became a zombie again. Kids stood around watching and rooting for her. I guess if I want to talk to Bunny, it will have to be at home if I ever catch her there. Her favorite game wasn't my thing. I scanned the arcade for easy games to play. I found "Centipede" and "Galaga". Next thing I knew Bunny was standing next to me. She's going to try to hit me up, I just know it. I don't want to hear it, she still owes me ten dollars.

"Hey Goldie, big sis," she said with a cigarette dangling out of her mouth. She patted her pockets and gave me the look.

"Uh-uh, no way," I said.

"Hey, don't you light that shit in here!" a short balding man yelled at her.

"Aw man, take a chill pill, I'm just holdin' it," she said.

"Anyway, you said you never lose, what happened?" I said.

"I don't ever lose, I'm tryna beat my own high score. Since none of these fools in here can beat it!" she said. A boy wearing a pistons jacket gave her a challenging look.

"I can beat it, I just don't want you jumping off the Ambassador bridge when you see my name above yours," he said. I reached into my purse and gave her a handful of quarters.

"Whoop his ass girl."

"Money talk and bullshit walk, let's rock and roll," she told the boy.

"A'ight bet that," he said popping his quarter into the slot. The game lasted for six minutes.

"Man, I can't believe you got beat by a girl," a boy said.

"You want a rematch?" she said.

"Nah man, later for you," he said.

"*Sugar's sugar, salt's salt if you didn't get off it ain't my fault!*" Bunny mocked the host from the local dance show called The Scene. It's just a poor man's Soul Train, but kids love it.

"It ain't my fault!" the other kids chimed in. On my way out, I spotted Matthew in a corner playing pool with the big boys. He's looking so good these days. Ever since I started hanging with Layla, we've drifted apart. I stood behind him and covered his eyes with my hands.

"Guess who?" I said.

"Uh, Janet Jackson?" he said. I nudged his shoulder.

"Is she who you want me to be?" I said.

"Nah, I knew it was you baby, I know your scent."

"And what scent is that?" He stared deep into my eyes without blinking.

"It's like cake," he said.

"Com' on lover boy, take your shot," his opponent told him. He called the shot and when the ball flew into the hole, he looked at me and winked. If I had been sitting on one of those stools, my ass would have hit the floor.

Beau came in and handed me one of Evelyn's notes. I realized he don't know what it says because he still can't read. Normally, on a Saturday night, I'd be out with Layla and praying to God to get us out of the trouble she liked to get us into. These notes don't scare me anymore. They certainly don't leave me drowning in tears, not like the first few times. Evelyn is a desperate woman to do something like this. I head up the steps to spend another lonely night. Once again, I thought I heard Aretha Franklin say, "*Rock steady baby!*"

I went into Evelyn's room. I hit the light switch. It flicked on, then off. The damn bulb is blown out. Thirty minutes passed and the party below me is in full swing. Evelyn's mystery man is laughing like Ricky Ricardo. I'd drop dead on the spot if one of them brought me a slice of pizza. I saw the delivery guy get back in his car and drive off twenty minutes ago. Why didn't I grab some food before I came up here? I ran my fingers over the dresser hoping to find Evelyn's cigarettes. Smoking curbs the appetite. Good, they're here, which means this one can't stand a woman who smokes. The second he's out the door she'll run in here and light two at once. It's a Newport. I prefer Salem cigarettes, the kind Millie smokes. They have a minty flavor, but these tastes like a tree stump. Most people smoke these because they're free. The green and white trucks come by and give them away all the time. There's always a mob of grown ass people, running behind the Newport truck, like kids trying to catch the ice cream man. I opened the window to blow the smoke out. I hate when the smell lingers in my hair and clothes.

"Hey girl," Matthew said from the sidewalk. I ignored him.

"I see you, put that thing out, you know you don't smoke." Still, I didn't utter a word.

"I know you see me down here, answer me."

"What do you want boy?"

"I just got paid, I want to take you to the candy shop."

"I don't want no ice cream, Matthew."

"Aw come on, a little ice cream ain't never hurt nobody," he said.

"You can't just waltz down here out of the blue, and expect me to go somewhere with somebody I ain't seen all damn week," I said. He laughed.

"Seriously, I can't go, maybe tomorrow," I said.

"Aw baby please, just for a little while." The tiny knot of balled-up paper in my pocket reminded me that I was stuck. But damn, look at him, standing under the moonlight, shining like a black diamond, and wanting me like he do.

"I'm sorry Matthew but I..." Wait, what is wrong with me? After all this time, whenever she sent a note, I stayed out of sight. I never knew what she would do if I didn't. I'm reminded of the one and only time I watched "Wild Kingdom". They were showing how they keep a nine -thousand-pound elephant from leaving a yard. While he's small they chain it to a tree or a pole or something. When he tries to break free and explore the horizon, the damn chain keeps pulling him back. So, once he is big and powerful he don't even try anymore because his will has been broken. He don't even realize the chain no longer exists. Anyway, that must be what happened to me. Oh my God, am I a fucking elephant girl? Suddenly, I felt sorry for myself. I put the cigarette out on Evelyn's floor.

"Yes, Matthew I will go with you," I said. "W*hose side are you on?*"I asked Aretha when she tried to warn me again. I skipped a few steps and stopped in the hallway to grab my pink sweater. "Who is that?" said my reason for having to hide. I felt Evelyn's evil stare burning a hole in my back. I ran my hand through my hair, and hoped she noticed my middle finger standing at attention. I ran outside where my man waited patiently.

At night, Sam's candy shop had a romantic atmosphere, with cream lighting, candy cane decorations and the heavy smell of sugar. We ordered milkshakes. Strawberry for me and vanilla for him. He offered me his cherry because he knew about my sweet tooth.

"You want it? Come get it," he said holding the stem between his teeth.

"A'ight now, you kids cut it out," the store owner said.

"It's getting late, you should walk me home now," I said. He helped me with my sweater and put his arms around me for a moment. We were quiet while he walked me home but when we reached the bottom of the steps we kissed like kisses were going out of style. I pushed him away gently and hoped he didn't get upset.

"A'ight then, I'll see you tomorrow, sweet thing," he said. A fat raindrop splashed on my forehead. He dried the drop with another kiss.

"You better hurry home before it starts," I said. I went inside, kicked off my shoes, and hung up my sweater. It was pleasantly quiet; the kids were in bed and the lights were low. I walked into the kitchen and reached into the top cabinet for a water glass. The glass fell into the sink and broke when I felt a sharp pain in my head. I collapsed onto the floor and crawled away while using my hand as a shield from the two by four. It feels like my pinky is broken. Evelyn made animal like grunts every time she brought the board down on me. I reached for the doorknob and ran outside.

The rain was in full force now. I ran to Millie's building and rang the bell frantically until I realized her car wasn't parked in front. I stepped back on the sidewalk. Her lights were off too. I didn't want her parents to see me like this, they're too old for this shit. I took off running until I reached Matthew's house. I knocked hard until his older sister answered the door. "Matt, your girlfriend is down here," she said without taking her eyes off me.

Matthew's got a big family, the kind I grew up in. They were all at home right now, probably because of the rain. I waited in the hallway, they were watching the movie "Sparkle". How many times have they seen it already? I have seen it three times. This is the part where the good-looking sister, whose name is also Sister, sits in the dressing room with a hundred black eyes. She tells her mother that her criminal boyfriend Satin is as big time as she could get. This part reminds me of Layla. I'm soaking wet, my hair pink with blood and rain and my feet are bare. They continued to watch the movie. No one stared at me or asked me a million fucking questions. They acted like nothing was out of the ordinary. I loved them for that. When Matthew saw me, he seemed confused. How could he not be? Twenty minutes ago, we were standing under the moonlight, falling deep in love.

"Baby, what happened?" he said.

"Yeah baby, what happened?" Matthew's adorable six-year-old nephew echoed from behind the coat-rack.

"Boy go in the room with your mama. Let's go upstairs," he said while taking me by the hand. He helped me out of my wet clothes and gave me some of his. I followed him into the bathroom where he helped me rinse the blood out of my hair.

"Ouch, that hurts."

"Am I too rough?"

"No, the water stings."

"Let me see." He tried as gently as he could to find out where the blood was coming from.

"Damn," he said.

"Is it bad?"

"You don't need stitches, but you might have a scar."

"Well, it can keep the others company. I put my hand on my head before she cracked it open, see," I said. My hand was black and blue. We went back to his room and sat on his bed.

"She only does this to you because she knows you won't fight back. She's a bully, I know she's your mother, but once you stand your ground, she'll back off," he said.

"That only works in the real world, not in mine."

"Why do you say that?"

"If I fight her, she'll make things bad for me."

"Not if you're nowhere near her. You know I'm enlisting. Just come with me."

"I should go back now."

"Stay here tonight," he said pulling me into him. We fell asleep holding on to each other. Matthew started kissing me in the middle of the night. Tender kisses turned passionate, and then too passionate for me. He pressed his hard body against my softness. I wanted to push him, but if I pushed too hard, he might fall off the twin bed.

"Please, stop Matthew," I told him.

"But we need each other, this is our time, I love you, I won't hurt you." Damn, I hated myself for saying no after that. When the morning sunlight flooded the room, I eased out of the bed. I slipped into a pair of Matthew's sneakers. I tiptoed down the steps and out of the door quietly without being seen.

Eventually, I lost Matthew for good, to a girl named Justine. She was always lurking around every corner. Just waiting and willing to do all the stuff I wouldn't do with him. Bunny said that Fredrick told her that Matthew finally joined the army. Now Justine's sneaky ass is having his baby in the spring.

"He gon' send for her as soon as he gets situated, and then they supposed to get married," Bunny said.

"Damn Bunny, I don't need to know every fucking detail, it's not like I care anyway," I lied.

"Okay, whatever. I'm just saying, I don't know why he picked her over you. You're like, way prettier than her. No offense Goldie, but you need to learn how to hold on to your man," said my tiny sister.

27

Every Man's Dream

"IS THAT SUPPOSED TO SCARE ME? Shit, we still got sixty days, maybe more," Evelyn said after I handed her the eviction notice. After about six months, the landlord realized he was never going to get the rent, no matter what excuses she gave him. We moved into a small one-story house in Southwest Detroit. Its main feature is the gaping hole in the dining room floor. None of that matters to me now. I don't live there anymore. One-night Evelyn came home with yet another broken heart. She galloped straight to the kitchen and came out with a knife in her hand.

"Get out!" she said like a crazed demon. We always kept our shoes on because it was early November. The frozen dirt under the house made the floor abnormally cold. My coat was draped over a chair. I would have grabbed it, but she saw what I was thinking.

"She did what?! And you ain't got on no coat?! Wait right there, I'm coming to get you," Millie said. I stood in front of the closed corner store and waited. Twenty minutes later a strange car pulled up in front of me. I was relieved to see Millie in the passenger seat.

"Hurry up, get in! Here put this on," she said while tossing one of her oversized jackets into the back seat.

"Can I stay at your house tonight?" I said.

"Tonight? No, you're staying with us from now on. But first, I'm going to put my foot in her ass," she said before she wriggled herself out of the car.

"Which house is it?" she said. I folded my arms and looked the other way.

"Fine, if you don't want to tell me, I'll knock on all these doors until her ass opens one up." The car rocked when she got out.

"Damn, she pissed off now," the driver said.

"Who are you?" I said.

"I'm Millie's cousin."

"Well can't you stop her?"

"Shit, I ain't tryna stop no bull. Now if I had a box of Twinkies or a slab of baby back ribs, then maybe, know what I mean?" he said. Hmm, he's right. I got out of the car in time to stop her from banging on the Garcia family's door.

"That's not it. Millie, just stop. Anyway, I'm okay now."

"What if I didn't answer the phone? You could have froze to death, you might still catch pneumonia. Fuck no, she ain't getting away with this, not this time!" she said. She opened the gate to Mr. Herrera's house. The idea of Evelyn getting a good old-fashioned ass-kicking, made my mouth water. I just didn't want Millie to be the one to try to do it. Honestly, I know she can't beat Evelyn. Millie's a big girl, but she's probably never had a fight in her life. Even if she could beat her, Evelyn would want revenge. And I know what she's capable of. We were standing next door from our house. I cried louder to distract her.

"Millie please, let's go," I begged. She stood unknowingly in front of our house. I saw the curtains move. I stomped my foot.

"Damn it, Millie get your ass in this car!" I said. When the car took off, she twisted her body and leaned out of the window.

"Don't let me catch you on the east-side, fucking psycho bitch! I'm sorry Goldie that just slipped out," she said.

"No, go ahead, express yourself," I said.

"Why do I have to be here in this basement, why can't I stay upstairs with you?" I asked Millie.

"Because I got to work, I can't watch you all the time."

"Since when does anybody have to watch me?"

"Since we became responsible for you." I looked around the room, it was as big as a single apartment, but it didn't have a ceiling. Basically, it's a vacant storage room.

"You'll be living with mommy and daddy, but this will be your room."

"What about that?" I said pointing to the missing ceiling.

"Girl, ain't nobody going to try to climb over this wall to get to you, just to get clobbered over the head by me," she said.

When word got out about the storage room, all the kids came here to chill without their mama's breathing down their necks. Some nights, we played "Why have I lost you?" by Cameo over and over. We would belt out the hook at the top of our lungs. Millie's parents don't care how much noise we make, all they expect me to do is go to school every day. Eventually, Millie's mom went downtown and signed a petition to become my legal guardian. Evelyn didn't come to court to protest. As far as she was concerned, anybody could have me. Believe me, I don't want her ass either, but my brothers need me. Not being there to protect them is killing me.

After a while, I stopped locking the storage room door. I know how it feels to be out on the street with no place to go. Bunny started coming over to be closer to the arcade and Fredrick. Speaking of Fredrick, that kid didn't have the decency not to rub Matthew and Justine's endless love in my face.

"Hey, where your girl been hiding these days?" That's the million-dollar question.

"Beats me," I say. Some kids told stories about her as if she were a phantom or something. They said they saw her riding in a Maserati, snorting white powder at a party at or turning tricks in the alley. I never believe their lies. She would have to be an octopus to do all that shit. Anyway. I got a true story about the last time I saw her. We were walking through a vacant lot and she told me to hurry up because she couldn't be seen on foot.

"So ain't you going to say nothing?" she said.

"About what?" I said.

"You are so full of shit Goldie," she said. She stood in front of me, hand on hip. I started at the top of her head.

"Honestly, I don't know what's different, you look the same to me," I said.

"I look the same?" Suddenly, I felt like a kid talking myself out of an ass whooping.

"No, I mean you look perfect in the same way." She shoved her purse in my face.

"This is a fucking Louie Vuitton! It cost over four hundred dollars. Do you know how many pickles I had to suck to get this purse? And you don't even say shit about it. I thought you was my homegirl, but you're just another jealous bitch!"

"Wait, you sucked some *pickles*?" I whispered. She stretched her eyes wide.

"Well, let me see it," I said.

"What for?"

"Please, I won't hurt it." She reluctantly handed it over. I unzipped it and checked the inside.

"What's so damn funny?" she said.

"I can't tell you."

"Just fucking say it!" she said.

"Okay, you played yourself."

"I what?!"

"It's fake Layla."

"How the hell would you know?"

"Adrian taught me how to tell. See, it says made in Honolulu."

"Who gives a shit?"

"I don't, but you should. Girl, they don't make no Louis Vuitton in Honolulu. It should say made in France." She flipped her hair and walked away.

"Do you even care what people say about you?" I said. She came back and got all up in my face.

"No, I don't give a flying fuck because I'm every man's dream!"

"So how come every man treats you like a ho?"

"I don't even know why I ever bothered with you at all. You ain't even on my level. Your own mama don't even love you," she said. A ton of bricks fell on my head, angry tears filled my eyes.

"Why didn't you come to my birthday party?!" She didn't have an answer, just a smirk.

"Okay, but know that one day when I'm old and gray, I'll think of my sweet sixteen, and you'll be there slurping up your own vomit. Yum-yum." She slapped me and turned her back. I yanked the back of her coat and we fell and wrestled in the snow. I sat on top of her with my fist in the air, ready to strike. She closed her eyes tight turning her head to the side.

"Don't mess up my face!" she said. I didn't want to mess up her face, but I owed her one. After that, I let her up. We brushed ourselves off. Adrian was right all she ever wanted was a sidekick. I miss him like crazy.

"All right, good-bye Layla."

"See you later Goldie."

"Girl, kiss my black ass," I said.

28

Ain't Nothin' Like Family

"HEY BUNNY, WHAT'S UP?" I said cheerfully.

"Oh, nothin' much, I just called," she said. I always knew when something bothered her. Besides, she never just called.

"What's wrong?"

"Um, can you come home?"

"I'm already at home Bunny."

"No, for real you got to come home. Mama's boyfriend is over here acting crazy. He tried to kill her, and she ran outside with no shoes on, and now she got frostbite." I want to say I don't give a flying fuck about Evelyn's toes.

"Are the kids okay?" I said.

"They're okay for now, but he said he gon' come back and shoot her." I called my friend Vincent who I met at the mall. He said he didn't mind taking me over there. Evelyn sat in a chair and her feet were all fucked up, just like Bunny said. Freezing cold air came out of our mouths when we talked. I looked toward the dining area. The hole in the floor was still covered with the same thick rug.

"Why is it so cold in here, and where is Beau?" I said.

"Jerome had the gas turned off 'cause it was in his name. Beau is probably gon' spend the night at his friend's house," Evelyn said.

"Keep your coats on and stay under the blankets," I told the boys.

"But we still too cold," Joshua said.

"I know, we'll get some heaters tomorrow," I said. I gave them each an ice-cold kiss. Me, Vincent, and Bunny were huddled in the same bed. Vincent's popsicle was pressed against my butt. It's too cold to move, but tomorrow, I'm going to cuss his ass out good.

"Y'all wake up, he in the house," Evelyn whispered in my ear.

"Who's in the house?"

"Jerome, he climbed through my window, he got a gun." I shook Vincent and Bunny. Only Vincent woke up.

"What's the matter?" he said.

"That guy broke in here," I said. He tossed the covers and coats aside and sprinted into the living room. I followed close behind him. Evelyn was in the closet shaking like a leaf. He was hard to find in the dark until his breath gave him away. Vincent grabbed him from behind. I saw their shadows tussling. The light came on, Bunny stood there wide-eyed. She was scared. The sight of the man startled me, with his oily skin and finger in a light socket hairstyle. I don't want this maniac around my brothers. He wrestled his way out of Vincent's grip and pointed a gun directly at his chest.

"Don't' you ever put your hands on me, I'll fuckin' kill yo' ass boy!" said the deranged man.

"No don't shoot him! Put that gun down!" we screamed. Without warning, he put his wild head on Vincent's shoulder and sobbed all over him. Vincent looked at me and moved his lips.

"*What the fuck is he doing?*" I shrugged and moved my lips back at him.

"*I don't know, get the gun, the gun.*" Evelyn limped in and stood behind us. The deranged man took one look at her and screamed like he saw Lucifer in the flesh. He shook his finger at her wildly. Man, you just don't know, she just, she, she won't stop, she keep messin' with my..." He kept hitting himself on the side of his head like he needed to shake some shit loose. *I knew exactly what he was trying to say.*

"Aw Jerome, I said I'm sorry, damn," Evelyn said. Vincent took the gun from him like candy from a sleeping baby. They nauseated me, turning off the gas, bringing guns into the house around the children. I can't leave them with her for a second, let alone for all these months, what if we hadn't been here?

The next morning Evelyn's deranged and poor excuse for a man, had the gas turned back on. I stayed with them all weekend. I stayed all day on Monday too. I went through the house looking for my Singer. It sat in a corner of the back room, broken.

"Evelyn, what happened to my sewing machine?!"

"How am I supposed to know?"

"I left it in perfect working condition."

"Girl I know you ain't tryna say I broke it, I know how much that thing mean to you. I can't speak for the kids though, they was probably back there playing with it."

"But you're supposed to tell them not to mess with it, how else would they know it's not a toy? Honestly, they could have lost a finger or something."

"Well it's done now, ain't no sense in crying over spilled milk, you can get another one. That guy you brought here Friday, he work somewhere?" she said.

"What's the use, you don't get it?" I mumbled.

Millie's mom called me Tuesday afternoon. I already knew what she was going to say.

"I know you want to spend time with your family, but you can't live here and there too. We were worried sick about you, we're too old for this," she said. She could have called me all kinds of things, like ungrateful, disrespectful. I deserved it.

"Yes ma'am I understand. I'll be home soon."

"Home? What the hell she talkin' about? You already home!" Evelyn said. I tried to cover the mouthpiece. Millie's mom spoke in my right ear while Evelyn put a bug in my left.

"You ain't got to sit here and beg nobody for no place to stay. To hell with them. Got you living in a damn storage compartment, actin' like they doin' you a favor. See, that's why I always tell y'all ain't nothin' like family. Is it Jerome?"

"Hell naw girl," he said.

"I can't believe you're going back," Millie said. Vincent and Bunny helped me carry my boxes out to his car.

"Millie, you know I love you and your parents, and I appreciate you looking out for me, but I have to be there for the boys."

"Well, what are you going to do the next time she decides to put you out in the cold?"

"I don't know."

"Please don't call me," she said. I knew she didn't mean it.

"You shouldn't say things you don't mean Millie. Please, just wish me well."

"I do, you know I do." We hugged tightly before I slid in the front seat of Vincent's car.

"Damn, Millie is ugly as hell," Bunny said. Millie isn't one of my sister's favorite people. Evelyn's enemies, outside of family are hers too, no questions asked.

"True beauty comes from the inside Bunny," I said.

"Beauty don't come from no damn inside, do it Vincent?"

"Nah, beauty make you want to feel a woman's insides."

"*Okay,*" Bunny said while reaching over the back seat to give Vincent a slight nudge on his shoulder.

"Y'all are sick," I said. I watched Millie from the side view mirror. She waved goodbye. I stuck my arm out of the window and waved back.

"What is that smell?" I said.

"What smell?" they said.

"Something's burning."

"I don't smell nothing," Vincent said. Suddenly my chest tightened. I could barely breathe.

"No, wait, something *is* burning!" I said.

"Aw Goldie, calm down, it's just another bridge. Ain't you used to that smell by now?" I thought I heard Bunny say. I peered back at her.

"What did you say?"

"I didn't say nothin', what's wrong wit'choo?" A million-dollar question that I don't have an answer to. Would somebody please tell me what in the fucking world is wrong with me?

29
Flight

"GOD MIGHT NOT BE a faggot after all," Evelyn said. We were sitting at the kitchen table, she held one piece of mail aside from the rest. *No, nothing she says shocks me anymore.*

"So, what made you change your mind?" I said.

"Don't get all excited, I said he *might* not be, I'm still not totally convinced. Anyway, about a month ago, I saw a commercial saying they help single mothers get a house of their own. I called the number, some lady told me I needed to bring a hundred dollars for some orientation fee. After I slammed the phone in her face, I turned around and fell through that big ass hole in the floor. I thought it was a sign. So, I got a money order and took it downtown to Woodward Avenue."

"That's good Evelyn," I said sincerely. She pushed the envelope toward me.

"This came in the mail today. I'm scared to open it. Here, you read it for me." I took the letter and opened it carefully.

"Okay, it says congratulations." She starts celebrating by screaming and jumping around before I finished. I continued to read the letter to myself.

"What else it say?" I hesitated to rain on her parade, but she's anxious to hear the rest of it.

"It says you have successfully met the criteria and you are indeed qualified for the housing program."

"Yes!"

"But, there's more."

"Well, what else?"

"It says you need a five hundred dollar down payment by the first of the month. And then you can move into the home of your choice."

"Ooh, them sneaky sons a bitches! I knew it. This ain't nothin' but a scam. They ain't say shit about no five hundred dollars at that orientation. They know damn well ain't nobody got that kind of fuckin' money just layin' around. Now they gon' keep the hundred dollars I already gave their scammin' asses."

"I don't think it's a scam Evelyn."

"How do you know it ain't?"

"I don't, but I guess it's the same way people got to pay to go to college, maybe it's just how things work."

"Well, how am I supposed to get that kind of money in thirty damn days?"

Thirty days later we loaded everything in a U-Haul. *How in the world did she get that money?* Before she started the truck, Evelyn started crying her heart out.

"What is you blubbering for woman?" Bunny said playfully.

"Wait until y'all see this house, I ain't never lived nowhere this good. Now I ain't got to worry about getting evicted 'cause they go by your income. So, if I ain't got shit, they don't get shit," she said. She pulled up in front of a house that had brand new light blue aluminum siding, and neat white shutters surrounding the windows.

"And there's four nice size bedrooms, a fenced in yard, and a finished basement," Evelyn said proudly. Our feet sank into the deep light blue carpeting. Every window had clean white Venetian blinds. There were no holes in the floor, and nothing needed to be fixed. Evelyn stood in the middle of the family room eyeballing everything. We only brought a few small boxes and a couple of plastic bags inside. Finally, Evelyn told me and Bunny to get back into the truck. She drove us around for a while before pulling alongside a huge vacant lot.

"Throw all this raggedy ass shit out," she said.

"God bless the child that's got his own," she said. The icing on the cake is that the neighbors are white and as pure as the driven snow. She believes that white equals peace and prosperity. Anyway, we stick out like sore thumbs around here. And none of the white kids want to rub elbows with us. But as far as Evelyn is concerned, we done moved on up like the Jefferson's.

Evelyn spent a lot of money and countless hours making sure that every piece of furniture, and every picture on the walls fit perfectly. But most of the time she sits on our enclosed porch. She glares out onto the street, puffing dramatically on a Newport one hundred, mumbling like Ebenezer Scrooge. That's because the private moving trucks come and take away her precious white families like thieves in the night.

"Just wait and see, I bet you their asses is black," she says every time she spots another U-Haul truck bouncing down our street like the Soul Train.

"Well you still got them white people next door," I said. She looks even more disgusted. That's because they're the only ones she hated because the mother is a hell-raiser. Sometimes, without warning, she'll stand back on her porch and give us a piece of her mind. "I'll be damned if I let a bunch of no good niggers run me out of my house!" We don't care, we know she's confused since nobody's trying to run her anywhere. "I ain't scared of nary a one of you black niggers!" She's around Evelyn's age, but she sounds horrible, like Granny from the Beverly Hill Billie's.

It was a hot June night. Inside the house felt like a sauna, so I went out and sat on the steps with Evelyn and Bunny. Tension filled the air when Granny pulled up in her brand-new black Saab. We knew she was going to start some shit. Although there was enough space for two and a half cars, she just couldn't calculate it. Evelyn had recently bought her first car, a black Delta eighty-eight that was born in 1972. We tried not to ever let her catch us making fun of it. She's proud of it. Anyway, Granny backed into Evelyn's delta, not once or twice, but four times. We watched the unstable woman with confused expressions. "You better watch whose car you backin' into!" Evelyn said. The car door opened, and stayed open for five minutes before she stumbled out. She stood three feet away from us, her face twisted.

"What did you say?" she said.

"I said you hit my car, you need to learn how to park," Evelyn said. Granny laughed like she heard a real gut busting joke. Then she turned her laughter off like a faucet.

"No-buddy cares about your old nigger car," she said.

"Who you talking to, you drunk white trash, raggedy house havin' bitch," Evelyn said way too slow. Oh shit, she's as high as Granny is. Five minutes later, they were still hurling liquor laced insults at each other. Neither of them were in any condition to back their threats up.

"Oh puh-leeze, I'll fuck your pasty ass up!" Evelyn said.

"Try it, and I'll sweep my floors with your nappy head!" she said before she laughed proudly. One of her three sons came out and stood back on their front porch.

"Ever'thang okay here Momma?" he said. He's a sturdy boy around twenty or so. He has a head full of thick flaming red hair. They all do. His name is Bubba. I know because one time him and the other two pulled up with a dead deer in the back of their truck, and Granny here said, "Damn Bubba, that's one big S-O-B!" His brother helped him get the animal on his back. He carried it like it only weighed twenty pounds. And the other one hopped out of their Silverado and said, "All right, let's get to guttin' boy." Hell, I been Texas Chainsaw Massacre scared of them ever since.

"No, everything is not o-fucking-kay!" she said. Bubba looked like he's been waiting for the day that he would have to straighten out the darkies.

"Wusta matter Momma?" he said.

"Yeah, so I get off work, something these porch monkeys know absolutely nothing about..." She stopped mid-sentence and punched her chest until she produced a solid belch.

"And um, this uneducated nigger accuses me of hitting her car. I told her no-buddy cares about this piece of shit car!" she said while kicking the poor Delta. It surprised me to see the woman still standing. Evelyn was paralyzed. I know why. Granny don't fight fair, throwing nigger around was like throwing sand in Evelyn's eyes.

"They put your welfare papers in my mailbox nig–" I used all my strength to slap the delicious taste of the word nigger out of her mouth. Now she's crawling around in the grass. She wants to scream, but it's stuck in her throat. Oh, shit, Bubba was coming toward me like Flash Gordon. I started moon-walking, but I didn't get very far. I turned and ran smack dab into the chest of a tall handsome guy, whose hair was in long braids. He was dark and the whites of his eyes and teeth sparkled. He smelled like a fresh shower topped off with Old Spice. I kept my face buried in his chest for a second before he grabbed my arm. He swung me aside as if I were light as a feather, all while keeping his eyes on Bubba. "What's on your mind boy?" he asked Bubba. There were about twenty people standing behind him. *Damn, where did they come from?*

Granny managed to stand up. She came toward us like she was walking on a tightrope. The crowd didn't scare her for a second. "All right, which one of you filthy black bitches hit me? Bubba don't stand there and let these niggers attack me, go in the house and call 911!" she howled. Bubba didn't bother with calling 911. He took a deep breath and coaxed his intoxicated mother toward their house.

"C'mon Momma let's go," he said.

"I got gasoline in my garage. I'm gon' to burn your house to the ground nigger bitch!" she said.

"Oh, hush Momma, you cause trouble ever' where we go," Bubba said. Damn, it seems I have something in common with a red-headed deer hunter.

Until tonight we didn't know any of our neighbors. Some said the slap brought them out onto the street. The neighbors went to their homes and returned with a variety of food and drink. We had a spontaneous block party in our backyard. Good music blasted from a loudspeaker. I bumped into Evelyn, she had sobered up and was having a good time.

"Wow Goldie, girl you slapped the stew out of that heifer. I never thought you would defend me," she said.

"Well you know what they say, ain't nothin' like family." This would be the perfect time for her to hug me. And maybe tomorrow we could go shopping, or to the beauty shop, or—"

"Oh shit, there go Cecil, with his fine ass, girl let me go mark my territory," she said before she sashayed over to our next-door neighbor. I should follow suit and go mark some territory of my own. I scanned the yard. My dream lover was nowhere in sight.

People love to tell stories. They say Granny couldn't live with niggers, but she was too stubborn and too full of pride to let niggers run her out. So, the four of them committed suicide inside the house. It sits far back from the street, and the yard is in front instead of the back. Now it looks like an old gray oil painting. One thing for sure is no one has seen nor heard from them since the fight. Common sense should tell them they took flight because the Saab, and the pickup truck are gone. But, everybody prefers the ridiculous suicide story. Nobody would dare go near the house now. People give directions by it. "You go three doors down from them dead white people's house." And when little kids start acting up, their mothers say, "All right, keep it up, I'm gon' leave you in them dead white people's house." It works like a charm.

"Girl I could really use some help with my mortgage this month, I can't hardly make ends meet. You and Bernard want to buy some food stamps?" Evelyn asked her friend Ava, who lives across the street. She never visits without a six-pack of Stroh's beer.

"Well you got to do what you got to do these days, but I get 'em from Wayne, he on that stuff, he damn near give 'em away," she said. She popped the top on beer number one and handed it to Evelyn. Carla's a hard-looking woman.

"I'm grateful for food stamps, even if I do have to sell 'em every now and then," Evelyn said.

"Mm-hmm I know you is, with all these crumb snatchers you got," she said.

"Shit, if it wasn't for Jimmy Carter, we would've starved to death," Evelyn said. *Evelyn worships the ground Jimmy Carter walks on.* She thinks he invented a big metal food stamp machine in the basement of the damn White House. And he stays up all night, cranking out food stamps, and personally hand painting the colors on each one of them, or something like that.

"If I ever catch that asshole who shot Reagan back in eighty-one, I'm gon' knock his ass upside the head," Evelyn said.

"Why, you got a thang for Reagan too?"

"No, because he had the chance of a lifetime and he fucked it up," she said, and they laughed.

"You want to see what starving is all about, go to Aliceville, Alabama where I'm from. At least here you can hustle, or get a job, or social security or assistance." She's on beer number three and Evelyn is still nursing number one. Evelyn never cared for beer, she can't stand the bloat that comes with it. Carla don't mind looking like a damn blowfish.

"If you ask me, Detroit ain't all it's cracked up to be," Evelyn said.

"Yeah well, the Mayor ain't nothin' but a crook, robbing this city blind," Carla said.

"Girl, I can't stand that shifty-eyed nigger. I should write Jimmy Carter about his ass."

"Mm-hmm," Carla said as she popped the top on her third beer. It's easy to tell what number she's on because she always crushes the can afterward, like a man.

"I got to find me another husband, a rich one this time," Evelyn said.

"Please, ain't nobody fixin' to marry no woman your age, 'specially after you been stretched out six times."

"Who you callin' stretched out?" I couldn't hold my laughter in after hearing that.

"And what you laughin' at?" Evelyn asked me.

"Gimme a break is on," I said.

"Anyway, how you s'possed to find a man wit' all these young fast tail heifers runnin' around here, spreadin' them legs for every Tom, Dick, and Dick," Carla said.

"You said Dick twice," Evelyn said.

"Did I? Well, you know what I'm tryna say," she said. I laid on the floor in front of the TV. I felt Carla's intoxicated eyes glued to my bare thighs. I turned my behind in their direction and hoped they got the message. Okay, now I'm laughing at Nell for real. She accidentally dumped a whole box of cleanser in the fish-tank. Poor fish.

"Girl you be better off finding you a little boy toy, or one of them married men to help you out."

"You mean somebody like Bernard?" Evelyn said.

"Yeah, like Bernard," she said. I glance over my shoulder in time to catch her putting the fourth can on the table. She ain't as stupid as I thought. She realizes she should slow down, or shut the fuck up. I pictured her catching Evelyn in bed with Bernard. Evelyn would say "See, I'm not all *stretched out*, am I Bernard?" Bunny came upstairs, and Carla got fidgety

"Damn, you still here? Ain't them your babies crying? You need to go home and change them diapers, I can smell them from way over there. Unless that's you," Bunny said. I'm sure Carla wanted nothing more than to give Bunny a good old- fashioned Alabama ass whooping, but she's outnumbered.

"Girl you gon' let her talk to me like that?" she said.

"Bunny don't talk to her like that. Anyway, I got to get ready for my date," Evelyn said while nodding toward the exit. Carla gathered her crushed cans and walked out.

"I don't even know why you friends with her," Bunny said. Evelyn grinned mischievously.

"Uh-uh, Mama what you up to?" Bunny asked her. She looked around like somebody might be spying on us.

"Her and her old man on social security."

"And?" Bunny said.

"And that's all I'm gon' say," Evelyn said.

On the 1st of July, Evelyn sat on the enclosed front porch with a cup of coffee and a cigarette. She got Beau sitting outside on the steps.

"Hurry up, don't let nobody see you," she told him after the mailman stuffed envelopes into Carla and Bernard's mailbox.

"Yes! Jackpot," she said when she found what she needed. She's dead wrong for that. Taking food out of those babies' mouths. People say Carla and Bernard will go around begging after their money is spent on alcohol. People give because they can't stand to see kids go hungry.

On Independence Day, Evelyn sponsored a neighborhood cookout. She put a big sign out front that said "Come one! Come all!" And they did. She splurged on cases of ribs, wine coolers, and beer. Carla wandered around the yard looking sad, and sober for once.

"What, somebody stole y'all checks? Girl it's a damn shame, this neighborhood is in decline. I don't trust none of these Negroes 'round here. You want a hot dog?" Evelyn said.

"No, I'll take a couple of them beers though," Carla said.

30

Here Comes Honeybaby

"MAN, SOMEBODY'S GONNA smoke that girl one day."

"What the hell is wrong with her?"

"No fuckin' home training." Those are the questions asked and things often said behind Honeybaby's back. She's a scrawny, bug-eyed, thirteen-year-old who lives one over. Somehow, she always seems to know what's happening on our street, and many others too. We call her the town crier because she's a living ghetto news bulletin. No one is safe from her. "Shit, here she come, she comin' right now!" people say when she's spotted at the top of the street. Some people want to hear her dish the dirt. But most are on edge. Just when they think their secrets are dead and buried, Honeybaby comes swinging a big ass shovel.

"Ooh, I saw Pastor McDuffie rocking his Cadillac with Mimi the prostitute last night! Shame, shame on you sir! All Sharon's kids got different daddies! Poor Miss Frankie, work all day while your man and your daughter be taking care of some business of they own! Mimi the prostitute got the HIV! If you ain't know, you know now!" That's what she says once her job is done.

"But, what the hell does she get out of it?" people ask. "She's a menace, a damn troublemaker," they say. She disappears around the corner leaving tension in the air. Some people try to deny Honeybaby's rantings.

"That little bitch is lying, straight up," they say. But I say she never lies. Mimi, who has been known to turn a trick or two, did disappear after a few guys got tested for HIV. One-day Miss Frankie came home early from work, and her daughter and her man ran out of the house butt naked. Miss Frankie put on quite a show when she threw all their shit out of the window. But, Sharon's eight kids having different daddies is hardly news. That bit of information applies to half the neighborhood.

"I saw her when we was riding down West Euclid about forty-five minutes ago," Phillyboy said.

"Uh-uh, I seen her down the street from my cousin's girlfriend's house off Seven Mile," Rasheed said. Obviously, she can't be in both places at once, but they swear on all they love, that it was her.

"So, what did she have on?" I said.

"A red and white striped shirt and blue jean shorts!" they said.

"Man, how she do that Houdini shit?" Phillyboy said.

Honeybaby sure ain't scared of a living soul. She will take on a whole family, and leave them all shaking in their boots. Just the other day, Mr. Jenkins took it upon himself to take a belt to her behind. *Damn*, he shouldn't have done that. Now he's where nobody ever wants to be, on Honeybaby's shit list. So here we are helplessly watching her with horrified expressions. She pulled out two cans of spray paint like they were pistols, fully loaded, with bright yellow and green bullets. She proceeded to shoot the shit out of his flawless candy apple red, 1985 Cadillac Eldorado.

"Man, that's a damn shame, Mr. Jenkins worked his old ass off to get that new car," Phillyboy said. Yes, we wanted to stop her, but the consequences would far outweigh our good deed. Mr. Jenkins looked out of his front window in time to catch her in the act. He came running outside and fell on his knees like somebody died on his lawn.

"Lord have mercy. Little girl is you done lost your mind?" he cried.

"Forget you, Mr. Jenkins, you started it!" she said. Poor Mr. Jenkins, he's over sixty, but that won't stop her from executing the big payback every chance she gets. He might as well call Harriet Tubman, go deep underground, and pray that she never picks up his scent.

"Hey, anybody seen that fuckin' Honeybaby? If you do, tell her I'm looking for her," Beau tells everybody he runs into. We stop and stare at him like he's E. F Hutton.

"Man, who in they right mind go looking for Honeybaby?" *Inquiring minds want to know.* Beau don't care about that girl one way or the other. Evelyn told him to find her and beat the black off her ass. He'll do anything for his mama.

"Why, what did she do?" I asked Evelyn.

"That boney bitch is out there lyin' on me, sayin' Miss Evelyn be stealin' checks from people's mailboxes. *If you ain't know, you know now,*" she whined, mimicking Honeybaby's famous line. It's funny because Evelyn always got a kick out of Honeybaby. She said the little girl reminded her of herself at that age. She would sit on the porch watching her terrorize the neighborhood.

"A'ight now lil' mama, talk your shit!" she always said. Once Honeybaby threw a brick at Evelyn's bedroom window and broke it. She was after Bunny that day. Anyway, Evelyn got the window fixed, and Honeybaby got a bigger brick for it. Now her room don't get any natural sunlight because that's the way that girl wants it. But even after all that, Evelyn still admired her. She would always stick up for her saying she wasn't all bad, she's just misunderstood and whatnot. But as far as Evelyn is concerned, she crossed the line with this stolen check thing.

"Thatlittlebitchdon'tknowwhoshefuckin'with!" Evelyn said.

"Well good luck finding her. She's probably in a tree or sitting on a rooftop, looking at you, looking for her," Phillyboy said.

"Goldie come to this house party with me tonight," Bunny said.

"No thanks."

"Why not?"

"Too many bad memories."

"Dang, you 'bout to be eighteen, but all you do is sit in the house, reading "Flowers in the attic" and shit. I laughed at her.

"I've only read it once."

"Well, that's still too many times. Or you always sitting around worrying about Mama's kids," she said.

"Bunny, I'm surprised to hear you say something like that."

"Why? I mean, I love Mama, I love my baby brothers, but them is her kids, not ours. Shit, I'm young and beautiful," she said playfully.

"Well, go be young and beautiful Bunny. I'm still not going to any fucking house parties."

"Girl, you need to let that shit go," she said. By that shit, she means the last time I went to a house party. We were having a good time until some guys rode by and shot at us for no reason. We ran for cover. When the bullets stopped flying, a nine-year-old boy lost his life. He didn't even bother to tell anybody he had been hit. He went into the basement to die in peace. When his mother found him, she sat in the corner and rocked him for hours she wouldn't even let the paramedics near him. I'll never really get over it.

"I touched a dead body before," Bunny said.

"You're lying."

"Please girl, I seen people get beat down, shot. I been shot at before too."

"When?"

"So, one night me and Fredrick was at White Castle. They just closed the inside, so we had to stand in the line outside the window. Anyway, some man got in line behind us, and he was like, "Kent State? Mother-fucker you must be out of your damn mind!" Fredrick had on a jacket that had Kent State on the back. Make it so bad, it was some old fart you wouldn't even expect to be startin' no shit. I told Fredrick to chill 'cause he wanted to whoop his ass for real.

Girl, we didn't think no more of it. Next thing you know, gran-daddy's doin' a drive-by." Bunny tells me all this in her usual casual way, but the thought of her getting shot at a fucking hamburger stand sends chills down my spine.

"So, what's wrong with wearing a Kent State jacket?" I asked.

"Damned if I know... Niggas is crazy these days," she said.

31
Jollies

POT AND PANS RATTLING in the kitchen. Evelyn in there singing "When somebody loves you back," by Teddy Pendergrass. All tell-tale signs that say she had a groovy time last night. It's too bad that Mr. Lover man loves to flirt with me and Bunny every time she turns her back. Bunny don't want to hurt her feelings, and I know she wouldn't believe me. She would say it was me who tried to entice her man. He sat himself down unnecessarily close to me. He leaned over and dropped his keys down my shirt. He got the nerve to pretend it was an accident when he tried to go fish. I grabbed his hand and dug my nails into his wrist with one hand and removed his keys with the other. I threw his keys across the room, grabbed him by the ear and whispered, "Touch me again and I'll get my boyfriend to murder you. He's a Vice Lord, he will blow your fucking head off." Honestly, I wished I had somebody like that to protect me. Evelyn appeared in the doorway holding a steaming plate of bacon, eggs, fried potatoes, and toast.

"What the hell is going on here?" she said.

"Ask your man," I said on my way upstairs. I slammed my bedroom door.

"I know what the fuck I saw!" she said. I breathe in and hold it in for a minute. I'm trying to calm my palpitating heart. *Okay, here we go.* I move my lips to say exactly what she's about to.

"Get the fuck out, you yellow whore!"

"Why Evelyn?" I ask as if she needs a reason to throw me out onto the street.

"You want to flirt with my man, in my house? Make a fool out of me? Go on, get your ass out! Go see how well you do on your own. See just how many friends your ass really got." It feels like I'm being swept up in a tornado. I don't know where I'll end up, or if I'll make it out alive.

For the rest of the week, I wore out my welcome on one couch or another. One night I stayed at a girlfriend's house, and her daddy came downstairs while I was asleep. He pretended to be looking for something, but really, he was touching my booty, having a good ol' time, until I opened one eye and stared at him without saying a word. That scared the shit out of him. He ran his ass back upstairs to his unsuspecting wife. I didn't bother to tell his daughter because she would have called me a liar. They always do. I got up and I wandered through our old neighborhood. I quietly walked past Millie's building. I wondered what she was up to, but how could I face her now? I could pretend to be just stopping by, but my uncombed hair, dirty ass clothes, and strong body odor would set off her alarm. Eventually, I bumped into a familiar face from Southeastern. She was a nice church girl. She invited me to stay at her house, but it's complicated.

"You have to sneak out at six o'clock in the morning before my mama gets up to go to work. Come back after school, but you got to find somewhere to go at five-thirty when she gets home. She goes to bed around ten o'clock. Wait by the back door, and I'll sneak you back in. Then on Friday, I'll ask her if you can spend the weekend with us," she said. Surprisingly it worked like a charm, but on Thursday night the back door never opened. That same night, I felt a piercing pain in my side. In the morning, I waited until I saw her mother leave before I banged on the door.

"Why didn't you let me in last night?" I said. She brushed past me without saying a word.

"Rachel, what's wrong? Why are you ignoring me?"

"I just don't understand why you did it."

"What do you think I did?"

"Please, save your breath Goldie, I know you took my mama's *Jean Naté* perfume off her dresser. When she finds out it's missing, she's going to kill me, and I'm going to kill you." I feel like a deer caught in the headlights. I went behind the garbage can to retrieve the perfume. I braced myself for the slap, she had every right to give me. Her face lit up, then she reached out and hugged me.

"Thank you, Goldie," she said. I broke down and cried.

"I'm so sorry Rachel."

"It's okay, I forgive you, but what's going on? Why did you steal from me when I'm risking my behind to help you?"

"Honestly, I didn't want it at all. I don't even like it.

"Then why take it?"

"I think sometimes, especially at times like this, I just need something to be easy, so I steal. It's how I cope with shit. I didn't mean to hurt you."

"Goldie, you have to go home."

"Rachel, you don't have to worry about me, it won't happen again."

"I believe you, but I can't risk you staying here anymore. Girl, you know my mama don't play."

I wandered through the streets with no place to go. My stomach started doing cartwheels as I approached Piggly Wiggly. But, I didn't have a dime to my name, so I didn't go in the store. I'll never steal anything ever again. I mean it. At least I'm gonna try. I ended up on Reverend Berry's doorstep, only because I happened to look up and see her house.

"Oh honey, I ain't got no extra space right now," she said. After thanking the Reverend for the sandwich, I prepared to move along. She gave me a look of pity. I'm used to it.

"Perhaps you should go and talk to William," she said.

"Who's that?"

"You don't know William?"

"No ma'am."

"He's your mama's boyfriend, he's a good man. I'm sure he would talk to her for you." *A good man my ass,* they ain't even her type.

"Okay, he's waiting for you. The place is called Jollies. It's a bar right off Gratiot," she said.

"Thanks again," I said when I stepped out onto the porch.

"You're welcome, honey. Oh, you'll see a naked lady sitting in a champagne glass on top of the building, you can't miss it." Maybe I deserved all this. I heard that if you did terrible things in your past life, you'll suffer in the next. Yeah, that must be why I felt another sharp pain in my side. Before I knew it, I was staring at the naked lady. I walked through the side door. A muscular dark-skinned man was washing glasses behind the bar. An older Italian man sat on a stool looking at a small TV that was high on a shelf.

"Excuse me, are you William?"

"In the flesh, how can I help you?"

"I'm Goldie, Evelyn's daughter."

"Wow, I didn't expect you to be so pretty, you look just like your mama."

"Thank you," I said while hoping he wasn't a pervert.

"Have a seat," he said. I only told William part of the story. Maybe someday he'll find out about all the men he's been sharing Evelyn with, but he won't hear it from me.

"So, Reverend Berry said you could talk to her for me. I ain't got nowhere to go. I wouldn't bother you, but I don't feel so good right now," I said.

"Wow, okay, I'm going to call her, wait here," he said.

"All right sweetheart, I love you too," he said before hanging up the phone.

"Hey Dino, I got to make a quick run, be back in a while," he told the older Italian man who waved his hand in the air as if he could care less.

"So, you talked to her, and she's going to let me back in, just like that?"

"She's waiting for us right now," he said. I stayed in his car while he went to the door. He knocked three times already, but the door remained unopened. He backed out onto the curb and looked at Evelyn's bedroom window. But why? It's still boarded up. Evelyn's odd behavior didn't surprise me, but William seems dumbfounded. He came back and slid into the car.

"She has to be in there, I just told her we were on our way." He turned toward me with a sudden look of suspicion.

"Your mama got to have a damn good reason for this. What exactly did you do?"

"I didn't do anything. I don't have to do anything, this is her way."

"I'm not buying it, Evelyn is the sweetest woman I've ever known. She would never do anything like this. Some of you teenagers are out of hand today."

"Okay if you say so, but did you even ask her why when you talked to her?"

"Well, what am I supposed to do with you?" he said. I was hit with another sharp jab. I grimaced and bent forward and waited for it to ease up. William drove us back to the bar. He placed a warm bowl of chicken soup in front of me.

"Maybe it's hunger pangs. When is the last time you ate?" he said.

"I had a bologna sandwich before I came here. Anyway, it's not hunger pangs, I know the difference."

"Okay, you can stay here with me tonight. He handed me his car keys. You can hang out in my car until the bar closes," he said.

"Why?"

"Because you're underage." I looked around the place. I could smell all the funky stuff they tried to cover up with heavy cleaning products.

"You sleep in here?"

"Sometimes," he said. I locked myself in his car and rolled the window down just enough, so I could breathe. As soon as it got dark the naked lady came to life, the hot pink flashing lights made her kick her legs up slow and sexy. It would be pretty from a distance. But sitting right across from it was fucking torture.

Hours had gone by. When I couldn't hold my pee anymore, I sneaked inside to use the bathroom. I shrieked when I opened the door to the stall and found some Italian guy, vigorously shoving his finger inside Mimi the missing prostitute. "Hey, kid get the hell outta here!" the man yelled. I ran out and peed behind a bush. I got back in the car and screamed at the top of my lungs. Later, William tapped on the window and I rolled it down.

"You okay?" he said.

"I guess so. How much longer do I have to stay out here?"

"About two more hours. Here I brought you some food," he said. I waited until he disappeared behind the door before I started screaming again.

"Come over here, we can share this," William said after he spread the blanket over a thin mattress he took out of a closet.

"No, I'm okay over here." Sleeping on the same mattress with Evelyn's boyfriend is the last thing I'd ever do. William patted the mattress.

"I'll sleep on this end and you sleep on the other end. It gets real cold in here at night, and I only got one blanket." Before I could protest, I heard him snoring. I sat there for a while, looking around the dark place. The only light came from behind the bar. I tried counting the glasses on the shelves. This is so stupid. I laid at the bottom of the mattress and covered myself with the part of the blanket he left for me.

When I woke up, William was standing by the bar talking on the telephone. I folded the blanket and went over there.

"Good morning, I got good news. Your mama said right after

we spoke on the phone yesterday, there was an emergency, and she had to run out," he said with a wide smile of relief.

"Um, William, you didn't tell her I stayed here last night, did you?"

"Of course, I told her, I have nothing to hide."
The pain in my side hit me like a bolt of lightning. I bent over and waited for it to pass.

"Is it getting worse?" he asked.

"Honestly, it hurts like fucking hell, I might throw up."

"The bathroom is that way," he said. Okay, so, this time when she didn't open the door, William knows he's been played.

"I got to go to the hospital today," he said.

"What for?"

"I got some water on my knee. They're going to drain it, no big deal. You can go through emergency and get your side checked out," he said.

"Why not? This is a hospital ain't it?" I asked a nurse who sat behind the small glass window.

"I'm sorry, but we can't treat you without a parent's signature. And besides, you don't have any insurance information."

"But, I'm in a lot of —" She closed the window as if to say not my problem. I waited for two more hours for William to come out of the operating room. He limped and grimaced with each step.

"You said it was no big deal, but you can hardly walk."

"That's what they told me, fucking liars. What did the doctor say about your side?"

"Nothing, I need Evelyn's signature since I'm a minor. And she said something about insurance."

"Come on let's go get something to eat," he said. He drove to a soul food restaurant in the middle of Gratiot Blvd. We both had roast beef, mashed potatoes with green beans, but we could hardly enjoy it because of all the pain we were in. I blubbered like a baby, while William cried Teeny like the Tin man.

"Why are you crying? You're supposed to be a man, ain't you?"

"I am a man...but if you pierce me, do I not bleed?" he said tearfully. He left twenty dollars on the table and limped, while I hobbled to the door.

This time William parked halfway on the curb like he didn't care anymore. I could tell he wanted to jump out of the car and kick the door in like a real gangster, but since he had his knee cut open, drained and stitched, he sat for a minute."

"I wanted to marry this woman, but I didn't even know her at all."

"Aw, William don't change your mind because of me, it's okay. I'm okay, it's just that she probably thinks we had sex. She always believes the worst."

"Well, I guess she don't know me either."

"She's not going to let me in William, I shouldn't have bothered you in the first place. He stared ahead and tapped his fingers on the steering wheel.

"That's what you think," he said. He endured the pain it took for him to get out of his car. William banged on the door over and over until it looked like it would come off its hinges.

"Open this damn door Evelyn!" he said. If I didn't know how kind he was, I would have been afraid of him right now. Slowly the lock turned, and he pushed his way in.

"What is wrong with you!" he said with his hand raised. He decided against hitting her when he saw my little brothers. They were sitting close together on the couch looking at us. He turned his attention back to her.

"Your daughter, who you forced out onto the street, where anything could've happened to her, needs to go to the hospital. She's in terrible pain. Get the insurance card," he said. She kept her eyes on me as she walked up the stairs. She looks so sad like she's been betrayed. I broke one of the secret rules of child abuse. *Never go running to someone who may care enough to help you.*

"When your sisters or brothers cry, you show concern. Get up, give her a hug," William told my little brothers, and they did.

They cut me open and took out my appendix, whatever that was. The hospital bed felt so comfortable, I didn't want to leave. They discharged me after two days. William brought Evelyn to pick me up. I listened carefully as the doctor told Evelyn how to take care of my incision and whatnot. Little did he know, she could care less. During the drive home, no one said one word. William slammed on the brakes when we got to the house.

"Goodbye Evelyn, have a nice life," he said.

"What, you ain't comin' in?"

"I said goodbye, Evelyn."

"William, I'm sorry I wasn't here to let y'all in, I told you somethin' came up."

"The sad part is you don't even know what you should be sorry for. Get your ass out of my car Evelyn." I sure didn't want the shit to go down like that. William is the kind of man Evelyn needed, he could change her. For a while, I'd hoped he would come back and forgive her. Lots of people break up and make up. But it's been months since they took my appendix out, so it's clear, he's never coming back. The last time I walked by Jollies, William stood outside leaning against the wall and twirling a toothpick in his mouth.

"Hi William," I said.

"Hey kiddo, how's it going?"

"It's going okay," I said.

"You still at your mama's?"

"Yeah."

"All right now, stay out of trouble. I love you," he said.

32
Boys

"WHO LET YOUR ASS in here?" I said, when I walked through the door. It's Vincent. He's sitting on our couch with his arms and lips stretched wide. Bunny was right, he looks like a black version of Frankenstein.

"Hello beautiful," he said.

"Hello, my ass, how did you even find out where I live?" He goes into this story of how he ran into "my mother" in a bar. She gave him our address and told him he's welcomed to stop by anytime.

"Oh, so you're here to see Evelyn? Good for you," I said. I headed up the stairs to my room. Once I reached the top, he called after me.

"Wait, Goldie, can I talk to you for a minute, please?"

"Hell no." I slammed my door, and hoped he got the message, *this time*.

Months ago, I ended my friendship with him because he started to get on my nerves. I should say he started to scare the shit out of me. I told him from day one that we could never be more than friends. He seemed okay with it. Eventually, I told him that I didn't want him hanging around anymore. That's when the begging started. Vincent had no shame. He came right out and asked me if he could have some pussy. "I mean make love to you," he said, after I slapped his cheek. He promised he would never ask me again, after I slapped his other cheek. One day we were hanging out at his friend Troy's house. Troy was twenty-four like Vincent, but *he* didn't live in his mama's basement.

"Troy, can you take me home?" I asked him after Vincent refused to.

"Sure, just let me get my keys," he said. Vincent was sitting in a corner and sobbing like his childhood pet just died in his arms. Troy looked down at him and shook his head.

"Aye-yo Vince, I'ma take your girl home man. Nigga we gon' have a little talk when I get back. Let's go, Goldie," he said. As we cruised down the street I felt proud of myself for not falling for the bullshit and leaving him in the state he was in. Troy started laughing.

"Fucking unbelievable. Seriously, what did you do to my friend? You some kind of witch?" he said, while looking in his rear-view mirror.

"What?" I turned around to look out of the back window. And there was Vincent, in the middle of traffic, chasing the car in the snow without a coat.

"Oh shit, just keep going please!" I said. Troy claimed he couldn't run a red light, so Vincent caught up with us. I rolled my window up. The light finally changed, but Troy hesitated. He drove slowly while Vincent jogged alongside the car. He shouted out a few please baby pleases, a couple of I'll buy you anything you want's, and a series of I love you's. Troy shot me a desperate look. I felt defeated.

"All right fine!" I said. That's why I never told him where we were moving to, and she goes and ruins everything. When Evelyn called out for us to come and get it, he was still here, sitting at the table, gazing at me like a silly lovesick puppy.

"Uh-uh get the fuck out of here Vincent!" I said.

"Vince, you welcome here anytime," Evelyn said. I sucked my teeth because that's all I can do. It's her house, I can't tell her who to have in it.

"Believe me, she'll change her mind. Give it time, right now she think her shit don't stink," Evelyn told him. At first, he would hang around for a few hours at a time, but now he's spending the night.

"Ain't it too late to drive all the way back to the west side?" she would ask him slyly.

In my sleep, I felt uneasy, I knew I wasn't alone. I opened my eyes. It's him. He's sitting on the floor caressing my foot. I kicked him hard on his shoulder.

"What are you doing?! You can't just come in my room, get out!"

"Goldie, can I make love to you, please?"

"Ugh go home, Vincent." I turned over and pulled the cover over my head.

"Your mother said I could stay," he taunted.

"Well go sleep in Beau's room."

"You so beautiful. You all I think about day and night." I started to wonder how I would dispose of his body if I were to put him out of his misery.

"Can I just taste you?" he whispered.

"Please leave Vincent, please," I asked nicely.

"You'll love it, I promise."

"Get the fuck out!" I yelled loud enough to wake the dead.

It's never easy to get him out of my room. I've been pushing my dresser against my door. One night I woke up because of a loud noise. I focused on my window, the rain beat against it forcefully. I loved rainy nights. I saw something hit the window. There it was again. It must be hail. No, someone is throwing rocks, I'm sure of it. I went over and opened the window. Vincent was standing down there soaking wet. I should have known it was his ass.

"Why are you throwing rocks up here? Have you lost what's left of your mind?"

"Blah, blah, blah?" was all I heard.

"What did you say?!"

"Uh, blah, blah, blah?"

"What?!"

"Can I please make love to you?!" he screamed so loud that the dark houses on the street started to light up. If I had slammed the window any harder, it would have shattered into a million pieces.

"Girl you should be grateful somebody love you like that," Evelyn said. I don't know what to do about the two of them. Vincent assumes I'm bought and paid for. He came close to raping me one night. I kicked him between his legs and damn near broke his thing. Now he knows better.

On Valentine's Day, Vincent came over and handed me a long white jewelry box. I have never been anyone's special lady on February 14th I tried to hide my green eyes when Bunny and other girls got candy and flowers and whatnot. I glanced around the room. Even Evelyn had admirers sending her that shit. I snatched the box and tore into it. It was a gorgeous fourteen-karat gold necklace with a heart covered in crushed diamonds. I love it. It's just like the one I always dreamed about. Every time I saw anything close to it in a magazine, I ripped it out and prayed I would have one someday. But how did he know? I glared at Evelyn. She told him. She gets on my damn nerves. But still, this beats some ol' dumb flowers and candy any day.

"Thank you, Vincent," I said while giving him a quick church lady hug. After that, whenever Vincent came bearing gifts, against my better judgment, I snatched them too.

The sun was showing us its natural ass today. Me and Bunny came out and sat on the front steps with our friend Phillyboy. I looked to my left and saw Vincent's car creeping toward our house. I tried to sneak onto the porch without him seeing me.

"Why you goin' in? It's hot as hell in that house. Oh, I know why now," Bunny said, once she spotted his car.

"Tell him I ain't here," I told Bunny.

'That ain't gon' stop him from waitin' for your ass to get home," she said.

"Vincent is good people. Why you duckin' him?" Phillyboy said.

"Because he's crazy. Always saying he love me and whatnot."

"So, what's wrong with that?" he asked.

"More than God, and air," I said, with a raised brow.

"Oh shit. Well, that's what you get for putting it on the man like that," he said. I backed up and stood directly in front of him to set the record straight.

"Vincent and me ain't never had sex, ever."

"Girl you a damn lie," he said.

"No, I swear."

"Then what this nigga trippin' on?" he said. Vincent was parking now.

"I don't know, we never even kissed." Vincent hopped out of the car.

"You better watch out, that mother-fucker might snap," he said through clenched teeth. Vincent approached us holding a bunch of Arab store flowers.

"What's up Bunny," he said.

"Nothin' fool," she said, while eyeing him up and down. Vincent and Phillyboy slapped hands. He held the flowers out to me.

"Hey beautiful, can I talk to you for a minute? In private?" he said.

"So, you see, it's not you, you're a nice guy. I just need time to figure out what I want to do with my life. I can't be tied down with anyone right now. So, I hope you understand," I told Vincent. I asked him to meet me at the pier of the Detroit River. I had been rehearsing this speech for a while. This is the perfect place to recite it. I knew Evelyn wasn't going to stop messing with his mind, or taking his money. So, I'm trying something new. It's called speaking from my heart. He's staring out at the water, not responding.

"Vincent, do you understand what I'm saying? I want you to stop drinking Evelyn's Kool-Aid because she can't make me be with you. And please stop coming by my house, okay?"

"Okay, Goldie—Fine, I'll leave you alone since you don't care about me."

"I didn't say I don't care, I just want...Oh, fuck it, goodbye Vincent." Swiftly I moved toward the renaissance center. I planned to hop on the elevator and scream at the top of my lungs. I think it worked this time. He should be holding onto my ankles by now, but he is not. Oh my God, he finally gets it. Don't do it, you might turn into a pillar of salt, I told myself. But curiosity got the best of me. I looked back. He's nowhere in sight. That simple son of a bitch. There was only one place he could be. To prove it to myself I walked back toward the pier. I looked over the safety bar and sure enough there he was, on the ladder with his ass halfway in the water.

"Vincent, what are you doing down there?!"

"Just let me die, I can't live without you." My screaming got the attention of some good Samaritans, who ran over and took turns trying to change his mind.

"Why don't you go home and sleep on it? The water still be here tomorrow," said a lady who was probably somebody's Big Mama.

"I'm gon' put it to you like this young blood, when you get to the bottom, you will realize there's plenty of fish in the sea. Exquisite, fine, sexy ass fish, but then it's gon' be too late," a man said. The crowd cracked up and tried to get serious again.

"I know this is about a woman, you remember them days?" he asked a man standing next to him who said he remembered them days and missed the hell out of them too. The crowd laughed again. Vincent went down a few more steps, now the water is under his chin.

"Honey you come on up from there," Big Mama said.

"I... I just need her to come back," he said. He could star in Days of our ghetto ass lives.

"Who you need son?" another man said.

"I need Goldie, she's my girlfriend," he said. He knows damn well that I was standing there looking dead at his lying, fake suicide committing ass. It's taking everything within me not to burst out into hysterical laughter and give myself away. When the panic-stricken crowd of strangers looked all around calling for "Goldie," I couldn't take it for another second. I turned on my heel and hustled toward Jefferson Avenue. Luckily a bus was approaching. I didn't bother to see where it would take me. Anywhere but here. When I looked back this time, Vincent was out of the water. He was blubbering on Big Mama's shoulder like he had known her all his life.

"Somebody run to Piggly Wiggly and get me some Italian bread for this spaghetti," Evelyn said.

"I'll go for you Miss Wallace," Vincent said. Nothing has changed since that day at the pier. Every day he comes around making himself available to her while keeping his eyes on the prize.

"No, I'll go, anything to get away from you. Give me some money Evelyn," I said.

"Give her some money Vince," she said. I rolled my eyes before snatching the ten-dollar bill from him.

I stood across from the grocery store when a small white sports car stopped at the red light. I recognized the driver, it's Mauricio. He's the last person I expected or ever wanted to run onto. Oh God, please don't let him see me. Damn, he saw me.

"Goldie what's up, it's been a while girl," he said.

"Yeah, well, hello and goodbye," I said. I tried to cross, but he eased up and blocked me.

"Will you move?"

"Why are you so hostile?" he said. He's got some nerve calling me hostile when the last time I saw him he kicked me in my ass.

"Give me your number and address," he said. What girl would pass on a chance to be with Mr. Mauricio Cordoba? He's father is half black and Indian, and his mama is Mexican. He thinks he's the finest man walking, and he is. But, he doesn't care about anybody except himself. He pushed a pen and piece of paper toward me. To get rid of him I wrote my business on the paper. I saw some lean brown thighs on the passenger side. I didn't bother to look all the way in. She must be young. No older girl would sit still while her man gets another girls phone number. Oh no, she would be dragging me up and down the pavement by my hair.

"This better be the right address," he said. Damn, why didn't I think to give him a fake?

On my way home from the grocery store, I reminisced about the good times I shared with Mauricio. I was fresh off the boat, walking around in my white pumps. He pulled alongside me and told me to stop and I froze. I was so shy, I didn't know what to say. He said a bunch of smooth shit while I nodded. A few hours later I was going on my first date. I stood on the porch, shifting my weight from one foot to the other. He took me to Royal Skate Land. The moment we got out of his car, he draped his heavy skates over my shoulder. "Thanks kiddo," he said. He proceeded to walk three or four feet ahead of me. He carried on like a rock star. He smiled, winked, and pointed at girls who waved, screamed and shouted, "There he is, Mauricio! Over here! Mauricio!"

When I got tired of skating, he grabbed the arm of a more willing girl and never asked me again. When he was leaving, I sort of had to remind him that I was his date. "Oh, right," he said, before draping his skates over my shoulder again. Anyway, we ended up at a Big Boy restaurant where he flirted with two other girls. He invited them to sit with us. They were so giggly. They showed him pictures of their adorable babies. He mentioned how my hips were wider than the both of theirs, yet I had no baby picture to show for it. *That bastard.* Once we got in his car I kept my lips locked and my arms folded across my chest. He stopped in front of my house. I jumped out and slammed his door. He shuffled up the steps behind me.

"Goldie wait, come here," he said, drawing me into his chest.

"No, let me go," I said.

"Are you upset about something?" I tried to free myself, but he held me even tighter.

"I'm sorry if you felt ignored tonight babe, but you see, I'm the social type. I'm outgoing, I love people, all people. Can you try not to become jealous when you see me socializing with other girls? I mean seriously, you're the finest girl I've ever laid eyes on, and the only one I want," he said. I'd only heard that kind of shit in the movies, so I forgave him on the spot.

Oh, not to mention the night we went to Kwong Tong's Chinese restaurant. I told him I didn't want anything, so he ordered everything on the menu for himself. I watched while he showed off his chopstick savoir-faire. When he finished, he patted the corners of his mouth, stood up and said, "Now my dear, if you'll excuse me," and headed straight out the door. It's okay, he must be going to his car to get his wallet, I reasoned with myself. I could hear the clock on the wall ticking away. Fifteen minutes passed. The Chinese people weren't paying me any mind. In fact, they were so still they reminded me of the statues Evelyn had back in the day. As I headed for the door, the statutes came to life and tried to kick my ass.

"You no pay, you pay, you pay!" they said.

"But I didn't eat nothing!" I pleaded before I broke free and ran into the parking lot. Mauricio was relaxed inside his car with his hands behind his head. I got in and gave him a look.

"What took you so long?" he said. *Okay, maybe that was kind of funny.* But the final straw was when he pulled up to my house and said, "Hop in, I want to show you something."

I got so excited when he turned into the parking lot outside of the mall. He's going to buy me something special, why else would he bring me here? Could it be the gold necklace I've always wanted? The one with the diamond heart? I asked myself. He walked three or four feet ahead of me as usual, but he waited for me to catch up when he stopped in front of JCPenny. Once inside the store, I got weak in the knees.

"Where is it?" I said excitedly.

"*She's* over there," he said, pointing at a sexy bleached blonde saleswoman with the perfect everything.

"Isn't she gorgeous?" he said.

"She is, but what did you want to show me?"

"That's it. Do you think she would go out with me?" he said. What a waste of my time. How stupid of me to assume he would do something nice for another human being. I followed him into a pizza shop. He flirted with two girls who were sitting in the booth behind us. *It was always two.* The waiter put the small cheese and pepperoni pizza on the table and walked away. After it cooled, I picked the whole thing up.

"Are you gonna eat that all by yourself, with those hips?" he said.

"No, I'm not," I said. I smashed the entire pizza into his face. I got up and sashayed what he considered wide hips, right out the door. The tramps started laughing at him. *Aw, he didn't get the chance to invite them to sit with us.* I found myself on the outside of the mall with no way home. I heard an awful screeching sound from behind. Mauricio pulled alongside me.

"Get your ass in!" he said. He looked ridiculous with the dried-up sauce all over his face. He took me to his house instead of mine. I ran straight to his room to avoid his mother who barely spoke English. That didn't stop her from trying to have a conversation with me. Mauricio went to the bathroom to wash off the sauce. I studied the collage of women and girls covering some space on his mirror. His reflection appeared behind mine. He put his paws on my titties and gently rubbed my nipples. I ignored the sensations running through my body.

"You know, I was really humiliated. So now, you're going to have to make it up to me," he said. I removed his hands and turned to face him.

"Just take me home Mauricio, I'm not making shit up to you!" I told him.

"Fine," he said. Now that I think about it, he didn't really kick me in my ass. He gave it a slight push with his foot, I lost my balance and fell into the hallway. That's not the same as an actual kick, is it?

"Where you been all this time?" Vincent said when I got back from Piggly-Wiggly.

"Damn, I should go live at your house, just to get away from you," I told Vincent. I looked at Jerome with as much attitude as possible. He's one of Evelyn's old boyfriends. He's back for round two. I guess Vincent forgot about Jerome pulling a gun on him. Now they're acting like blood brothers.

"Why are you still here?" I asked Jerome.

"Don't ask me no questions little girl, I'm your daddy. Lease I will be when I marry yo' mama." I put the bread on the table while laughing at his stupidity. Jerome knew not to flirt with Evelyn's daughters, or his ass would be out. He had a good thing going on here. A place to stay rent-free. He may not get three square meals a day, but he knew a crumb would fall off the table at some point. On my way to my room I heard a familiar horn blowing urgently. Shit. He said he would call me sometime, not show up in front of my house in thirty minutes. Vincent was peering through the blinds.

"It's somebody out there in an old white Jaguar," Jerome said.

"Who is it?" Vincent said like a well-trained, overly suspicious guard dog.

"I don't know. Look like some silky smoove nigga with curly hair cascading all down his back and shit. That punk better not be here for you Evelyn," Jerome said.

"Damn, move Jerome," I said pushing past him. Mauricio was approaching the house when I got to the screen door.

"What are you doing here?" I said. He flashed his irresistible smile. He was wearing all black and dark sunglasses like a movie star.

"I couldn't wait to see you," he said. Vincent and Jerome were on the porch listening until I gave them an evil eye. Mauricio sat on the steps and made himself at home. He removed the sunglasses.

"You put on weight girl," he said.

"You couldn't wait five minutes before putting me down, could you?"

"You know what pleases me most about you?"

"No, what?"

"Your lovely shape. So, I beg you not to gain another ounce. You're almost straddling the fence."

"Whatever Mauricio."

"Hey, you know honesty is one of my best attributes. But, for the record, you are blossoming into a very alluring woman. The world could be your oyster. Why blow it for an extra piece of cheesecake?"

"So, you came here just to talk about how fat my ass is getting?" He laughed and leaned over and kissed me on the lips. Years ago, I would have been paralyzed by his words. But today, I'm relaxed and enjoying his visit. The last time I was in the company of such a fine man, it was him. There was a brief pause in our playful banter. That's when I noticed that the atmosphere on our street had shifted. Men were standing outside staring at us, some were pointing. The girl next door came outside.

"Where he at?" she said. Some other wild girl must have called and told her about Mauricio.

"Dayum," she sang when she spotted him.

"What the hell you foamin' at the mouth for?" Our neighbor Rodney asked his woman. Bunny appeared in the doorway.

"What's wrong with all these heifers around here? *Oh, well all right,*" she said, when she saw him gazing up at her. Mauricio loves being the center of attention. I shook my head. *Some things will never change.* Bunny winked and gave me a thumb up before she went back in the house. Minutes later, the screen door swung open and Vincent stormed past us. He paced back and forth, like a stone-cold retard. He charged back into the house. Mauricio laughed.

"What's so funny?"

"As if you don't know."

"I don't."

"Please tell me you are not with that guy."

"So, what if I am?"

"Hey, it's your life, but if you want my opinion." *I wanted his opinion.* He lifted my necklace with one finger.

"This is nice, but even if he gave you a thousand more, he would still be beneath you."

"Look, we're not together, but I wouldn't say he's beneath me."

"Open your eyes, you're a golden goddess, and he's a rusty nail."

"You're crazy."

"No, seriously, have you ever seen a swan in the coop with the chickens?"

"Oh, so now I'm a swan, like you? Like Marilyn Monroe at the mall?" I said. He smirked and shrugged his shoulders.

"Come on, imagine what your kids would look like." I heard muffled voices inside. Jerome was throwing shit in a pot and stirring it up.

"Mauricio, you should go," I said. He knows what's got my street in an uproar. He finds it all amusing and ego boosting.

"I'm not ready to go just yet, I've missed you."

"Okay suit yourself," I said.

"I'm thirsty. What do you have to drink?"

"We got some beer, Kool-Aid, or water."

"Grab me a beer, make sure it's cold." I stood in front of him and put my hands together and bowed.

"I aim to please you, your highness," I said playfully.

"Very good, and pour it in a glass," he said.

"You mean to tell me you 'bout to let some nigga, who's prettier than she is, roll up and make a fool out of you, in front of the whole damn world?!" Jerome asked Vincent.

"I'm not, it's just, she ain't my woman yet."

"Shit, at the rate you goin' she never will be. All the money you done spent on her ass. Man, I'm tellin' you, these slick ass, Smokey Robinson, "Purple Rain" type niggas will sneak up, and snatch the cootie cat right from under you!" I reached into the cabinet for a glass.

"Shut up Jerome, you don't know what you're talking about!" I said, when I pushed past them.

"That ain't right how you doin' this man girl, you know you wrong! Boy that's why I can't fuck with no young bitches, 'cause they don't 'preciate shit," he said. I glared at Evelyn, she was sitting in a chair crocheting, and pretending not to hear her man talking about my cootie cat, and calling me a young bitch. When I got back outside, the street seemed more crowded than before. I felt like I was in the twilight zone. Mauricio was leaning in his car, so I met him curbside with the foam topped glass of Stroh's.

"Here's your beer," I said.

"Great timing," he said. He reached for the glass, but it exploded.

"Vincent, what the fuck?!" I said, when I realized he was the culprit. I attempted to apologize to Mauricio, but he was suspended in air, and flying backward for a moment before he hit the ground.

"Yeah, that's it, show that son of a bitch he can't come 'round here startin' no shit!" Jerome said, from behind the screen door. Men on the street crowded around and added their two cents.

"Yeah kill that nigga!"

"Kill him for what? What did he do to you?" I asked.

"Knock his ass out!" another man yelled. Mauricio struggled to get off the ground and regain his composure, but Vincent hit him again causing his blood to splatter onto the crowd. I went deaf for a second while I watched the crowd of men cheering in slow motion. I ran in the house.

"Evelyn, you got to stop Vincent!" She didn't look up at me, instead, she kept moving her lips, *knit one, pearl two*. I started to cry.

"Evelyn this is really bad." Knit one, pearl two, my ass. I ran to the kitchen and got a knife. *I'm going to have to kill Vincent.* I dashed through the screen door.

"Vince that's enough," Evelyn said, barely above a whisper and his fist froze in midair. *What the fuck?* When he came out of his trance, he seemed shocked by his own blood-soaked hands. He looked at the crowd of people for a moment before he took off running. Mauricio tried to stand and fell back onto the sidewalk a few times. I reached out to help him.

"Stay away, don't you fucking touch me!" he said.

"No, please let me help you." He managed to stand on his own. His body bloody and shaking.

"You should have warned me!" he said.

"I tried to, but I didn't know anything like this would happen." He staggered to his car leaving bloody prints all over the hood.

"Mauricio, wait, I didn't know, I swear," I pleaded. He gave me a looked that sent chills down my spine before he drove away. I turned around and gave that same look to the men who encouraged Vincent to become a monster.

"I hope you're all satisfied!" I said. When I went back into the house the boys were at the table quietly eating spaghetti with Italian bread. Evelyn and Jerome were off somewhere hiding like the devils they were.

I haven't seen hide nor hair of Vincent since that day. It feels good to live my life without him lurking around every corner, or sitting on the couch waiting for me when I walked through the door.

For Bunny's sweet sixteenth birthday, we rented a banquet hall and threw her a party fit for a princess. She had on a pale pink strapless gown that made her reddish-brown skin shimmer. It took me two weeks to make the darn thing. Everybody loves Bunny, so this place is jam-packed. Somebody bumped into me when I came out of the ladies' room.

"Hey Goldie," Vincent said.

"Don't hey Goldie me, you got some nerve to show your face after what you did. Mauricio filed a police report on you," I lied. Vincent had a chip on his shoulder like he's the man or somebody.

"I don't care, pretty boy had it coming for disrespecting me like that. Anyway, I didn't come here for you. I don't love you anymore. I came to wish Bunny a happy birthday."

"Please, she ain't expecting to see your ass ever again," I assured him. When a well-built girl walked by, he dramatically twisted his spine to scope her booty. He looked at me to see if I cared. I shook my head in pity.

"You couldn't even get me, let alone make me jealous. Get the fuck out of here Vincent."

"All right fine, give me my shit, and I'll be on my way."

"What shit?"

"All the shit I gave your ass for nothing, like that necklace around your neck. My money bought that, so check it in." I just had to laugh. Out of habit, I played with the necklace.

"This ain't enough for putting up with your crazy desperate sex fiend ass. I was so tired of seeing your ugly face every fucking minute of the day."

"If you give me some pussy, I'll let you keep it, whore."

"Whore?" The DJ played "Young love," by Teena Marie. I peered around the hall for a second. Kids were having a good time. Bunny and Fredrick were in the middle of the stage slow dancing. They held onto each other like their lives depended on it. So, I hope the birthday girl don't catch me doing this. I reached up and slapped a deep scratch into his cheek.

"You fuckin' bitch!" he said. I moved backward. I just couldn't believe this asshole who claimed to love me more than God, and air to breathe, is now charging at me, and calling me whores and bitches.

"I'm glad I didn't give you no pussy, you weirdo," I said, with a smirk on my face. He resembled a mangy dog when he tried to yank the necklace off my neck.

"Nigga, I know you ain't put your hands on this pretty ass girl!" A guy with a deep voice said. My heart pounded in my chest. It's been a year, but I know who belongs to that voice, and that scent. *Old Spice.* I stood up and started checking my olive-green halter dress for dust. I turned around to give Vincent another piece of my mind, but he was already in the wind.

"You all right baby?" said the man of my dreams.

"I'm fine."

"Do I seem blind?" he said.

"No, well, thank you. I just hope it don't cost you later." He cracked up.

"What's so funny?"

"You're funny, to say that shit. You must not know who I am."

"Who are you?"

"I'm Elijah Kingston baby." I have never heard his name before now, but I like it. *Mrs. Gwendolyn Renee Kingston.* I can live with that.

"I'm Goldie. So, how do you know my sister?" I asked.

"Who's your sister?"

"Bunny, it's her party."

"Get the fuck outta here, y'all are sisters?"

"Yeah, we are." We stood there for a moment, taking each other in. It feels like a rollercoaster ride. I want to get off, but it's too late. I'm locked in. The DJ changed the record to "Tender Love" for kids who weren't done grinding on each other. Elijah lured me toward the dance floor without asking. I didn't put up a fight. The least I could do is dance with the man. After all, he's the reason I placed a pillow between my thighs every night. Twice he came to my rescue, and he just called me a pretty ass girl.

33

Being Strong, and Keeping My Head Up

I AM NOT IN THE MOOD for her shit today. I was in the bathroom undoing my braids. All I want is for my hair to have deep waves, instead of tight curls. "Oh, fuck it!" I said before grabbing my jacket and stomping down the steps. Evelyn was sitting on the couch watching me like a hungry hyena. She wanted to even the score.

"I said I'm sorry Evelyn."

"Sorry my ass, don't come back in this house unless you get another one!"

"Where am I supposed to get one?"

"I don't care where you get it from, go in one of them abandoned houses and get one or don't come back."

"I ain't going into any abandoned houses."

"Okay, come back here empty handed and see what happens," she said. I stormed out the door and headed to school with one side of my hair still braided, the other side flowing free like I couldn't commit to one style.

All this over a stupid toilet cover. Okay, I was in the bathroom at the time, but I didn't break it. The picture above the toilet fell on top of it, and the damn thing broke. I took a shortcut and told her I did it.

"I didn't break it! And you can't break me!" I cried. I felt like a fish out of water. Tears stained my blouse. If only I could get out of my body, I wouldn't have to feel whatever this is.

"I hate you!" I yelled out against my will. People walking by had trouble minding their own business. I tried to straighten up, but I couldn't.

"You stupid fucking bitch!" *Damn, I didn't mean to say that out loud.* What is happening to me? I can't control anything. A little voice whispered in my ear, it told me to let go because things would never get better. I watched the traffic and fought the urge to throw myself into it. I lifted my head up and saw my Nana is in the clouds talking about,   "Be strong, keep your head up, honey."

"I'm fucking trying Nana, shit!" I yelled into the sky. People walked around me. They looked over their shoulders and whispered to each other like I'm strange. I guess they don't see my grandmother up there as plain as day.

I found myself sitting outside the principal's office. My body had tied itself into one big ass knot. I don't know if I've been here for a few minutes or hours.

"Don't forget what I told you, Darnell," the Principal told a chubby boy who came out of the office. He looked at the secretary's desk and back at me.

"Are you here to see me young lady?" he asked. I struggled but managed to shake my head.

"Right this way," he said. I understood him, but I couldn't unravel myself from the knot. A minute later he came back for me.

"I said I'll see you now," he said. Move it, I told my stubborn body. He knelt in front of me and gently placed his hand on my shoulder.

"I can't' help you unless you stand up and come into my office, do you understand?" he said. By the time I got inside, he was already seated behind his desk.

"Which of your teachers sent you?" he said. I trusted the words would come out smoothly when I tried to express myself.

"I came on my own," I said like I had strep throat.

"That's fine, how may I help you my dear?"

"I don't know."

"Why don't you have a seat, and tell me your name?" Sure, I can do that. I tried to thrust my body into the chair. Instead, I accidentally knocked over a silver swinging pendulum on his desk. At least I got my real voice back.

"Oh my God, please sir, I'm sorry, please don't be mad, I can fix it! I can fix it!" I screamed as I struggled to get it to balance again. It kept falling back on the desk, but I was determined to fix it. Damn it, it fell again

"Dear, it's fine," he said. He spoke in a patient tone that soothed me. He reached across the desk and pried the thing out of my tightly closed fist. He put the thing back together in one smooth move.

"See, there's no harm done," he said. When he sat back in his chair, I followed suit by letting my body fall back into the other chair. I watched his lips move, but I couldn't hear a word he said. The silver see-saw thing had hypnotized me. How does it stay up there like that without falling? Look at it. It seems like it might fall at any moment, but it never does. It teeters back and forth, and back and forth and... The earth-shattering scream that escaped my belly had been a long time coming. Once it started I couldn't stop. I was still screaming when a policeman stuck his head inside the office. I was afraid to go to jail, so I managed to stifle my screams by biting into my arm. They stepped outside the door to talk about me.

"What are we dealing with, the kids pretty banged up huh?" the officer said.

"Well, not exactly, I didn't see any bruises anywhere. You know I've been principal here for damn near twenty years, I've seen hundreds of kids come through my office with everything from black eyes, to broken arms, to cigarette burns. But, I have never encountered a child who has been emotionally traumatized like this," he said.

34
Independent Woman

"HUSH CHILD, EVERYTHING will be all right," said a petite lady wearing a canary yellow sweater and tan pants. The officer gently handed me to her like a newborn or a ticking time bomb. I cried while chanting stupid fucking bitch the whole way here. Now my throat is dry and I'm exhausted. The sign on the dark green door of this three-story warehouse building said Prospect Place. Thankfully, she didn't stop to ask me what brought me here. Instead, she led me to a room with three beds and let me lay on one of them. She covered me with a blanket and turned off the light. The room went completely dark when she closed the door. I awoke to the sound of two girls rushing into the room. They were laughing, but their smiles faded when they saw me sitting on the bed. "Oh shit," the tall one said. I couldn't blame her. Finding a stranger in your house, but not being able to tell them to get the fuck out is a nuisance. The woman who brought me here appeared in the doorway.

"Hey, Miss Tangie," both girls said.

"Hello Monique, Nicole have you introduced yourselves to our new girl?"

"Yes, ma'am," they lied.

"If you're up to it, we can go in my office for a little chat," she said. After the thirty-minute tour, I knew all I needed to know about my new institution.

The girls at Prospect Place attend East Catholic High School. I can't believe I made it to my senior year. Catholic school curriculum was a breeze. It seems like the nuns would rather force us to watch documentaries about aborted babies than to teach Algebra or History. Some of the girls would run out of the classroom in tears during these horror films. The nuns give each other the wise eye. Not being able to stomach mutilated babies whose bodies were broken and bloody, body parts, proved you were guilty.

"Don't you try to sneak peeks at me, Sister Granada. Bitch, I ain't no baby killer," Skylar said.

"I guess I'll see you at home," she told me when Sister Granada put her out of the class. Skylar's family is rich, and she is spoiled. Her mama died three years ago, she was fourteen. Then her daddy married some girl seven years older than her and all hell broke loose. For years her father tolerated her many rebellious acts. But, putting hair remover in his hot new wife's shampoo bottle got her ass kicked out. Now she knows how good she had it.

I'm the only girl here who thinks about sex all day and night. The other girls are too busy doing it to fantasize about it. I'm pushing eighteen and I'm embarrassed about being almost a virgin.

"Well, you must be a dyke," Sky said when I told her I never done it before. I didn't tell her about Dirt.

"I keep telling you, I'm not into girls."

"What other reason could there be? I mean, are you confused about what the pussy is here for?"

"Gone are the days when a lady had class," I said pertaining to her choice of words.

"Anyway, if I was that way, wouldn't this place be like candy land? Wouldn't I have tried to get with your ugly ass by now?"

"Girl don't front, you know you want this," she said. I laughed.

"Goldie, you got a phone call!" somebody yelled from the break room.

"Who is this?" I said. I knew it was Elijah, but he needs to know that I'm not sitting around waiting for him to call, although that is exactly what I do all day.

"It's me, come braid my hair," he said. Ever since the night of Bunny's party, we have been inseparable.

"Will you bring me back before curfew?"

"Yeah, girl hurry up," he said. I don't like this one damn bit. Elijah lives with this older woman. He told her we were cousins. She knows we're not cousins, but obviously, me taking her man don't make her list of things to worry about. She ain't nothing but a sugar mama. Anyway, he loves me, he never said so, but I can tell.

"You could have at least taken these braids out first," I told him after I spread my legs and he got comfortable between them. We're sitting outside on his front steps. My complaining is all an act, I'm glad he left the braids in, he'll be sitting between my legs forever now. When things were getting good, Sugar mama rode up in her cream-colored Audi 5000. She hopped out and sashayed her wide hips and high booty past us and through the front door without saying a word. She's old, but she's still attractive. And she smells like tropical grown woman fruit, like kiwi and papaya. I was aggravated so I pushed his head and pulled his hair to show it. He ignored the unnecessary roughness. I jerked his head back, so I could see his eyes. They were blank, his mind was elsewhere.

"Are you even listening to me?" I said even though I didn't say anything.

"Huh, what?" he said.

"Forget it," I said. He stood up. He needed to stretch.

"Sit tight, I'll be back in a second," he said. How many seconds are there in forty minutes? I'm a damn fool for staying out here this long when I know Sugar mama is in there making him forget all about me. I put the hand towel, hair grease, afro pic, and comb back in the bag, and headed to the bus stop.

"Goldie, you got a visitor!" I told Bunny about Prospect Place, so it must be her. I was wrong.

"What do you want Elijah?" I said. All week I told the girls to tell him I wasn't here if he called.

"What up, you rollin' out with me or what?" he said. He's got some damn nerve, acting all innocent after the shit he pulled last week. My sassy inner me put her hand on her hips and twisted her lips. "*Girl, tell him to go straight to hell,*" she said.

"Wait until I get my purse," I said. We went to Belle Isle because he loves the water, he's a Pisces, but I don't bother getting in because it's disgusting, you shouldn't have to clear a space to swim in. I remind myself we're just friends. I never had a male friend who wasn't gay. Elijah hasn't even tried to kiss me, but he's nowhere near gay. Sexy as hell is what he is. He's chatting with a girl in a firetruck red bikini. She's all up in his face, batting her eyeballs, and touching his soaking wet chest. I laughed out loud when a hungry fifty-foot shark jumped out of the water and swallowed her ass whole. He spit out the red bikini. *Okay, stop fantasizing, shake it off, act natural,* I told myself when he came toward me. He playfully popped my thighs with his damp towel.

"Would you stop please? That hurt!" I said.

"You didn't want to get in the water?" I folded my arms and turned my back to him.

"I told you I never get in that water, it's full of bugs, and piss."

"What's with the funky ass attitude?" Oh, I get it now, you're mad about the other day. I told you I'd be right back, all you had to do was wait."

"Like how long should I have waited, maybe until you and your grandma came out of your comas? And why are you laughing?"

"You're funny. I mean, you're the last one I expected to get all weird on me." He grabbed my legs and swung me around, so I'm facing him.

"Listen, princess, you made it clear you weren't interested in me."

"I never said that."

"Every time I tried to get close to you, you pushed me away. Stop Elijah, boy quit, move, no stop," he said in an exaggerated girly voice.

"So, I was like cool," he said.

"Really, just like that, you were like cool?"

"That's right baby because I'm a real man, in case you haven't noticed."

"I've noticed that you like your cookies stale," I said with a smirk.

"So what, she's thirty-one, who gives a damn? At least she's a real woman who ain't afraid to take what she wants. And her cookies are fresh to death."

"Okay Elijah, good for you. I'm done, take me home," I said heading toward Sugar mama's car while he walked a few paces behind me.

"Aw baby, you mad? I know what you're used to, but I ain't in the Sahara, and if I was, you ain't no damn oasis. You're fine as hell, I'll give you that. But I'll be damned if I start falling all over you, stalking you like what's his name, acting like you the last piece of ass on earth. You ain't nothing but a Barbie doll anyway," he said. I spun around too quickly, and he bumped into me. We were staring into each other's eyes.

"What you mean by that?"

"You know Barbie, she's got a pretty face, hair stretched to her waist, and a body like *damn*, but when you get them panties down, you realize that she's just a fucking dummy," he said with a mischievous grin. His analysis paralyzed me. Now he's walking ahead of me.

"Then why are you always with me?" I said.

"Because you my nigga."

"Fuck you, Elijah."

"Promises, promises," he said. I rode back to Prospect Place with my hands folded across my chest. When he entered the parking lot, I opened the car door and threw my leg out before the car made a full stop.

"Goldie wait a minute," he said. I gave him a mean five second glare, before I hopped out of the Audi and bolted toward the door. He put the high beams on and had the nerve to sit there laughing at me. *Asshole.* So much for my grand exit since I had to wait to get buzzed in. The girls were in the common area debating about which one of them Kenneth really wanted to take to paradise. Most of the time, I avoided the passion filled arguments like a plague. But since I was in a foul mood, I went in. I sat next to Sky and she gave me a little nudge. Kenneth is the only young male worker here. Sure, he looks like El DeBarge, but still, these horny toads go overboard sometimes.

"He wouldn't touch your ugly ass with a ten-foot pole!" Nicole told Robin.

"Bitch please, my kitty is so good, I don't need no pretty face! Plus, I ain't ugly!" Robin lied. She looks like a damn seahorse. Poor Simone, she's madly in love with Kenneth who is twenty-eight. She's only seventeen. She said she's walking right out the front door the minute she turns eighteen. And the next day she's coming back here to get her man. But every time she confesses her love for him, he says stuff like, "First, you're too young for me, and second, I don't shit where I eat."

Me and Sky sat in my room flipping through this old nasty book called "*The Joy of Sex*". I found it in the Prospect library.

"Done this...done that, and this, but in reverse," Sky declared, as she turned the pages. I studied a picture of a woman with her hands wrapped around her man's manhood.

"Damn, they could have at least washed their asses first," I said. Sky laughed.

"Okay, I've memorized all the positions."

"But what about this one?" she said. A man and woman were going to town on each other. I pretended not to be intrigued by it.

"Ewe skip it, I'm never doing that shit."

"Oh, but you shall, in time my child, in time. Damn, I almost forgot," she said before giving me three condoms.

"Thanks, Sky," I said.

"Did you bring a stiff banana from the kitchen?" she said. I laughed again, and reached into my desk drawer to retrieve the fruit. We practiced until I successfully put the condom on the banana with the light off.

"Last thing you need is a big belly, it's always the nice ones who get caught," she said."

"I know girl," I hugged her. I like Sky because we're equal. No sidekicks here. I read somewhere a friend is a gift you give to yourself. I would choose Sky as a friend outside of Prospect Place. If I don't want to do something, she doesn't call me names. She understands that I'm a late bloomer. Besides, I love how she talks like a fortune cookie sometimes. Moments later she had the painful look in her eye again.

"You have to stop thinking about it Sky."

"But it's my fault, ain't it?"

"We had no way of knowing." Deep down I knew it was more my fault than hers. I should have given her one stupid cigarette. This all happened about a week ago. I was in the bed trying to sleep. Sky stuck her head in from the bathroom doorway that adjoined our rooms.

"Goldie give me a cigarette," she said.

"No, get out," I said.

"Why not? After all the times I hooked your ass up Goldie," she whispered.

"Well I ain't got none," I lied because she always smoked me out of house and home, and I was flat broke.

"Please, I need one, bad," she said.

"No, and you better get out of here before you wake up the Statue of Liberty," I said referring to my twelve-year-old roommate Monique. She's six-feet-two and she didn't know how to control her emotions or her temper. So, if she felt like you did her wrong, she came at you like a tornado, no questions asked. Kenneth came in for the night shift. Every counselor had to do a body count at the beginning of their shift. He knocked on our door before sticking his head in.

"Hey, is Skylar in here?" he said.

"No, she's in the bathroom, but she'll be back in here when you leave."

"Skylar, I know you're not in your room, I'm going to write you up!" Monique jumped out of her bed and stomped over to the door. Kenneth looked up at her the way we all do, with fear and trembling.

"She ain't in here!" Monique said before she slammed the door in his face, causing our room to vibrate.

"Was that necessary?" I said.

"Shut up," she said.

"Girl, if you weren't a wide receiver, I'd whoop your ass."

"What you say?"

"Nothing." Kenneth was out there laughing like a maniac.

"Thanks, Monique, now I'll never play the bass again!" he said from the other side of the door, but I didn't get the joke. After that, Miss Tangie starts screaming like she's auditioning for a horror movie. We jumped out of our beds and ran to the door. *Uh-uh, this isn't happening.* Miss Tangie's running around the common area screaming. Poor Kenneth, he stood still while beaming at his bloody hand. His middle finger had popped off. Miss Tangie needed to be slapped out of her hysteria, but we all loved her too much to do it. We called Miss Harper from downstairs, she's the only other counselor in the building at night. "Oh Lord!" she said when she saw what happened. She instantly took charge by slapping Miss Tangie.

"Calm down Tangie," she said.

"Why is he standing there like that?" Nicole said.

"He's in shock, hurry, go and get some towels!" Miss Harper said before she draped a towel over Kenneth's hand. He had a frozen smile on his face, like a scary clown.

"Oh Lord, Kenneth, come with me honey, I'm gon' drive you to the hospital," Miss Harper said. A few hours later we huddled in Miss Tangie's office, anxiously waiting for her to finish the phone call with the hospital.

"What they say?" Sky said. She took a deep breath.

"The good news is they can re-attach his finger." We cheered.

"The bad news is it's still here, somewhere. Ladies we've got to find it and put it in a container with ice right away.

We were crawling around looking under everything. Monique was somewhere in the building hiding. Simone was out there going crazy.

"Monique, get out here, I got something for your gigantic ass!" Simone said.

"Man, Simone needs to chill out, the girl is only twelve," I said. Sky crawled into the bathroom behind me.

"I can't believe we're looking for a damn finger. Did the mother-fucker have legs too?" she said.

"Were there any windows open?" I said.

"I hope not." I pulled down my night shorts and sat on the toilet to pee. I screamed.

"Where?" Sky said.

"In the bathtub." She pushed the shower curtain back further.

"Wow, how the hell did you get way in here?" she asked the finger.

"Don't stand there talking to it, pick it up."

"No, you do it."

"Simone!" we yelled. She came running in with the ice. She didn't hesitate to pick up the finger, she stared at it lovingly and handled it with care. It was at that moment that I realized I'm in love with Elijah. If he ever needed me to deal with his amputated finger, I would.

"Come here and sign me out for the weekend," I told Elijah over the phone.

"Are they going to let you leave with me?" he said.

"No, get your woman to come here and sign me out. Tell her to say she's my dear ol' Gramma, they'll believe her."

"You're funny."

"Seriously, why can't she come and help your cousin out?" I said.

"All right, but where you going to be all weekend?"

"With you, where else?" I said.

The next Friday evening, Elijah and his old lady came and signed me out. She's never even bothered to say one word to me. That's why I don't feel bad for what's going down tonight. I don't care how fresh her cookies are supposed to be. Mine are fresher because I'm younger, I think. Anyway, I hope Elijah has money for a motel. I slid into the back seat quietly. When we pulled up in front of her house, she got out and went inside. I hopped in the front seat.

"The Golden Child" was playing in the theater and we were both excited. Elijah doesn't know that I know that he idolizes Eddie Murphy. Halfway through, Elijah claimed he couldn't take the shit no more.

"You were expecting Axel Foley or Reggie Hammond, but this is good too," I lied. I wasn't paying attention to the movie, but I wanted to stay. I thought he would at least try to kiss me in the dark theater. But he didn't seem to notice how I stared deep into his eyes every time he leaned over to make fun of the movie. What about the lip gloss? He knows damn well my lips ain't never been this greasy. We found a small carnival in Greek town. He won a huge pink teddy bear playing basket toss. He hit me in the chest with it.

"You want this shit?" he said. I did want the shit, but he could have been a little more romantic. We headed back to Sugar mama's house at around one in the morning. Getting a room never crossed his mind.

"Come on, there's a bed in the basement, you can sleep there. I'll be back with some blankets and shit," he said. I expected him to be able to read my mind, but I guess it don't work like that. If I don't make my move right now I'm going to die almost a virgin. I eased my white t-shirt over my head and unhooked my bra.

"Can't you wait until I leave before you change your clothes?" he said.

"Who cares if I change in front of you, we're niggas, right?" I unraveled the band that held my hair in a high ponytail. I shook it out slowly until it fell all around my shoulders. I stood facing him, topless and nervous. I'm blessed upstairs, so there's no way he can resist me now. I only wished I had a mirror to see how seductive I must look to him. Elijah stood in front of me and stared deep into my batting eyes. I felt the heat from his body leaping all over mine. I closed my eyes, arched my back, tilted my head, and puckered up. This will teach him for underestimating me. What is taking him so long to kiss me? I felt a breeze, my skin cooled in an instant. I opened my eyes.

"Oh, you funky ass son of a bitch," I mumbled. How could he leave me standing here, half- naked? Wow, what a fool I am, he really doesn't want me. That's it, as soon as the sun comes up, I'm out of here, and I never want to see his ass again.

In the morning, I felt Elijah sliding into the bed behind me. He snatched my new teddy bear from between my thighs. I tried to pull away, but he had his hand where the teddy bear had been. His lips were on my neck. He planted soft sweet kisses there. *God, I hate his ass.* I shifted my shoulders, so our lips could touch.

"What about her?" I said.

"Her, who?" he said.

"Girl, they all do that shit after they slay the dragon," Sky said after I told her I hadn't seen Elijah since we made love a hundred times in the two days Sugar mama was out of town.

"His cousin Ray-Ray said he got a job somewhere. He won't say where," I said.

"So, when you say a hundred, you mean like six, seven maybe?" she said.

"Is that too much?"

"No, that's about average?" she said. She cleared her throat and gave me a look.

"Oh, you want to know how it all went down?"

"Yes slut, you're supposed to brag." I laughed at my friend.

"I can't describe it, but I'll try. He made me feel like a natural woman," I sang. Girl, he was everything I held out for. I'm so in love.

"Aw, that's sweet, but how big was it? Did he make you come?"

"Sky, if I tell you more than that, you'll fall in love with him too. Damn, did you not read the warning page?"

"No, I wasn't aware of it, what did it say exactly?"

"It said never tell your horny best friend every fucking detail."

"Touché bitch, touché," she said.

East Catholic High School graduating class of '86. I did it! This is my first real accomplishment on paper. It feels good. Miss Tangie took me to Sindbad's for a celebratory dinner. We sat by the window, so we could look out at the river. Once we got settled in, she told me that because I'm eighteen, and a high school graduate, my room, and board would no longer be funded by the state.

"Are you serious, where the hell am I supposed to go?!" I said.

"Calm down and mind your language. Swearing is simply a sign of a limited vocabulary," she said. She scanned the room in hopes that the other patrons we not disturbed by my outcry.

"I'm sorry Miss Tangie, I'll try to remember that. But, how do you expect me to react when you tell me that you're throwing me out on the street?"

"No one is throwing you onto the street. Yes, you've aged out. The good news is that I put in a recommendation for you with the Independent Living program. Last week I received a letter stating that you have been accepted."

"Well, what is it?"

"It's a program that gives foster kids a fair start once they've aged out. You'll have an apartment, a job, and a full college scholarship. Congratulations Gwendolyn, you're on your way to becoming a fine independent woman," she said.

"Wow thank you Miss Tangie. This is the best news ever!" I said. I went over to her side of the table and gave her a bear hug. People stopped what they were doing, and smiled at us. They probably think we're mother and daughter. I wished we were. Damn, how did I lose the mother lottery? Why isn't this lovely lady my mother?

"Now, don't forget, the key word here is independent. It won't be easy, and it won't happen overnight, you must be willing to work hard and always persevere," she said.

"I know Miss Tangie. I'll do my best." The waiter brought our food out. We didn't hold back, we dug into our prime rib. Halfway through our meal, Miss Tangie wiped the corners of her mouth with the fancy napkin.

"And don't worry about your plane ticket or meals, we've got it covered also," she said. I placed my fork on my plate and wiped my mouth with my fancy ass napkin. *I smell a rat.*

"Please Miss Tangie, I would ride a shopping cart before I ever set foot on a plane, what for?" She took a sip of wine and cleared her throat.

"The program is based in Houston Texas. They sponsor young men and women from all over the world," she said.

"But you know I can't move so far away from my family."

"You can't pull anyone out of a hole if you're standing in the same hole. You need leverage. This is an opportunity of a lifetime," she said.

The next day I signed the papers and left them on Miss Tangie's desk. She's right, I need to help myself first. After that, I'm coming back for them like the fucking Terminator. The question is, can they survive until then?

Finally, the agency came across a family who wasn't afraid to adopt Monique. It was probably the Detroit Lions trying to get a free mascot. Kenneth came back to work a week later, so they must have planned it that way. His finger had been sewn back on. It was slightly crooked and darker than all the rest. Sky avoided being anywhere near Kenneth. She wouldn't even look at him.

As hard as I tried, I still couldn't get Elijah out of my mind. Why did he bail on me like this? I guess his dumbass chose Sugar mama over me. I'm not cut out for this love shit. I rushed to Sky's room. I needed her comical view of the situation. I was shocked to find her side of the room all cleared out. There was a small pink envelope on her bed with my name on it. I tore it open. *"Hey, Goldie, what's up? Sorry I had to vanish like a thief in the night. But, I got some shit to figure out, you know? I'm thinking it's time for me to act my age and not my shoe size (Ha-Ha). What I did to my father's ugly wife was real fucked up. My mama, God rest her soul, didn't raise me like that. I miss her. So, I'm going home. Anyway, I'm glad we met in this cold ass place. Always remember, it's up to you to create the happiness you long for. Love Skylar. P.S. Don't worry about Elijah. Bitch, he's with me."*

35

Have You Seen Him?

HERE I GO AGAIN, running through these concrete hallways like Franco Harris. My goalpost is in the telephone room. I told myself I would never let a boy have me acting a fool like this. When I enter the room, my housemates roll their eyes and turn their backs to me. That's because I used to call them desperate and stupid for being how I'm being now. But, they must understand, I had never been in love before.

"Elijah, where are you? I miss you," I said shamelessly.

"Goldie it's me," Evelyn said.

"Oh...what do *you* want?"

"I need you to come home." She got some nerve. I was just about to experience the pleasure of hanging up on her ass.

"It's about Beau, he been missing for about three weeks, ain't nobody seen him," she said. I stiffened out of concern for my brother.

"Did you call the police?"

"I been callin' for two weeks straight. They keep telling me to wait it out. They claim kids his age run away every day."

"What did you do to him?"

"I didn't do nothin' to him. You comin' to help us find him or not?" I headed straight to Miss Tangie's office.

"We don't give out any special passes until the weekend, you know that," she said.

"I know, but this is an emergency, otherwise I wouldn't ask." She studied me carefully.

"I'm sorry there's nothing I can do. Once again you're allowing yourself to be entangled in other people's tribulations." I headed for the door. She stood at the top of the steps shaking her head.

"Have yourself back here before curfew young lady."

"I will if I find my brother by then," I said.

"For goodness sake, you've come so far. Please don't ruin things for yourself now!" she said.

When I walked through the door, Evelyn was balled in a chair. Her face was wet from crying, her eyes filled with worry.

"Where are the boys?" I asked.

"They went to a free summer camp."

"Where?"

"The one over in Kalamazoo."

"Have you talked to them?"

"I talk to 'em every day."

"Did you check it all out before you let them go?"

"Stop givin' me the damn third degree, they all right. Beau the one we got to worry about," she said.

"Sorry. Where's Bunny?"

"She out there tryna see what she can find out. I hope they ain't killed my child."

"Who would want to kill him?"

"Ain't nobody got to want to kill him for him to end up dead around here. All these goddamned drug houses sproutin' up like wild mushrooms. These niggers runnin' around here shootin' and shit, the kids ain't even safe in they own backyard."

"I know Evelyn. Let's just calm down and wait for Bunny." An hour later the front door opened.

"Bunny is that you?" Evelyn called from upstairs.

"Yeah Mama, it's me," she said. She came into the dining room.

"Hey Goldie, I ain't know you came home."

"I'm here, but I'm not home." The clock on the wall said past curfew. I didn't bother calling because Miss Tangie's shift had already ended. I'm sure she would do the same if her brother went missing.

How did I get here exactly? It certainly was not intentional. As soon as the sun came we went looking for Beau. We decided to split up to cover more ground. I went left when somebody said they might have seen a boy like him over there. I got on a bus, got off and walked for ten blocks. Now here I am, in the Brewster projects. I've only been here once before. I told myself never again. I'm starting to sweat. From a distance people often mistake me for a white girl with a good tan. I'll be okay if I keep my rough girl façade. I'm just a tough girl, which means I got what it takes to survive an ass-kicking. The rough girls just got a kick out of kicking somebody's ass.

I made sure to bring a good recent picture of Beau. I stopped everyone I bumped into.

"Hi, I'm looking for my brother, have you seen him?" They all did the same thing. They look at the picture, try to recall if they ever seen him before. They shake their heads no. They all say they're sorry, and they hope I find them. I stopped in front of three old men who were sitting on some rickety lawn chairs, and they responded a little differently.

"All them little nappy headed niggas look alike to me," number one said while two and three cackled like some old hens.

"Stop clowning this little girl," number two said. He reached for the picture and talked with a cigar dangling from his lips.

"All right let me see here. Oh no ma'am, you ain't gone find nothin' like this around here."

"What you mean by that?" I said.

"Well if you look close you'll see this is one of them young black males. These wild animals is extinct," he said. The silly old trio slapped their knees and shook with laughter. I snatched the picture from his old crinkled fingers.

"Gimme my picture back. Assholes," I said. I could still hear them laughing from a distance.

I wanted to get out of there before it got dark. I walked by some guys who were gangster leaning on cars. They just couldn't resist asking about my nice ass. "Damn girl, you know you got a nice ass?" Somebody grabbed me from behind and forced me into an open door. How could this go down in broad daylight? Why isn't anybody helping me? I fought for my life by kicking and swinging violently. I stopped fighting once I heard the familiar voice.

"You're busted! What are you doing over here?!" Elijah said.

"What? You scared the shit out of me!" I swung at him without landing a blow. He grabbed my arms and held them down.

"Seriously, what business you got in Brewster?" I looked sideways and raised an eyebrow. He grabbed my face.

"Stop it, Elijah!"

"Let me see your eyes!" he said.

"What for?" I heard a loud cheering in the other room, like a bunch of men watching a good game or something.

"All right, you're still you," he said.

"I know I'm still me. What are you talking about? I only came over here to find Beau, he's been missing for weeks. Have you seen him around here? Wait, what are you doing here, and why haven't you called me in all this time?" Someone tapped on the door before he could explain.

"Sit at the table and don't say shit," he said.

"Hey partner', a man said before he came into the tiny kitchen. He was an old guy, about forty, dressed in a business suit and tie.

"Hey, let me holla at you for a second partner," he said. He followed Elijah upstairs. A few minutes later Elijah came back alone. He sat at the table across from me. Eventually, Mr. Suit and tie came down looking glassy-eyed and whatnot.

"A'ight partner, take it easy," he said before closing the door behind him. Elijah counted back from sixty. The group in the next room seemed out of control, they screamed obscenities at each other.

"And one," he said at the same time the man knocked on the door.

"Hey partner, let me holla at you for a minute," he said. Up they went. Elijah came down. Moments later, Mr. Suit and tie shuffled down the steps.

"A'ight partner be easy," he said like déjà vu.

"Why don't he get it all at once?" I said.

"He is getting it all at once, but he got bills to pay. He goes out to his car and tries to figure out which bills can wait, and how many rocks he can buy today. He's one of my funnier customers.

"Why?"

"Because he's in denial, he'll keep coming back 'because he ain't got no control over it. In a few days, he'll come here asking for favors, he'll force me to take his keys and the title to his car. He works at city hall, he got a wife and three kids. He would blow me if I was into that kind of shit. Don't worry, I'm not," he said once he saw the disgusted look frozen on my face.

"I'm just telling you what this shit will make a man do."

"I don't believe you." Somebody knocked on the door and he jumped up.

"Hey partner." Elijah sat and added the money to the wad he took from his pocket. I'm seeing another side of him right now.

"If you ever touch this shit I'll kill you myself. When I saw you walking by, all kinds of shit ran through my mind. Somebody knocked again, but it wasn't who I expected. Elijah stood to the side while two school girls hurried in. They were about twelve, or thirteen.

"Tyrone here?" said the one carrying a "Thriller" book bag.

"Yeah, he's in there, go on in," Elijah said.

"Did you see their eyes? They all got the look, don't matter how young or old, rich or poor, black or white," he said. The boys got even rowdier since the little girls went in there.

"What's all that about?" I asked him. He pulled me into the doorway between the kitchen and the living room and put his hands around my waist.

"Aye you ho's got my money?" one of the boys asked them. They kept their heads down like children being scorned.

"Man, you know they ain't got shit. Broke bitches," one of

the boys said. I recognized Tyrone from around the way. I never liked him.

"This what y'all want?" he said while shaking the small baggie with the little pieces of dried out crumbs. The little girls shook their little heads like their necks didn't have any bones. *Where are their mothers?*

"Okay, I'm gon' hook y'all young ho's up. What y'all gon' do for me?" he said.

"What you want us to do?" said the one with the blue butterfly- shaped barrettes hanging from her ponytails.

"See this fat nigga over here?" Tyrone said while pointing to Elijah's cousin, the only fat boy in the room. The girls directed their attention toward Ray-Ray.

"If y'all lick his booty you can get it." He threw two packets on the table while the others fell out laughing.

"Man, you crazy," one of the boys said.

"Okay," they said.

"Drop them draws Chubby Checker!" Tyrone said excitedly. The boys waited in anticipation, all eyes were on Ray-Ray.

"Y'all niggas is loco, straight up," Ray-Ray said.

"Pussy!" Tyrone said.

"Nigga, I ain't about to sit here and let no base heads lick my booty, y'all some sick mother-fuckers. Aye Tyrone, call me a pussy again!" he said while lifting his t-shirt up and showing them the gun he had tucked into his jeans.

"A'ight y'all break this shit up, get back to work," Elijah said.

"So, you the ringleader of all this insanity, huh Elijah?" I said.

"What you talking about? I'm doing this for us, baby." He tried to get close to me, but I put my hands on his chest to keep him at bay.

"I see, we're back to square one, you're pushing me away," he said.

"Why do people always think they can wallow in shit, and still come out smelling like roses?"

"What are you whining about?"

"I think power is a drug too Elijah. How long do you think it will be before little girls are offering to lick your ass? Or grown men are...I'm just saying you got to stand for something. I wasn't getting through to him. "I wish I had time to deal with you Elijah, but I have to find my brother before he gets sucked up in the devil's vacuum." On my way out, Mr. Suit and tie bumped into me. "Hey watch it, *partner*," I said.

"Beau, where you at?" Evelyn said when he called her the next day. Me and Bunny ran to the other phones to listen in.

"Please tell me you ain't joint no gang," she said.

"No, Mama I ain't in no gang, that's played out."

"You ain't sellin' no drugs, is you?"

"Everybody be sellin' drugs. How else am I'm gon' get paid?"

"Boy, you know I ain't raised you like that."

"But Mama, I get tired of seeing you struggle all the time. I'm gon' buy you a new washing machine and some stuff for my brothers."

"Listen, I don't need all that. I just want you to come home in one piece," she said.

"I can't come home right now. I'ma call you back later, I got to go, plus ain't nothin' gon' happen to me, I got a gun," he said.

"What you need a gun for Beau? Beau!" Bunny came back down the steps.

"Mama he hung up already," she said.

I called Prospect Place first thing in the morning.

"I'm sorry, those are the rules. I stuck my neck out for you and you've disappointed me," Miss Tangie said.

"Miss Tangie you should understand. You know where we live. You watch the four o'clock news every night. Shit, you're acting like I'm doing all this on purpose."

"You must learn to recognize when a situation is beyond your control. You have what's called a savior's complex."

"I don't."

"Yes, you do, you need to save others because nobody has been there to save you. Let somebody save you this time honey, better yet, save yourself. Come back right now, and we'll work—" I put the phone on the receiver as nicely as I could.

Three days later Beau walked through the door. He put a finger to his lips. He wanted to surprise his mama. When she saw him sitting beside me on the couch, she lit up like she won the showcase showdown on "The Price is right".

"Oh my God, Beau?" she said.

"See Mama, I told you nothin' was gon' happen to me." He spun around slowly so she could get a good look at him. He had on a brand-new green and white Adidas tracksuit, some white Nike's, and a white Kangol hat. He looked proud to be so fresh.

"Y'all look outside and see what else I got," he said. A brand new black and yellow moped was parked in the grass. He had been begging Evelyn to get him one for a few years, but she couldn't afford it.

"Wow that's nice," Evelyn said.

"Pittsburgh Steelers baby! And I got this for my brothers, where they at?" he said while showing us a nice electric train set.

"They're at summer camp in Kalamazoo," Evelyn said.

"You sent them way out there?" Beau said.

"I needed a damn break," Evelyn said.

"Where his ass at?" Bunny said as soon as she came through the door. She called earlier from Fredrick's house, I told her the good news. She said she came home to kick his ass for the shit he pulled.

"You just missed him, he took his mama to the mall, like he's her sugar daddy. Them tears dried up quick when she saw the money he spread out on the table," I said.

"I bet, she said, and we laughed.

Later the phone rang, I answered it cheerfully.

"Yo this Mad-dog, let me talk to Beau," he said.

"What you want with him?" I said.

"Look here bitch don't ask me no questions, just put that lil' muthafucka on the phone."

"He ain't home," I said. The Mad-dog hung up.

I waited until my brother to came through the front door.

"Beau, some guy called here while you were gone. He said his name was Mad-dog, who is he? He sounds like a demon."

"What he say?"

"It's not what he said but how he said it that bothers me."

"Man, forget him. That's that nigga I was working for. He just mad 'cause I quit."

"Why is he calling you if you quit?" He shrugged his shoulders like he ain't got a care in the world. I stomped my foot.

"Beau why the hell is he calling you?!"

"Okay, this is what happened, one day he rolled up on me in a shiny ass black Benz. He said he would pay me five hundred dollars a week to work for him. But I had to decide right then, so I decided. He showed me the ropes and shit. I stayed for like three weeks before I asked him about my money. He told me when I start pullin' in some real cash, I would get paid. So, I worked for another week, I took my two stacks and bounced. I put all his money, his gun, and the crack in the hiding spot. Plus, I locked his door behind me, so he can't say I stole shit from him."

"Two thousand dollars? Beau you know people get killed for less than that."

"Man, he had me sittin' in that hot ass apartment by myself all day, no girls can't come over. Them fiends be kickin' the door nonstop. And you got to worry about one of them robbing you or killing you."

"Now you got to worry about this Mad-dog."

"I keep tellin' you I ain't done nothin' wrong, plus I ain't scared to die."

"Well good for you. Now can you think of somebody besides yourself?"

"A'ight, I'ma call this fool right now. Aye man, my sister said you called over here looking for me." I grabbed the phone from the kitchen wall and stretched the cord into the living room. Bunny ran upstairs while Evelyn sat with him on the couch.

"You got less than thirty minutes to return my shit lil' nigga," the Mad-dog said.

"Man, I ain't got nothin' of yours, matter of fact I think you under paid me, *nigga*." Bunny flew down the steps and bopped him upside his head.

"What you hit me for Bunny?" Beau said.

"Don't say that shit, you crazy?" she whispered. I kept my ear pressed to the phone in case the Mad-dog mentioned what time the massacre would be taking place.

"Do you know who the fuck you fuckin' with?" he said. Lil nigga still wet behind the ears. Don't make me come and blow your mutha-fuckin' lights out permanently!" he said.

"If you do you ain't no man," Beau said. Neither of them said anything for fifteen seconds.

"Man, I kept asking you about my money, you tried to play me close, so I took mine. A man only got three things in this world, his word, and his balls," Beau said. Bunny ran down the steps to bop him again, but he put his hand out to let her know she better not.

"What, you some kind' a comedian?! Oh, I get it, you believe that shit you see in them movies. This ain't "Scarface" lil midget ass muthafucka!" The Mad-dog said.

"Aye man, calm down. I took what you owed me no more or less, if you wanna kill me instead of paying me, hang up the phone and come on," Beau said. The Mad-dog started laughing. We waited for him to regain his composure.

"Today's your lucky day, I ain't had a laugh this good in a long ass time. I'm gon' let your narrow ass slide, but don't call me when those pockets get flat muthafucka." Eventually, the Mad-dog's laughter turned into the buzz of the dial tone. Nana always said that God takes care of babies and fools.

36

Remain Silent

"WHAT'S UP APOLLO, WHERE have you been hiding?" I said. The inside of the house was too muggy. I was forced out on the steps where Beau was hanging out with his best friend.

"I been around. You're the one who been M-I-A-S," Apollo said.

"M-I-A-S?" I said.

"Missing in action sexy."

"Apollo who are you calling sexy?" I said.

"Goldie don't front, age ain't nothin' but a number. You ain't but four years older than me. I can handle that, so anytime, anywhere," he said.

"Yo man, chill, that's my sister," Beau said.

"I know, but I got to set her straight," he said. It's a good thing we're not the same age because Apollo is already going around making young girls cry, with his almond smooth skin and rare green eyes.

When I saw Honeybaby walking towards our house, I got nervous. I hadn't seen her all year. She had a new swing in her walk. She traded in her pigtails for a greasy Jheri curl. Her face was framed by baby hair that was laid down and swirled perfectly. One thing for sure, she's still up to no good.

"What up crack baby?" Beau said.

"I know you ain't talkin', you the one sellin' dope out here." She swung her neck toward Apollo. "You too boy, you ain't slick." Then she swung her neck toward Beau. You know some niggas is lookin' for yo' ass," she told him.

335

"Shut up, ain't nobody lookin' for me."

"Man, move on, you cock-a-roach," Apollo said. She must have had a bigger fish to fry because she went on her way. The Honeybaby I remember would have at least knocked the moped over. There was an empty forty-ounce beer bottle on the ground, but she ignored it. Maybe she's got a man. Oh Lord, please don't let her multiply.

"I can't stand her ass, her mamas on the pipe too," Beau said.

"I know, one time she tried to get at me for a rock," Apollo said.

"Ewe, and you let her, huh?" Beau said.

"Nah man, that's nasty, lettin' some old base head do that, I ain't desperate. I don't want no AIDS and shit."

"You better not let her hear you talking about her mama like that, or there will be hell to pay," I said.

"Man, I ain't even worried about that skeezer," Apollo said. He looked left and right to make sure "That skeezer" wasn't lurking anywhere. Some other kids came by to check Beau out, his new clothes and the moped made him the man of the hour, for the moment. I went inside when shots rang out in the distance. Beau and his boys were playing guess that gun. A few hours later I went back out to tell Beau I was locking the house up for the night. Evelyn said not to wait up.

"Where did Apollo go?" I said.

"He had to get in the wind," Beau said.

"Bring your bike in it's getting late," I said. He looked at me and grinned before turning his attention back to his boys.

"Um, did you hear what I said?"

"Man, you can't tell me when to come in 'cause I'm grown," he said.

"Last I heard, you were only thirteen."

"Thirteen and a half, get it right girl."

"Okay Mr. Grown ass, you stay right there, I'll be right back you little..." His friends were laughing hard until I came through the screen door.

"Oh shit, look out man, she got a bat!" they warned him. It was a plastic bat, a Savage specialty. I knew it wouldn't hurt him, but it would help me get my point across.

"Damn, girl what is you doing?" he said. He ran around the outside of the house, forcing me to chase his little ass. He embarrassed me in front of his friends by running in slow motion and taking off when I got too close. I wasn't going to catch him, so I did the next best thing. I sat on his moped.

"I guess you won't be needing this," I said.

"Aw, that's messed up. A'ight, I'm goin' in 'cause I'm sleepy, not 'cause you said so."

"A'ight man, we'll catch you later," the boys said.

"Peace out," he said. I held the doors open while he brought the moped inside.

"You better not get no grease on this rug mutha- fucka this Mad-dog," I said.

"What, you think you Tony Montana nigga? Or Super Fly? You Gary Coleman lookin' muthafucka!" Beau said. He had the Mad-dog down pat. I howled with laughter.

I fell asleep on the couch since I didn't have a room here anymore. I put a pillow over my head to escape the annoying morning sunlight. I wanted to ask Evelyn more about this summer camp she sent the boys to. Bunny came creeping in this morning as if being seventeen makes her a full-grown woman.

"So, you be staying out *all* night now?" I said.

"Well, how old was you when you gave birth to me?" she said.

"Hey, you little fass ass hussy, don't come in here smellin' your own piss!" I said playfully. Beau's moped was gone, he must have gone out early to see what mischief he could get into. Speak of the devil. He came in and dashed upstairs without saying hello. I heard him vomiting in the bathroom. A few minutes later he came back and sat on the last step.

"Are you okay?" I asked. He sat there for a while, staring at the door.

"Goldie, you know Apollo?"

"What kind of question is that?"

"He died."

"What? Boy, it's too early, I don't have time for games. Damn, he would never play about something like that.

"How?"

"They found his body in the apartment he was working at." I went over to put my arm around him. He jumped up.

"I gotta go, I'll be back," he said. Minutes later, Bunny came upstairs from the basement.

"Where's Beau?"

"He ran out."

"Dang, I wanted him to go to the Arab store to get me a pack of *Newport's.*"

"Bunny, wait, I need to tell you something."

"If it's something bad keep it to yo' damn self," she joked.

"Sit down please." She started to panic.

"Where Mama at?"

"It's not about her."

"Oh, okay," she said before she sat.

"Apollo's gone. He was found in some apartment somewhere." She covered her mouth with her shaking hands.

"What? No...no." She slid onto the floor and cried. I got down and put my arm around her. I thought about Apollo's mother, Miss Ruby. She called the girl's in the neighborhood daughter, because she didn't have any. "Hey there daughter, come on in. I could use some sugar and spice, all these musty behind boys are driving me to drink," she teased. We look up to Miss Ruby because she's a registered nurse, and she always taking classes. She encourages us to be something in life. Besides that, I couldn't think of a kinder person. The extra weight on my shoulders made it hard for me to stand.

"Where you goin' Goldie?" Bunny said.

"I'm going to see Miss Ruby, she'll need her daughters by her side," I said.

"I'll go with you," she said. Somebody pinch me. Either I'm dreaming, or the front door just came flying into the living room.

"Where the fuck he at?!" Brick screamed. He's Apollo's oldest brother. In seconds, the other four stormed in.

"Is he here?! Find his ass!" Rasheed yelled. His face was plastered with tears.

"Is who here?" I said. I know why they're wailing like they're in hell, but why are they here? Bunny ran upstairs.

"He didn't do it!" she screamed. Lance took off running behind her.

"Please don't hurt Bunny!" I shouted. I felt crazy for saying that. Lance would never hurt Bunny. We're all friends here, aren't we? I stood in the middle of the room paralyzed while they turned the house upside down.

"Check the fuckin' basement!" Demetrius said. They came back into our living room screaming, falling out like they were standing on a linoleum floor soaked with oil. They picked each other up and held onto to each other. I didn't have the strength to hold back my tears. After not finding who they were looking for, they moved out like a pack of hungry wounded wolves out for blood. Seconds later, Bunny crept down the stairs looking wide-eyed at the damage they caused.

"They gone?" she said.

"Yeah, they're gone. Come help me fix this door, please."

"Who were they looking for?" I asked her.

"Damn Goldie, seriously? They're lookin' for Beau, they think he killed Apollo.

"That's bullshit, everybody knows that Beau and Apollo were like brothers, they were inseparable.

"Well, brothers fall out sometimes. Remember how Apollo used to push Beau around?"

"He just wanted to toughen him up, he didn't mean anything by it," I said.

"Anyway, after you left, they got into it. Beau got Mama's rifle and pointed it at Apollo. He was like, "Man I'ma blow your fuckin' head off!" Apollo was shook, but he told his brothers not to touch him. Anyway, they ain't said a single word to each other since."

"Did you know Apollo was out on the steps with Beau last night?" I said.

"What? So that explains why they busted up in here."

The news about Apollo has traveled far and wide. Our street looks like a carnival. People standing around like buzzards. The brothers were parked two doors down. They were standing outside of a green pickup truck waiting and still wailing.

"Beau did it. He shot Apollo with a rifle!" Honeybaby yelled.

"That raggedy bitch. That's it, I'm gon' strangle her ass," Bunny said.

"Wait, he's coming down the street right now," I said. She came and stood next to me. He had no idea that his own life was in danger.

"Where's Evelyn's rifle?" I asked her before Beau parked on the grass.

"Oh my God. Please don't come up here. Run Beau run," Bunny said through clenched teeth.

"What you talkin' about?" he said.

"Apollo's brothers are after you," she said. Beau walked steadily toward the house. Now that he can see how terrified she is, he stopped.

"Just listen to me for once in your life," she pleaded.

"A'ight, what?" he said.

"Go to Fredrick's house, don't stop for nothin', and don't come back until I come get you." The fear in her eyes told him to trust her now, and ask questions later. He got back on his bike and took off.

"You think they gon' stay out there all day?" Bunny said.

"Where would you be if you knew who killed your brother?"

"This shit is unreal," she said.

"Come on, let's sneak out the back," I said.

"No, we can't leave yet."

"Why not?" I said.

"I don't want Mama to come home in the middle of this, she don't even know what's going on." While Bunny went on about her mama, I stood on the porch. Shit, God only knows how much I love my baby brother. I just want him to live a long happy life. But maybe there ain't nothing I can do about it. Maybe God wants him in heaven. Today. How else can I explain the black and yellow moped bringing his ass back toward the house? I just started fucking crying.

"Bunny, come here, look," I said. She stood next to me and saw exactly what I wanted her to see.

"Beau, what you doin'?" she said.

"I don't know where Fredrick stay!" he said.

"There he go, right there!" Honeybaby said. Beau looked to his left and saw the brothers jumping in their truck, and it all became clear. This wasn't the time to beat on his chest and proclaim his innocence. This time he kicked up some dirt, and high tailed it down the street. The buzzards started buzzing. Brick banged on the side of the truck. "Let's go, let's go!" he yelled. They turned the truck around in the middle of the street and drove recklessly after Beau. There was no way he could get away on the miniature motorcycle. I grabbed my shoes.

"Stay here and wait for Evelyn," I told Bunny.

"They gon' get his ass!" Honeybaby said when she saw me. I headed toward Gratiot. My heart raced. Apollo's brother Omar didn't realize I was walking with him, or maybe didn't care. Beau's head on a silver platter is all he wants. I didn't dare try pleading with him now. When Omar started to run, I ran too. The traffic on Gratiot was heavy as usual, but something on the far-right side of the street kept the cars from moving past the green light. I didn't see the truck, the brothers or Beau. But when I saw the bumblebee colored moped in the middle of the street spinning all by itself, I fell to my knees and screamed.

I wandered around the streets for a while half out of my mind, looking in dumpsters and behind buildings for Beau's body. I had no idea where people put bodies after they murder somebody. After hours of searching, I went back to the house.

"Who's that?!" Evelyn yelled when I tried to open the unstable front door.

"It's me," I said. Evelyn sat by the window clutching her shotgun.

"Where you been all this time?" Bunny said.

"I couldn't find him, they must have caught him. Did y'all call the police?"

"They didn't catch him, he over Shirley's," Evelyn said.

By morning, the threatening phone calls poured in.

"We're coming over there right now, we gon' kill all y'all niggas, a guy with a raspy voice said.

"Who is this?" I said. He hung up. I hung up. It rang again.

"Better run while y'all still got legs," he whispered like a snake. I knew the brothers weren't sitting around making threats over the phone. Right now, they were at home, doing all they could to keep Miss Ruby from sinking in quicksand. Everybody loved Apollo. We loved him too. People are out for our blood. The calls continued into the night, each threat more terrifying than the last. I went upstairs to Evelyn's room. She was stretched out on her bed, reading a magazine like she didn't have a care in the world. As far as she's concerned, the shit is over. Beau's safe at Miss Shirley's. She's arranged to send him to Pittsburgh by Greyhound tomorrow.

"Evelyn, we should probably get out of here. Somebody keeps calling, making threats, saying they're going to kill us and burn the house down," I told her.

"Let 'em try. I ain't gon' let them niggers, or nobody else run me out of my damn house!" she said.

"Seriously Mama, we need to get up out of here, before we wake up dead," Bunny told her.

"All right goddamn it!" she said. We sneaked out the back door and went through the dark alley. Evelyn walked backward clutching her rifle the whole way.

"Evelyn, you are my dear friend and I love you, but I can't get involved in no mess. I'm still trying to recover myself," Miss Shirley said.

"I need to lay low 'til all this mess die down. Girl these kids ain't nothin' but trouble," Evelyn said. Miss Shirley knew trouble all too well, both her sons were murdered. They were born and buried two years apart. Beau sat at the kitchen table. I sat across from him.

"How did you get away?" I said.

"I kept cuttin' through the alleys. I even ran through somebody's house. I felt like a runaway slave, but I couldn't let 'em catch me. I had to leave my bike though."

"I know, I saw it in the street."

"Did you get it?"

"No, I didn't get it, I was too busy trying to *get* you." Evelyn came into the kitchen.

"Ma's gon' be waitin' for you at the terminal in Pittsburgh. Boy, you killin' me. I'm a peaceful person, I don't bother nobody, you brought this shit to my doorstep," she said.

"What you gettin' mad at me for? I ain't kill Apollo."

"Boy, I know that," she said.

The next morning, Apollo's handsome young face was plastered all over the news.

"Police are searching for a suspect," they said. Beau's big brown eyes were glued to the TV.

"You ready?" I asked him.

"No, but I ain't got no choice, do I?" We jumped out of the cab and headed toward the counter to buy a one-way ticket. We only had fifteen minutes.

"It says gate twelve, let's hurry," I said. A man in a brown tweed suit stepped into our path.

"Are you Robert Savage? Well, are you, or aren't you?" he said.

"Who's asking?" I said. He flashed a badge like they do in the movies.

"I'm Detective Malcolm Calhoun. I'm with the Detroit Police Department," he said.

"What do you want with him?" I said. He turned back to Beau.

"Are you Robert?"

"Man, you keep saying my name, instead of telling us what you want."

"I'm going to have to detain you. I need to talk to you about Apollo Haywood."

"But he has a bus to catch in ten minutes, our Nana will be waiting for him," I said. He nodded toward the ticket I held in my hand.

"One-way to Pittsburgh, right?" he said. I looked at him sideways, I didn't appreciate him spying on us.

"And, what is your name, miss?"

"I'm Goldie, I'm his sister."

"Delighted to make your acquaintance. You're certainly welcome to tag along, but Robert's not getting on any bus, not until he's been questioned," he said. We didn't know if we should protest, or what our rights were. We followed this Detective Calhoun into a room where he locked us in.

"Goldie, you think they gon' put me in jail?"

"No, you didn't do anything."

"How they know we was gon' be here?"

"I don't know, but I need to call Nana and tell her you won't be on the bus, or she'll be worried to death."

The Detective came back with a stack of papers in one hand, and a cup of coffee in the other.

"Okay Robert, or should I call you Beau?" he said.

"Whatever man."

"Okay, Robert it is." He handed Beau a sheet of paper and sat on the wooden table facing him.

"Read it aloud, would you?" Beau stared at me for a moment.

"I'll read it," I said.

"No, he has to. Go on Robert, read it." I felt embarrassed for him. Now, this asshole will know he's illiterate. I cast my eyes toward the floor while Beau struggled with the first line. I looked up and watched his lips move, as he read the rest of his rights effortlessly. He must have been arrested before and memorized the whole thing.

"That's right, tough guy, you have the right to remain silent, but in my experience, innocent people don't mind talking. So, unless you have something to hide."

"Um, I object to this line of questioning," I said. The detective chuckled.

"Do you understand your rights Robert?" he said.

"Not really, since I didn't do shit."

"So, what can you tell me about the murder of fourteen-year-old Apollo Haywood?"

"I don't know nothing about it, just like you."

"I have signed statements from people in your neighborhood. They say they saw Apollo sitting on your steps at about nine-thirty last night. Is that true?" Beau shrugged.

"So yesterday afternoon, I swing by your house, and I find the place abandoned. Why are you running if you're innocent?"

"Apollo's brothers came after me, so I had to jet."

"You are the last person to see Apollo alive, correct?"

"Nah man, whoever killed him was the last person to see him alive," Beau said.

"Oh, you're real clever. How did the fight start?"

"What fight?"

"The fight which led you to kill Apollo."

"Man, I didn't kill Apollo, he's my best friend!"

"Well, he *was* your best friend. Do you always threaten to shoot your best friends with rifles? Oh yeah, I know all about it." He skimmed over at the paper in his hand.

"Let's see here, last summer, you threatened to blow his fucking head off."

"Nah man, I ain't stupid, you playin' mind games. I ain't kill

Apollo, but if you think I did, prove it then!" Mr. Detective Calhoun raised his hands.

"Whoa big man, I'm only doing my job, wouldn't want to get on your bad side." Beau wanted to go off. I gave him a look that said, *"Boy chill your ass out."* Calhoun turned his attention toward me.

"So, sis, tell me, do you know where your brother was between ten and midnight last night?" he said.

"Yeah, I know."

"Would you care to enlighten me?"

"He came in at ten o'clock on the dot."

"How can you be so sure?"

"Because at nine-fifty-three, I was outside chasing him with a plastic bat."

"Why were you chasing him?"

"To make him come in, and he did."

"He could have gone out while you were asleep."

"I would have heard him taking his moped out of the dining room. I slept on the couch by the door. He just got that thing, he wasn't going anywhere without it." The detective ran his hands over his tired and frustrated looking face.

"Would you lie for your brother?" he said.

"I'd do anything for my brother."

"Including lie for him?"

"Yes, I would lie for him, but I'm not lying now. Even if I couldn't tell you where he was between ten and midnight, I know my brother. He would never hurt anybody, especially not Apollo. They were close, and please don't bring up the rifle stuff because it happened last summer. Last night they were laughing together like they always did...I think God was giving them a chance to say goodbye. And now nobody will even let him grieve properly, he's just a fucking kid!" I said. My tears ran wild. "Goldie, you don't have to cry," Beau said. Detective Calhoun stayed on top of the table for at least thirty minutes, he stared down at the dingy linoleum floor and let his legs swing. We sat quietly, hoping we said all the right things. I shouldn't have told the truth by saying I would lie for him.

"Okay, you two, sit tight, I'll be back in a minute," he said. When he returned, he wasn't alone. A young white man who looked like he was on his way to the Tigers stadium was standing with him.

"This is Stanley Peterson, he's an undercover police officer. There's an express bus leaving in thirty minutes, we can put Robert on it. Officer Peterson will also be on the bus to make sure he arrives safely in Pittsburgh. One more thing Robert, did Apollo happen to tell you the name of the man he worked for? No one else knows, not even his family." He handed Beau a pen and paper. He scribbled something on it and gave it back. The detective shook Beau's hand. I looked at my brother sideways. *Who are you?* I ask him with my eyes.

"Good luck son, and try to stay out of trouble," he said.

"I try, but trouble always finds me."

"Well you've got to learn to bob and weave," the detective said while throwing a few jabs at Beau.

"It was my pleasure to meet you, Goldie, you're one hell of a sister," he said before walking away.

"Hey, Mr. Calhoun!" Beau said. The detective stopped and faced us.

"You gon' get 'em?"

"If it's the last thing I ever do," he said. The undercover police officer walked right past us and got on the bus without saying a word.

"We should all leave Detroit," Beau said.

"We are, but first we got to get the kids from that camp."

"At least they had a good summer."

"Oh, I almost forgot. How did you memorize all those words?"

"I ain't memorize 'em, I know how to read and write."

"How?"

"When my teacher found out I couldn't read, he started teaching me. I couldn't go to lunch, and I had to stay after school sometimes. Anyway, you was right, it is like a puzzle."

"Aw, you remembered. But why keep it a secret? You should be shouting from a mountaintop."

"You know how Mama is, she want me to play dumb, so she can get that money, but I ain't no dummy for real, I wanna be somebody," he said.

"Wow, you never cease to amaze me. I love you, Beau."

"Me too sis," he said. He got on the bus and we waved until the bus turned the corner. Four to go, I told myself.

37
Parasite

"IT'S JUST A HOUSE. You can get another one. What good is it anyway without a moment's peace?" I told Evelyn.

"I know damn well you ain't tryna school me. Anyhow, they was after Beau, he gone now. On top of that, them kids is comin' home from camp next week. Where am I supposed to take them, huh?" she said.

"Home where they belong." She gave me her signature evil look, but I pressed on. Any other time she would chase me through the front door. But she can't put me out of Miss Shirley's house. Speaking of Miss Shirley, she was slamming the kitchen cabinets this morning, and then the front door when she left for work. She wanted our asses out ASAP. I guess she had enough of other people's tribulations.

I've been cooped in here with Evelyn all day. She hasn't said one word to me. She's got some damn nerve. When she needed a fool to do her dirty work she called me. She should have been the one getting interrogated by detectives and whatnot. I stood in the doorway of the room she shared with Bunny. Evelyn was standing in from of the mirror brushing the ends of her shoulder-length hair. I'm trying to give her a taste of her own medicine. I hope I'm creeping her out.

"What you standin' there watchin' me for?" she said.

"Why don't you love me, Evelyn?"

"Girl, I got too many other things to worry about for you to be askin' me dumb ass questions."

"Okay, what did I ever do to you?" She kept brushing and staring at me through the mirror.

"The least you could do is tell me why." Still nothing.

"You're such a coward," I said before I went and fell back onto the old easy chair. My eyes were shut tight, but I felt her standing over me. I laughed inside.

"If you touch me, I will fight back, so make my day," I said without ever opening my eyes. Fuck her, she's a bully. I bet she won't lay a finger on me. So, she reached down and pulled a different rabbit out of her hat.

"Okay, you want to know why I don't love you? I'll tell you. You old enough to know now," she said. I looked at her.

"The floor is all yours," I said.

"All right fine, smart ass. When I was seventeen, Ma was doing domestic work for some rich white folks in Warrington. Ernest won the lottery, so he was shipped off to Vietnam, and Thea was just born. Then daddy lost his job at the mill and they started fightin' all the time. When he found out that Kevin wasn't his, he cut her face." I stretch my eyes wide.

"Mm-hmm, then one night he walked out on us. She couldn't make ends meet and everything got cut off. We struggled through the coldest winter ever. Long story short, she made me go with that old white man she worked for, and told me he was gon' buy me a car," she said.

"I asked you why you hate me, please don't go telling lies on Nana," I said.

"See that's why I never told a soul. Who would ever believe that precious Pearl would ever do somethin' so foul? I'm only telling you because I want to be free," Evelyn said. She dragged me down memory lane. I didn't want to hear her story because I don't care. If she is looking for sympathy, she came to the wrong place.

"Anyway, I tried to put it all behind me and look on the bright side. Come spring I was gon' get my car, and me and my girlfriend was gon' drive up to California in style. We had big plans. We was gon' be in the movies like Judy Pace. People always said I looked like her," she said.

"So, what did you do with the car? Did you go to California?" I said. She started laughing.

"I never got no damn car, they used me! Maybe we ate better that week, or a few bills got paid, I don't remember. What I got took nine months to come."

"What was it?"

"Look in the mirror and see for yourself, start from the top of your golden head," she said while smirking at me. I admit I can be naive at times, but some shit is so unbelievable. Once it all sank in, I gasped.

"Oh no, don't you dare, you hate me because you're evil, just admit it!"

"How else could I come up with a nappy headed blonde baby? Every time I look at you, I see him. I feel betrayed," she said.

"Too bad because I'm nobody's trick baby, David is my father!"

"Ma always tried to convince me that you was some gift from God. She just wanted to ease her guilty conscience."

"You know what? I'm sorry I asked. Besides it's all in your head, I know who I am."

"I told David you was his 'cause I needed somebody to blame it on. Don't look at me like that, hell, at least I didn't kill you, give me some credit."

"Mothers kill their kids every day, so it was God's grace that kept me alive, not you. All I want to know is why you never told me you could never love me?"

"I tried to tell you, but you kept coming back, that's your own damn fault!" She shook her head.

"You was too damn stupid to take a hint. Every time I thought I got rid of you, I turned around and there you was, like a damn parasite. Just the sight of you makes me want to scratch 'til I bleed," she said.

"Okay Evelyn just stop, I get it. You won't have to scratch or bleed anymore because I'm through with your ass." I started rubbing my temples.

"I can't believe this shit, all this time you hated me because you didn't get a stupid car? Well boo fucking hoo. I will help you get the kids out of Detroit. There's something in the water here. They would never survive this place." She let out a dismissive laugh.

"I'm serious Evelyn, it's not safe here. If you were any kind of mother you would see it, and you wouldn't need me to tell you."

"I *see* you smellin' your own piss, tryna tell me what to do with my damn kids. I ain't leavin' my fuckin' house, after all the time and money I put into it!" Who am I kidding? She will never see things my way. I thought about slapping some sense into her, but unfortunately, Bunny bolted through the door. She rested her eyes on her mother's stressed face. She looked at me with suspicion.

"What was y'all talkin' about?" she said.

"Nothing, where you been all day?" I said.

"With Fredrick, I ain't about to be in them streets by myself."

"They find out who killed that boy?" Evelyn said.

"I ain't heard nothin' yet, but you'll never guess who they found shot in the head last night."

"Who is it this time?" I said.

"That fuckin' Honeybaby."

"So, you're saying she's dead?" I asked.

"As a doorknob," she said without sympathy.

"Well don't act happy about it, she was just fourteen years old," I said.

"I ain't actin' happy Goldie, I'm just tellin' y'all what happened, damn."

"See what I tell you, karma's a bitch. Too bad she can't run and tell who laid her ass out," Evelyn said.

Where did I first see those dolls? Oh yeah, at Gramma Betty's, a long time ago. She had this funny looking, egg-shaped doll on her dresser, and every time I opened it, there was another one inside. I can't remember what they're called. I wanted to keep them so bad, but Gramma Betty said it wasn't a toy. Anyway, this day reminds me of those dolls, but not in a good way.

When I got out of the shower I looked in the room Bunny and Evelyn shared. Bunny had the luxury of sleeping at Fredrick's house whenever she wanted, but tonight, she's sleeping here for some reason. Evelyn's bed was still made up, I checked the time. It's 1:18 am. *Great, another fucking doll.* I shook Bunny. As expected, she didn't budge so, I shook her harder. She groaned and flung herself in the other direction.

"Stop, leave me alone," she said.

"Okay, but Evelyn's not here, do you know where she went?" She bolted upright like a jack in the box. She frantically looked around until she saw Evelyn's empty made bed. She laid on her back and kicked her legs wildly.

"Shit, shit, shit!" she said, before putting both feet on the floor.

"You think she went back to the house?" I said.

"Let's just go get her. I tried to tell her how serious this is, but she so fuckin' hardheaded. She pulled some sweats over her night clothes and slid into her sneakers and tied them in about thirty seconds. She took the sleeping scarf off her head and threw it to me because my hair was dripping wet. She ran through the streets like Carl Lewis, I could barely keep up with her.

"Please God, I'll do anything you say, just let my mama be all right," she said. Damn, I bet God gets tired of prayers like that, especially since nobody ever keeps their end of the bargain. Bunny would keep her end though. I followed her through all the shortcuts, there were dogs barking into the night. She knew which backyards were free of Pit Bulls, or Doberman's.

"You hear that?" she said.

"What, the fire trucks? That ain't nothing new," I reminded her. We reached the top of our street, and things didn't look good. Once she knew for sure that the fire trucks were in front of our house, she took off running again. I tried to stop her.

"Bunny, wait!" Our burning house brought the spectators out of their beds. Several firefighters were hard at work while two others struggled to keep Bunny from running past them. She would run through the blaze to save her mama. She wouldn't care if she was scarred for life.

"Let me go please, my mama is in there!" she said.

"Miss, stand back, you can't go in there!" a firefighter told her. She looked at him with panic filled eyes. He took her by her shoulders.

"Hey, we don't know if anyone is inside, they have to extinguish the flames first," he said in a soothing manner.

"Bunny come on, let them finish," I said. She buried her face in my shoulder.

"I know she's in there, I can feel it, can't you? Mama's gone Goldie, she's gone," she said.

I patted Bunny's forehead with a soft warm towel. She's lying in this hospital bed like Sleeping Beauty, except for those breathing tubes in her nose. She said she knew Evelyn was gone, she could feel it. But, when she overheard them say they found a woman inside the house, *unresponsive*, she became hysterical. She swung on them and called them fucking liars. That led to a life-threatening asthma attack. They put her in the ambulance and brought us here.

They couldn't confirm or deny that it was Evelyn's body they carried out of our house. A relative must go to the city morgue and identify her for it to be official. Miss Shirley quietly entered the room. She walked directly toward me with arms open wide.

"Oh honey, I'm sorry," she said putting her arms around me unnecessarily. I called Miss Shirley early this morning and told her what happened and where we were. I asked her to call my family, but not to talk to anybody but Uncle Nolan. Miss Shirley stood by the hospital bed staring at Bunny's sleeping face.

"What the doctor say?" she said. I wanted to say she's playing possum. I mean, how can she just not wake up?"

"They said she's traumatized, and she'll wake up when she's ready to deal with reality," I said. Miss Shirley started crying. I tried to comfort her.

"I made her feel unwelcome," she said.

"Don't blame yourself, Miss Shirley, besides they don't even know if it's her for sure."

"Who else could it be? Oh lord. You want to come back home with me for a while?"

"No thank you, I have to stay with her. Did you talk to my Uncle Nolan?"

"Yes, I did honey, he said they should be here between nine, and ten o'clock tonight."

I fell asleep for a few minutes, so I thought I was dreaming when I opened my eyes and saw my Nana, Uncle Nolan, and Aunt Sylvia peering down at me. Their heads looked like question marks.

"Goldie, what the hell happened?" Uncle Nolan said. His eyes were bloodshot from crying or drinking or both.

"Um, there was a fire, they found Evelyn in there, she wasn't supposed to go back. Bunny passed out, she had a real asthma attack." I couldn't think straight, I hadn't slept all night. Nana went over to the bed. She gently rubbed Bunny's hand.

"Come on baby, wake up, I'm here now," she said. I saw a tear escape her closed eyelids.

"Come on honey let it out," she said.

"My mother," she said with her eyes still closed. Nana scooped her up and gently rocked her.

"All right baby let it out," she said. Bunny released a shrill scream that made me feel sick inside. I ran to the bathroom. After I emptied my stomach, I sat against the door and wept silently.

"Hey, you okay in there?" Uncle Nolan said.

"Yeah, um, I'm okay, I'll be out in a minute." We were at the morgue sitting in the gray, fluorescent-lit, and putrid smelling hallway. Nana said she didn't have the strength to view the body. Besides, she still had hope. Bunny stayed in the car, she refused to play dumb like the rest of us. Uncle Nolan took on the burden of finding out for sure. Minutes later, he came out with his hat in his hand, and tears in his eyes. Nana almost hit the floor, but we caught her and held her up. Her screams echoed and bounced off the walls. We carried her dead weight through the front door and put her in the back seat. The inside of the car wasn't big enough to hold their grief. Uncle Nolan pulled up to a lot between two houses and they jumped out. People came out and stood on their porches. They didn't say a word because they knew what the matter was. Once they got back in the car, Uncle Nolan studied the map for a minute before folding it up and driving straight to that camp in Kalamazoo.

38
Butterfly

EVELYN'S BODY WASN'T BURNED. Thank God, she died of smoke inhalation. They found her in her bedroom balled up in a corner. "She might have survived if that damn window hadn't been boarded up," they told Nana. According to the Fire Marshal, it was arson. They knew that the gasoline had traveled from the garage of the abandoned house next door to our house. But they couldn't say for sure if whoever set the fire intended to kill her. They assured Nana they will investigate. They mean well, but they'll never get around to it.

The church was crammed full of elegant orange and blue floral arrangements. A poster of a teenaged Evelyn was placed on an easel. I didn't know her then, she seemed sweet. The words "Gone too soon" were captioned above her head. Next to the photo lies the real thing. She's stretched out in an expensive mahogany casket. The family spared no expense on her ass. I greeted people as they came in. I swear if one more person asks me if I'm Evelyn's daughter, I'll scream. *They know damn well who I am.*

I didn't go up to the casket, but from where I stood, I could tell her lips were glued shut. I know she didn't appreciate that shit. I hope she likes the dress, it's a vibrant orange with gold and pretend diamond studs around the neckline and wrists. Nana wanted to send her home in all white. She thought she would look angelic. I talked her out of it. Evelyn never cared for white, she thought it was boring.

There ain't nothing I can do about her hair though. It's in a tight bun on top of her head like an ice skater. If she were alive to see it, somebody's ass would get kicked.

Seeing all these people from years ago feels strange. They seem so harmless now, smaller even. They're all oblivious to the memories they left imprinted on the heart and soul of a certain innocent little girl. Mr. Graham is sitting in the third row. There are no kind words to describe his appearance. Why is he here? Perhaps to spit on her grave? I see Josiah sitting with a young woman who I recognized. Her name is Naomi, she used to work at the restaurant in South Carolina. How scandalous, he's got some nerve bringing her here. He must have sensed someone sending him a bad vibe because he turned his neck and caught me. He smiled. I looked the other way. I know exactly why he's here.

I saw a woman in the third row wearing a show-stopping white wig. Miss Gazelle? She's ten years older and twice the woman she used to be, but it's her all right, sans the bikini top and hot shorts. Aw, how kind of her to take time out of her busy schedule to attend the funeral of her maid. I laughed, but I wondered if things might have been different if she had been a better friend. Maybe she was the original yellow bitch in Evelyn's life.

Poppa and Nana are sitting in the front row holding hands. So, this is what it took for them to realize what they have in common. Aw, look at all my Aunts and Uncles sitting side by side in the second row. They're all staring straight ahead stoically and quiet as church mice. That's because they viewed her body last night. As soon as they saw her lifelessness laid out in that fancy box, all nine of them lost their minds. They raised such a ruckus that the funeral director rushed in and defused the situation. *Actually, he threw their asses out.* He said he's never had to do anything like that before. He apologized profusely. A heavy hand landed on my shoulder. I looked and saw my daddy.

"Hey baby, how you holdin' up?" he said. I gave him a tight hug. I really missed him.

"I'm fine daddy, really."

"When did you become a grown woman? Seem like just yesterday you were sittin' in your little rockin' chair. You remember that little rockin' chair, don't you?"

"Yes, I remember."

"Look here I'm real sorry about your mama, she was a mighty fine-looking woman," he said.

"Is that all?"

"Well, I'm sure there was more to her as time went by, but when we was young she was a doozy. If you need anything you call me, you hear me?" he said. I couldn't help but laugh inside.

"I hear you, daddy."

"Here take this," he said as he pressed a powder blue envelope into my hand. I'm sure there was money inside. People have been laying it on me, along with their condolence this whole time. My daddy headed for the door.

"Aren't you staying for the service?" I asked.

"Oh no baby, I got someplace I need to be. I just stopped by to see you, and pay my respects," he said.

Evelyn's funeral turned out to be a total fiasco, the kind I'd only heard about. I couldn't take it anymore. I didn't mean to disrespect the dead as they say, but it was getting hot in there. I could hardly breathe. I ran outside and yanked off my black patent leather pumps, they were killing my feet. I walked right past the shiny black stretch limousine, it looked eager to get to the cemetery.

So, people lined up to get their chance to stand at the podium. They each told personal stories of a fun-loving, God-fearing woman who was so gentle and kind. *Gentle and kind?* I looked at the person on the obituary to make sure I was still in the right place. I waited for somebody to slip up and call her a virgin.

A well-groomed woman wearing a royal blue silk dress walked

slowly to the podium with her nose up in the air. Anticipation filled the room. She began to sing "His Eye Is on the Sparrow" like nobody's business. Her voice was sweet and eerie, like an opera singer. I tried not to cry, but I couldn't help it. I dried my tears quick, so nobody got the wrong impression and rushed over to comfort me. Heads turned after a wailing woman burst through the closed doors. Oh God, it's Big Bertha, Evelyn's least favorite, and most dramatic cousin. *Okay, here we go.*

"My God, it should 'a been me!" she cried dry tears. The gifted songstress wasn't disturbed, she seemed to be in sync with Big Bertha's theatrics.

"Woo-hoo-hoo, say it ain't so! My God, she was too young! What about them babies? Raise her up Lord! Raise her!" Big Bertha begged. By the time Jesus' eye got back on the sparrow, the middle aisle was crawling with fools. Josiah, Naomi, and the few white folks in the room were the only ones bold enough to step over them, and walk out. Just when I thought things couldn't get any worse, they closed the casket, and Poppa sprang to his feet.

"Open up that box!" he said. The ushers panicked. Their eyes stretched wide, heads tilted in question.

"Do what I tell you, that's my child. I want to see my child, I got somethin' to say to her!" he said. So, they had no choice but to open it.

"Lord no, Henry no," Nana said quietly. I put my head down in shame.

"Good God almighty, somebody stop her! Hurry up, get her!" people yelled from the pews. Uh-uh, don't do it, girl, mind your business, I told myself. However, I rarely ever listened to my inner voice. I looked up anyway. Just as I thought. Bunny already had one leg in the goddamn casket before Uncle Nolan, and Uncle Paul got over there and snatched her ass out.

Two days later I got a chance to sit down and open the envelopes from friends and family. I saved the best for last and opened the one from my daddy. There was two hundred-dollar and a and a slightly damaged photograph inside. Tears formed in my eyes. I stared at the woman holding a baby boy on her lap. If I didn't know any better I'd say she was me, except I haven't live long enough. Her hair was a halo of gold and her eyes were like mine. I turned it over and read the fading words. Clara Mae Guthrie, and grandson David 1947.

There was an unfamiliar van parked outside the big house when I got home. I went inside. Josiah was sitting in the downstairs living room with Nana. There were some garbage bags, better known as poor people's suitcases sitting in the corner. A few of their cheap toys were piled on top. Nana refused to look at me. "Mm-hmm, you should feel guilty," I told her subliminally.

"No, it's not happening," I said before Josiah could open his mouth. Joshua and Joseph were sitting on his lap. "Go to our room right now!" I told them. I didn't want to yell, but they were certainly under Josiah's spell. Joseph went right away but Joshua hesitated until I gave him the look.

"Where is Jeremiah?" I asked Nana.

"He in the room takin' a nap. Give him a chance honey, just listen to what he got to say. Child them boys need they daddy!" she blurted out. I shook my head at her disapprovingly. Nana tried to act normal, but I know she's miles away from sober town. I'm not going to let her give my brothers away, especially not to that fucker. Not after the way he abandoned them.

"You can leave now, they're not going anywhere!" I yelled and slammed our door. Pulling the dresser in front of the door is a bit dramatic, but I was caught off guard by all this. Josiah could have called first. I could have saved him the trip and told him to go to hell. Joshua and Joseph were staring at me. They seemed confused by my behavior. "Play with your cars," I told them. If I didn't know any better, I'd say they wanted to be on the other side of the door with Josiah. I dismissed the thought. They don't know him. I watched them play. They were all his spitting image. Maybe they do know him, and they're connected to him. I could feel Josiah standing on the other side of the door. He wasn't going to just disappear just because I wished he would. Suddenly, I felt tired and much older than my nineteen years. *Damn.*

I pushed the dresser back where it belonged and opened the door. Josiah stood there patiently waiting to be invited in. I stepped aside. I can't help the way I feel, he's number one on my shit list now. He sat in the chair by the window. I sat on the edge of my bed.

"Wow, Goldie, you're not a little girl anymore," he said.

"Man, could you please cut the small talk, and get right to it. Why are you trying to split us up now Josiah?"

"Well let me just say I'm sorry about your mom, she was—"

"She was a mean and hateful bitch. Sorry, that slipped out."

"You'll get no argument from me," he said.

"Well, where the hell have you been all this time?" I said.

"Believe me I tried, but Evelyn made things impossible. You were too young to understand what happened with us back in those days."

"Please, I understood so much more than you think, like when they took Joshua and you didn't even..." I turned my head toward my precious little brothers. Their eyes were glued to our lips. I must remember to be careful of what I say in front of them. No matter how bad she was for them, they still loved her. Last night they kept crying for her and asking when she was coming home from heaven. It broke my heart to explain that heaven was her home now.

"Hey, you guys go outside and play for a little while," I said. After the kids were gone. Josiah got straight to the point.

"I was only seventeen when I married Evelyn. I didn't care about our age difference. I didn't care that she had three kids. She was the most beautiful woman I'd ever laid eyes on, she was my first. But, I wasn't prepared for everything else that came along with her."

"Wait, you were ten years younger than Evelyn when you got married? So, that would make you —"

"I'm twenty-eight," he said. That bit of information made my head throb, I rubbed my pulsating temples.

"I wanted to be there, but after she shot me, and left me to die in that vacant lot, I was afraid of what I would do if she ever tried to harm me again." I tuned him out, so I could hear myself think. *No, we belong together. I can't let go, I won't.* Josiah must have read my mind.

"Goldie you're a young woman. I know what you've been through, but my sons are not your responsibility. All you have to do is be what you were meant to be, a great sister. And you are, but I'm here now, you can let go."

"Well before I let go, I need to know that you won't hurt them because if you do..."

"I promise they'll be safe with me, I'm their dad. I was your dad once, you know I'd never hurt them."

"So, you married Naomi. I bet you're glad Evelyn's gone, huh?"

"I take no pleasure in any of this, but for years I have been praying to God to bring me and my sons together. Evelyn swore that if I ever saw my boys again, it would be over her dead body."

The six of us spent the rest of the week together. We tried to get the little ones used to the idea of living apart from us. Letting go is breaking my heart, but they belong with Josiah. Thank God, I still have Bunny and Beau.

"Why are you running off to some Decatur Georgia, wherever that is, to get married? You're not eighteen yet," I reminded Bunny.

"Aw Goldie, don't be jealous just 'cause you didn't stand by your man," she half-joked.

"There was more to it than that Bunny. Anyway, don't you want to get your education and whatnot?"

"I'ma still go to school and get my edumacation and shit."

"Child please, you're gonna be somebody's mama same time next year."

"Maybe I will, so you better babysit," she said. Evelyn's death hit

Bunny hard. If I could turn back time, I would, just for her. Fredrick waited patiently in the driver seat.

"You better take care of my baby sister, I don't want to have to hunt your ass down," I told him.

"I ain't gon' let nobody harm a hair on my baby's head," he said. I believe him. Bunny handed me a copy of the Detroit Free Press."

"Fredrick saved this for us. Make sure you ain't standing up when you read it," she said.

Later that night I got a chance to read the paper. Inside told the gruesome details of Apollo's death. This can't be real. I will never be the same after reading this, I mean, what kind of a world are we living in? How could anyone do such horrible, unspeakable things to a child? Heaven help us all. I felt sick. I ran to the bathroom. I ripped the article to shreds and flushed it down with everything else. Beau can read now, but he can never ever find out about this.

"Why is everybody leaving?! No, you can't go period. I want you to stay. You're all I have now," I told Beau.

"Goldie calm down, I ain't all you got, you so dramatic. I'm just goin' to Philadelphia with my pops," he said.

"Damn, pops, already huh?"

"His name is Robert too. Did you know he got in a bad accident back in the day?" he said.

"Is that what he told you?" I asked skeptically.

"Yeah man, he all messed up on the outside, but he's a cool cat. He funny too."

"Now you know where you get it from…Please don't go," I said.

"Man, you act like I'm gon' be a million miles away. It's only a five- hour drive. Plus, my pops said he gon' buy me a car if I get good grades and pass the driver's test."

"So how do you feel?"

"About what?"

"You know, about Evelyn, you gonna be okay?"

"I'ma miss her, but she gone. Plus, we all got to die someday."

"Wow."

"What? It's true. We gon' see her again. Anyway, she ain't really dead for real. Her soul probably got transferred to a ladybug or a leaf. Something that's alive, but not human." He walked to the doorway.

"Boy you're so crazy, you made that up," I said.

"Nah, for real, Mama could be in here spying on us right now," he said before he disappeared.

Rita stepped over the broom instead of jumping because she's six months pregnant with a little Savage, so her wedding dress looks like a small tent.

"I can't believe Uncle Nolan's married now," I told Auntie Althea.

"I know. I like Rita, she's perfect for him. He's finally in a good place," she said.

"So, what's it like, living on your own and being a sophomore at Penn State?" I said.

"It's hard, but I'm not going to let anything stop me. I'm going to be a successful business woman someday," she said.

"You will Auntie, I just know it."

"What about you, what do you want to do with your life?"

"I want to be a fashion designer. Now that I have all this time on my hands, it's all I think about."

"Follow your heart, Goldie. No one deserves to be happy more than you," she said.

"It sure wasn't easy, was it?" I said.

"What?"

"Growing up Savage."

"No, it was really hard at times, but we survived," she said.

Nana's favorite gospel song "I've been in the storm too long" could be heard from the front porch. I went inside and headed for the kitchen. Nana stood at the sink pouring whole bottles of "good liquor" down the drain. Sorrow filled tears stained her cheeks. I know I shouldn't have, but I stopped believing that this day would ever come. I stepped back even further so she wouldn't see me. She always said some things should be between you and God alone, and what he does in the dark always comes to the light.

The last time I checked it was eighty-six degrees outside. So why am I suddenly shivering from a cold wind? *Someone is here with me.* Suddenly the air smells like sugar. I scanned the entire room. There is a bright orange butterfly sitting on the armrest of my light blue chair. I was drawn to it because its wings were perfectly aligned and as still as can be. Call me crazy but I think it's watching me too. Staring deep in my eyes like I owe it something. I remembered everything Beau said before he went to Philadelphia. I glanced toward the door to make sure the coast was clear.

"Evelyn, is that you? Did you hijack that butterfly?" I whispered. She flapped her wings just once like bitch you know who it is.

"Well, get your ass out of here. You know it was an accident. How was I supposed to know you were there? You should have listened to me. Who's gonna find out Evelyn? Nobody, that's who. Detroit is crawling with pyromaniacs. And for the record I ain't sorry, but I always knew you would—" Suddenly she fluttered its wings and headed through my open window like she didn't have a care in the world. I couldn't help but laugh. It was just an ordinary butterfly, and I just told it all my fucking business.

"Goldie? Sister girl, I can't believe it!" Adrian said. After many nights of asking God to show me where I belonged. I couldn't get him out of my mind. It's been over a year since we last spoke. He says he absolutely adores San Francisco. For twenty minutes, I held my breath while he described the picturesque landscapes, beautiful beaches, talented musicians, visual artist, and great food.

"And child it's raining men!" he added. In a month or two, he's opening a small boutique to display and sell his designs. He invited me to come and be his protege. I screamed yes!

"You better work it. You understand?" he said, when I told him I was too afraid to fly. I thought I would be stuck here forever, but now it feels like life has finally rolled out the red carpet for me. If there is one friend in this world I trust, it's Adrian. And for once in my life, there are no chains holding me. Child, I'm free at last!

Nana is preparing Sunday dinner for tomorrow. She's resting in between chopping, mixing, and mashing. I tapped on her door. Seeing her like this warms my heart. Ever since she started going to AA meetings at the church, she's looking fabulous. When she brought home the thirty-day disc, we dressed up and took her to her favorite soul food restaurant. I never told her about California, but today is the day, so it's now or never. I just don't want to break her heart. Honestly, I don't know what she's going to do without me. We're so close. Lord, please don't let her turn back to the bottle, I pray.

"Nana, do you know there are plenty of starving kids in Africa."

"Lord knows there is."

"Then why do you always burn the cornbread? Don't you know they would appreciate what we waste?" I said playfully. She sat up and forced her feet into her house shoes and hurried toward the kitchen. The bread looked perfect from where I stood. She put it on top of the stove while I dropped my suitcases on the old hardwood floor to grab her attention. It worked. She looked at my luggage and came toward me. I knew when this moment came, she would cry a river. I imagined prying myself from her tight grip, and begging, *"Please let me go, it's my time now, you're gonna have to try to live without me!"* To my surprise, my Nana didn't do any of that shit. Instead, she seemed happy to see me go. She placed her hands on my shoulders and looked in my eyes.

"Call me the moment you step foot in San Francisco baby," she said. She chuckled because she knew about it all along. One of these damn Savages has betrayed me.

"You're pushing me out of the nest, just like that? Whatever, bye Nana. I love you." We hugged tightly. Hopefully it will last until I see her again.

With one foot inside the cab, I looked back at the big house. My memories are bittersweet, but mine to keep. This was home. Home was safe. But, now home is shrinking and fading away too fast to stop it. When we walk across the floors, open a window, or close a door, all home does is complain. That last rainstorm turned the basement into an Olympic sized swimming pool. When the wind blows at night, home sounds like a woman ghost moaning. Soon home will be marked condemned and demolished, like so many others. I blew home a kiss.

"Hey, you're Evelyn's daughter, ain't you?" a lady asked me as she passed by. I held back the overwhelming urge to scream. I smiled and replied, "Yes, I was."

THE END

Talissa Tillman resides in Pennsylvania. She attended college in Erie County. She has a degree in criminal justice. Evelyn's Daughter is her first novel. In the future, she looks forward to becoming a source of encouragement, and healing for those who were afflicted during childhood all over the world. Readers may reach her via e-mail at talissatillman@gmail.com.